To Sto[...]
Much At[...]
and to Ed. Sit back.
Take The Ride!

The Ragged Edge

Richard Nisley

The Ragged Edge

A racing novel by

Richard Nisley

For more information, visit our website at
www.racingfiction.com

Racecar artwork by Laura Lea Evans
(www.autoartink.com)

ISBN 1-58500-495-2

1stBooks - rev. 02/21/00

To Cindy,
who never lost faith

Special thanks to Avie and Jerry Blount for suggestions and help with editing; Jon Lang for timely criticism, advise and encouragement; Danny Ongais for taking time out from his busy schedule to read an early draft; and "the real guys," John, for dropping everything to go with me to Europe; David, for true friendship; and Rob and Charles, for those Porsche nights in the streets and hills of Southern California.

"To be on the wire is life; the rest is waiting."

--Karl Wallenda

Chapter 1

Nothing could touch him now. Before, there had been the crowd pressing him, wanting his autograph, journalists questioning him, and the sickness in his stomach that always plagued him before every race. Now, all that was gone. He was seated inside his machine, cutoff from the outside world, his mind cold, empty, yet sharply focused.

The starter, a man dressed in a trim blue suit, held up the two-minute sign.

Wagner reached out and adjusted the right sidemirror, but otherwise remained perfectly still. It was a bright, hot day in Johannesburg, South Africa, the kind that made the skin sweat from the slightest exertion, but for these final minutes, at least, in the shade of a sun umbrella, it was almost pleasant.

"You gotta win this one," Hacksaw said, holding the sun umbrella over him. "You probably don't want to hear that, but it's a natural fact."

Wagner closed his eyes. He did not want conversation, not now, not this close to the start, or to think, or to strategize, or do anything but wait.

"Shut up, Hacksaw," he said quietly.

An engine fired up and began revving, joined by another, and another, in a gathering chorus of throaty growls and shrieks. Wagner looked at the switches on the dash panel, crossed his arms, and waited.

One minute.

He tugged at his gloves and checked the vision in both sidemirrors. He was ready, really and truly ready. He flipped switches for the slave battery, fuel pumps, and ignition. He stabbed the starter button. He couldn't hear his engine fire for the rage going on around him, but he could feel it in the pit of stomach, feel it lurch, clear itself of unspent fuel, and come to life.

Hacksaw folded up the umbrella, leaned over and shouted what sounded like "Good luck" and disappeared.

Thirty seconds.

Wagner grasped the small padded steering wheel and watched the starter step out onto the tarmac.

Ten seconds.

He upped the engine to a steady 8000 RPM and engaged first gear. He looked at the gap between the cars ahead of him-- between Evans' Lotus and Bogavanti's Ferrari. If somehow he could squeeze through that gap, he would lead right off. It was possible. If he timed it right. If he was lucky.

Five seconds.

The starter looked over the field, making sure everyone was set, and then raised both hands. In one he held the South African National Flag. In the other he held five outstretched fingers, and began closing them one after the other--four, three, two, one....

Wagner released the clutch, felt his wheels spin and ... nothing. He was left standing at the grid while the cars in front and beside him burst away. He feathered the clutch as several cars from behind screamed past. Moving now, picking up speed, he upshifted. Two more cars passed him but not as fast. He nailed one of them braking for Crowthorne Corner and passed the other one coming out.

So much for timing. So much for luck. So much for grabbing the damn lead. How far back was he? Eighth or ninth? The cars ahead darted back and forth and kicked up dust negotiating Barbeque Bend and the Jukskei Sweep. He could see Evans' green Lotus at the head of the pack, before it disappeared into Sunset Bend. A moment later, setting up for the Leeukop Hairpin, he saw it again, accelerating up the front straight already leading by a sizeable margin.

Wagner shook his head grimly. He had to act fast. He passed a car at the start of lap two, passed two more on lap three, another on lap five, and another on lap six. That put him fourth, where he'd started the race. The next car ahead of him was a BRM, driven by Parks, the reigning world champion. Good old Mal Parks, never an easy man to pass. Wagner had no time to waste on him. He made a run on the BRM braking for Sunset,

2

t the curve too fast and had to back out of the throttle to keep
om spinning. Two laps later, braking for Crowthorne Corner,
e tried again, got crossed up as the corner tightened, and had to
rake to keep from spinning. Before he recovered, two cars
ipped past.

Nuts. He was trying too hard. When everything was
licking, speed came effortlessly, at will, but not now. The
orld was rushing at him in a blur. What else was new? The
hole weekend had been one big blur. Driving for Garret-Hawk
acing Enterprises had been a last minute deal, arranged hastily
ere days before the race, with details to be worked out later,
ich as a contract and money. He'd barely had time to be fitted
the cockpit, bed in a set of tires, and qualify, with no time for
ill fuel-load tests, no time to practice accelerating off the line,
o time for all the little things that went into winning.

"Take it easy," he muttered. "There's plenty of time."

He forgot about passing cars and concentrated on driving as
moothly as possible, easing in and out of the curves, feeling the
uspension and tires work as he braked, cornered, and
ccelerated, getting his rhythm. Laps clicked by. The car behind
im began to press. He looked in the mirror and smiled wryly.
)an Phillips back there, his ex-boss, trying like hell in an
nderpowered car to overtake him. Only two days ago, after the
iorning practice session, Wagner told him he was leaving. It
/as a rotten thing to do, but Phillips was nice about it. He
nderstood. Repco Brabham was no longer a front-runner. If
Vagner had a better deal, go for it.

"But remember one thing, Johnny," Phillips said in that
wangy, outback way Aussie's have of talking. "If things don't
/ork out, I can't take you back. Business, you understand."

Wagner understood. He absolutely must win today.

He upped his speed and Phillips' Brabham faded from his
iirror. Four laps later, he repassed the two cars that had
vertaken him earlier. That put him in fourth. Again. He felt
omewhat better. His fuel tanks had lightened and his driving
ad settled into a nice steady groove. The world was no longer
assing in a blur, but sharply detailed, an ever-unfolding tableau
hat he controlled.

Only now he could no longer see any sign of Evans. He could see the backside of Parks' dark green BRM, maybe dozen car-lengths ahead, and Bogavanti's blood-red Ferrari maybe another dozen car-lengths in front of it, but nothing of Evans' Lotus. Had the Scot dropped out? That would certainly make his job a whole lot easier. Accelerating up the front straight, he checked the lap board hoping, praying that maybe the Scot's number was no longer there.

No such luck. Number Five was still on top.

The Crowthorne right-hander loomed at the end of the straight, demanding his full attention. There would be no hanging back now. He waited very late to brake, downshifted from fifth gear directly to third, and leaned the Garret-Hawk into the long right-hander. Immediately he felt centrifugal force pull at his head, felt his tires begin to slide. He fed in power and kept his machine pointed deep into the curve. Past the apex, he let drift outside. Exiting, his outside tires thumped against the low curb that ran along there. Yeah. That was the way to take that curve.

He lifted slightly for the Barbeque Bend right-hander, and again for the Jukskei Sweep left-hander, but after a few laps, if he got it right--if his line was dead solid perfect--he would nudge the curb exiting Crowthorne, upshift to fourth gear, and in wonderful rush, take these two corners flat-out. He began gaining on Parks' BRM, and soon had his nose pressed up against the green car's tail. The Englishman was lifting for Barbeque Bend, so next time around he built up a head of steam through Barbeque Bend and Jukskei Sweep and passed the BRM easily, wondering why he'd had trouble with Parks earlier.

More laps clicked by, and he began feeling the intense heat inside the cockpit. He glanced down at his fireproof coverall and saw they were soaked through with perspiration and clinging to his skin. Coming up the front straight, he could see heat waves radiating up from the blacktop, and amidst the heat waves, phantom-like, Bogavanti's red Ferrari. He still couldn't see Evans' green car, but Hacksaw was feeding him information now, and he knew he was catching him. Lap 40--the halfway point--came and went. Bogavanti's Ferrari drew clearer as he

4

grew closer, until Wagner could see the Italian's dark eyes in the sidemirrors, every few seconds glancing back at him.

Wagner smiled slightly. "That's right, Bogo. It's me, and I'm going to nail your ass."

The big Ferrari looked twitchy and unsettled rounding corners ahead of him. He moved closer, got a run on the red car through Barbeque and Jukskei, and passed it on the straight to Sunset.

Wagner was feeling much better now. Evans was somewhere up ahead, no doubt aware that his old nemesis was chasing him. More laps passed, and he could no longer ignore the excruciating cockpit heat. On the straights, he braced his knees against the steering wheel and lifted his hands to cool them in the wind stream. He wished he could do the same with his feet, which were mere inches behind the broiling water radiator, and throbbing with pain.

A green speck appeared in the heat haze. Hacksaw signaled the gap was down to eight seconds, with 22 laps remaining. Still plenty of time. The green speck took shape as Evans' Lotus. Moving closer, Wagner could see Evans' little yellow helmet sticking up above the injector stacks, bouncing stiffly over the bumps. Closer still, he could see Number Five painted on the Lotus' flanks. Hacksaw signaled ten laps remained. Still plenty of time. Wagner moved closer. Bearing down on Crowthorne Corner, he thought about trying to outbrake the Scot, decided against it, and followed him around the long curve. Setting up for Barbeque Bend, the Lotus fell back slightly. Wagner nodded to himself. Evans was lifting here too. He followed him through Jukskei, on around Sunset, Clubhouse, and The Esses, up to Leeukop, and back up the front straightaway, confident of what he was going to do. Crowthorne reappeared. He downshifted directly to third and followed the Lotus into the corner. Feeling centrifugal force pull against his body, he eased on the throttle and watched the snake of curb slither around to meet his far-side tires.

Ka-thump! The jolt rocked the chassis and bounced him in his seat. He twitched the wheel to steady it, glanced in the mirror and saw a puff of dust rising from outside the corner. What the hell? Had he run over the curb?

Ahead, Evans slowed for Barbeque. Wagner kept his right foot planted. This was it. Nail him. He eased the Garret-Hawk into the fast right-hander, felt the tires slide, and ... oh, shit, he was losing it. Big time. He flipped the steering wheel opposite the slide, hoping to force a spin and not put any scratches in that shinny steel guardrail outside the curve. He was a passenger now, at the center of the gyro, watching the world spin past: the blurred yellows and browns of sun-dried grass, the reds and browns of sun-burned faces watching him from the infield, and the long streak of silver that was the guardrail. Then a cloud of tire smoke descended as his machine slowed and slid to a sudden, jarring stop.

He looked around him quickly. Could it be? He hadn't hit a thing. He was parked past the guardrail still pointed in the right direction. He spun his tires getting away, hurrying to get back up to speed, back in the race, back in the hunt. But why? Evans was on the other side of the circuit by now. The race, or what was left of it, was over.

So was his career. Garret-Hawk wouldn't be signing him now, not without winning the South African Grand Prix.

He rounded the lower half of the circuit, accelerated up the front straight, past the pits, and back to Crowthorne, to where it had all gone wrong. Had he gotten off line, or had the corners become too slick to hold him? He didn't know. It didn't matter. A great weight seemed to settle on his entire body. He felt utterly drained and depressed. Would the race ever end? Hacksaw signaled that Evans' lead had stretched to 20 seconds, and that Bogavanti, in third, was 40 seconds behind him. Second place was a sure thing, at least, if it had mattered. He could practically get out and walk and still finish second. Nuts.

Coming off Jukskei Sweep, a backmarker arrived in his path, spewing a fog of black oily smoke. It was a Lotus, one of several in the race similar to Evans'. He swooped past the green car and looked back in his mirror, stunned.

"Can't be."

Driver in yellow helmet. Number five emblazoned on the nose. It was.

"Evans. The poor bastard."

He accelerated up the front straight, saw the looks of incredulity on the faces of Hacksaw and the crew, as they too realized what had happened. He waved a clenched fist, and in his mirror saw his crew jumping and dancing wildly. The final laps came and went, he took the checkered flag, and the race was over. Today, he had won. Tomorrow, it would sink in. Right now, it was time to celebrate, and to see team owner Edward W. Garret about the little matter of a contract.

Chapter 2

Susan Jennings grabbed a pencil and paper pad, filled her mug of coffee, and walked down the hall to her boss's office. The door was open. She entered and walked directly to the window and looked out. It was raining in Chicago, and Grant Park looked as it had all winter--gray, cold, lifeless.

"Good morning, Susan."

She turned around. "What's good about it?"

Jeremy Sterns, associate editor at <u>SportsWeek</u> magazine, and her immediate superior, drummed his fingers on the desk. "Well, for one thing, it's not raining in California."

She put her mug on the edge of his desk and sat down, suddenly interested. She'd give anything to travel to a warm climate. Her previous two assignments had taken her to merely smaller versions of Chicago--Cleveland and Buffalo. "Is that where you're sending me, to California?"

Sterns leaned back in his big leather swivel chair. "This is a very special assignment, the kind I would've loved getting when I was in your shoes. The guy's a personal friend of mine. I guess you could say we go way back. My very first byline was a story about him."

She placed her pad on her knee, poised to write. "Great. Who is he?"

"John Wagner."

"Who? How come I've never heard of him?"

Sterns was a great bear of a man, with light-blue eyes that transmitted sensitivity. She detected a trace of annoyance in those sensitive, light-blue eyes.

"He's a race driver, Susan. One of the best in the world. He drives Formula Ones and lives in Europe most of the year, but right now he's staying in California."

Susan nodded. Now she understood. Sterns was the resident gearhead, the guy who was passionate about motorsports. In his lexicon, everyone else at <u>SportsWeek</u> was a "jock-sniffer,"

someone who grew up worshipping ballplayers and didn't hav
the slightest understanding of motorsports, even questione
whether or not it was a sport. With rare exception, it was th
same attitude with sports writers across the land. That's wh
motor racing results were buried in the back pages of the spor
section, if at all, unless, of course, a driver was killed, in whic
case it was front-page news. "Never mind that motorsports is th
second biggest spectator draw in the country, and the bigge:
worldwide," she recalled Sterns often saying, "every damn spor
writer and every damn sports editor I know is a bloomin' joc
sniffer. Why is that? Can someone tell me that, because I sur
would like to know?"

Susan put down her pad, no longer quite as enthralled wit
the idea of going to California. "Somehow, I don't think th:
assignment is right for me, Jeremy."

"Susie, please. Hear me out, first."

"It's Susan. Listen, Jeremy, I don't know the first thin
about auto racing, and I've never even heard of him. What's hi
name again? Bob Wagner?"

Sterns nodded patiently. "John. John Wagner. Remembe
when you begged off covering that chess tournament over i
Stockholm, between Bobby Fischer and that Russian, Bori
what's-his name, because you said you knew nothing abou
chess? That turned out to be the best thing you've written."

"That was different, Jeremy."

"How was it different? Think of John as just another jock
Ask questions. Let your natural curiosity guide you."

"Auto racing is a `guy' thing. He won't relate to me. Don'
you have a car-guy to cover this?"

"There is no `car-guy.' I was doing all the motor racin,
stuff, remember, before I was made associate editor?"

She tossed her head. "Oh, great. Does this mean I have t
cover the Indianapolis 500 too? Just what I've always wanted t
do: hear Jim Nabors sing `Back Home Again Indiana' to 300,00
gearheads."

Sterns chuckled. "I see you do know something about racin;
after all."

"Be serious."

"You won't have to cover Indy, okay? I'll get someone else to do it, I promise. But I do want you to take this assignment. It would mean a lot to me."

"He'll think I'm a bimbo, what do you bet?"

"No, he won't. Trust me on this one. A lot has been written about him. You'll bring a whole new perspective."

"A woman's perspective? You're patronizing me, Jeremy."

"That's not what I mean. I mean ... what do I mean? I mean you always uncover little things about people that others miss. You'll do a really terrific job, Susan, I know you will." He reached for the candy jar on his desk, removed the lid, and offered it to her, a peace offering.

She folded her arms and shook her head.

"Susan," he said quietly, helping himself, "it's true you don't know much about motor racing, but you do know a lot about people, what motivates them, makes them tick, and how to draw them out. It's your strength, and it's all you'll need to write this story."

Susan dropped her arms. Jeremy was a sweet man, an unrelenting sweet man. "Do we have a file on this guy?"

"You know we do." He removed a thick folder from a stack and slid it across the desk to her. "Look, I even pulled it for you. John's sort of the hard-luck type, and I want you to play it from that angle. He's with a new team and he's won the first race of the season. Can he keep it up, can he win enough races to finally win the world championship, lick his history of hard-luck? Those are the kinds of questions I want you to raise in the story. We'll do a follow-up later, say the Monaco Grand Prix in May, and the United States Grand Prix at the end of the season. You know, it could be kind of exciting, watching him make a run at the title, sort of like watching the Cubbies making a run at the pennant, and maybe getting to the World Series."

"I doubt if the Cubs will be making a run at the pennant any time soon," she said, scornfully.

"True," he said, "but I really think this could be John's year. He's due. What do you say, Susan? Does this sound like something you can sink your teeth into?"

She started thumbing through the folder. "You know him pretty well, huh?"

"Hey, the guy flew all the way from England to be an usher at my wedding, a couple years back. John's sort of the loyal old-fashioned type; your type, Susan, now that I think about it."

"You don't know my type." She pulled out one of the photos and gazed at it a moment. "He's nice looking, I'll say that much for him."

Jeremy sucked on his candy. "He's single."

"He's too old." She closed the file and stood up. "All right I'll do it." She turned to leave but stopped at the door and looked back. "Auto racing. This will be a first. You owe me one, Jeremy."

Sterns leaned back in his swivel chair, a satisfied look on his face. "You'll thank me someday, Susan. Oh, and one other thing."

She eyed him uneasily. "Yes?"

"It's `motor racing,' not `auto racing.'"

* * *

The wind that blows on the California High Desert was utterly still, the air dry, warm, crystalline as only desert air can be. Wagner turned the hose on his Porsche Speedster and watched the water bead instantly on its waxed finish. Using a soft sponge and no soap, he rubbed down the entire body, once again becoming acquainted with all its little dings and dents and scratches, the only evidence of two years' heavy racing. The Speedster still bore the original Bali blue factory finish, a source of pride to him. The few scars were nothing compared with the smashing and bashing many Speedsters had been put through in club racing. Anymore, it was hard to find a Speedster that wasn't loaded with bondo or lead and several coats of cheap enamel. Wagner knew body men who could smooth out the dings and dents without using an ounce of bondo or lead, but he liked his Speedster the way it was. Each ding and dent told a story, and coming across them again was like encountering old friends and reminded him of just how far he had come in 14

12

years of motor racing. He'd made his share of mistakes along the way, certainly, but buying the Speedster wasn't one of them. Mastering it, winning with it, had given his life purpose and direction--and had been his ticket out of the High Desert.

He wiped away the water with a chamois and rubbed in a fresh coat of wax. Then he scrubbed the tires and wiped down the aluminum wheels. Lastly, he vacuumed the floor board, ran the chamois over the dashboard and seats, checked the oil and tire pressure, and topped off the battery. Now he was done. He started the engine, backed the Speedster into the barn, and switched it off. He closed the barn door, thinking how good a shower would feel, and headed to the house. At the door he saw his mother walking up the long gravel drive, holding up a letter.

"You'll never guess who it's from," she said.

Wagner opened the door for her. "You're right," he said without interest. "I won't."

"Come on, guess."

"I'm taking a shower."

"It's for you. Aren't you going to open it?"

"Later."

"It's from Tina."

His face hardened. Why was Tina writing him now, after all these years? What could she possibly want from him?

He opened the letter and removed a snapshot and a brief note. He glanced at the photo and read the note without emotion.

"What does she say, dear?"

He handed her the photo. "Ron's gotten his driver's license. I guess that's him."

"Of course, it's him," gushed Katie, admiring the photo. "He looks just like you, too, except for those brown eyes."

Wagner started up the stairs.

"He's your son, John, your own flesh and blood. Aren't you the least bit curious about him? Tina says he wants to meet you. I think that's marvelous."

"Well, I don't want to meet him. And I don't want to see Tina. The whole thing never happened, as far as I'm concerned. She's remarried. Ron wouldn't know me from Adam. Why can't they forget about me? I forgot about them--years ago."

13

"You knew this day would come eventually." She held out the photo. "Look at him. He's almost a grown man. Won't you go see him?"

"Forget it." He walked upstairs and shut the door to his room. It was his childhood room, and he felt like a child, running away from something he deeply regretted and tried never to think about. Now, unwanted as they were, memories flooded his consciousness, memories of long ago, before the Speedster, before he joined the army, when he still worked as a mechanic at his father's car dealership. That's when he met Tina. He was a year out of high school, attending night classes at the local junior college, and she was a senior at Antelope Valley High. He was skinny and awkward and hadn't dated much, and couldn't believe someone as lovely as Tina Gonzalez was interested in him. She was Mexican-American, with haunting dark eyes and a flowing mane of black hair. In makeup and heels, she looked as sophisticated as a woman. No matter what Wagner did to himself, he still looked the gawky kid, although she often said he looked like Gary Cooper in a Frank Capra movie. He took her everywhere in his '32 Ford coupe, to Friday night dances, to the beach--where she showed off her busty figure--and especially to a secluded spot on the top of Diablo Pass. But after a year, the magic wore off and the relationship deteriorated to where it revolved around little more than quarreling and sex. When at last he broke it off, she countered with news she was pregnant. It was the worst day of his life. He married her and joined the army, and was away when Ron was born. He took no interest in his son, and lived with Tina only a short while after his Army discharge. Buying the Speedster: that's what precipitated it. He made alimony payments faithfully until she married a cop named Steve Reynolds, who adopted the boy.

Wagner dismissed the whole sad affair as the folly of his youth. Once his racing career took off and he moved to Europe, the memory of it seemed so remote, so like a bad dream, that it seemed he had never met Tina Gonzalez, or had a son who was growing up without him. He never talked about it, so that even friends such as Jeremy Sterns weren't aware he had ever been

14

arried--or had a son. Through the years Katie had stayed in ontact with Tina and Ron, and sent presents at Christmas and irthdays.

Wagner left his room and walked back downstairs. He ooked at Ron's photograph again. "How old is he?"

"He'll be eighteen in August."

"Draft age. All ready." He shook his head. "This time next ear he could be in Vietnam. Maybe I should see him."

"It will mean so much to him, John, and to you, you'll see."

"I don't know where I'll find the time." He looked at his atch. "That gal from SportsWeek will be here in about an our. That'll knock out the rest of today, and tomorrow I have a est session at Willow. It'll have to be Sunday, because after at, I'm off to England and who knows when I'll be back here gain."

"Then Sunday it will be," said Katie. "I'll call Tina and set up."

"Let me do it." He smirked. "Tina: I wonder what she looks ke, after all these years?"

"She's as pretty as ever, John."

Chapter 3

"What have I gotten myself into?" Susan wondered, as her plane descended through a layer of clouds and the urban grid of Los Angeles appeared. She had read Wagner's file twice and still didn't have a clue as to who he was. What was she going to write about him but the usual tripe? He loves speed. He has grease under his nails, scars under his coveralls. He's won ex-number of races, survived ex-number of crashes, and has a reputation for bad luck. Yawn. She wasn't having much luck understanding his sport either. Out of desperation, she'd read two racing novels and learned absolutely nothing.

She claimed her bags, rented a Ford sedan, and headed north on the San Diego Freeway. North of the San Fernando Valley, she switched to Highway 14 and followed it over the San Gabriel Mountains. Cresting the final rise, a broad arid valley opened before her, with a checkerboard of crop farms on one side, an aerospace complex on the other, and in between a few widely dispersed towns. She followed Highway 14 across the valley, to Lancaster, and checked into the hotel Wagner had recommended. She ate a tuna sandwich in the coffee shop, chased it with black coffee, and returned to her room. She leafed through Wagner's file once more, stopped herself, and put it down.

"It's too late for that." She noticed her hands were shaking. "This is crazy. He's just another jock I have to interview." She looked at herself in the mirror. Lots of red hair, hazel eyes, fair skin, no makeup except lip color. "Pale," she said, brushing a red curl out of her eye. "You're too pale."

She found Avenue J and followed it out of town. The mountains to the southeast were snowcapped and stood out. Everything else was desert--sand and sagebrush, and an occasional wire fence jammed with tumbleweeds--until she reached the alfalfa farms on Lancaster's east side. This was unexpected. They were green from regular irrigation and looked like a parcel of midwestern flora that somehow had been transported here and grafted into the desert. It was here she found a silver mailbox bearing Wagner's number. "Edington Farm" read the sign above the mailbox. Up a long gravel drive was the house, an old white victorian set among mature cottonwoods, with a white barn behind it. She parked in the shade of the cottonwoods, climbed out and stretched. The air was warm and still. The only sound was the crunch of gravel beneath her feet.

"Any problem finding the place?"

The voice was coming from the porch. She turned to see a tall figure, lanky as a cowboy, step down to meet her.

"None. Your directions were perfect." She extended her hand. "You must be John Wagner."

"That's right." He smiled. It was the same boyish, crooked smile she recalled seeing in many of his photographs. She felt his eyes looking her over.

"So, you're Susan Jennings. Jeremy didn't tell me you were tall."

She raised an eyebrow. "Just what did Jeremy tell you?"

"Oh, you know, the usual bull."

"I suppose he said I didn't know a lot about your sport."

"No, he didn't."

"Like heck, he didn't." She looked at the vast green fields. They felt cool, and smelled faintly of mint. "Somehow, I didn't picture you as a farmer."

"I'm not. This is my mother's place. I live in London most of the year. I've been staying here while we've been testing at Willow."

"Willow?"

"Willow Springs Raceway. I'm taking you there tomorrow, remember?"

She removed her briefcase from the car and said nothing.

"Here, let me take that," he said.

He led her into the parlor, an uncluttered room, bright with afternoon sunlight. Against one wall was an antique cupboard on which china plates were displayed. In the center of the room were facing sofas. He placed her briefcase on the coffee table between the sofas, and motioned her to sit down.

"Have you had lunch, dear?"

Susan turned around to see a woman as fine and fragile as a porcelain doll, smiling benignly.

"Yes, thank you, I have."

"My mother, Katie Wagner."

"You have a lovely home, Mrs. Wagner."

"It's Katie. Iced tea, then?"

"Maybe later, thank you."

"Then a tour of the house?"

Susan looked at Wagner with questioning eyes.

He shrugged, noncommittal, plopped down on one of the sofas, and removed his shoes.

*   *   *

The interview was into the second tape, but the conversation was in fits and starts, going back and forth in time, without continuity. Susan kept looking at her notes, trying to direct the conversation without asking dumb questions. She sensed she was losing him, and she was beginning to harbor a grudge against Jeremy for insisting she take this assignment. Wagner seemed bored, and probably was, for all the times he'd rehashed this information. He lay lengthwise on the sofa, feet draped over one end, eyes closed. She tried another question. This time, he didn't answer. She repeated the question. He didn't stir. His breathing became rhythmic.

"John? John? Oh, great, he's fallen asleep. Hello, John? Are you still with the living?" She sat back and crossed her arms. "Now what am I supposed to do? Jeremy, I swear. Hey, John. Wake up."

Katie entered balancing a pitcher of iced tea and two glasses on a tray. "How about that tea now?" she said cheerily.

"I think he's fallen asleep."

"No, I haven't." Wagner grunted and sat up. "As a matter of fact, I would love some tea." He took the pitcher and poured them both a glass.

"Have you asked him about the early days when he raced his Speedster," Katie suggested. "That always gets him talking."

19

Wagner smirked. "I'll bet she has no idea what a Speedster is, do you, Susie?"

She shifted uneasily on the sofa. Wagner was on to her: she didn't know what she was talking about, didn't have a clue, in fact. So, what if he was? She wasn't going to try to bluff him. She wasn't going to guess and give him that satisfaction, or worse, be caught faking it. Thankfully, he didn't wait for her answer.

"Hell of a car, the Speedster. Small, lightweight, engine in back." He took a drink of tea. "Remove the windshield and bumpers and you had yourself a racecar. Porsche made them only for a couple of years. My dad bought one of the first ones to come into the country. He raced it a couple of times, but he really couldn't be seen driving it because he owned a British import dealership--bad for business. Anyway, after I was discharged from the Army, I started driving it. One thing led to another, and I ended up buying it from him. A real competitive guy, my dad."

"Is that where you got your competitiveness--from your father?"

Wagner fished the lemon out of his glass, squeezed the juice out, and placed it on the tray. "I'm not nearly as competitive as my dad was. He got upset if anyone tried passing him on the highway. I can remember when I was about fourteen taking a trip with him up to Frisco and never being passed once. He always had to be first in everything. I suppose that's why he was such a great salesman. Me, I preferred working in the backshop, which was a big disappointment to him. He wanted me to sell cars, learn the business, and run it someday." He smiled ruefully. "Yeah, for a long time I was a big disappointment to him."

Susan sipped her tea. "Did you two ever race against each other?"

"Racing cars was about the only thing I could do better than him. It burned him, too, until he realized racing might take me places. Anyway, that's how I got started, with the Speedster. I used to take it out on the backroads at night, just going like hell.

here was one road I especially liked, called Diablo Pass. I
)ent a lot of hours going up and down that road."

Susan scribbled down "Diablo Pass" and underlined it.
Where is this Diablo Pass? I'd like to see it, if you have time."

He looked at his watch. "It's about 30 miles west of here.
here's a place out there that serves a pretty decent steak. We
ould have dinner and afterwards I'll show you the road. How
oes that sound? We'll take the Speedster."

"The Speedster?" Susan sat up. "You mean you still have
1e Speedster? After all these years?"

"Washed it this morning, as a matter of fact."

*   *   *

The ringing metallic whine an air-cooled engine makes at
600 RPM was dulled by the rush of wind. The cloth top was
own, but the windshield--a mere slip of glass--was doing an
mazing job of keeping the wind off Susan's hair. She could
eel every crease and bump in the road, as if the chassis springs
ad been discarded and the frame was resting on the suspension
ump stops. Other than that, the Speedster was a comfortable
ar to be seated in. It had plenty of room for her long legs, and
he liked the way the small bucket seat hugged her hips and
nade her feel planted and secure. It was a peculiar looking car,
) be sure, with its inverted bathtub shape, but she could see the
ppeal.

They drove back through the alfalfa fields, past the
torefronts and gas stations of downtown Lancaster, and into an
xpanse of sagebrush and spiky Joshua Trees that cast long
hadows in the afternoon sunlight. The lumpy San Gabriel
Mountains drew close. Avenue J ended. They turned south and
notored up into the San Gabriel foothills. It didn't seem they
vere going particularly fast, until she noticed the speedometer
udging 90 mph. Cresting the hill, a grass valley revealed itself
n the other side. Susan saw the sparkle of a lake before it
isappeared behind a stand of ponderosa pines. When they were
n the valley, Wagner turned down a gravel drive that passed
hrough the pines. A hundred feet in and the lake reappeared.

21

Against the shore was a weathered A-frame house that had bee converted into a restaurant. A sad-eyed man in white jacke greeted them inside.

"Monsieur Wagner. Is so good to see you again."

"How are you, Michel. Can you get us a seat by th window?"

"For you, my friend, always."

He seated them beside a window that overlooked the lake.

"Can I get Mademoiselle something from the bar?"

"No, thank you, but I would like some coffee, black."

Wagner flipped open his menu. "Beer."

Susan watched him leave. "A French waiter, out here That's unexpected."

"I've known Michel for years. Owns the place."

Susan looked out at the lake dreamily. The last rays c sunlight glittered as gold on the water. Above the lake, the Sa Gabriel Mountains cast shadows that touched the far shore. Sh turned back to him. "Thank you for bringing me here."

"My pleasure."

She glanced at the menu. "How's the fish."

"Trout is Michel's specialty."

"Then trout it is."

Michel returned and placed their drinks on the table. H looked at Wagner expectantly. His mustache twitched.

"The lady will have the trout. I'll have the New York strip rare. Baked potato. Forget the asparagus. Slice up a tomat instead." He handed him the menus.

"Trout stuffed with crab meat is the day's special, or woul mademoiselle prefer the fish prepared in some other way?"

"Stuffed with crab sounds wonderful."

The shadows were stretching fast across the water, coverin the gold in a veil of black. Susan sighed and turned back t Wagner. He too was staring at the water, lost in thought. Sh studied him a moment. For a guy who'd spent most of his lif around cars he had remarkably clean fingernails, and smelled o some subtle cologne. She could see a girl falling for him quit easily. Under different circumstances, she could see hersel falling for him, but allowing something like that to happen, sh

22

knew, would never do. This was an assignment, not a date, and she never allowed herself to confuse the two. Still, what if he should express interest in her, maybe tried to kiss her? It was a delicious thought.

"You were telling me that you raced on public roads," she said.

He winked. "Still do."

"Yes, but isn't that against the law?"

"What isn't? Look, Susie, let's not get into that. Back then they didn't have racing schools, so you had to learn any way you could. I came out here and practiced. Nobody was harmed. Few people travel over Diablo Pass, especially at night, so I wasn't endangering anybody. After about a year, I entered my first race, and stopped coming out here."

"You won your first race, didn't you?"

"I won a lot of races in the Speedster, but it was strictly club event stuff. There was a lot of cheating going on in those days-- still does--and guys would blow me off on the straights who obviously had tweaked their engines in some way. I still beat them, and wouldn't you know it, the bastards would turn around and accuse me of cheating."

Susan laughed. "Were you?"

"Everyone's looking for some type of an advantage over the next guy, but no, I didn't cheat."

"How did you beat them then?"

"In the corners. That's what road racing is all about, Susie-- cornering. But it's more than that, it's about braking, and how you come off the brakes, and using the throttle, being precise, consistent. It's little things that add up in the course of lap. I was winning races pretty regularly and started getting offers to drive faster cars--Jags and Allard J2s mostly. My dad had a friend who owned a four-nine Ferrari, and he talked him into giving me a tryout. Our first race was at Palm Springs, and I smoked the field. It was my first big win--and it opened a lot of doors for me. Within a year, I was living in Europe racing for Ferrari."

Michel returned and placed their dinners before them.

"Can I interest Mademoiselle in a nice white wine to go along with the fish?"

"Thank you, but coffee will be fine."

Michel looked at her with questioning eyes.

"This is a business meal."

"Oh, I'm so sorry." He turned to go.

"On second thought," she said, "maybe I will."

*   *   *

It was dark when they returned to the Speedster and the paving beneath their feet was uneven. Susan struck her toe on something, pitched forward, and felt Wagner's strong hands catch her by the waist.

"A little too much wine, maybe?" He released her.

She felt embarrassed, clumsy, stupid, and angry. Worse, she detected a smile on his face. "You call two glasses too much?"

"Was it two?"

"Okay, three."

She stepped into the Speedster. He closed her door, reached behind her and pulled the canvas top up and over her head and latched it at the windshield.

"Look," he said, climbing in beside her and slamming his door. "I'll bring you back here tomorrow when it's light."

"It's my fault," she said. "I should have stopped after one glass of wine and insisted we leave. It just seemed so pleasant sitting there by the lake and listening to you talk. I do want to see Diablo Pass tonight, the way you used to see it."

"Are you sure? It's no big deal coming back here tomorrow." He turned the key. Behind them, the engine spun to life.

"Yes, I'm sure."

He switched on the headlights and drove back through the pines to the highway. Within minutes they crossed over another hill and followed the twists of a narrow valley. The lights of a country store and a few houses winked past. The curves tightened as they climbed a steeper, higher hill. At the top Wagner pulled over, turned off the engine, and suggested they

24

get out. Standing in the light of the headlights and remembering the feel of his hands around her waist, she wondered if he might try to kiss her, and wondered if she should let him. She could almost feel him taking her into his arms. Maybe it was the afterglow of the wine, because she decided she would let him.

"This is it," he said, looking down the road. "Diablo Pass. From here down to the bottom, it's nothing but curves."

She looked around. It seemed very lonely up here and far away from everything. A breeze hissed through the pines. The road dropped down the hill, out of the reach of the headlights, and disappeared in blackness, the white center line, like an arrow, pointing the way: this way to your doom.

"But what if you had crashed out here?" she said. "Who would ever find you?"

He shrugged. "I was 23. You never think about things like that when you're 23. I could tell you about some circuits--Spa, for example--that are just as dangerous as this road, that have places where, sure, if you left the road, you might not be found. But this very road was probably the best preparation I could have had for Europe.

"Come on," he said. "Let's get back in the car. We've been standing here long enough."

He started the engine and revved it menacingly. "You ready for Diablo Pass?"

Before she could answer, he launched them down the hill, the engine whine high and shrill in their ears. Susan was not ready for this. Her head was too full of wine, her stomach too full of dinner. The Speedster weaved from curve to curve. At the first corner she felt queasy; at the second corner sick. What if this was the night Wagner screwed up and left the road? Just her luck. She could see the headlines: "Race driver and female companion killed on public road." Oh, her head was going round and round. She was going to vomit, right inside the Speedster. Then Wagner did something totally unexpected--he backed off the gas and drove the rest of the way slowly.

Chapter 4

If you weren't looking for it, you would drive right past Willow Springs Raceway and not know it was there. The sagebrush along the highway disguised a good part of it. There was no gate or guardhouse to mark the entryway, and the narrow road leading in was not promising. The only marker was a small, weathered sign. It read: "Willow Springs Raceway."

Wagner turned into the entry and Susan's big white Ford began to rock and shake over the potholes in the road. Two hundred yards in and the first signs of life appeared: a few weathered shacks that passed for a control tower, administration office, and a garage, and after that a strip of asphalt that was the front straightaway. Susan spotted the large Garret-Hawk transporter and several cars parked at the back of one of the shacks.

"That's Michael's car," Wagner said, parking the Ford beside a red Corvette. He smirked. "My teammate." He reached in the back seat and grabbed his helmet and a nylon bag containing his driving coveralls. They walked around to the front and saw two racecars parked on the pit apron. They were open-cockpit, and long and pointed as a pair of missiles, painted white with blue center stripe and blue sidetanks, and exposed wide, flat-treaded tires.

"This must be the scribe," came a voice from inside the garage. Susan turned to see a short man, as plump and pleasant looking as a teddy bear, walking into the sunlight to greet her. "Hi. I'm Eddie Garret, the team manager. And you are? Sorry, but I'm bad with names."

"Susan Jennings."

"Susan Jennings, that's right, from SportsWeek. Let me introduce you to my crew. You don't mind, do you, John? Everyone, listen up. We have a visitor. Her name is Susan Jennings. Be careful what you say around her because she's a writer." He chuckled, to let Susan know he was joking. She

smiled politely. "Let's see," Eddie said, looking over the crew
"The guy in glasses there is George Gilbert, better known a
Hacksaw, our crew chief. His cars used to win pretty regularl
at Indy, until we hired him away, that is. You've heard of him
no doubt."

"I'm sorry, but I haven't," Susan said.

Hacksaw shrugged. "That's okay. My wife barel
recognizes me either, I'm away so much."

"Our engine man is J. Renwick Jackson. Used to be wit
BRM. We found him turning wrenches in a car dealership dow
in San Pedro, if you can believe it. One of our bargain finds."

"Call me Rennie," said the short Englishman. He smilec
revealing two prominent front teeth.

"Then there's Ray Springer, like John, a California boy
Worked for Carroll Shelby when Carroll was still racing Cobra:
He does suspension and brakes. And there's Dave Milzarek
clutch and transmission. He was with Jim Hall until the
switched to that slush box. He's from somewhere on the eas
coast, I forget where."

"Philly," said Milzarek, inhaling on a cigarette.

"Right. And Tom Faber. Just back from Vietnam. How ol
are you, Tom?"

"Twenty-one."

"Tom loves Chevies more than he does the ladies. He's ou
apprentice."

"Gofer is more like it," said Faber. "I'm always going fo
stuff--parts, cigarettes, you name it, I get it."

"And when we're done testing today you'll go for beer,
laughed Rennie.

Susan shook hands with each crewman. They all had th
same rough calloused hands, and were all dressed in white shirt
and blue pants. Over their left breast pocket was the tear
emblem--a black hawk with outspread wings, and, below it, i
big gold letters, G-A-R-R-E-T--H-A-W-K.

"And, of course, there's Michael Bravo," said Eddie. "Ou
number-two driver. Dad discovered him last summer racing
Formula Fords. He'll make his first race start next weekend a
Oulton Park."

28

Susan said hello. Bravo was small and fragile looking, with big blue eyes and a moptop of jet-black hair. Standing beside Wagner, he looked like a boy.

"Let's see," Eddie said, thinking, "back at the shop there's Travis Olson, our design engineer. If you want to know the truth, it's Hacksaw who designs our cars; Travis merely inks in the details. And there's Walt Balchowsky and Zeke Barnette, our two fabricators, and an old German named Leo Schwartz, our machinist. Who am I leaving out, Hacksaw?"

"Huey, Dewey and Louie."

Eddie chuckled. "Right. Our engine builders. Their real names are Chuck Cecil, Gary Washburn, and Lou Downey. All English lads, like Rennie, with about 50 years experience among them. And, of course, there's my father, Edward W. Garret. The team is really his baby. He couldn't be here today--business. But I believe you have an interview set up with him for tomorrow morning."

"Eight o'clock," said Susan.

"Be on time," Eddie said gravely. "My dad expects promptness."

Wagner disappeared inside the transporter and emerged wearing his white driving coveralls. Over the left breast was the Garret-Hawk emblem, on the right breast an emblem for Unirich Tire & Rubber Co., the team's main sponsor, and on the sleeves various smaller patches for lesser sponsors. He pulled on his black helmet, eased his goggles down over his eyes, and slipped into car number 36. He fired the engine, revved it for several seconds, nodded at Hacksaw, and screamed away. Bravo followed him out in car number 37.

Susan removed her hands from her ears and watched the two cars disappear around Turn One. A moment later they reappeared on the hill, slowing and dipping into Turn Three. They accelerated uphill, rounded Turn Four at the top, and barreled back down, sounding fierce and determined. They reached the desert floor and disappeared again, but Susan could hear the rise and fall of the engines as the drivers lifted and accelerated through Turns Seven and Eight, moving from her left to her right, and reappearing out of Turn Nine. She cupped her ears again as they came around and rocketed past at 180 mph. A second later, she felt their tail-wind ruffle her clothes and hair.

"Johnny's about two seconds a lap quicker than our dear Michael," someone said, standing beside her. It was Rennie. He was about a head shorter than she. He had thick black hair, dark skin, and those prominent upper teeth that showed whenever he spoke or smiled.

"Michael is learning, but it takes time," he said. "John is just toying with him."

They watched the two cars bear down on Turn Three. Number 36, in front, slowed and rounded the curve smoothly, but smoke flared from the tires of number 37 as it slowed and turned.

"Aye," said Rennie. "See there? Michael locked his brakes. Trying too hard, he is."

They watched the cars sweep down off the hill and disappear into the desert again, heard them go past on the backside of the circuit, round Turns Eight and Nine, and come back around into view again. Number 37 emerged first--and alone--and flashed past.

Rennie's dark brows raised with concern. "Where's Johnny?"

"I see him," said Tom Faber.

Susan craned her neck and saw a racecar roll slowly into view, trailing a plume of black smoke.

"Looks like one of your engines, Ren."

"Aye," he said. "I can see, thank you very much."

Wagner turned down pit lane and stopped. He removed his helmet and climbed out. "Lost all power backing off for Eight," he said, tight jawed.

Rennie removed the engine cover and peered around. "She's not dropping oil. Could be a valve or a piston. In any event, I think your day is done, Johnny, sorry to say."

Wagner sat on the tarmac. Susan watched him. He seemed tense. Rennie and Tom Faber pushed the car toward the garage. Far off, she could hear Bravo backing off for Turn Eight, then gun the engine turning in. The engine grew louder as he circled around Nine. A moment later, he screamed past again, six feet from where Wagner was sitting.

Susan went over to him. "Can your car be fixed?"

"No, engine's blown. They didn't bring a spare, so that shoots today. This was our last day of testing before Oulton Park." He stood up, exhaled, and smiled at her.

"Lunch?"

*   *   *

It was late afternoon. Inside the farmhouse, shadows stretched from the furniture like silken hose. Wagner lay sprawled on the sofa, his stocking feet dangling over the side. "Listen, forget all that psycho-babble about why people race, you know, that it's a death wish or a substitute for sex. That's a bunch of baloney. And it's not about speed either. Speed is relative. It's about controlling the car, making it do exactly what you want it to do. When I go through a corner, knowing I've taken it on the absolute limit--that I can't go one-mile-an-hour faster--that's it. That's what it's all about. There's no feeling like it in the world. None." He paused, thought about it, and smiled mischievously at Susan. "Well, almost none."

She picked up an eraser and flung it at him.

He caught it easily. "Not much of an arm for a pitcher, Susie."

"That wasn't my high fast one. One last question."

"Shoot."

She handed him a photo. It was a group shot of eight drivers, all hamming it up for the camera. Wagner studied the photo a moment. "This must have been taken my first year in Europe. Gad, I look young. I still had my crewcut."

"Who are the others?"

"Let's see. Bogavanti, Lafosse, me, Calti--what a character he was--St. Onge, Torrez, Forgue, and Hermann."

"How many are still alive?"

"Bogavanti, Lafosse, me, of course, and Forgue." He handed the photo back to her.

"That's it? You mean, the rest are dead?"

He leaned back and closed his eyes. "Yes."

"That's half the group." She placed the photo on the coffee table. "It's the inherent danger that makes racing so different from other sports. Baseball, football, hockey, even boxing--none of them are as inherently dangerous as motor racing. What if baseball were as dangerous? Half of my childhood idols might be dead today. Think about it."

Wagner frowned at the ceiling. He didn't want to think about it. He didn't need reminding that racing was dangerous. "You said you had one last question."

She clicked off the recorder. "You've answered it."

Katie reappeared at the door, wiping her hands on her apron. "I do hope you're staying for dinner, Susan, dear."

Susan rose. "No, I'm sorry I can't. I have an interview tomorrow morning with Edward W. Garret that I need to prepare for, and I want to go over my notes from today and write down some things."

"You have an interview tomorrow?" asked Katie. "But it's Sunday."

"Sunday's just another workday for me. And it's the only time Garret had available."

"I think that's awful. John, make her stay for dinner."

"You heard her She has work to do."

Katie gave Susan a hug. "I do hope we meet again."

"I hope so, too. Goodbye, Katie."

Wagner took her briefcase and carried it out to her car. "You won't change your mind about dinner, will you? There's a Mexican restaurant in town over on Avenue I that's a favorite of mine. They make great margueritas."

"Thanks, but I can't." She looked up into his eyes. "I'm sorry if that last question offended you."

"It didn't, but I have the feeling you don't exactly approve of what I do."

She removed her keys. "Whether I approve or not isn't important. You're the story, John Wagner. I'm merely the writer."

"You sure you don't want a marguerita--to help take off the edge?"

She smiled. "I'm going to need that edge to get through my work tonight."

"How about lunch then--after the interview tomorrow? It would give us a chance to talk about something besides racing. You know, we've spent the last couple of days together and I feel like I hardly know you."

She thought it might come to this. She had sensed his growing interest in her throughout the afternoon, seen it his eyes, in the way he looked at her, as if he had discovered for the first time she was a woman. She had mixed feelings about this. On the one hand, she would love having lunch with him tomorrow, drifting through the afternoon hours in quiet conversation, without thought of interviews or deadlines. On the other hand, she couldn't. After her interview with Garret, she would have tapes to play back, writing to do, a story to shape. Besides, it meant crossing over the line and getting involved personally. She had almost done that the night before. She wasn't about to let it happen again. And it would happen. The attraction she was feeling was too great.

"I'm going to have to say no."

"Is it work? Forget the work."

"It's more than work."

"It is? We're only talking lunch."

"You know what I mean." She climbed in the car.

"No, I don't. Explain it to me. Look, Susie, I like you, and I'm pretty certain you like me. Is that a crime?"

She started the engine and pulled away without another word. Through the dust, he could see the brake lights come on, the car turn onto Avenue J and accelerate back to Lancaster.

Chapter 5

Garret-Hawk Racing Enterprises was headquartered in a long white factory building in North Hollywood, two blocks east of Lankershim Boulevard. Her interview with Garret over, and having been given a tour of the shop where the Formula Ones were built, Susan pushed through the big glass door of the main entrance and walked across the parking lot to her car. Parked beside her Ford Sedan was Wagner's Bali blue Speedster. The Californian was seated behind the wheel reading a newspaper.

He looked up. "How'd the interview go?"

"He's a jerk, if you want to know the truth." She climbed in beside him without hesitation.

Wagner started the engine. "Tell me about it over lunch." He cut over to Ventura Boulevard through a dizzying series of side streets, never coming to a complete stop despite passing a dozen stop signs, knifed through traffic on Ventura Boulevard, and whipped into a parking lot behind a small French restaurant called Maison Misslin. Facing the street was a garden terrace with seating around a half-dozen wrought iron tables, each with a sun umbrella. Only the tables were vacant and the sun umbrellas folded down, due to a stiff wind blowing down from the foothills. He told the waiter to seat them on the terrace, which he did, raising the sun umbrella above them.

Wagner looked at her a moment. "I thought it would be nice to sit outside in the sun. I hope you're not cold."

Susan squirmed to get comfortable in the metal chair and buttoned up her sweater. She was cold. "I'm fine."

"You sure? We can always go inside."

"I'm sure."

"So, tell me about Garret?"

She shook her head. "You wouldn't believe it. I was at his office at eight sharp, like he asked, and he made me wait two whole hours before he would see me. Then, for 40 minutes, he rambled nonstop about his dream of building the first American

Grand Prix car to win the world championship. When I tried questioning him about you, he said he had pressing business and dismissed me. He said Michael Bravo was the future of the team."

Wagner snickered. "Michael? You're kidding."

"No, I'm not. Afterwards, Eddie took me around the shop. He's a gentleman."

"Eddie's all right, a bit naive, but all right."

"Hacksaw speaks very highly of you, by the way."

"Yeah? He's the reason we're winning."

The waiter took their order. Only in a French restaurant in Los Angeles can you be served a hamburger, which is what Wagner ordered, with the works--mustard, ketchup, mayo, pickles, onions, cheese. And a beer. Susan gave up looking over the menu and ordered the same thing--with red wine. When the wind didn't blow, she could feel the sun's warmth; but mostly it blew, rattling the umbrella pole and whipping her red hair into her eyes.

"Jeremy said you played ball as a kid."

She nodded. "I could outhit and outrun most boys my age. My dad used to play in the minors. The poor guy wanted a son and kept having daughters. I'm the middle of five girls. I was also the most athletic, so I guess I became the son he never had. He even tried to get me into little league, but since I was a girl, they wouldn't take me. So I pitched in an all-girls' softball league and still hold the record for the most strikeouts. And ... why are you looking at me that way?"

"I was just trying to imagine you giving those poor boys a hard time."

"It wasn't like that. They razzed me constantly."

"I wouldn't have razzed you."

"You would have been the most unmerciful."

"How do you know?"

"I can tell about these things."

"You got me wrong. I would have asked you to go steady."

"Even if I could outhit you?"

Wagner smiled. She had a point there. "How did you get into writing about sports?"

"I started in junior high, as a stringer for the local paper. Right away, I knew this was for me. I went to college on an athletic scholarship, but dropped out after my first year and went to work full time for the <u>Chicago Herald</u>. It nearly broke my father's heart, but it was the best thing I ever did. <u>SportsWeek</u> liked my work and offered me a job a couple years later, and there you have it."

After eating, Wagner looked at his watch. "The day's still young. How about if we go somewhere? Maybe drive over to the beach?"

Susan smiled. "I really have enjoyed this, but I can't, John."

"What's stopping you?"

"Well, for one thing, I have work to do."

"Here we go again--work. What do you have to do, play back Garret's tape? Waste of time."

"It's more than that. Remember last night? I wanted to go over my notes and write down some things, but I got to my room and couldn't keep my eyes open. And I still have to listen to your tapes."

"Listen to them on the plane. It's a sunny day. The Speedster's got a full tank of gas. When's a chance like this going to come along again?"

Susan looked at her hands. They looked empty without her pencil and notepad. She had none of the trappings to stop her, nothing of her job to lean on and support her in saying no.

"All right. But drive slower this time."

The Speedster again, the harsh ride, the rush of wind, zooming in and out of traffic on the Ventura Freeway. Offramps whipped past for a succession of Valley towns--Sherman Oaks, Encino, Tarzana, Woodland Hills. The freeway rose gradually to Calabasas and out of suburbia, crossed Simi Hills and descended into a narrow canyon en route to Thousands Oaks and points beyond. Wagner wasn't going that way, and turned off onto Malibu Canyon Road. Within minutes they were over the Santa Monica Mountains and facing the blue-green Pacific. He pulled into the Surfriders State Beach parking lot and stopped. Slow rollers crashed against the shore.

He turned to her. "Do you feel like walking?"

"On the beach? I'd love to."

A wet breeze blew in off the water. Overhead, seagulls faced the wind with wings outspread, but not advancing, as if suspended by invisible strings. Occasionally, one would veer off and wheel around back into formation. The beach was empty except for a few hearty sunbathers and an old man walking his dog.

They left their shoes inside the Porsche and walked barefoot along the beach, holding hands, kicking up sand, sidestepping an occasional mound of kelp the waves had washed ashore. They climbed an outcropping of rock, giggling as they steadied themselves. Susan missed a step, reached for him, and felt herself being pulled gently into his embrace. Then she felt a finger lift her chin and welcomed a kiss, tender but not lingering. Susan surprised herself by pulling him back for just a little more.

Everything flowed naturally after that. Susan would no longer deny her feelings. She wanted to be held by him. They put their arms around each other walking back to the car, taking their time, as if to make the moment last as long as possible. Back in the Speedster, they kissed like teenagers.

"I wanted to do this last night," he said.

"Why didn't you?"

"You weren't exactly encouraging, remember?"

"No, I guess I wasn't." She kissed him again, a very long and passionate kiss. "How's that for encouragement?"

Instead of going back over Malibu Canyon, Wagner went south on Pacific Coast Highway. They drifted through Malibu and Pacific Palisades, enjoying the broad sweep of the Santa Monica Bay. Somewhere around Venice they turned inland. It wasn't long before Susan saw the commercial jetliners gliding down out of the sky and disappearing into the horizon of hotels and office buildings near Los Angeles Airport.

"Where are we going," she asked.

"To a nice hotel."

"Don't you have an apartment near Garret's plant? I would prefer going there, if you don't mind."

"Haven't had time to find one. No need, anyway."

"I don't want to go to some hotel, John."

38

"But you would go to my apartment. I don't see the difference."

Susan said nothing.

"No one cares, if that's what's bothering you."

Susan still said nothing.

He pulled into the front of the hotel. A doorman dressed up like a royal guardsman stepped out to open Susan's door.

"Take me back to my car," she said, ignoring the doorman.

"Susie."

"It's Susan. Take me to my car, please."

A bellhop arrived for their bags.

Wagner looked at his hands gripping the steering wheel, shook his head.

"Sir?" said the doorman.

"I guess we're leaving," he sighed.

The following morning, Wagner boarded a jetliner for London. The plane took off over the Santa Monica Bay, made a -turn, and headed inland. Above Los Angeles, the plane slowed as if someone had hit the brakes, and seemed to hang in the sky. Wagner had no fear of flying, but wished the pilot would get back on the throttle and fast. A few minutes later, crossing the San Gabriel Mountains, he felt a surge of acceleration pull him gently back into his seat. That was better. He settled back and said softly, "Go like hell, plane." Then he chuckled. Go like hell? That was the story of his life. The only time he truly relaxed was when he was going like hell.

It was later, somewhere over the Atlantic, that he remembered his son. He'd forgotten to go and see him.

Chapter 6

As dawn crept over London early Tuesday morning, the Boeing 707 carrying the Garret-Hawk team touched down at Heathrow Airport. Hacksaw and the crew spent the day transferring the racecars and equipment to their summer headquarters, an old brick hanger beneath the glide path of Heathrow's busiest runway. Susan checked into a hotel and in the afternoon dropped by the hangar. The moment she heard the deafening whine of a jetliner coming in for a landing--flying directly overhead--she just knew it was going to crash into the building, and ducked under a work bench.

"You get used to it," Rennie said, taking her hand and helping her to her feet. "Eventually."

The following morning, the team moved again, this time by highway and only for the weekend, to Cheshire, for the Oulton Park Gold Cup. Wagner picked up Susan in his other Porsche, the black 911S he used to travel around Europe, and started up the M1. To Susan, after the exposed, bone-jarring Speedster, the 911S was like riding in the lap of luxury. The low-slung coupe was quiet, air-tight, and best of all, rode smoothly. Further along, they switched over to the M6, passed through industrial Birmingham, and into Northwest England.

This time, Wagner was determined to get it right and had reserved a room for them at the George Inn, a wonderful old half-timbered house dating from the seventeenth century, the type known locally as a "magpie" due to its scheme of black beams and white plaster. It was the perfect romantic spot, on a narrow tree-lined street within the medieval walls of old Chester. Wagner reserved the best room in the house, the one with a private bath. When they arrived it was dark, and raining. They made a mad dash for the door, giggling as they ran. Inside, a log was blazing in a big open fireplace. Susan was enchanted until learning Wagner had reserved only one room.

"John, I don't know how to say this. I'm sorry, but I must have my own room."

Wagner was signing the register. He asked the desk clerk to excuse him a moment. He turned to Susan. His eyes narrowed. "What?"

"I know it sounds old-fashioned, and maybe it is, but I must insist on having my own room."

Annoyance, anger, disbelief; she could see it all in his eyes. He spoke in a forceful whisper. "This is nuts. I go out of my way to bring you here. I even get us a room with a private bath. What am I supposed to do now?"

"I don't care about a private bath. Just get me my own room."

"Why?"

"We're not married."

"Not ... what does marriage have to do with it?"

"I'm not some cheap floozy who sleeps around."

Wagner didn't say anything. His eyes said volumes.

"But you're making me feel like one. Please, do as I ask."

The desk clerk was watching them with some curiosity, but looked away whenever Wagner glanced in his direction.

"They won't have another room--there's a race this weekend, remember--then what?"

"Then take me to another hotel."

"That's just great, Susie. It's raining. It's dark. There won't be another vacant room in Chester. We'll have to drive out into the countryside and hunt."

"Ask if they have a room."

"Look, you sleep on the bed," he said. "I'll sleep on the floor, if that will make you happy."

"Ask."

"They don't have a room. I guarantee it."

"Ask."

"They don't. Watch." He turned to the clerk. In a calmer voice, he said, "You wouldn't happen to have another room, would you?"

"As a matter of fact, a gentleman called not five minutes ago to cancel."

42

Susan nodded. "See."

"This must be your lucky night," said the clerk.

"I'll take it," Wagner said, feeling anything but lucky.

After dining, they drifted downstairs to the bar where four men in tweed coats were playing billiards. Susan sat at Wagner's side, enjoying the game. A waiter arrived and Wagner ordered a dark ale for himself and a white wine for her. No sooner had the drinks been served when one of the gentlemen offered Wagner his cue. He shook his head. "Thanks, no."

"I'll play," Susan said, brightly. "Do you mind, John?"

Wagner sipped his ale. "Don't let me stop you."

For 60 minutes he watched her shoot the eyes out of the gentlemen in tweed coats. It depressed him even more.

"I have a practice session in the morning," he said, when the clock struck eleven. He rose and turned to leave. "I'm heading up."

"Wait." Susan put down her cue and took his arm. "I'm with you, remember?"

At her door, he kissed her, a perfunctory kiss without feeling. Then he continued down the hall to his room, the one without the private bath. He undressed, donned a robe, and went searching for someplace to brush his teeth. When he returned to his room, he found Susan in his bed.

*   *   *

The sidemirrors on Wagner's racecar vibrated with the pulse of the engine, blurring the image of the car behind him. It was another Garret-Hawk, driven by Michael Bravo, falling back as the two accelerated out of Esso Bend. Huge black oaks, bare from the long winter months, loomed on the rolling terrain. Their limbs curved down to the road and looked like arthritic hands reaching out to snatch a car, should it stray off line. The trees flew past like a gallery of phantoms. The road dipped and curved right for Knicker Brook. On either side a small dark body of water winked and flew past. The road climbed, crested a hill, and Wagner felt a moment of weightlessness, as his machine soared above the road, and jarred his backbone as it landed. A puff of white smoke in his mirror drew his attention. He looked and saw Bravo's car swerving back and forth across the road, recover and motor on. It was Bravo's fourth trip around the 2.8-mile Oulton Park circuit and already he was having trouble. Wagner took the next corner slower, and the next, and Young Michael closed up on his tail again, following him like some obedient puppy dog.

Setting up for Old Hall Corner, to begin another lap, Wagner was stunned to see Bravo moving up on the inside, trying to pass him. Turning in, Wagner managed to squeeze him out and stay in front. He shook a fist. "Stay back, jerk. You might learn something. Nuts. What's he think, I'm slow or something?" Exiting, he wound the engine out through the gears. A moment later, he felt the chassis lift and become light plunging downhill into the Cascades left-hander. Outside the curve, the terrain sloped down to the cattails that thrived in the shallow waters of Upper Lake. Dropping down into the curve--feeling the chassis settle back on its springs as he braked and downshifted--the lake with its cattails filled his vision, then veered off to his right as he rounded the curve and accelerated away.

After Cascades, Bravo disappeared from his mirrors. He backed off and waited for the familiar white-and-blue machine to reappear. It never did. He rounded bowl-shaped Esso Bend and winged back through the gallery of black oaks, down to the opposite end of Upper Lake. It was here, setting up for Knicker Brook, he saw his teammate, standing up in the seat of his cockpit, his racecar half-submerged in water outside Cascades.

*   *   *

"Don't worry about it, Michael," Edward W. Garret said, as a big tow rig dragged the racecar slowly from the lake. "You were going flat out and you lost it. It happens."

"I'm really sorry about this," said Bravo, fighting back tears.

"Don't be. Once the car's outta there and cleaned up and you're out running laps again, no one will even remember."

44

A crowd had gathered. It wasn't every day someone plunged into Upper Lake. The white and blue machine was pulled up on dry land now, water pouring from its seams.

"What do you think, Hacksaw?" Wagner nodded towards Bravo's car. "Can you fix it, or is Michael a spectator this weekend?"

The crew chief rubbed his chin. "Won't know till I've had a closer look. But right now, I'd say the chances of having that car ready are slim and forget it."

"I told you we should have brought up one of the Mark Fives, as a backup." Wagner frowned. "This is ridiculous."

Susan watched the crowd. Everyone had come out to see: drivers, officials, journalists, even some stunningly beautiful women who were so much a part of the Formula One scene and often in the company of wealthy older men, some old enough to be their grandfathers. She could hear derisive comments and squeals of laughter, all directed away from Bravo, lest he connect a face with someone making fun of him. The whole sad affair had turned into a sideshow. She shook her head. "Poor Michael."

Wagner smiled wryly. "Every driver spins once in a while. Sometimes no one even knows about it. Not Michael. Nope. He has to go and spin into a lake."

Hacksaw picked up a cattail dragged up with the car, and speared the water repeatedly. The veins on his neck were showing. He'd be getting no sleep tonight. He and his five-man crew would have to strip Bravo's car, clean it, and put it back together again, all in one night. He nudged back his horn rims and eyed Wagner. "You know what this could mean, don't you?"

"It means we should have brought up one of the Mark Fives, like I told you."

"It could mean sharing your car with Mikey, if Garret has anything to say about it, and he will."

Wagner's face hardened. "You just see to it that Michael's car gets fixed tonight, so I don't have to face that prospect."

"Why didn't you bring a backup car?" Susan looked at them both with questioning eyes.

45

Wagner sighed. "It's a long story. The fact is, Bravo's car is the backup. This was a one-car team, before Garret decided to add Michael. Anyway, once the Mark Fives are sorted, it won't matter, because three have been built--one for me and one for Michael, and one as backup. The chassis we're running here is last year's car--the Mark Four."

The show was over and the crowd dispersed. Bravo's car was loaded onto a trailer and wheeled back to the paddock. The crew began taking it apart but stopped when Hacksaw discovered a crease in the magnesium skin. The monocoque chassis tub--onto which everything was attached--had kinked in the mishap.

"John's gonna love this," said the crew chief, shaking his head.

Edward W. Garret and his son Eddie were having lunch in the transporter when Hacksaw entered.

"No way can we fix that car in time for the race," the crew chief said, watching them eat.

"And why is that?" Garret asked, between bites of food.

"Tub's bent. Only way we can fix it is back at the shop. I guess that means Mikey will sit out his first Formula race. Want me to tell him?"

"No need." Garret pushed his plate away. "I want Michael to drive John's car. He needs the experience. The race is merely a tune-up and doesn't carry any points, so John won't mind."

Hacksaw shoved his hands into his pockets. "If he's a race driver he'll mind plenty. Listen, boss, Wagner's your home-run hitter. He can win this thing...."

"He's right, Dad," Eddie chimed in. "Let's go for the win. It'll establish a winning attitude."

Garret put up his hands. "Don't tell me about winning. I wrote the book on winning. Find John and send him in here. It's better that he hears it from me."

"I think you're making a mistake, boss."

"That's your opinion Hacksaw and you keep it to yourself. Now, get me John."

*   *   *

Wagner watched Bravo take out his car in the afternoon session. It pushed in the tight curves, but with stiffer front springs the front tires began to stick and he managed a respectable 1 min 36.3 sec, for eleventh fastest. The second day of practice, in the morning, Wagner drove the car again, changed the front anti-roll bar, added a touch more negative camber to the front wheels, and recorded 1 min 33.9 sec--a new lap record.

"Let Garret chew on that a while," he said, turning the car back over to Bravo.

"You know, you got a mean streak in you, boy," Hacksaw said, amused. "I kinda like that."

As morning turned to afternoon, black clouds gathered in the west. Before the circuit was drenched in rain, Bravo recorded 1 min 35.2 sec, for eighth spot on the starting grid.

Tired, cold and bored, Wagner returned with Susan to the Inn. The desk clerk handed him their room keys, and a message. Wagner opened it. It was from Herb Cook, the president of the Unirich Tire & Rubber Company. Cook rarely attended races, but since he was in London for a meeting with his European sales directors, he'd decided to see this one. Would Wagner meet him at seven for a drink at the Boar's Head Tavern, on Lower Bridge Street?

Wagner crumpled the note. "Nuts."

"Who's it from?" Susan asked.

"Only our biggest sponsor. He wants to meet me for a drink. There goes our dinner, Susie."

"What time does he want to meet with you?"

"Seven."

"We can have dinner afterwards. Most places around here don't start serving till eight, anyway."

"No, Cook will want to have dinner, too."

She smiled wistfully. "Oh, well, maybe it's for the best. I need to work on your story."

47

"Why bother? I'm not racing tomorrow."

Wagner walked up to his room, grabbed his robe, and went down the hall to shower. He owed Cook a lot. It was Cook who stepped in to save Brabham, when the small English team lost its biggest sponsor and was about to fold. Brabham started winning after that--and Wagner almost won the world championship. That was the year he lost the title to Evans at Watkins Glen. When Brabham was no longer a front runner, Cook stepped in again, and set up the deal with Garret-Hawk. Unfortunately, the deal didn't go smoothly, but that was no fault of Cook's. At first, Edward W. Garret agreed to the deal, then changed his mind, saying he'd decided to go with youth and was hiring a 22-year-old driver named Michael Bravo. Cook upped the ante, offering to finance a second car, making Garret-Hawk a two-car team. Garret thought about it, agreed--and changed his mind again. Weeks went by, then months, with Wagner's career hanging in the balance. Cook told him to be patient, that a deal was pending, but Wagner could no longer wait and renewed his contract with Brabham. Then, mere days before the South African Grand Prix, a deal was reached, but it came with a condition--Wagner had to win the race. He tested the car before committing, decided it was worth the risk, and severed ties with Brabham (again, thanks to Cook, who got him out of his contract). Later, after Wagner won the race, Cook told him there had been no such condition, that a contract was forthcoming regardless of where he finished, that talk of having to win was merely unfounded rumor, but Wagner knew better.

After showering, he returned to his room, unpacked the blue suit he wore to banquets, decided it was too formal, and instead dressed in a pressed tattersall shirt, pressed Levis, and white low-cut sneakers, clothes he felt comfortable wearing. The moment he stepped inside the Boar's Head Tavern he knew he'd made a mistake. It wasn't just Cook he was meeting for a drink, but two of Cook's sales directors, and--to his surprise--Garret. They were all dressed in businessman's uniform--three-piece suit, starched white shirt, and regimental striped tie. Cook was tall, lean and angular, with hollow cheeks and a full head of salt-and-pepper hair. The sales directors were both trim and silver-haired.

One was English, the other French. Garret was Garret: short, bullish, with red face and bulging eyes, as if his necktie were knotted too tightly.

"Sit here next to me, John-Boy," said Cook, rising. Wagner slid into the booth beside him. Facing him were Garret and the two sales directors. Garret looked like he wanted to be somewhere else.

"You know, Ed," Cook said, drawing Garret into the conversation. "I never told you this before, but once upon a time I raced against John."

Garret's face registered no emotion.

Cook stopped a waiter. "Get my friend here a dark ale, will you? And another round of martinis for the rest of us. Ale's what you want, isn't it, John, or are you drinking something stiffer these days, now that you're driving for Garret?"

"Ale's fine."

Cook turned back to Garret and continued. "It was in the mid-fifties, when I was managing the Coast Division for Unirich, and living in Los Angeles. I used to race a Porsche Speedster on weekends, strictly club races, you understand, although somewhere in my thinking I suppose I thought I might be the next Rex Mays." Cook chuckled at the irony.

"That was back when you were young and full of piss and vinegar," laughed one of the directors.

"I still am full of piss and vinegar," Cook growled. He winked at Wagner.

Garret said nothing. Now he understood why Cook had wanted Wagner as his driver--he liked him.

"Hell of a car, the Speedster," continued Cook. "Wish I still had mine. Anyway, one weekend this skinny kid driving a Speedster like mine shows up and blows my doors off. Embarrassing as hell, let me tell you, because I had a Super and this kid was driving a Normal. I thought, he can't beat me, I got more horsepower. He's gotta be cheating. So I complained to the tech inspectors and they looked over his Porsche pretty good and could not find a damn thing illegal about it. You tell them what happened after that, John."

"I don't remember."

49

The waiter returned with their drinks.

"Sure, you do. I asked you to show me how you drove so bloomin' fast, remember?" He looked at the others. "As a favor, he drove me around the track--I think it was Pomona. He was so smooth with the brakes and so smooth with the gas it hardly seemed we were going fast at all. What was that you used to tell me, John?"

Wagner sipped his ale. "Take the corners with power on."

"Yeah, that's it. See, I was hitting the corners so damn fast, with the chassis cocked over and the tires sliding--looked as impressive as shit, let me tell you. But I couldn't get back on the damn gas until I was practically out of the damn corner, I was sliding so much." Cook shook his head. "John here was getting back on the gas <u>before</u> the corner, and hardly slid at all."

"Did your lap times improve after that?" asked the French sales director.

"Some, but not enough to keep up with this guy." He nodded toward Wagner. "I just didn't have it. But I was smart enough to know it." He looked at Garret evenly and said without inflection: "Being a keen judge of talent is one of the key management skills, isn't that right, Ed."

Garret folded his arms. He sensed where the conversation was going and didn't like it. "Bravo needs the experience."

"My tires need the victory." Cook pointed to his sales directors. His hollow cheeks quivered. "Ask them if they care a damn about Michael getting experience tomorrow. All they care about is winning, and what it can do for sales. Why do you think a U.S. company spends millions over here on Formula One--for fun? I can't make you, but John here better be driving in that race tomorrow. Michael has a whole season ahead of him to get his precious experience, for all the good it will do him; parks his car in a damn lake. Incredible, Ed, just incredible."

Garret's eyes had been focused on the wall behind Wagner's head. Now they looked at Cook. They had a tinge of anger burning in them. "You don't think much of Michael, do you?"

"Let's just say, I don't think he's ready for Formula One, and leave it at that."

Garret stared back at the wall behind Wagner. Gradually his eyes focused on the driver. Very slowly, he said: "You drive the car tomorrow, John."

Cook grinned. "Now, that's the kind of talk I like." He threw down the last of his martini. "I'm starved. Can we get any beef around here? I mean real beef, not any dinky little piece of stewed meat covered with gravy; I want steak, cooked over a flame, an inch thick at the very least, and large enough to cover a damn plate. Is that too much too ask?"

"I know just the place," said Wagner, rising.

Cook had intervened, but Wagner sensed there was a limit to what he could do. Maybe that was good. He didn't want to be calling on Cook every time Garret pulled one of his little surprises. Next time, Wagner knew, he would have to fend for himself.

Race day, the sky over northwest England was clear and bright. At two PM, as international flags snapped in a stiff breeze, the cars were waved off. Wagner jumped into the lead, extended it, and appeared to have the race won until an injector pump seized forcing him to pit. Up in the press box, where Susan was seated, journalists muttered to themselves, "Wagner luck." Parks inherited the lead and won the Oulton Park Gold Cup.

*   *   *

Susan had to admit it was a lovely room. Packing her bags, she wished she didn't have to leave it. She swung open the casement windows to let in the morning sunlight. Every time she walked past the open window, she stopped and looked out into the English garden below. In the center, was a small fountain, and around it were rose bushes and hedges, a gravel path, and freshly spaded flower beds awaiting the planting of annuals. In about two months, she imagined, with summer in full bloom, the garden would be breathtaking. She felt a longing to return.

Susan also had to admit she was very much in love. It was a wonderfully light-headed feeling that made her want to dance

51

around the room. It seemed crazy, reckless, to be in love with someone she had known little more than a week, and be the subject of her article. Yes, she had let herself be drawn into the very relationship she had intended to avoid. If she blamed herself--and she didn't--it wasn't for sleeping with Wagner, or even for that first kiss on the beach, but for accepting Jeremy's assignment in the first place. Meeting Wagner and being with him, that's what did it. She resisted her feelings at first, but once he pursued her, she gave in. Now all she did was think about him.

Somehow she had remained objective enough to finish the article, and had it filed away in her briefcase, 12 pages, typed double-spaced. All of her questions had been answered save one, and she still intended to ask it, when the time was right.

Two knocks at the door, quiet but firm. It was him. He took her bags and headed downstairs to pack them in the front of his Porsche. She looked around the room one last time. "It's such a lovely room," she said when he returned. "Thank you for bringing me here."

Inside the Porsche, she reclined her seat just a bit, felt the engine spin to life behind them, the tires begin to roll along the uneven cobblestone street. Wagner turned onto Grosvenor Road and followed it out of the city. She had a 7 PM flight out of Heathrow, but had looked forward to this trip, just the two of them, traveling back through Cheshire and its dairy farms, past Birmingham with its smokestacks, back through the Warwickshire countryside, on down to the wide Thames Valley back into London. For a long time she said nothing. Wagner was quiet too, his eyes trained on the road.

"I have something I've been dying to ask you," she said after what seemed like a millennium of silence.

He turned to her. "Don't tell me--another question?"

"Yes. Something personal. If you don't want to answer, understand. Why haven't you ever married?"

He seemed surprised by the question, but not wanting to seem surprised. He didn't answer.

"You haven't been married have you?"

He said nothing.

She persisted: "Have you?"

"No."

"I didn't think so. Why not? I mean, it's unusual for a man of 40 not to have married."

"I don't know. I just haven't."

She watched him. He seemed annoyed.

"You have been married, haven't you?"

"I thought the interview was over."

"That's not an answer."

He exhaled, turned to her. "How did you know?"

Now it was her turn to be surprised. "You have? I don't believe it. Why didn't you tell me?"

He shook his head. "What's the point. It ended years ago. I was 19, a kid. What do you know when you're 19?"

Susan looked at him as if seeing him for the first time. "Why weren't you going to tell me?"

"It's not something I go around advertising. To tell you the truth, until very recently, I haven't thought about it much at all."

"Why did you separate?"

"It was a mistake me getting married to her. Last I heard, she remarried and is happy."

"Were there any children?"

"No, no children."

It became quiet again. Susan looked out at the rolling terrain. Sheep grazed, still clad in their thick winter coats. It seemed strange his not wanting to tell her about it. Except out of curiosity, she didn't care a whit about his past, who his loves were, or whether or not he'd ever been married, but she did care about his future--their future. Certainly, if they shared a future, there should be no secrets between them. She still didn't know where she stood with him, or if even she would see him again. In a few hours she would board a big impersonal jetliner and they would be separated. Near Stratford, Wagner broke the silence.

"What's next for you, Susie?"

She brushed a red curl out of her eye. She hated being called Susie, but somehow, coming from him, she didn't mind, and was beginning to like it. "I'll spend tomorrow at the office, then take

Tuesday and Wednesday off. After that, I'll probably be assigned to a weekend series somewhere, now that baseball's underway. What about you?"

His jaw tightened. "Madrid, in two weeks. After that it gets crazy." He turned to her. "I want to see you again, Susie."

She touched his cheek affectionately. "Oh, John, I feel the same way."

"Maybe Jeremy will send you to Monaco next month."

"I don't want to wait for another assignment from Jeremy in order to see you again. Can't we do something about this?"

She felt his arm slip around her shoulder and pull her close to him. "Something will work out," he said, softly. "I promise you."

Chapter 7

Wagner rolled off Viraje del Tunel and tried pushing his right foot through the floor. Inches behind his head, throttle slides drew open, exposing 12 shiny round ports, each one the size of a silver dollar, each one sucking air and fuel with hurricane velocity. He felt his body weight triple as speed exploded past 100 mph and within seconds touched 180 mph. On either side, the world blurred past. Ahead, at the opposite end of the front straight, Viraje Nuvolari leaped out at him, a speck one moment, huge and menacing the next. But his mind was fully absorbed and he was seeing the corner arrive in slow motion. He had plenty of time to brake and downshift. With the curve dead in his face, he even had time to come off the brakes gently, so the chassis wouldn't lurch up on him, but remain steady and balanced for a smooth, swift entry into the curve. Turning in, he fed in throttle and felt the tail slide, the car shift into oversteer. Coming out, Viraje Fangio winked into view. He stayed in second gear, accelerated, backed off, and eased on the brakes. Turning in, he felt his rear tires slide again, saw the guardrail spin past his eyes. Calmly, in complete control, he powered out, upshifted to third, and stayed left for Viraje Varzi. It was broader, faster, and taken in a heartbeat. He was on a chute now, speed climbing, wind pressing against his goggles. The magnesium-and-aluminum chassis enclosing him, containing a mere eight gallons of fuel, vibrated like some big empty can.

The car was better, but still far from perfect. Despite all the work of the previous day, it was still unpredictable around <u>Circuito Permanente del Jarama</u>'s stop-and-go curves. If he got on the throttle too soon, the car wanted to understeer--go straight on--rather than turn. If he got on it too late, it wanted to oversteer--the tail slide out on him. He was having to finesse the car to get it through the curves reasonably quickly, and to guess, because in every one of Jarama's 14 curves the car responded differently. But with the morning session about to end, and desperate for a quick lap, he was hustling the car, pushing it faster than it wanted to go.

He braked very late for the first of a pair of sharp left-handers called the Le Mans Corners. He felt the tail become light, saw smoke flare from his front tires. Too fast. Too damn fast. With no time to steady his machine, he inhaled deeply and steered into the first left-hander. His inside tires ran up the curb. The car bounced, skidded, threatening to spin on him, but he caught it and angled out of the curve under increasing throttle. Now, for the second Le Mans Corner. Still in second gear, he braked and turned in. He clipped the inside curb again--harder this time. The car bounced up, airborne, hung there a moment, landed sideways and spun around backwards. All he could see was the white of tire smoke but he knew where he was headed. He switched off the ignition and fuel pumps, and braced himself.

The tail struck first, slamming his head back against the roll bar. The tail crumpled and the soft metal of the transmission casing split open and spewed out hot oil. The Garret-Hawk bounced off the rail and spun in the opposite direction, striking the rail again, nose first. The nose cone flattened, the radiator smashed and sprayed steam and scalding water. The car spun another half-turn and skidded to a stop, its path delineated by heavy skid marks, blotches of smoking oil, and steaming water.

In an instant, he was out of the cockpit, walking around the car. He didn't look at the damage. He knew it was bad. He removed his helmet and did something he hadn't done in 14 years of racing--slammed his helmet against the pavement.

It felt good.

*   *   *

"Yep," said Hacksaw, peering at the chassis; it was dangling by a hook on back of the wrecker, swaying back and forth. "You banged it good, Big Guy. The right-side a-arms are bent and it's going to need a new radiator and new trans and maybe a dozen other things I haven't seen yet, but I think the tub's straight. I hope so, anyway. I think we can have her ready in time for the

ur o'clock session." He looked at Walt Balchowsky, the
abricator. "What do you think, Walt?"

Balchowsky kneeled beneath the car and grunted. "Hard to
ay until we get it inside and look closer. But overall, it looks
retty decent. Wait. Aw, shit. Looky here, George."
Balchowsky was probably the only person who called Hacksaw
y his first name, other than Hacksaw's wife. The crew chief
neeled beside him and looked where he was pointing. "See
aat?" Balchowsky pointed to the front lower right a-arm
aounting point. It was pushed in, forming a one-inch divot in
ae outer skin. "Sheee-it."

Hacksaw rose and hitched up his pants. "Tub's damaged,
Big Guy. Looks like you're stuck with the Mark Four."

Wagner shook his head. It was going to be that kind of
veekend, where nothing went right. "It can't be any worse than
ais pig," he said, and walked off to the team's transporter. He
eeded aspirin for his headache. And time alone to regather
imself. One practice session remained, one last chance to
edeem himself. Somehow. He had to do well at Jarama.
Monaco was in two weeks and it promised more of the same,
rying to hustle a chassis that didn't like stop-and-go curves. He
ould see it: Parks or Evans or Bogavanti winning both races and
etting a firm grip on the championship, his championship. He
ad to do better in the afternoon session, move up, get in the first
r second row and be in position to pick up points in tomorrow's
ace.

Inside the transporter, he drank down some aspirin and lay
ack on the sofa. He couldn't relax. His mind was racing. He
ould hear engines revving over in the garage. He rose and went
ack to the garage, where his crew was prepping the Mark Four.
he smashed Mark Five was shoved off to one side. The crew
vas working with purpose.

Hacksaw grinned. "Good news, Big Guy."

"Yeah? They're cancelling tomorrow's race?"

"Mikey's ninth quickest."

Wagner nodded. "So."

"It's a damn sight better than what he was yesterday--las
They got the front tires to stick. Unless you got any better idea
we're setting up your car the same way."

"What have we got to lose? Do it."

Wagner was first out in the final session. Tires and brake
were new so he spent four laps bedding them in. Then he pitte
He stayed in the car while his crew made a quick check for leak
retorqued the wheels, and added ten gallons of fuel. Then h
was away again.

The corners named after the legendary race drivers
Nuvolari, Fangio, Varzi, Farina, Ascari--flew by with less effor
than before. Then it was downhill through the Bugatti Esse
around the hairpin, up to Viraje de Monza, on to Viraje de
Tunel, and onto the front straight again. The machine wa
cornering smoother and flatter, without a lot of fuss. Wagne
allowed himself a small smile, then noticed his wate
temperature was rising quickly. Nuts. Nothing ever came eas
in this business. He pitted, knowing he'd been quick, but hov
quick?

Hacksaw handed him his lap chart and nodded. "Not bac
Big John. A minute twenty-eight-eight. Sixth fastest."

"It's overheating," Wagner said, climbing out. He remove
his helmet. "If it's something simple, I'm going back out. I ca
beat that time. Where's Michael?"

He found his teammate back in the garage, sipping on a col
while Rennie and Ray lay beneath his car repairing an oil leak
Wagner put out his hand. "Nice work, pal."

"Don't thank me. Thank Ray. He kept making changes an
I kept telling him what it was doing to the car. Little by little
the car got better and better."

"Ain't it a bitch?" said Ray, from beneath the car. "Seem
like every race we got to start all over again."

A food wrapper had found its way into Wagner's radiato
inlet causing the engine to overheat. That removed, th
Californian went out again. He knocked another four-tenths of
second off his time, then the engine lost power. There wasn
time to change it. But his latest time put him inside Row Two.

The first three rows looked like this:

<u>Spanish Grand Prix</u>
Sunday, May 12

EVANS	BOGAVANTI	PARKS
Lotus	Ferrari	BRM
1 min 27.9 sec	1 min 28.1 sec	1 min 28.3 sec

WAGNER	EDWARDS
Garret-Hawk	Cooper
1 min 28.4 sec	1 min 28.7 sec

PHILLIPS	GREENMAN	LAFOSSE
Brabham	Lotus	Matra
1 min 28.9 sec	1 min 29.2 sec	1 min 29.5 sec

*   *   *

Edward W. Garret looked down imperiously from the VIP suite, atop the main grandstand. It was race day. Below, on the starting grid, a field of 16 cars was lined up in rows of three and two, revving, fuming, anxious for release. The starter signaled them to take a warm up lap. Garret watched them go around the 2.1-mile desert circuit, and return to the grid like birds returning to the roost. Engines switched off, crews returned, and several drivers climbed out and stretched. Garret's eyes were not on Wagner in Row Two, but further back, on Bravo, in Row Four. The Spanish Grand Prix marked Michael's Formula One debut, his grand entrance onto the world stage, and Garret was as nervous as an expectant father. Bravo was his discovery, the driver he had plucked from obscurity and intended to groom into a world champion. Wagner? He was the team veteran who would win some races, but not the championship. Guys like Wagner, who'd been around awhile, who'd never truly fulfilled their talent, their luck never changed.

Waiters in white jackets moved unobtrusively around the room, serving champagne and canapes to the guests businessmen, promoters, and high-ranking functionaries, men of wealth and influence, with interests in the sport. Although they were Dutch, English, French, German, Italian, and Spanish, they all spoke the current language of Formula One--English.

Garret had arrived in Madrid the night before, establishing a pattern he would follow throughout the season: fly in for the weekend, see the race, and return to Southern California to run his business, Garret-Hawk Racing Enterprises, the largest U.S supplier of performance and after-market auto parts. Eddie managed team affairs in his absence, or did so on paper anyway Everyone knew it was Hacksaw who really directed the team and that Eddie was little more than a glorified secretary who answered the telephone and kept lap charts.

On the grid, crews topped off fuel tanks, retorqued wheels checked tire pressure, and gave the bright finishes a last wipe down. Drivers climbed back into their cars, engines started, and crewmen hurried off to the side. The final seconds counted off. the flag waved, and the Spanish Grand Prix was underway.

Wagner watched Evans, Bogavanti, and Parks burn away, in front of him, and followed them over to the left setting up for Viraje Nuvolari. Loaded down with 43 gallons of gasoline, his car felt like some heavy bloated animal, wallowing this way and that through the slow, tight curves. He could feel his tires strain under the increased load every time he braked and turned, which was every second or two, the way the corners kept coming. On the short Pegaso straight, he had a brief moment to take stock. Parks' BRM was in front of him, running third, emitting puffs of blue smoke between gear shifts, and behind him was Edwards' Cooper-Maserati. Edwards seemed to be having a problem, because every time he braked smoke flared from his right-front wheel. In the split second Wagner looked back, he could detect nothing visibly wrong with the Cooper. Oh, well. It was Edwards' problem, not his.

The sharp Ascari right-hander rolled into view, demanding Wagner's full attention. Setting up, out of the corner of his eye, he saw the same telltale smoke flare off Edwards' right-front wheel. Exiting the turn, he hammered the throttle for the fast downhill run to the hairpin, felt the chassis lean side-to-side through the Bugatti Esses, and hunker down as he braked for the hairpin.

The next instant, he was slammed from behind, head flung back, stunned, uncomprehending, feeling his car lift, becoming very light, tilting lazily into a spin.

The thing's gonna flip, he thought, realizing what was happening, but no, the car was settling back on its springs just as it veered off circuit. He switched off the ignition and fuel pumps, released the steering wheel, and made his body as limp as possible. Dust and sand began swirling up around him, the car kicking and bouncing, rocks beating against the magnesium exterior. A tire ripped loose, banged against the side, and flew away. The car slid, dug into the sand and stopped. He heard steam hissing from somewhere and smelled something burning.

Fire! The mere idea of the car catching fire sounded an alarm in his nervous system.

He lurched forward trying to get out and to his horror discovered his legs were pinned. Something wet and stinging began running down his back. What the hell? He turned around to see a torn fuel line dumping raw gasoline into the seat. Frantically, he looked around for help. No one within 50 yards. Where were the bloody marshals? Damn it all. He had to get out of here. Now. This instant. He pulled and squirmed trying frantically to free his legs. Nothing doing. He pulled harder, felt movement, pulled harder still, one loosened. He wedged it free, which freed the other. He slid them both clear and raised himself up in the seat, and shit his back was on fire, and his arms too. He dove from the car into the sand and rolled over and over in it until the flames were out. Then he jumped to his feet and ran as hard as he could to get away from the car. When he was 30 feet away he turned and looked back. His car was fully engulfed in flames now, a thousand man hours of careful work, exotic metals, delicate castings, burning to the ground in seconds. He looked across the track at Edwards' Cooper, shooting flames 20 feet into the air.

A marshal ran up to him. "You all right?"

"Where's Jimmy? Did he get out?"

"Jimmy?"

Wagner pointed at the blazing Cooper. "The other driver. Did he get out?"

"He got out. I saw him."

That's what they always said. Wagner didn't believe him. He knew Edwards was still inside that car, past saving.

* * *

The accident was cleared and the race resumed. The two wrecked cars still lay on either side of the road, charred and smoldering throughout the afternoon. Bogavanti tried putting the whole sorry sight out of his mind, but each time down to the hairpin, the two blackened hulls rolled into view reminding him of what had taken place there. He hadn't seen either driver escape the carnage, but he had seen Edwards climb into an ambulance. The fate of his friend, Wagner, haunted him. He'd known the American for a decade, since their days as Ferrari teammates. Evans, in front, was drawing away, but Bogavanti didn't care. Parks passed him, then Phillips. The Italian did nothing. Ferrari team manager Zilli wrote a message on the pitboard: "Wagner OK." Bogo didn't believe it. Drivers were never told the truth until the race was over. The Italian soldiered on. Zilli held up a new message. "Evans Out." A few laps later, Phillips pitted, then rejoined the race. That put Bogavanti back in second place. Then smoke poured suddenly from Parks' BRM and he slowed down. Bogavanti repassed him and found himself leading the race, and not caring very much about it.

* * *

Wagner was relieved to see Edwards alive and unhurt in the trackside medical facility. The Canadian approached.

"I'm sorry, John," he said, looking very sorry indeed. "My brakes bloody well gave out and there was nothing I could do, everything happened so quickly."

"Don't sweat it, Jim." Wagner grimaced. The pain on his arms and back made him want to scream. He hissed through his teeth, "I'm just glad as hell we're both around to talk about it, know what I mean?"

Edwards nodded. "I'm really, really am sorry, John."

"That's racing," he hissed. "Forget about it."

Wagner was given temporary treatment and put in a helicopter bound for a Madrid hospital. Garret appeared and climbed in beside him.

"I saw the entire accident," he said, as the helicopter lifted off. "Thank god you're all right. Jesus, what an unbelievable thing to happen."

Wagner nodded, turned and looked out the window. The circuit was shrinking beneath them. Whatever they'd given him was working, because the pain was subsiding. "If I never see this place again, it won't make me unhappy."

"I'm going to have you flown back to London tonight," Garret said in a grave voice. "A burn specialist I know will see you in the morning."

Wagner nodded. "That's very kind of you. But my car...."

"Eddie will drive it back. Listen, those burns might be worse than anyone thinks. My experience has been that it pays to get an expert's opinion."

Wagner looked back out the window. Rows of small houses rolled by as the Madrid skyline grew larger. The race, the accident, both seemed surreal. Only now did he have time to think about it, to grasp the reality of it, to feel truly frightened. And sitting beside him was Garret, acting strangely human.

The finishing order and standings after two Grands Prix:

| Spanish Grand Prix | | Championship Point Leaders | |
| Top Six Finishers | | Race Two of Eleven | |

Driver	Points	Driver	Points
Bagavanti	9	Bagavanti	15
Parks	6	Parks	10
Phillips	4	Wagner	9
Lafosse	3	Phillips	7
Greenman	2	Lafosse	5
Van Zwet	1	Greenman	2

Chapter 8

It was 9 PM when Wagner's plane taxied up to the gate at Heathrow. Under his shirt, the Californian's arms and upper torso were wrapped in bandages. The flight had been smooth, but uncomfortably warm. He was exhausted and depressed, but relieved to be home at last. He cleared customs but rather than take the tube as he normally did, he called a cab. When he reached his flat in South Kensington, he called Diane, his secretary. She said 32 calls had come in.

"Did Susie call?"

"Yes. She's in Cincinnati, Ohio. Let me give you her number there."

He wrote it down, hung up, and dialed. A hotel operator connected him with her room.

"Hello?" The voice sounded distant yet familiar.

"It's me, John."

"John. Are you all right? The wire service said you received second degree burns in a crash."

"First-degree, mostly; on my arms and back. I would love a beer about now, but the doctor said not on pain killers. What's happening in Cincy?"

"Figure skating. It's the nationals. I can't tell you how good it is to hear your voice."

"I suppose I was lucky to get off with first-degree burns. Nothing went right. I couldn't get the Mark Five to handle, and banged it up pretty good trying too hard, and then I got rear-ended in the race and destroyed one of the Mark Fours."

"I'm so sorry, John, but at least you're all right. I wish I had some good news on this end. Your story didn't make the cover. In fact," her voice dropped, "it didn't make the issue."

"I don't care, Susie."

"I feel just sick about it, John." She sighed. "And, well, Monaco is out too."

"Monaco?"

"Jeremy says if you win a lot of races, the stories will follow. So win a lot of races, will you? so I can see you again."

"You'll be seeing me, all right," he said, "one way or another."

"Soon, I hope?"

"Soon."

"Is that a promise? I miss you, John."

"That's a promise."

*   *   *

Wagner visited the burn specialist Monday morning. The doctor saw nothing requiring his attention, but asked him to return daily for fresh bandages, until the burns healed. The Californian spent the next few afternoons at the hanger watching Walt Balchowsky perform surgery on the crashed Mark Five. The fabricator opened up the monocoque tub, straightened the bulkhead bent in the accident, and sutured the magnesium skin back in place with 274 rivets. The damaged area was repainted. Then Ray and Tom replaced all the bent and broken pieces-- suspension arms, trans, water radiator, etc. When the machine was finished, mounted with wheels and lowered to the floor, Wagner felt the urge to jump in and blast away. The latter part of the week, and all that weekend, he spent at Silverstone, watching Bravo test. They tested on the shorter 1.6-mile club circuit, with its two hairpins, in preparation for Monaco. The Mark V was handling the tight curves well now, and Wagner was beginning to think he might have a chance of actually winning the race.

Nine days after the crash, he climbed back into car number 36. Most of the bandages were off. His skin was scratchy and sore, but he felt good being back inside the cockpit, his nostrils tingling from the smell of raw gasoline. This was what he lived for, driving a racecar. He pulled a white handkerchief up around his mouth, slid his clear goggles down over his eyes, grabbed the small padded steering wheel and smiled to himself.

Time to go like hell.

66

It was cold, gray and windy, as only Silverstone can be, but he motored away in high spirits. The wind blew in spurts and tried to unsettle him at the worst possible times, such as sliding through Copse Corner at 120 mph. Undaunted, he pressed for the limit. Toes dancing on the pedals, spinning the wheel side-to-side, he found his rhythm quickly. Within eight laps, he took nine-tenths of a second off Bravo's time. Everything felt perfect. He ran another half-dozen laps--just joy-riding and feeling glad to be alive--and pitted.

Hacksaw kneeled beside him, the concerned professor, peering at him through horn-rimmed glasses. "How you feelin', Big Guy?"

Wagner removed his goggles and grinned crookedly. "Never better."

The skin crinkled around Hacksaw's blue eyes. He patted his driver on the helmet. "That's my boy."

*　　*　　*

Cloud cover was heavy and low, but not low enough to stop flights in and out of Gatwick. Wagner was wearing a wool overcoat and still felt chilly in the dank morning air. It was Spring everywhere but in England. He handed his bags to Mal Parks, who shoved them into a compartment behind the cabin, and climbed aboard Mal's Piper Twin Comanche. Mal's wife, Irene, was seated ahead of him, in the front passenger seat. Monaco was the only race she attended outside England. Mal climbed in behind the controls. He taxied out to the runway, received clearance from the tower, and within minutes they were above cloud cover, feeling the warmth of morning sunlight.

Irene turned around and gave him a big smile. "So, tell me, John, who are you seeing these days?"

Oh, no, here we go again. Irene always wanted to know everything about his love life. Ever since Mal had bought his plane and learned to fly, each year, the three of them made this trip down to Monaco together, and each time Irene grilled him on who he was seeing. He and Mal once had shared a London flat, until he introduced Mal to Irene. That was eight years ago.

Wagner was best man at their wedding. Mal was tall and blond, with a long chiseled nose. Irene was tiny, had short dark hair and a cheeky pretty face. She favored red-red lipstick, and had big green eyes. Her shapely body had once had a touch of baby fat that Wagner suspected would balloon out after she bore children. It hadn't. After bearing two daughters, her body had become thinner and firmer. With age, she had grown more attractive. She knew it, too.

"Are you still seeing Carol, the actress? No. That ended, didn't it?"

"Three years ago." He looked out the window.

"Has it been that long? Whatever happened to Lisa, the one who went with us to Monaco last year? I liked her very much, you know." She giggled. "We had fun shopping."

Wagner put his legs up on the seat and sat sidesaddle. "She's getting married."

"Pity for you. Are you going?"

"To the wedding? Naw."

"All your old girlfriends get married, John, but you stay single. Hard to get, aren't you?"

He shifted in his seat uneasily. "How are Mary and Beth?"

"Mary is five, and quite the little lady, very dainty and mannered; Beth is seven and is going to be tall like her father; she has a big crush on you, by the way, ever since the last time you came to dinner. She's been begging me to have you again. I dare say, John, if you hold out very much longer, she'll be old enough for you to marry."

She laughed, but Wagner didn't see the humor.

"What about Linda?" she tried again. "Now, there was a sweet girl. What was wrong with her?"

Wagner closed his eyes. "Linda?"

"You remember, Linda. Linda Hamilton. That was her name, I believe."

"I always felt suffocated around her. She was always trying so damn hard to please me." He folded his arms. "Can we talk about something else?"

"You must be seeing someone."

68

"Yes, John," Mal broke in. "What about that journalist girl? Susan. Susan ... oh, what was her last name? I can still see her face. Striking red hair."

"Jennings."

"Right. Susan Jennings. What about her?"

"She's not bad."

Irene frowned. "She's not bad? Is that the best you can do? You are hopeless, John. Utterly and completely."

Wagner smiled.

"Tell us about her? What's she like?"

"What's there to tell? She has her own career to worry about, otherwise I would be seeing more of her."

"Don't keep her on a string, John. Go and see her, or you'll lose her for sure, just like all the others."

Mal removed a briar pipe from his breast pocket, tapped it full with tobacco, and lit up. Between puffs, he said: "We're over the English channel just now."

Wagner looked out. The cloud cover was behind them now, clinging to the coastline. The channel waters sparkled like sequins on a blue cloth. Several craft were making the crossing, each leaving a long white trail.

"Will your father be at the race, Mal?"

Parks removed his pipe. "Oh, my goodness, yes. Every year, you know. He and the Prince go way back."

"The Prince has invited us to dine at the Palace Saturday night," Irene said with satisfaction.

"Officially, it's to commemorate my world championship," said Parks, "although conversation will invariably be about the race. My father doesn't think my career will be complete without winning there, you know."

"I haven't won there myself, Mal. Does it have anything to do with the fact that your father and the Prince are close friends?"

"Oh, I'm sure that's part of it," said Parks. "But the biggest reason is because my father broke the bank at the Monte Carlo Casino once upon time. He used to be quite the gambler, you now, until he met my mother and began running her family's banking empire. I think he would like me to win the race for

69

good measure, as a way of father and son leaving their indelibl mark on the Principality, as if it really mattered to anyone."

"The pressure on Mal is terrible," Irene confided. "I doubt Joseph realizes it."

Wagner looked at Parks intently. "I hope you're not tryin to win it to please your father."

"That would be silly of me, wouldn't it?"

Later, after they landed and drove to Eze-sur-Mer, an checked into the Cap Estel, Parks took Wagner aside and tol him he was planning to leave Irene.

"Why, Mal?" Wagner was stunned. "I thought you guy were happy. Is it another woman? Don't tell me its anothe woman."

"No," Parks replied bitterly. "Irene's been seeing anothe man. A younger man. I've known about it for some time. thought it was just a sort of fling, you know, and would pass But the other day, I found some of his clothes in her closet. Th bloody clot is staying there while I'm away. Well, that was jus too much."

Wagner shook his head. "I'm sorry, Mal. Does she know that you're leaving?"

"No."

"When will you tell her?"

"I don't know. After the race, maybe. I've only jus decided. I thought you should be the first to know, as you di introduce us, and all."

Chapter 9

The timing was going to be tight. It was Saturday noon, and one practice session remained. Eddie picked up his father from the airport in Nice. Driving his yellow Saab, he raced along the Mediterranean to Monaco, whipped through a series of narrow city streets and turned into a garage beneath a ten-story hotel. An area right of the entry was cleared of parked cars and enclosed by temporary fencing. This unlikely place was the Garret-Hawk garage. Other teams were set up in similar unexpected places around town, as Monaco was too cramped for a single garage to house all the teams together. Garret jumped out and hand-carried the valuable parts the final few feet of the journey.

"Thank you, Mr. Garret," said the crew chief. He popped the latches and opened the suitcase. "You are a lifesaver." He picked up one of the halfshafts and felt its heft. It was thicker in diameter than the old ones, counter-balanced and beautiful to a man who appreciated fine machine work. On very short notice, machinist Leo Schwartz had outdone himself. Immediately, Hacksaw and Ray went to work installing one set in Wagner's car, while Dave and gofer Tom began installing the second set in Bravo's car. Outside, racecars began howling through the streets.

"Shit," Garret said. "The session's started."

Twenty-four hours earlier, the team had been in a state of crisis. First, the left halfshaft snapped on Bravo's machine. Nobody thought much about it. But before the tow rig could bring him back, Wagner rolled to a stop with his right halfshaft broken. Two halfshafts broken. Okay. Circuit de Monaco was tough on halfshafts. And gearboxes. And suspensions. What else was new? Then Wagner's left halfshaft broke and in the process stripped the ring gear. That was enough for Hacksaw. He called Schwartz in California and asked him to make a

71

beefier set for both cars and ship them post haste. Garret moved up his flight and brought them himself.

"Damned cobbled-up flight," Garret said, watching them work. "I need a drink and a bath. How's Michael doing?"

"Hasn't made the cut yet," said Hacksaw. "Only 16 open spots makes it kinda tough on the kid."

"He'd better make the cut, after dragging my ass half-way around the world. And hotshot?"

"Eighth quickest."

Garret sniffed. "What's his excuse? He's supposed to be the veteran around here."

Garret checked into the Hotel de Paris and watched the rest of practice from his balcony window. Cars swung into Casino Square, made the sharp right turn directly beneath his window and blasted downhill to Mirabeau Corner, where they disappeared. Passing beneath him, he could look right into the cockpits and see drivers change gears, even see the tach needles leap up as they accelerated. The high winding engines made an awful racket between the tall buildings.

Wagner and Bravo were circling now. Wagner cornered smoothly, although his hands did seem busy, on the same line, to an inch, lap after lap. Garret clocked him at 1 min 30 sec flat. "Still not setting the world on fire," he noted with distaste. Bravo slammed into the corner, tail jerked out, then jerked in. Sometimes he hit the apex, sometimes he didn't. His hands were even busier. Garret clocked him at 1 min 32.5 sec.

"Shit, Michael," Garret muttered. "You're losing a damn second right under my window."

He left the balcony and ordered a bourbon from room service. When he returned, the two Garret-Hawks were running in tandem, Wagner leading the way. Bravo looked steadier, quicker, following his teammate. His lap times picked up too. His best time: 1 min 31.7 sec. Garret put away his stopwatch, satisfied Bravo was in the show. Feeling better, he showered. After practice, he checked with timing and scoring for the official results. Sure enough, Michael was in. Garret had him right on the button--1 min 31.7 sec. Sixteenth fastest and last on the starting grid. Wagner's time: 1 min 29.6 sec. He'd improved too, and would be starting on the outside of Row Three.

The first three rows looked like this:

<u>Monaco Grand Prix</u>
Sunday, May 26

EVANS
Lotus
1 min 28.1 sec

PARKS
BRM
1 min 28.6 sec

BOGAVANTI
Ferrari
1 min 28.8 sec

LAFOSSE
Matra
1 min 29.1 sec

EDWARDS
Cooper
1 min 29.2 sec

WAGNER
Garret-Hawk
1 min 29.6 sec

*   *   *

It was typically hot and sticky on race day. Wagner checked in the with the team, and 20 minutes before the start, sat alone in the shade of a tree, on a cool patch of grass. People were everywhere he looked, on rooftops and balconies, peering from doorways and windows, on ledges and in trees, perched like birds on the rocky cliff below the Palace. A privileged few watched from yachts in the harbor. Many more were cordoned off in bleachers around the circuit. One of those bleachers was directly across from where Wagner was sitting, facing Boulevard Albert I, pit straight. Officials, crewmen, and other drivers, milled nearby, awaiting the start. He felt cut off from them and quite alone, a feeling he nurtured in the waning moments before every start.

His race plan was simple. Stay out of trouble, preserve his transmission and brakes, and move up as others had difficulty.

Evans or Parks would likely win the race. It was their race to lose, at least. He was shooting for a podium finish--second or third. Monaco was the one Grand Prix he'd never won. He could baby his car, or drive it flat out; it didn't matter. Something always broke. Nine years of trying had produced one fifth place finish and eight DNFs.

He heard race director Louis Sainjon's high pitched voice call the drivers to a meeting. The Californian rose and joined them. It was Sainjon's usual speech. Admonishment not to attempt winning the race on the very first lap. "Watch your passing. And remember, the streets are narrow." The meeting ended and drivers dispersed to their cars. Evans and Parks brushed past Wagner with blank stares, mindless of everything but their innermost thoughts. In contrast, Bogavanti was smiling.

"Here we go again, eh, Giovanni?" He looked around, taking it all in. "Ah, Monaco. The wealthy mistress."

"You mean the cruel mistress, don't you?"

The Italian laughed, but he could afford to, having won the race three times. "Shall we wager on the winner? It certainly won't be you or I. I will pick Evans. How does ten of your American dollars sound?"

"Twenty." Wagner put on his helmet.

"Twenty? On Parks? Or me? Ha! Ha!"

"On me."

"On you?"

"That's right. It's time my luck changed around here."

*   *   *

Parks settled into his cockpit, knowing he mustn't let Evans out of his sight today, that he must stay glued to his tail, must harry him, must push him, must somehow force him into a mistake. That or hope his car broke. It was Parks' only chance. He couldn't beat the Scot straight up. Not at Monaco. He grasped the steering wheel and stared straight ahead while crewmen finished with his car. He sneaked a look at Evans. He

74

o was staring straight ahead. Sainjon held up the two-minute ign. Parks heard engines start behind him. At the one-minute gnal, he started his engine and began revving it. He felt the ercussion of Evans' Cosworth fire up beside him.

Ten seconds.

He engaged first gear and sensed Evans creeping forward. He saw Sainjon's steel-gray eyes glower at the Scot, heard vans' RPM drop slightly. Out of the corner of his eye, he could ee Evans looking around for someone to push him back into lace.

"Forget Evans," he told himself. "Watch Sainjon. Get off leanly and quickly."

Sainjon's fingers counted the final seconds. The Monegasque flag dropped and Parks blasted away, rounded St. Devote, and shot up the hill past the high-rise apartments and alm trees that lined the walk. He was leading. Ahead, at the op of the hill was what appeared to be a cathedral but was in act the Monte Carlo Casino. He checked his mirror surprised to ee not Evans' slim green Lotus glued to his tailpipes but Lafosse's chunky blue Matra. Evans had blown the start. The ery break he needed. With growing confidence, he negotiated he left-right turns around Casino Square and swooped downhill o the Mirabeau Hotel. The curves began coming in rapid-fire succession: a sharp right in front of the Mirabeau Hotel, left round Station Hairpin, then steeply downhill to another right urn, practically in the Mirabeau's basement. In his reclined eat, he was riding around the circuit on his back, peering out ver the windscreen at his front tires, cutting them within an inch f the curbs. The chassis enclosing him was alive--vibrating, ouncing--transmitting the "feel" of the road as his tires slid round the curves and squirmed and wandered over the uneven oad surface. He didn't fight his machine, but sort of guided it long in a hurried fashion, knowing if he forced matters he vould only scrub off speed and maybe spin.

A narrow railway arch flew overhead and the broad, glittering Mediterranean spread before him, and blurred off to his eft as he rounded Portiers. He was on Boulevard Louis II now, ollowing the seashore back around to the harbor. Below the road, waves crashed against the rocks. He checked his mirror again, relieved to see a gap opening between himself and Lafosse. Ahead, the Tir Aux Pigeons Tunnel yawned opened and swallowed him. One second he was in sunshine, his engine sounding dull and distant in the rush of wind, the next he was in the glare of artificial lighting and about to go deaf from the scream of exhaust blaring off tile walls. Another tick of the clock and he was back in sunlight again, with the harbor--and the Chicane--directly ahead. He checked his mirror again: a dozen car-lengths back, Lafosse burst from the tunnel, chased by Evans, Bogavanti, and Wagner.

At 130 mph, the Chicane looked impossibly small. The clearance on either side was, in fact, large enough for just one car. Parks braked to 65 mph, made a quick left-right flick of the wheel, and darted between the barriers with maybe four inches to spare on either side. Yachts danced past on his left. He braked for Tabac and drifted lazily around the left-hander. He could feel the eyes of crewmen and officials peering at him from pit row, beneath a row of umbrella pines. Almost at the end of the lap now. He braked and changed down to first gear, almost coming to a stop rounding Gasworks Hairpin. A stab of throttle and he was away again, speeding in the opposite direction, up Boulevard Albert I. The start-finish line skipped beneath his wheels. He guessed his lead was two seconds. Heading uphill to the Casino, he checked his mirror again. And cursed silently. Evans had moved up to second place.

*　　*　　*

Race Director Sainjon wasn't ready to completely relax, but he was feeling more at ease. The race had started cleanly. There had been no accidents in the early laps, when they most often occurred. The race was on lap ten, cars spreading out. A Sainjon relaxed he found himself drawn into the drama of Evans catching Parks. Evans had nearly spun somewhere and fallen six seconds behind, but was closing the gap. At the start of lap 11 Sainjon noticed something amiss. The anti-roll bar at the back of

Evans' Lotus had broken loose and was dangling. Sainjon grabbed the black flag and marched to the Lotus pit.

"I'm black-flagging Evans," he shouted to Kevin Revette, Lotus Team Manager, over the scream of passing cars.

Revette's small round face registered mild surprise. "Why, for heaven's sakes?"

"A piece of your car is falling off, or haven't you noticed?"

"Now see here, Louis. Let's not be rash. I've seen it. It hasn't affected Ian's performance. He's about to take the lead. For heaven's sake, man, how much of a problem can it be?"

"If the bar falls off--a very big problem. It's a menace to everyone on the circuit."

Revette smiled. Being diplomatic always worked with men of Sainjon's refinement. "Let's have a closer look when he comes by again. What do you say, old boy?"

"Don't `old boy' me. I'm flagging him in."

Revette shrugged. So much for diplomacy. He grabbed his crew chief by the lapels. "Listen to me, Big Jim. When Ian stops, be prepared to remove that roll bar at once. Tear it off if you must, but get it off quickly. Understand?"

Big Jim nodded.

Sainjon stepped out onto Boulevard Albert I and waited for the leaders to round Gasworks Hairpin. He saw them flash behind the pits, engines blipping between downshifts for Gasworks. Evans Lotus appeared first, having passed Parks half-a-lap earlier. Sainjon held up the black flag and pointed his finger at Evans as he sped up Boulevard Albert I. Then he waited. The 90 seconds it took seemed an eternity. At last, the British car reappeared and dipped into the Lotus pit. Parks' green machine blared past, alone, in front again. Big Jim removed two small bolts holding the bar and Evans was away again. Revette placed an arm around Big Jim's shoulder. "It's not over yet, my friend."

"Not as long as Ian 'as breath in 'im," replied Big Jim.

Parks resisted the urge to let up. His lead over Lafosse, in second place, was 15 seconds, and over Evans, now back in eighth, 30 seconds. He wasn't about to relax and let the Scot back in the race. Not today. Not at Monaco. He continued pushing, driving as if Evans were pinned to his tail. Several laps passed. Exiting the Tir Aux Pigeons Tunnel, he spotted a racecar up ahead going very slowly. It was a two-year old white Brabham, driven by Erich Lehmann. Realizing he and the slow-moving West German were going to arrive at the Chicane at once, Parks slammed on the brakes, saw there was no avoiding a collision, and turned down the escape road, where he skidded to a stop. With reverse gear locked out, he couldn't back up under power, so he jumped out and began pushing his car back up the escape road.

"Lehmann, the bloody twit," he muttered, deeply agitated. Two marshals ran up to help him push the car. "Keep back. The rules, men, the rules. You want to get me disqualified? Blimey. Has the whole world gone daft?"

Panting hard, he pushed the green car back onto the circuit. Before stepping in, he glanced up at the tunnel. No one was coming. He slid under the steering wheel and sped away. Something flashed in his mirror. Another car was closing in fast. A green car with driver in yellow helmet.

*   *   *

Wagner's plan was working to perfection. At the start, he passed Edwards to move up to fifth. Bogavanti's faster Ferrari was ahead, in fourth. Wagner remained patient. When Bogo's engine soured on lap 18, he passed him. Thanks to Parks' and Evans' mishaps, he picked up two more places. Now, running in second place, five seconds behind Lafosse's Matra, he decided it was time to quit babying his machine and take some chances. He braked later for the curves, getting his tail to slide, pushing, probing, riding the ragged edge. Within four laps he was on the Frenchman's tail, following him in and out of the curves, looking for passing room, looking to grab the race by the throat and not let go until he was holding the winner's trophy.

Setting up for St. Devote, he dipped inside Lafosse's sky-blue car, got on the throttle too soon, lost traction, and fell back. Next time, he told himself. Next time he would make clean work of it. A moment later, his plan, working so perfectly, began to unravel. Rounding Mirabeau, he reached for second gear and his shifter balked.

"What?"

It was a fluke--had to be--something that wouldn't repeat itself. Be more deliberate, he told himself. Ease the shifter into gear, don't slam it. Seconds later, at Station Hairpin, with the sensitivity of a safe cracker, he tried easing the shifter and the damn thing still balked before engaging. His heart sank. He was losing second gear--and precious fractions-of-a-second fighting to get it to engage. Around the circuit, those fractions began piling up into whole seconds. The backside of Lafosse's Matra, so enticingly close one moment, was drawing away the next. Soon after, Parks and Evans passed him.

"There goes third," Wagner muttered, trying to shift gears. Sweat was pouring from his face now, not the usual sweat from cockpit heat, but a special kind of hot sweat, from being as gentle and careful with something and knowing at any second it could blow up. With each shift, he could feel the gearbox tighten, feel gears grind dryly. In his mirror, Edwards' green Cooper-BRM closed in and began sniffing at his tail. Behind Edwards was Greenman, in the second Team Lotus. Using first and fourth gear now, he kept them at bay, lugging the engine at times, burning the clutch at other times, knowing it was pointless. On lap 62, sliding into Station Hairpin, two gears engaged at once. He declutched to avoid locking the wheels and rolled to a stop at the curb.

"Monaco," he muttered disgustedly, climbing out. He wiped his mouth and looked up at the Casino, glistening clean and white in the bright afternoon sun. "I wonder if I can get a beer in there, dressed like this?"

*   *   *

An hour after pushing his BRM up the escape road, Parks was still panting, working harder than he ever had in a race before, and still that man Evans pressed from behind. On lap 70, he looked at the lap board, saw ten laps remained, and wondered if he could hold out. He was past exhaustion, driving on nothing but a burning will to win. Every second or third turn, he would see Evans' green nose move up beside him, the Scot probing for passing room. Bloody nerve-racking it was. The narrow streets were growing slicker by the lap and he could feel his rear tires nudging the curbs now as he exited curves. Bloody, bloody nerve-racking.

With two laps to go, Evans' managed to pull even with Parks as the pair set up for St. Devote. Parks drifted over ever so slightly to pinch him against the curb and rounded the curve in front. At the top of the hill, Evans moved out again, and the Englishman drifted over in front of him again, and rounded Mirabeau still leading. Exiting, Parks checked his mirror and saw Evans follow him back across the road, setting up for Station Hairpin. Dropping down into the hairpin, Parks braked, downshifted to first gear, and....

Ka-womp!

The impact sent him skidding wide of the turn. He laid on the brakes harder, managed to get his car to turn, and romped on the throttle, but it was too late.

Evans was past.

"I don't believe this," he said. "He ran into me. The bloody clot actually ran into me."

Bounding down beneath the railway arch, he saw Evans' tail weave braking for Portiers. He saw it weave again, braking for the Chicane, and for Tabac. Evans' rear tires were pitching at odd angles at every corner. Parks looked closer and saw what the problem was: the rear anti-roll bar was missing. Now he understood. Powering up Boulevard Albert I, to begin the final lap, he drew even with the Lotus. He saw the grandstand crowd rise in unison as the two cars sped side-by-side up the boulevard. Setting up for St. Devote, he had position and led coming out. Up the hill, he could feel the wind in his face, a cooling, refreshing wind. He was going to win this race. He led over the top of the hill, past the Casino, down past the nightclubs, to the tight right-hander in front of the Mirabeau Hotel. Setting up, he checked his mirror, not at all surprised to see Evans staying back.

"He's helpless," thought Parks. "He can't do a thing but follow me now."

Exiting Mirabeau, he darted back across the road. Right here, coming down to Station Hairpin, it always felt as if he were standing on his heels, such was the steepness of the grade and extent of weight transfer as he braked. He grabbed the shifter and slid it into first gear. He turned in, and....

Ka-Womp!

Harder this time, much harder. As he scrambled to recover he saw Evans' Lotus was dragging fiberglass. Bits and pieces of flew off as it went by.

"The bastard," Parks shouted. "That was deliberate."

He followed the Scot around Portiers, through the tunnel and he Chicane, and onto the harbor quay. It was here he was going to make his move, here, in full view of the yachts, and the people jammed around the tobacco kiosk, for which Tabac corner was named, and the people looking down from the high-rise apartments and hotels. He watched Evans move over to the right to take the fast line into the curve as he knew Evans would, but he stayed on the left, drawing even with the Lotus.

From 100 yards out, Tabac looked about as big as the eye of a needle. Parks kept his eyes glued on the turn, an image of disaster forming in his mind. He still had a micro-second to back off, to avoid trouble, and finish safely in second place. But he didn't. He had come too far and invested too much emotionally to give away the race.

Suspensions compressed and tires clawed as both cars braked and leaned into the curve, Parks' dark green BRM clinging to the inside. He felt his machine slide out towards the Lotus, sensed wheels within wheels. This did not make sense, he thought, too late. In one second both cars would tangle and become junk. Only Evans could control his car no longer. The Lotus skidded away from Parks' BRM, looped once, and crashed nose-first into the haybales.

Parks saw it all in his mirror as he exited.

| Monaco Grand Prix | | Championship Point Leaders | |
| Top Six Finishers | | Race Three of Eleven | |

Driver	Points	Driver	Points
Parks	9	Parks	19
Evans	6	Bogavanti	15
Lafosse	4	Wagner	9
Edwards	3	Phillips	9
Phillips	2	Lafosse	9
Greenman	1	Evans	6

Chapter 10

The prize-giving ceremony at the Hotel de Paris ended at 1 AM. Parks left his wife and father and walked down the hill to Tiptop, the watering hole for the British racing crowd. The BRM crew and several of his friends awaited him there. He bought the first round of drinks. People began crowding in. Tobacco smoke and rock music mingled in the air. Parks sat at a table smoking his pipe, the center of his own little universe. His hands were blistered and his muscles were sore and stiff, and he was utterly exhausted from the race, but he'd never before felt this good, this happy, this light, this free. He seemed to float above the room, still not quite believing he'd won the Monaco Grand Prix.

The sun was rising when he left Tiptop and walked further down the hill, to the Mirabeau Hotel, where earlier he'd reserved a room. He ordered up a big breakfast of fried eggs, bacon, hashbrowns, a stack of toast, and tea, and watched the Principality's narrow streets come back to life. Later, he called the Cap Estel and told Irene he was leaving her. That afternoon, she didn't return with him in his Piper Cub Twin Comanche, but returned to London aboard a commercial airliner. The marriage was over. There was nothing more to be said.

London was gray and misting rain when Wagner arrived home Monday evening. The papers in the South Kensington Station newsstand all carried Parks' Monaco victory as front-page news. He bought <u>The Times of London</u> and flipped through it as he walked across the street to his flat. Inside he saw this heading: "Wagner Luck Sidelines Yank Again." He closed the paper and folded it tightly. Wagner Luck. Whoever dreamed up that idiotic phrase ought to be shot, he thought. Inside, he opened a beer and rummaged through his mail. He remembered he hadn't eaten dinner and was about to step out for a sandwich when the telephone rang.

"John, thank goodness you're finally home." Irene sounded breathless. "I know my split with Mal must have come as a terrible blow to you, but it's been coming for some time, and I simply must tell you my side."

Wagner slumped down onto the sofa. "Can this wait? I just got in. I'm tired, I'm hungry."

"No, it can't wait. Mal has told you some dreadful things about me, and I want to set the record straight. It's only fair."

"Irene, really, this is none of my business."

"I love Mal. I always will. But it hasn't been easy all these years, what with him being away so much. I am a woman--an attractive woman. Men notice me. Well, I couldn't stand being ignored any longer. Even when he was home, Mal didn't give me the kind of attention I need; the kind you always gave me, John."

"What are you talking about? We only dated a couple of times."

"Mal never said he loved me, or said that I looked pretty. And," she added with some hesitation, "he wasn't the most dutiful of lovers--in bed, I mean."

Wagner looked around. Where was that beer he was drinking?

"Surely, you of all people know how it is. You can just pop in and out of some girl's bed whenever you want, and no one thinks the lesser of you. But for a woman, especially if she's married, it's positively scandalous. Well, it's not fair, I tell you. I'm not some whore."

"I know," he said. The beer was in the kitchen. He could see it on the sink, beads of moisture forming on the bottle. He stretched the cord, reached around the corner, stretched his arm, stretched, stretched, and reached it. That was better.

"Well, Mal thinks I am."

"Is that what he said?" He took a long drink.

"In so many words."

"Look, Irene. I'm sorry. We've known each other a long time. If there's anything I can do...."

"You're such a friend, John. I knew you'd understand. Our marriage has been a lie, one big lie, and it had to end, sooner or later. I feel better having talked to you."

"What will become of Beth and Mary?"

"Mal wants them, and I quite agree. The nannies have been their parents, really, not Mal or I. They'll be attending boarding school soon, so our divorce won't matter to them, not really. They'll still see each of us regularly, I'm sure."

"And you? What about you?"

"Me? Oh, I'll be fine. I would like to see more of you. Except for our trips to Monaco each year, I rarely see you anymore. When can we get together for a drink?"

*   *   *

Susan's plane set down at Chicago's O'Hare Airport late Monday morning. She took a cab into the city and stopped by SportsWeek's editorial offices on Michigan Avenue. The story she'd filed the night before had been edited and typeset. She poured herself a cup of coffee, picked up a proof, and read the first half-dozen paragraphs. Satisfied Jeremy hadn't made too many changes, she headed to her office. She passed Jeremy's large office and thought of his unobstructed view of Lake Michigan. It must be nice, she thought, having that view. Her office was at the end of the hall, near the copy machine. It had no window, no art work on the walls, no knickknacks or family photos on the desk, no plants, nothing to liven up its stark white walls. Several memos and a few letters were piled on her desk. She set down her coffee and began flipping through the memos. Jeremy's large frame appeared in the doorway.

"Lunch?" he asked.

"No, I couldn't possibly."

"Some of us are going to walk to Piccalilli's and sit outside. It's a nice day. Why don't you join us?"

"I don't have a lot of time and I want to stop by my apartment and take care of a few things before I leave again." She went back to reading.

Jeremy watched her a moment. "Nice piece on the Celtics-Lakers game. Think it'll go to seven?"

"No. Yes. I don't know."

"Too bad about Monaco. I watched it on TV. For a while there it looked like John had a chance."

Susan continued reading and said nothing.

"I saw you walk past my office. I was hoping you would stop in and maybe chat a little. You know, about how things are going."

Susan looked up distractedly. "I don't feel like talking right now. Some other time, huh?"

"Something wrong?"

"Nothing's wrong."

"Something's wrong. You're not your usual sunny self."

"I just, you know, wish he would call me once in awhile. Is that such a hard thing for guys to do? I can't believe I let myself fall into this. I hardly know him. The only photo of him I have is a clipping from our magazine. I'm pining for some guy I don't know and never see."

Jeremy nodded. "John's not real big on telephone calls. Heck, sometimes I don't hear from him for a year or more. He never sends me a Christmas card."

"Yes, but you're buddies. Buddies do that sort of thing. I'm supposed to be his ... I don't know what I'm supposed to be."

"Give him a call, Susan. Tell him you were thinking about him and that you just wanted to say hello; something like that."

"I'm not going to call him. He'll think I'm some clinging vine, which I'm not. Besides, he should be calling me."

"Want me to call him, put a bug in his ear?"

"No I do not."

"I could ask him how you guys are doing, that sort of thing. Of course, knowing him, he would say something smart like, `Ask Susan.' I guess I'd have to come at him somehow differently, with something like ... `I bet you miss Susan.'"

"He doesn't miss me, or else he would call. He keeps me hanging by a string, promising he'll see me. The dirty rat."

"...He'll never even know we had this little discussion, Susan. Did you call him a dirty rat just now?"

Susan rose. "He is a dirty rat, and if you call him I'll break our neck."

"I take that as a `yes.' Your heart's not in it, Susan. Let me o call the dirty rat and see if I can't get him to give you a oller."

Susan walked around from behind the desk. "Jeremy. No. I on't know how to make it any clearer. I will call him. Okay? I ill make a fool out of myself and call him. Will that make you appy?"

"Yes. That would make me very happy. Now, about lunch. our plane doesn't leave until eight tonight. I know, 'cause I aw your itinerary. I do read my mail, contrary to what everyone ays around here."

"Oh, all right."

*   *   *

Wagner backed his 911S out of the narrow garage at nnismore Gardens Mews, turned onto Cromwell Road and eaded in the direction of Heathrow Airport. Susan had called nd left a message. Had it been a month since he'd seen her ast? It didn't seem that long. He felt trapped by the call.)bviously, she wanted to get together, and he had promised to ee her. Why did he always make promises and not keep them?

The gate to the hangar was open. There was no sign in front o announce this was headquarters for Team Garret-Hawk, only a treet number. Wagner drove in and parked away from the other ars--so no one could open their door and ding the side of his 'orsche. The sun was peeking through the clouds and the air hrobbed with the sound of commercial jetliners taxiing nearby n the east runway.

Inside, everyone was busy. Testing was scheduled for ioodwood that weekend, but the racecars looked far from ready. Iravo's machine was mounted on a heavy jig, stripped of ngine, transmission, and suspension. Walt Balchowsky had the uter skin removed on one side, the side where Bravo had macked the guardrail at Monaco, and thrown away a sure six-place finish. Fat Walt saw Wagner enter, spit, and frowned menacingly.

"Another race, another wreck. I can't believe they pay you guys."

Wagner smiled broadly. "Nice to see you, Walt." He patted the big man's belly. "Looks to me like you need the exercise carrying all that weight around. You ought to be thanking us."

"I will--if you ever win another race." His belly began to convulse. "Ha-Ha-Ha!"

Wagner's machine lay on a similar jig. The suspension arm had been removed and sent out that morning to be magnafluxed. Non-ferrous metals, such as suspension uprights, which were cast from magnesium, were zygloed. All parts that bore a load were inspected for metal fatigue. Wagner heard the crackle of welder coming from the purge box. Ray was inside, no doubt making a new set of titanium suspension arms for the right side of Bravo's car. In another part of the shop, Rennie and Tom Faber were uncrating the latest batch of engines to arrive from California. The engines had been dyno tested and tagged with the horsepower rating. Some engines delivered more horsepower than others, even though, ideally, they were all built to identical specs. The most powerful engines went into Wagner's machine, the team leader. But Rennie had reason to believe the tags were inaccurate and dyno tested the engines once they arrived in England. Sure enough, when he compared his readings with those on the tags, they invariably were reversed. Rennie suspected Garret had something to do with it. The Old Man wanted Bravo, his pet, to have the best engines. Only Rennie was wise to him. He retagged the engines with the correct readings. To be certain Eddie didn't change them back, he also put a small identification mark on the cylinder block, as a backup, where only he could see it.

Dave Milzarek waved Wagner over to his workbench, where he was examining a transmission case. "Have a look at this, John. You won't believe it."

"Try me."

Milzarek pointed to a blemish on the outside of the case. "See that? That's a crack, a very fine crack. Lubricant leaked

88

out of it, the box overcooked, and that's why you started losing gears. Makes you wanna puke, don't it?"

"A crack? The sucker was brand new, wasn't it? How on earth did it crack?"

"Casting flaw. I checked the other cases. None of them have it. I called the manufacturer and told 'em about it. Know what they said? Ship it back; we'll send you a new one no charge. Big deal, I said. You bastards cost us the damn race."

Wagner found the man he was looking for leaned over a lathe. Hacksaw looked up from his work and nodded. While he waited, Wagner looked through the big glass window into Eddie's office. It was a spacious office with racing posters on the walls. Eddie wasn't in.

"Where's the kid?" Wagner asked, when Hacksaw switched off the lathe.

"Doing us some good for a change. I sent him out to run down some parts. Usually, all he ever does is sit in that office all day and read magazines, or talk to his girlfriend on the telephone. What's up?"

"I have a favor to ask."

Hacksaw removed his glasses and with his sleeve wiped his brow. "A favor, huh?"

"I would like to take a pass on testing this weekend."

"Is it important?"

"I don't know how important it is. It's Susie. I haven't seen her in awhile...."

Hacksaw's eyes narrowed with thought. "You going to Chicago to see her?"

"Yeah."

"Go ahead and go. Mikey needs the work. But you be at Goodwood bright and early Monday morning, hear?"

*   *   *

"I'd love to see you, John," Susan said, her voice competing with line static. "But the way the Celtics-Lakers series is going, I don't see how, unless you want to be traveling back and forth across the country with me, while putting up with me trying to

89

write a story. I'll be in Los Angeles another night and then I'll have to fly back to Boston for game six on Saturday. And Sunday is iffy, too, because the series might go to a seventh game."

"When I got your message, Susie, I thought you were free."

"No, I only called to say hello. How have you been?"

"Fine."

"I'm sorry about Monaco. How are your burns healing?"

"Healed, pretty much."

"I'll be free next weekend. How about then?"

Wagner sighed. "I've got a race. In Holland."

"How about during the week then? I'm free Tuesday and Wednesday."

There was always some demand on his time--a test session, an appearance somewhere for one of the team's sponsors. "I don't know," he said. "I'll have to see."

"You don't sound promising."

"Yeah, I know." He needed to say something encouraging, something that said, `I love you' without actually saying those words. He didn't know if he loved her, only that he didn't want to lose her. Thinking about it now, where he was placing his priorities, he knew how she must be feeling. He cared more about racing than her, she was thinking, and it was true. The only thing that mattered to him was winning the world championship. Everything else--Susan included--was secondary.

"I want to see you, Susie, very much. Something will work out."

"You've said that before."

"Have I?"

"Look, John. I didn't mean to put you on the spot. I just wanted to say hello, that's all. I know you're busy. I'm busy. One of these days we'll get together."

"I miss you, Susie."

"It's nice to hear you say that. I miss you, too, John. Now, go win that race in Holland."

He hung up feeling ugly and empty. He stared out the window. "I'm going to lose her. I can hear it in her voice. It's just a question of time."

90

Now what? He had the weekend off and nothing to do. He was about to call Hacksaw and tell him he was available after all, when the phone rang. For a moment he feared it was Irene and debated whether or not to answer. Feeling edgy, on the fourth ring he picked up.

"Big John! Boy, am I glad to reach you."

It was Paul Spencer, a rival from his Speedster days, ex-Ferrari teammate, ex-F-1 driver, and ex-most everything to do with racing. His career was on the ropes.

"Want to have some fun?" Spencer asked. "I'm at the Nurburg Ring and I've got myself this big ol' Ferrari P3 and no one to share it with. Why don't you come? It'll be like old times. You know, drink beer, chase women, win the race. What do you say, partner?"

Wagner rarely drove prototypes anymore, but the idea of racing for the sheer hell of it, with nothing riding on the outcome, sounded inviting, even if it was for an independent.

"How much?"

"Six-hundred, plus expenses. It ain't much, I know, but who can put a price on fun, right?"

It wasn't much. Garret was paying him $2500 per race, plus half of the purse, plus expenses.

"What happened to your co-driver?"

"Busted his arm playing around on his motor bike, the dumb shit. Hey, we're up against the factory Porsches, and the P3's a little tired, but we got a chance. What do you say?"

"Save me some beer."

* * *

It rained on and off all race day afternoon, causing a jam up in the pits as teams switched back and forth between wet and dry tires. Wagner and Spencer were both contracted to Unirich, but somehow a set of Dunlop wet-weather tires got mounted up on Ferrari rims and ended up on their car. Wagner noticed the change immediately. The Ferrari suddenly felt stable in the wet, and the rear tires gripped when he accelerated. The Ferrari P3 was more than a little tired, and on the Ring outclassed by the

91

sleek Porsches. He was running tenth, but on Dunlop wets moved up to fourth, before turning the car back over to Spencer. Spencer was forced off the road overtaking another car and that ended their race. But Wagner came away deeply impressed with Dunlop wet-weather tires. If it rained during a Formula One race, his main rivals--Evans, Parks and Bogavanti--all Dunlop users, would have a serious advantage over him.

*   *   *

It was still raining Sunday night when he arrived back in London. The next morning, as promised, he was at Goodwood, testing. Tuesday and Wednesday, back at the hangar, the crew prepared the cars for the next race. Thursday morning, they loaded up the transporter and departed for a small resort town on the North Sea, for Zandvoort, home of the Dutch Grand Prix.

Chapter 11

"I suppose it was bound to happen," Hacksaw said, looking dolornly at the latest from Norfolk, England, the Lotus 49B. It was newly repainted red and gold, the colors of the team's new sponsor, rather than the familiar British Racing Green, but there was something even more unusual about it. It had airfoils: canard wings on either side of the nose and a wide upturned lip in the tail. Airfoils created downforce on the suspension, so tires would grip better thus allowing the car to corner faster. They weren't new to racecars. Mercedes Benz experimented with them in nineteen-fifty-five; Ferrari ran them on their GTO in sixty-two; and Chaparral mounted one high above the rear of its Group Seven racer in sixty-six. But never before had they been tried in Formula One--until now.

Hacksaw walked around the Lotus and shook his head. "I had the idea. I just didn't have the time. Now I guess I'll have to make the time."

Practice was about to start. All the cars along pit row were warmed up and ready to go.

"Sure, the things work," Wagner said, stuffing cotton into his hears. "On sportscars. But the suckers create drag. Chaparral runs the big Chevy so it doesn't matter, but on a Formula One, with everything maxed-out, the drag will just kill us."

Hacksaw rubbed his chin. "Maybe you're right, but I think we're in for a long weekend myself. Old Chappers wouldn't run them if they didn't make some kind of difference."

Wagner put on his helmet, fastened the strap, and slipped down into the cockpit. "Chapman's always experimenting," he said, adjusting the side mirrors. "Half the time he gets it right, and half the time he gets it wrong. This time, I guarantee you, he's wrong."

A pretty girl in shorts walked past, showing long tanned legs. Hacksaw looked her over and smiled. "Not bad."

Wagner ignored the girl and got his bearing. Time to fin
out how the Garret-Hawk handles <u>Circuit van Zandvoort</u>'s subtl
curves. He liked the seaside circuit, not because he alway
performed well here--which he did, always finishing in th
points and winning once--but because it required absolute
precise driving to go quickly. The 2.6-mile circuit was not th
stop-and-go madness of Jarama and Monaco, or a showcase fc
speed and steely nerves such as upcoming Spa-Francorchamp
and Reims. The circuit's deceptively simple curves flowe
around sand dunes in a series of left-and-right handers that kep
drivers busy lining up for the next curve, and the next, lik
skiers, slaloming back and forth. Miss an apex, and you miss th
next three as a consequence.

It didn't take him too many laps to realize the suspensio
needed fine tuning. When he pitted, Hacksaw handed him
scrap of paper. Scribbled on it was Evans' time: 1 min 23.5 sec.

Wagner handed it back. "So."

"So, that's two seconds under the old record. What do yo
think of them wings now?"

The Californian scowled. "What do you expect ... they'v
been here two days testing all ready. Give me an hour then as
me again what I think."

Wagner glanced at the wings on the Lotus and shook hi
head. Maybe they do give Evans an advantage, he thought. A
if he needed one. Beating Evans. That was the game. It wa
always the game. The Scot was always that tiny bit quicke
sometimes as little as a tenth-of-a-second quicker around a five
mile circuit. Take a corner flat out, on the absolute limit o
adhesion, and the guy would find a way to take it quicker. It wa
frustrating. On top of that, Evans had Chapman's genius behin
him, always dreaming up new ways to make his cars faster. An
now this. Wings.

"Wings belong on airplanes," he muttered, trying to reassur
himself. "Not on Formula Ones."

He spent all that first day in and out of the pits, searching fo
the right gear ratio, the correct tire pressure, the best roll-ba
stiffness, the perfect camber setting--for little things--because th
Garret-Hawk chassis was handling well. Late in the afternoon

with the sun low over the North Sea, and the wind blowing in, he got within .9 seconds of Evans' time.

"The car's got more speed," he said afterwards, satisfied with his day's work. "It's just a question of finding it. Tomorrow we'll nail Evans' butt."

Hacksaw furrowed his brow. "Think so? What are we talking about? Another half second at most?"

"I'd say a good second."

"Even if you do, all Evans has got to do is turn the wing up another notch to beat you. Listen, we'll make us some airfoils and beat his sorry hide at Spa."

Wagner smiled wryly. "I'm surprised at you, Hacksaw, giving up this easily."

"Just being realistic, that's all."

The sun glistened off the cars as they were rolled out for practice Saturday morning. The wind was calm and there was the smell of kelp in the air. Rennie sipped coffee while warming up Wagner's engine. The Californian eased down into the cockpit and wasted no time recording 1 min 23.9 sec for second fastest, then went back to work making more adjustments. In the afternoon session, with the wind blowing out, he pushed harder than he knew was safe, running a tire up the curb here, sliding out to the grassy verge there, riding the dunes at full tilt. At times, gusts nearly blew him off the road. Each time, he steered out of it, maintaining his fine edge of control. In the end, he came within two-tenths of a second of Evans' time.

Pulling into the pits, he saw the Scot seated on the pit counter, grinning with satisfaction, as if to say, "Nice try, John, better luck next time."

"Next time, I'll have wings," Wagner muttered to himself.

The first three rows looked like this:

<u>Dutch Grand Prix</u>
Sunday, June 9

EVANS	WAGNER	PARKS
Lotus	Garret-Hawk	BRM
1 min 23.5 sec	1 min 23.7 sec	1 min 23.9 sec

BOGAVANTI	LAFOSSE
Ferrari	Matra
1 min 24.0 sec	1 min 24.2 sec

GREENMAN	PHILLIPS	EDWARDS
Lotus	Brabham	Cooper
1 min 24.3 sec	1 min 24.4 sec	1 min 24.6 sec

*   *   *

Everyone connected with the race was staying at the Bouwes Hotel, which was walking distance from the circuit, everyone except Ian Evans. The Scot was staying five miles down the coast, at the Fairview, which had a restaurant overlooking the sea. When the weather was nice, the owner opened the large glass doors facing the sea so Evans could hear the sea as well as see it. Race day morning, the weather was cold and overcast, and the glass doors were closed, as Evans sat down to a meal of one hard boiled egg, cold cuts, toast, and tea with cream and sugar. Across from him sat a very pretty English girl named Sarah Luck. She was a model, and had been seen in his company for about a year. Evans ignored her most race-day mornings, but this morning he was feeling particularly confident about the race.

He gazed at her while sipping his tea. "Do you know what it is that I love about you?"

Sarah perked up. Ian was speaking. She smiled and shook the blond locks out of her blue eyes. "No. Tell me."

"It's that you're so unspoiled, so pure, so innocent. Did you know that?"

"No." She giggled. "I thought it was my beauty and charm."

"Oh, that too, certainly. But it is your innocence and purity that I find most appealing. You know, you are not like the other girls that sit around the pits, clocking laps for their men, always looking into the mirror to see if their makeup is on straight, their hair in place, that sort of thing. They're always competing with one another. You don't compete. You don't have to. You are above them. I love that."

Sarah laughed. "But I'm rarely in the pits."

"Yes, but when you are, you are above them. Do you know what I mean?"

Sarah appeared confused. "I think so."

Evans smiled. "Oh, Sarah, you are such a child, but that is what I love about you."

"What else do you love about me?"

Evans thought a moment. "Oh, you know, your clothing, your hair, your teeth."

"My teeth?"

"Yes. They are so straight and so white. Perfect, like you."

Sarah pouted. "They're not mine."

Evans raised his eyebrows. A pained look came over his face. "They're not? Do you have false teeth? Don't tell me."

"No, silly." She tapped a front tooth with one of her long enameled nails. "They're capped. My real teeth were so small and ugly." She crinkled her nose. "Ugh. My agent insisted I have them capped. You wouldn't believe the difference it's made to my career."

"That's so interesting," he said, his voice flat and emotionless. "I never would have guessed."

Sarah touched his nose. "You are a silly man. A thoughtful but a silly man." She giggled. "And you leave me breathless."

*   *   *

97

The paying public--Dutch, German and English--turned up their collars against the stiff wet wind blowing in, and huddled in the grandstand or crouched along the high sand bank that separated the circuit from the choppy North Sea. Below them, 19 Formula Ones surged forward in another kind of sea, a sea of reds, greens, whites, blues, and yellows; they circled Tarzan Corner two- and three-abreast and sped noisily behind the pits, Evans out in front.

Wagner clung to the Scot's tail, feeling his machine bounce and skitter around Hunze Rug, the hook-shaped turn. Clearly, Evans' Lotus cornered smoother, flatter, and faster than Wagner's Garret-Hawk, thanks to the downforce provided by those wings.

The field flowed up and down through the dunes, veered right, then left, then right again, and over Tunnel Oost, barely discernable at 140 mph. They negotiated another right-left-right combination before entering Pulleveld, a circular right-hander that brought them back around to the front straightaway. Wagner followed Evans down the straightaway, around Tarzan and Hunze Rug, and into the backside of the circuit again. He tried keeping up, but was sliding too much in the curves, scaring the hell out of himself.

"The guy's got you beat today," he thought. "Finish second and take the frickin' points."

He reduced speed and stayed mentally alert, not liking to give up, but not wanting to give it away either by making some foolish mistake. First Bogavanti, then Parks, made a run at him, but couldn't pass him. Both fell back, Bogavanti with a failing engine and Parks with a slipping clutch. Evans' lead stretched to a minute and more. The race was down to the final laps when Wagner saw the Scot's red-and-gold car moving up in mirrors.

"The bastard wants to lap me, does he?" he muttered. "We'll just see about that." He jumped back on the throttle, but the slow laps had thrown off his rhythm. He whipped into Hunze Rug a tad fast and felt the tail let go. He had about four-tenths of second to decide whether to fight the car and maybe save it--and maybe end up parked in the sand--or let the foul thing have its way and spin. He chose the latter, controlling the

ar with throttle as it spun around and stayed on the track. A
econd later, Evans motored around the curve wagging a finger
t him playfully.

"Screw you, Ian."

Wagner turned around and crossed the finish line a lap
own, but in second place at least, earning his first points since
he South African Grand Prix way back in April. It moved him
nto a three-way tie for second place in the championship
tandings. The fast circuits were ahead--Spa and Reims--and a
etter than even shot at picking up some wins.

Dutch Grand Prix Top Six Finishers		Championship Point Leaders Race Four of Eleven	
Driver	Points	Driver	Points
Evans	9	Parks	23
Wagner	6	Bogavanti	15
Parks	4	Evans	15
Edwards	3	Wagner	15
Giraud	2	Phillips	10
Phillips	1	Lafosse	9

Chapter 12

As the three o'clock start neared, eyes peered up at the sky; the questioning eyes of team managers, crew chiefs and tire engineers, and the uneasy, worried eyes of drivers. Rain was forecast. But here and there slivers of blue sky shown through the dark clouds, promising sunlight. Should they switch to rain tires? Or not? If there was one thing more dreaded than rain at Circuit National de Spa-Francorchamps, the fastest road circuit in the world, it was the threat of rain, because it created the element of uncertainty in the hearts and minds of drivers.

"What do you think, Big Guy?" Hacksaw looked up at the clouds and rubbed his chin. "Should we make the switch?"

Wagner walked around his racecar, giving it one final look over. "The decision's made, Hacksaw."

Two Ferrari crewmen pushed Bogavanti's red machine past. Wagner nodded. "See that? Ferrari's on dries. So's BRM and Lotus."

Hacksaw glanced up at the sky once more, as if it might yet yield an answer. "The other teams will have to pit, if it rains. That'd cost 'em a minute, at the very least. You'd have that advantage over 'em."

"We lose either way, if we switch." Wagner removed his wallet, watch and keys and handed them to Eddie for safekeeping. He took a final sip of mineral water, looked around to make sure he had everything. Gloves, two pairs of goggles, and a wrist band containing his blood type. Yes, he had everything. He nodded to Hacksaw.

The crew chief motioned to Ray and Dave to push Wagner's car out to the grid. The wait was over. There would be no more agonizing over the weather or over tires. It was up to the drivers now.

Wagner was starting from pole. Further back, in row seven, Ray and Gofer Tom pushed Bravo's car into position. He was starting 16th. The only surprise of qualifying was Ian Evans, who was starting eighth, instead of first or second, as he usually did. But it wasn't that much of a surprise. Evans never qualified well at Spa--but usually won.

Wagner slid beneath the wheel and got his bearing. On either side of the Garret-Hawk nose were canard wings. Each displayed a large, orange-and-blue Unirich logo. In the rear, the tail cone had an upturned lip, like a ducktail. The team had spent many hours perfecting the surface angles of these airfoils and it had paid off. Around Spa's 8.7 miles, Wagner was nearly four seconds quicker than the next man.

Team Garret-Hawk wasn't the only equipe to have followed Lotus' lead. In the fortnight between races, a strange variety of tabs, fins, winglets, and wings, had sprouted from racecars. Ferrari and Brabham had taken Colin Chapman's innovation a step further and mounted a single wing above the engine, giving these cars a peculiar aerial look. But not everyone was convinced airfoils made the slightest difference. Mal Parks' BRM had no tabs, fins, wings or winglets--and was second fastest.

Belgian Grand Prix
Sunday, June 23

WAGNER	PARKS	BOGAVANTI
Garret-Hawk	BRM	Ferrari
3 min 28.6 sec	3 min 32.3 sec	3 min 34.3 sec

STOCKTON	TAMBALA
BRM	Ferrari
3 min 35.0 sec	3 min 35.4 sec

LAFOSSE	EDWARDS	EVANS
Matra	Cooper	Lotus
3 min 37.1 sec	3 min 37.2 sec	3 min 37.8 sec

Two minutes.

Hacksaw kneeled beside his driver. "Keep an eye peeled, hear? It might be raining down in the valley. Don't get caught with your weeny hanging out."

Wagner nodded. He knew. All too well he knew. He had been one of Spa's victims in 1966, when he and half the field were eliminated in a first-lap accident caused by a surprise downpour.

"On wets you'd at least have some kind of chance. It's still not too late. We can make the change in two shakes."

Wagner stared ahead, getting his focus. His mind had no room for doubt or second guessing. Right or wrong, the decision was made. He shook his head.

The crew chief looked at his driver a moment. There was nothing more to say. He arose. "Okay, Big Guy. Go get 'em."

Like a slow beating drum, the final seconds ticked off. Crews dispersed to the side. Engines fired, filling the air with their pungent gray fumes. The crowd rose in anticipation. Wagner glanced up at the sky one last time and wondered if he should let someone else be the hare--the one to find the rain--if it was raining down in the valley. He looked ahead at the high ridge. Beyond it was the valley, and mystery. Engaging first gear, he decided he was going to lead. He had the fastest car. It was his race to win. He wanted it. Badly.

The flag whipped down. Cars scrambled forward, funneled through the Eau Rouge esse curve, and bolted up the ridge.

There was nothing in front of Wagner but daylight. He upshifted to fourth gear, then fifth, and watched his tach climb to 9500 RPM--160 mph. He could feel the uneven road beneath his wheels, pitching the chassis, keeping his hands busy steadying it. Pines whipped past on either side of him. He checked his mirror: Parks' green BRM was behind him, maybe a half-dozen car-lengths back, followed by Bogavanti's Ferrari. Was that a red-and-gold Lotus behind the Ferrari? Had Evans moved up that quickly? Wagner gripped his steering wheel tighter. No one was catching him today, not Evans, not anyone. He eased his machine over to the right for the fast left at Les Combes, tapped the brakes and shifted back down to fourth. In a moment he was in the pull of the curve, drifting lazily, the car under his spell. Exiting, he moved back across the road, setting up early for Burnenville, which he could see curling to the right, at the bottom of the hill. No sign of rain so far. He upshifted back to fifth and watched Burnenville grow. It was one of two curves that it was absolutely essential to get right. He eased up on the throttle, dropped 800 RPM, and pointed his racer into the long curve. As it tightened, he made a series of quick, delicate corrections to the wheel. He could see the front suspension arms vibrating over bumps, feel his tires strain against the road. A small cafe and stone barn scrolled into view, facing each other from opposite sides of the road. Aiming a racecar between them at 150 mph, at this, the tightest point of the curve, always reminded him of threading a needle. He was positioned on the road exactly where he wanted to be--right of center. As he neared the cafe, he felt G-loads build against his body, felt the steering wheel strain against his fingers, the footprint of the tires distort. The cafe doorsteps appeared, and flew past, not one yard away from his inside wheels. Feeling G-force ease, he let his car drift outside, near a single row of haybales that passed for a safety barrier, mildly aware of cows grazing in a pasture outside the curve, and of a farmer, gnawing on a straw, watching him impassively from the porch of his house. Another barn and farmhouse, both close by the road, flew past. The line of haybales ran out and the curve opened. He pressed the throttle fully and felt the chassis lift under a surge of horsepower.

Still no sign of rain, but this far down in the valley the low clouds were allowing no light to pass. It was eerie dark--but dry. He straight-lined the Malmedy esse curve and fields of green appeared. He was on the bottom half of the circuit now, on the long Masta Straight, crossing a valley of rich farmland. His tach climbed to 11,200 RPM and hovered there--196 mph. Terminal velocity. At that speed, he didn't hear his engine as much as feel it, drilling away at his spine. The chassis hull was awash in currents, floating over the road, wanting to fly, his helmet being buffeted. It didn't take much strength to keep his racecar pointed own the center of the road at this speed, but it did take every ounce of his will.

Midway across was the second curve he must get absolutely right, a gentle esse bend through a Belgian hamlet, called the Masta Kink. The posted speed limit was 50 kph, but he would be taking it considerably faster than that. He checked his mirror again. It was vibrating so profusely he could not make out the image of the car behind him, but he could see the color--Napier green, BRM's color. Parks was still behind him, shrinking in size. No sign of rain.

With the care and precision of a brain surgeon, he inched his car over to the right, setting up for the Masta Kink. Resisting a powerful urge to back off the throttle, he began the turn in, tach still hovering around 11,200 RPM. A farmhouse directly in his path moved off to his right and flashed behind him. A section of steel guardrail--the only such guardrail anywhere on the circuit-- raced up to meet his outside wheels, maybe six inches away, flashed brilliantly, and it too disappeared behind him. Another farmhouse--three stories of red brick--stepped out in front of him. Facing it head on, he calmly eased the steering wheel back the other way. Staring at that red brick house, waiting for the nose to point away from it and into the second part of the esse curve, always seemed to take forever, but in fact took three-tenths of a second. At this speed, with his mind fully absorbed, he could count the tenths as if they were seconds--one, two, three. The farmhouse vanished off to his left and reappeared in his sidemirror, shrinking rapidly to a red spec before vanishing all together, while ahead, at the opposite end of the valley, Virage de Stavelot grew in size, another curve demanding his full attention. He braked hard briefly, made the turn, and started back up the valley. The sky was brighter ahead, showing slivers of blue that he had seen earlier in the pits. Great, he thought, with a slight shake of the head. Just great. The threat of rain is on the lower half of the circuit--at Burnenville and the Masta Kink--the most dangerous parts.

The road rose quickly, climbing through pine forest and the last, gentle curves of La Carriere, Blanchimont, and Seaman. Nearing the top, he could see the backside of the pit complex, see the control tower with its big clock, see the main grandstand and the row of international flags that fronted pit straight. La Source Hairpin, the final curve, was ahead. He hadn't touched his brakes since Stavelot, three miles back, and they were cold as ice. He stabbed the brake pedal several times, to heat up the pads and discs, so they would grip evenly. That done, he braced himself and laid hard on the brakes, cutting speed from 170 mph to 35 mph, in all of five seconds. He swung around La Source as if suspended by an invisible cable and got back on the gas. The row of flags he had seen from afar mere seconds ago, flapped in the breeze above him, marking the way down the hill, past the grandstand, past the control tower and pit row, and over the start/finish line. Hacksaw had no message for him. The time on the tower clock was three-oh-four. It was early. There was a lot of racing yet to do.

* * *

Cradled in the buzz of the narrow BRM cockpit, the race was going about as Mal Parks expected. He held a clear lead over Bogavanti and Evans, in third and fourth respectively, but he could make no dent on Wagner's lead. In fact, the American was pulling away at an alarming rate. No question, Wagner's Garret-Hawk was dialed in perfectly, and Parks felt a little envious. Gradually, the white-and-blue car vanished from his vision, while behind him Evans had passed Bogavanti to take over third, which concerned Parks. He monitored his mirror, to see if the Scot was gaining on him. By the start of lap three, it was clear Evans was losing ground, and Parks worried less. Then, setting up for Les Combes, he caught a glimpse of Wagner's car, darting into the left-hander ahead of him. Accelerating down the hill to Burnenville, he saw it again, larger than before.

"Something's wrong," thought the Brit. "I shouldn't be catching him this easily." The distance between the two stayed the same through Burnenville, but on the long Masta Straight, Parks closed the cap. He followed the American through the Kink, and on the straight that followed, drew even.

106

That's when he heard it, a skip coming from the Garret-Hawk V-12 engine. At 200 mph, the sound was a fierce, high, metallic, deeeeeeee-da-deeeeeeee-da-deeeeeeee. Awful.

Parks grimaced. "He won't be around long."

He moved past the American, rounded Stavelot, and stretched his lead to four seconds before reaching La Source at the top of the valley.

By then, he had troubles of his own.

He rounded the hairpin and motored easily down the hill, switching off the engine as he rolled into the pits. His crew surrounded him immediately, anguish on their faces. Their man had just taken the lead. Why on earth was he pitting?

"No oil pressure," he said, calmly. He stepped from the car and could hear a collective groan coming from the grandstand, as Wagner, too, slowed and pitted; the first- and second-place cars exiting the race on the very same lap.

In the Garret-Hawk pit, it was the same scene repeated all over again: crewmen surrounding their man, wanting to know what the devil was wrong. Meanwhile, Evans and Bogavanti screamed past, suddenly one-two.

Wagner kept his engine running and with heated emphasis pointed behind him. "Misfire," he yelled. "The damn thing's misfiring again."

"How's that?" Rennie leaned closer to hear what the driver was saying.

Wagner scowled, pulled the bandanna down from his mouth, said louder. "Misfire. You didn't fix it."

Rennie nodded. It was the same problem that had plagued Wagner's engine during Friday's practice session. Rennie replaced filters, pumps, metering unit, injector nozzles, everything. That cured it. The engine ran perfectly all day Saturday, but now, for some reason, the misfire was back, and at the worst possible time. Obviously, the problem went deeper than mere filters, pumps and nozzles, but lay with some fundamental design flaw. "There's nothing we can do about it now, Johnny. Just drive the bugger."

"What?"

"He's right," yelled Hacksaw, leaning in from the other side "Try to finish."

"Try to finish?" Wagner looked at them both in disbelief He pulled his bandanna back up over his mouth, then yanked i back down again. "You guys are useless. Hear me? Useless Why the hell did I even stop?"

Parks watched the American exit the pits, swoop down over the Eau Rouge Bridge, wing up the far ridge and disappear into the pines. By now, his own crew had removed the engine cover and tail section from his car and were searching frantically for a quick fix, but there was none to be found. The problem was inside the engine. Slowly, with resignation, they buttoned up the BRM and pushed it back to the paddock and into the transporter.

Parks removed his earplugs and gloves and stuffed them into his helmet, his workday over. He looked up at the lap board to see number five--Evans' number--placed at the top, the new race leader.

It had been a month since Parks and Irene had separated. His life really hadn't changed much. He came to Spa-Francorchamps like he did to most races--alone. He ate alone, slept alone, and before the race, secluded himself in the team's transporter. Empty marriage or not, with Irene he still had someone to go home to after each race. Now, he didn't even have that.

Unlike Monaco or Zandvoort, there were no hotels within walking distance, or a helicopter to shuttle him off, as at Watkins Glen. Spa-Francorchamps was isolated in the wooded hills of the Belgian Ardennes. With public roads operating as part of the circuit, he couldn't even beat the traffic back to his hotel. He felt suddenly tired and wondered what to do with himself. The public address blared something about Wagner that elicited a roar from the crowd, but the Englishman wasn't listening and missed what was said. Then he remembered there was a VIP lounge up the hill that had an open buffet. He stepped inside the BRM transporter, changed into his street clothes, combed his blond hair, and walked up to the lounge.

Inside, the atmosphere was reserved and quiet. Several patrons were seated beside a broad window that faced pit

108

straight. They were mostly corporate types, dressed expensively, chatting quietly among themselves, occasionally watching the cars speeding past. A few came over to express their regrets that Parks had dropped out, and to cordially invite him over to their table. Parks thanked them but said he preferred to be alone just now. They understood. He seated himself at the bar and ordered a sherry. It was then he noticed all the women gathered at the back of the room, young and pretty, showing lots of leg, decked out in baseball caps and tee-shirts displaying various corporate logos. Parks remembered seeing several of them working booths near the paddock gate, before the race. One in particular had caught his eye, a short, busty brunette, with big brown eyes and hair worn in a pageboy cut. Parks looked down the line of pretty faces until he saw her, with two other girls, giggling over something that was said. She must be no taller than five-foot-three, he thought. Her tee-shirt came almost to her knees and bore the green and yellow BROCO insignia, for British Oil Company, one of BRM's sponsors. Parks couldn't keep his eyes off her. She was chatting and giggling and becoming aware of his stare. She smiled back, expecting him to come over, but Parks didn't move. After a few minutes, she became self-conscious and a little nervous.

Parks still didn't budge. He couldn't. He was a public figure, had made countless speeches, but for some reason he didn't have the nerve to approach her and introduce himself.

"You're just out of practice, old boy," he said to himself, sipping his sherry.

Chapter 13

Deeeeeeee-da-deeeeeeee-da-deeeeeeee.

It was an agonizing sound, the sound of an engine running lean, burning fuel at a higher temperature than it should, scorching valves and piston tops, dying a slow, painful death. Wagner reduced RPM, hoping it would go away, but it wouldn't go away, not at Spa-Francorchamps, not with its long curves and longer straightaways, where engines labored all day long at peak RPM. He drove several laps this way, nursing his engine while falling further and further behind. Every lap he saw Evans' number atop the lap board, a constant reminder that another victory was slipping away, and with it maybe his last shot at the championship.

By lap eight, he'd had enough of this hanging-back-doing-nothing nonsense, and for what? To finish out of the points?

Go like hell. That was his style. He stuffed the gas. "Screw it. If the sucker blows, it blows."

The engine pitch rose several decibels. The chassis lifted from acceleration. Yeah. That was more like it. It felt good, the mind alert and sharp again, acting instantly, instinctively, precisely, unencumbered by the slow, sometimes errant, thinking process. His heartbeat jumped up too, leveling off at 200 beats per minute, normal for a healthy race driver going full-tilt around the Spa-Francorchamps madhouse. The engine made the same shrill, tortured "deeeeeeee-da-deeeeeeee-da-deeeeeeee" sound, and he hated it as passionately as ever. At any second, the whole thing could go up in smoke--a massive meltdown--but, hey, it was out of his hands.

Laps began spinning by. Hacksaw showed him ninth, then sixth, then fourth. By lap 14--the half-way point--he'd cut Evans' lead to 43 seconds. On lap 15, coming up the valley, he caught Pete Stockton, Parks' teammate, running third. He stepped out to pass him and Stockton slid over and blocked him. What the hell? He tried again and Stockton blocked him again.

The jerk had a reputation for doing this, and Wagner didn't have time to waste. He considered nudging him once from behind--to let the Welshman know that he meant business--but at Spa, a 170 mph, such a move bordered on homicide. No, he would have to try something else, something more subtle.

He drafted the green car to the top of the valley, made the turn at La Source, and started back down the other side, all the while breathing its noxious fumes and being zinged by every stone thrown up by the BRM's wide tires. He feinted a pass here, a pass there, making Stockton be everywhere at once. Setting up for Les Combes, he feinted another pass, to the outside. The moment Stockton moved outside to block him, Wagner veered back inside to fill the lane. Turning in, he forced Stockton further outside, to a point where the Welsh driver had no choice but to back out of the throttle. Coming off the curve, Wagner led, and Stockton faded from his mirror.

* * *

Edward W. Garret could no longer sit still. The VIP booth was just that--a booth--small, cramped, with cheap wood paneling. Rain was beginning to fall outside. He went down the single flight of stairs, entered the door leading to the Garret Hawk pit, and joined his brooding crew chief at trackside. In the Lotus pit next door, Kevin Revette and Big Jim huddled beneath an umbrella. Further down, in the Ferrari pit, team manager Ludovico Zilli paced somberly in a hooded raincoat, his gray stony face looking grayer than usual.

"How we doin', Hacksaw?"

The crew chief looked cold and worried and his glasses were beaded with raindrops. "Not good, boss. John's made up a chunk of time, but I don't know." He looked up at the low ceiling of clouds. "Until this confounded rain hit, he had a chance. Now ...."

"How's his engine? Will it last?"

Hacksaw grinned slightly. "That's the ironic part. The rain's had a cooling effect. I was hoping Evans and Bogavant might pit for wet tires and let him back in the race, but so far

112

everyone's sticking with what they got. It's still dry down in the valley. That's where John's making up time. But if it rains down there, it's over."

With two laps to go, Bogavanti passed Evans to take the lead. Accelerating up the ridge, he rounded Les Combes and the valley below came into view. Was it raining at Burnenville too? He had all of three seconds to decide. Speeding downhill at 165 mph, about to begin the turn in, he decided he was taking no chances and backed off the throttle completely. The moment he did, Evans screamed past him so fast his Ferrari shuddered in the turbulence.

* * *

Except for the pitter-patter of raindrops, the pits were utterly quiet. All the racecars were somewhere down in the valley, faced with the ever-changing elements, the drivers hoping, praying, to finish the race in one piece. Eddie, manning the stopwatches, listened closely. He could hear a car roaring up the valley, the engine pitch high and clear and unmistakably V-12, a familiar sounding V-12, one he'd heard on the dyno many times, a Garret-Hawk V-12. It was too early to be Wagner, so it had to be Michael Bravo in the second Garret-Hawk, plodding along in eighth, wet, tired, no doubt shaken by his first race at Spa. Bravo's engine grew louder and was joined by two other engines, then by a fourth engine, joined together in a kind of dissonant four-part harmony. Bravo exited Seaman Curve and appeared on the road behind the pits. Two seconds later, running in tandem, Evans and Bogavanti appeared. Another five seconds and Wagner appeared. One-by-one they braked for La Source, rounded the hairpin, and shot downhill past the pits. Bravo had two laps to go, but Evans, Bogavanti, and Wagner each received the white flag--one lap.

"Five seconds," Eddy cried.

That's how much Wagner still had to make up.

Garret rubbed his face and turned to Hacksaw. "You ever get used to this?"

Speeding up the ridge, Evans and Bogavanti blew past Bravo--one to the left of him, one to the right of him--and made the left turn at Les Combes. Coming down the ridge, Evans upshifted to fifth and planted his right foot. At the bottom of the hill, the entry into Burnenville was shrouded in mist now. Uncertainty gnawed at him. He felt very much alone, thinking of how fragile was the aluminum cocoon that surrounded him, of how fragile was his small, compact body, and of how the slightest rain drops could send him spinning into trees or maybe against a stone barn or brick farmhouse. He checked his mirror, to see what Bogo was doing. The Italian's red car was fading. Bogo had backed off. Good idea, thought Evans. Wonderful idea. Beautiful idea. His decision was made for him. He backed off too, felt the Lotus slow from wind resistance, and eased into the curve at a sluggish 135 mph.

Like a bullet shot, a car screamed past him. A white-and-blue car. Wagner. Good lord. Evans' mind scrambled. Where on earth did he come from? Wait. No. The driver was wearing a red helmet. It wasn't Wagner at all. It was Bravo. The bloody fool was unlapping himself, here, why?

Four seconds later, Wagner arrived at Burnenville, eyes hard and searching. Finishing third or even second, was not in the cards today. He hit Burnenville as he had all afternoon.

Flat out.

*   *   *

The pits were silent again. Hacksaw stood motionless in the rain, while nearby Garret shuffled nervously. Eddie remained seated, preoccupied with his lap charts. In the Lotus pit, Revette marched up and down, in front of his crew. In the Ferrari pit, Zilli folded his arms and leaned against the pit wall in seeming meditation. The seconds passed like minutes.

A voice boomed over the Public Address, speaking excitedly in French, then calmer in English: "We have report of a car leaving the road, at Burnenville."

Zilli stood up erect and stared blankly. Revette's marching stopped, his small round face twitched. Evans? Bogavanti?

114

Silence.

Eddie jumped down from the pit counter. Cars were coming. He could hear them buzzing up the valley. Across the way, in the stands, eyes turned toward Seaman curve. Everyone could hear them now, the high wail of stampeding engines, drawing closer. Garret and Hacksaw looked at one another, lines of worry etched on their faces.

The PA came on again, first in French, then in English. "We have no report on whom the driver is, but we do have report of the car. It is one of the American Garret-Hawks that has left the road at Burnenville."

Hacksaw shook his head slowly. "Damn."

"Wagner?" Garret could barely get the word out.

"Yep."

*　　*　　*

Wagner felt his suspension arms tremble over the bumps, his tires distort and slip. Burnenville was dry as far as he could see which wasn't far, but at this point it was too late. He was committed. The cafe and stone barn appeared in the mist, on opposite sides of the road. He shot the gap, one last threading of the needle. Further ahead, his eyes were drawn outside the curve. There, in the cow pasture, with wheels still spinning, was a car flipped over on its top. The scene flashed by in an instant, but he knew who it was. He blocked it out of his mind immediately. He couldn't think of accidents, think of someone being hurt or even killed, and still try to win the race.

*　　*　　*

Parks ordered another sherry. It wasn't like him to order a another drink, but it wasn't like him to be nervous either.

News of the race diverted his attention from the girl. If there was one driver Parks wanted to see win, it was his friend John Wagner. Parks had always admired his driving. There were certain unwritten rules about racing in close quarters, rules about passing and respecting the other guy's line. Wagner never

115

violated those rules. If you stuck out your neck a bit, as they all did, Wagner was never one to chop off your head. He always gave you room, gave you a way out. He was a gentleman in the truest sense--an English gentleman--even if he was American.

News of the crash elicited looks of concern and speculation from around the room.

Parks moved closer to the speaker, to hear any news. He feared it might be Wagner, a known risk taker. After a moment, he sensed someone standing beside him.

It was the brunette. "Who is it?" she asked. "Do you know?"

Parks looked down at her. Her red lips were slightly parted.

"Hard to say, really," he answered distractedly. He looked back at the speaker expectantly, forgetting the girl. When it was announced that the car had been identified as car number 37 Parks relaxed. He remembered the girl. She was still beside him.

"Do you know who it is now?"

"Yes. It's the young American, Michael Bravo."

"I hope he's not hurt."

Parks studied her face a moment and frowned. She was as pretty as a pixie, but that baseball cap just wouldn't do.

"Why don't you take off that silly hat and let me buy you a drink or something? What's your name?"

*   *   *

Rain. Hard Rain.

At 180 mph, it fell horizontally and exploded off Wagner's windscreen and goggles, and felt like bee-bee shot against his covered face. He nudged the steering wheel this way and that, gently, easily, keeping his wandering machine from veering off the wet Masta Straight. He could see a car up ahead--or was it two cars?--kicking up a great cloud of spray. Backmarkers? Or was it Bogavanti and Evans? Had he caught them? He watched the ball of spray divide and disappear into the Masta Kink. Clearly, it was two cars. Who else could it be but Bogavanti and Evans?

116

Now it was his turn to face Masta, and a chance to pick up more ground. He reduced speed even more, to 160 mph, and eased into the first curve. He felt the chassis lean, his outside tire treads burrowing down on the wet road. But instead of gripping, they were riding a film of water.

Too fast. He'd hit the esse bend too fast.

Through the mist he glimpsed something long and gray and hard, rushing at him. Beyond that, looking ghostly in the rain, was the first farmhouse. There was no time for fear, only detached observation. The guardrail streaked past. His tires settled--finally--drawing him out of the first curve and pointing him towards the second farmhouse. He eased the wheel the other way. Chassis weight shifted from right to left. He felt the same sickening sensation--treads not settling but riding a film of water. There was no guardrail to stop him this time, merely three stories of red brick, coming at him at lightning speed. His eyes focused on the front door. It was wood, with old black hinges and a bronze latch. An image flashed in his mind of smashing through that wood door, a sudden, unexpected dinner guest. Only he wouldn't be staying but passing through ... at 160 mph. An angel must have been watching over him--or maybe his speed was just this side of the limit--because again his tires settled against asphalt. Off to his left, the farmhouse flew past like some red phantom that had released him from its death grip.

Another mile of straightaway splashed beneath his wheels. Setting up for Stavelot, he saw Evans and Bogavanti make the turn and accelerate up the valley. Bogavanti's red machine was second, looking none too steady in the wet, and Evans' Lotus was in front, water streaking off its red-and-gold finish.

Fighting a thick veil of spray, Wagner moved ever closer, following the Ferrari's high red airfoil as it floated above the spray. He sensed Virage de la Carriere coming up. Seeking passing room, he moved right of the Ferrari and felt his near-side tires rabbit at the edge of the road. He had his nose up with the Ferrari's mid-section when Bogavanti steered over into his path. Wagner braked and fell back, one chance wasted. There wouldn't be many.

Past La Carriere, the road straightened, veered gently right then swept left, for Virage de Blanchimont. Using the tops of trees as a guide, he moved up again, this time to the left of the Ferrari. Blanchimont was 200 yards away, and already he was beside the red car. He sneaked a glance and saw Bogavanti crouched low in the seat, rain sheeting off his powder blue helmet. What was this? The Ferrari V-12 engine was sputtering now, as if water had gotten into the ignition, or was running short of fuel? Bogavanti looked back at him, and seemed to shrug.

Wagner shook his head. Tough luck, my friend.

The view ahead was clear, such was the extent Evans had stretched his lead. Wagner leaned on the throttle more and felt his rear tires shift from side to side. Any faster and he might spin. But he had to go faster. Through Blanchimont and Seaman, he closed the gap. Speeding back behind the pits, he latched onto the Lotus' tail. His only hope of winning was a long shot--outbraking the Scot. In the wet.

What the hell. Go for it.

He darted out from behind the Lotus and gradually drew up even with it. La Source appeared out of the mist, coming on fast. Wagner inhaled deeply and focused his eyes on it. This was it. His concentration was so deep he almost forgot a small but important task he always performed at this point: heating up the brakes. He eased his foot against the pedal and could almost feel the discs expand with heat and fill the calipers. Staring La Source dead in the teeth, he bore down on the brakes for all they were worth. The Garret-Hawk nose dropped and the tires throbbed, flinging spray. Evans' Lotus leaped ahead, the Scot having braked two-tenths-of-a-second later, and, in those two tenths, having won the race. Wagner accepted this, and so was shocked to see the Lotus swerve wildly, almost spin, and shoot up the escape road.

The poor bastard had forgotten to heat up his brakes.

Garret, Hacksaw, Eddie and the entire crew stared in wonder as the Californian took the checkered flag. Except for Garret, they danced and hugged each other. After the initial excitement wore off, they wondered what had become of Evans. They could

118

near an engine revving atop the hill, perhaps from a car turning around. They looked up toward La Source and saw a red car coming. Evans? No. Bogavanti, coasting downhill, out of gas. Then Evans reappeared, screaming downhill after him. The flagman raised the checker for Bogavanti, but waved it for Evans, who beat the Italian at the line.

Belgian Grand Prix Top Six Finishers		Championship Point Leaders Race Five of Eleven	
Driver	Points	Driver	Points
Wagner	9	Wagner	24
Evans	6	Parks	23
Bogavanti	4	Evans	21
Stockton	3	Bogavanti	19
Tambala	2	Phillips	10
Lafosse	1	Lafosse	10

* * *

Rain was falling at Burnenville when Wagner arrived on the cool-off lap. He pulled over and stopped. In the pasture, the crumpled Garret-Hawk had been righted, but there was no sign of his teammate, no sign of an ambulance having come and gone, no tow rig, no marshals, just farmfolk standing around in the rain, looking at the wrecked car. Then Wagner heard a voice from behind.

"John. Boy, am I glad to seed you."

He turned around to see Bravo climbing from a ditch below the road. His uniform was splattered with mud and grass.

"Michael? You all right?"

"Yeah, I think so." He walked with a decided limp. "I mean, I'm not sure. My legs are sore, and I lost one of my shoes. Probably still inside the cockpit."

"What happened?"

Bravo looked down. "My stupidity, that's all. I tried unlapping myself and flat lost it. The next thing I knew I was

119

upside down in that pasture over there. A couple farmers ran up and one of them peered underneath at me and asked me what I wanted. I said, `Get me the hell out of here.' They tipped the thing back on its wheels and here I am."

Wagner shook his head. "You're lucky, my friend. Climb on back."

"Shouldn't I wait for the ambulance?"

"You'll be here all day. Come on, Eddie can drive you to the hospital."

Before Bravo could climb on, an ambulance sped around the curve and ground to a stop behind them. A paramedic jumped out to intercept him.

Wagner gunned the engine. "See you later, Michael."

"Wait! Who won?"

Chapter 14

Hacksaw threw three chips on the pile and glared at Balchowsky. "Be glad I'm not raising you, Walt. I know you don't got nothin'."

Balchowsky laid down his cards gleefully. His voice sounded as raspy as an old file. "Read 'em and weep, George. Three whores. Ha-ha-ha!"

Hacksaw slid his cards back in the deck. He shook his head. "Luck. That's all it is, luck." He went into the kitchen for a beer just as Wagner was hanging up the phone. He eyed the driver. He seemed defeated by the call. "Well, what'd she say?"

Wagner stared at the wall a moment. "She wants to see me regularly or call it off."

Hacksaw rubbed his neck, thinking. "Hmm. What did you say?"

"I told her about the new wings Fat Walt fabricated and that we'll be doing a lot more testing now, to stay ahead." He shrugged. "And, well, she didn't want to hear about it."

Hacksaw removed two beers from the refrigerator, popped off both tops, and handed one to Wagner. "Can you blame her?"

"No."

Hacksaw took a swallow of beer. It was icy cold, the way he liked it. "Ever think of inviting her over here?"

"Sure, but she's got her own career to worry about. In a way, I like it that way."

"Call her in a couple of days, John. She'll act like nothing ever happened and be glad as heck to hear from you. What do you bet?"

Wagner smiled ruefully. "That's another thing. She's mad because I haven't been calling her enough." He looked at the bottle he was holding. "It's over, Hacksaw. She didn't come right out and say it, but it's over."

"You going to drink that beer or just stare at it? Do you want it to be over?"

"Not really."

"Then do something."

"Like what, for instance?" He took a drink of beer.

"Send her flowers."

"Flowers? Susie would never fall for anything as obvious as that."

"She's a woman, isn't she? Whenever my wife gets sore at me, I send her a dozen yellow roses. Works every time. What do you got to lose?"

They rejoined the poker game. It was Tuesday night, two days after the Belgian Grand Prix, and a rare day off for the crew. They were in Wagner's third-story flat for their weekly poker game. Wagner looked at the faces around the table. Ray, Dave, and Gofer Tom, looked back at him hungrily, each having a bad night. Rennie was about even and Hacksaw was eight dollars to the good. The big winner was the big man, Walt Balchowsky. He sat smugly in his chair with arms folded over his belly. Wagner was down twelve dollars. He usually dropped twenty-to-thirty dollars most poker nights and considered it a good investment. Another hand was dealt. Bets were placed. Systematically, players began folding, cursing as they threw their cards on the table, until only Rennie and Balchowsky held cards.

"Dollar to play poker." Balchowsky tossed a chip on the table and grinned evilly.

Rennie smiled toothily, counted out six chips and pushed them to the center of the table. "Here's your dollar, and five more. What do you say to that, Walter."

Balchowsky grunted, measured off five more chips and tossed them on the pile. "I say `call', Runt."

Rennie laid down two jacks and two tens. He smiled at Balchowsky triumphantly.

Balchowsky spread his cards on the table. "Three aces." His big hands surrounded the pot and pulled it toward him. "Like taking candy from a baby."

Rennie looked at his dwindling stack of chips and shook his head sadly.

The phone rang. All heads turned toward the kitchen.

"If that's Carol, I'm not here," Gofer Tom shouted.

Hacksaw held up a poker chip. "I've got a dollar here that ays it's Susan."

"You're on." Wagner picked up the receiver.

"John. I must see you. Now."

Wagner turned to his crew chief and shook his head: it vasn't Susan.

Hacksaw flipped him the chip.

"Look, Irene," he said, fingering the chip, "I have a poker ame going on. I can't see you now."

"How about later, then. Can I come over later?"

"What's this all about?"

"I just want to see you, that's all. Does it have to be about omething?"

"Some other time, huh?"

"Tomorrow then."

"I don't know, Irene..."

"In the afternoon. I'll come to you. We can meet over at the 3rig & Age. It's just around the corner from you."

"I know where the Brig & Age is," he said impatiently.

"How does four o'clock sound?"

Another hand was dealt. Balchowsky raised the betting to ive dollars. There was the usual chorus of swearing as players hrew in their cards. "Call," said Rennie, counting out five chips nd pushing them forward. Wagner detected a look of panic on 3alchowsky's big bearded face.

"Four is fine, I guess," he said. "Look. I'll see you later." Ie hung up the phone and immediately wished he'd had the guts o say no, but something within him intervened. Did he want to ee her?

"Queen-high straight," said Balchowsky, laying down his ards one at a time. Only where the jack should be was the eight f spades. Fat Walt had a nothing hand.

Rennie held up two cards--a pair of deuces--and smiled his toothy smile. "Sweet, eh, Walter?"

*　　*　　*

Wagner did not arrive at four, but at five-fifteen, hoping Irene had given up on him and departed. He surveyed the pub. As London pubs went, the Brig & Age was typical, with heavy stuffed furniture, tiffany lamps, brass rails, and old posters and assorted Victorian bric-a-brac adorning the wallpapered walls.

"Over here, John."

There she was, smiling warmly, as if he wasn't a minute late. He sat down beside her, and felt her hand squeeze his thigh.

"You look positively wonderful, John. Good enough to eat, in fact."

Wagner cleared his throat self-consciously. He ordered a dark ale and another red wine for her. He had to admit, she looked pretty wonderful herself. Her skin looked as white and as delicate as whipped cream, and her emerald earrings were a magnificent match for her big green eyes.

The bartender smiled, placing down their drinks. "Cheers," he said, and departed.

"Was there something you wanted to see me about?" Wagner took a large swallow of ale.

Irene's fingers rubbed her glass thoughtfully. "Nothing in particular. I did hope we would get together occasionally, now that Mal and I have separated." She lit cigarette. "I do find you very attractive, you know." She blew a smoke ring. "I always have."

"You don't beat around the bush, do you, Irene?"

"I never was big on foreplay, or don't you remember?"

Wagner put down his glass. "I have a girlfriend."

"A girlfriend, yes, I remember. What was her name again? Sheila?"

"Susan."

"Susan, yes. An America girl. I bet you haven't seen her since our trip down to Monaco, have you? You don't really care about her, otherwise she would be over here, with you."

"You don't know what you're talking about."

"I'm here, and I will see you whenever you want, no strings. Susan will never know, and if she's like the rest of your girlfriends, she'll tire of your inattention and leave you. Me, I'll always be around, whenever you want me."

Wagner said nothing. He felt a sudden, deep inner physical attraction for her and, at the same time, disgust with himself. He was defeated, and sensed she knew it, too. Still, he didn't want to yield, to give her that satisfaction. There was pride at stake here--and something else.

"Oh, come, come, John, you've slept with plenty of girls. You slept with me, once upon a time. Remember? I can't forget."

He rose suddenly, paid the bill and went out to the street. Cars pushed past in the summer heat. He walked in the direction of his flat.

"You don't like my being so direct, do you?" Irene said, walking fast to keep up with him. "If only I was a little more demure, a little more hard to get, a little more of the sweet innocent girl, then you would be interested, because then I would be your little conquest."

"That's not it," he said.

"Then what it is?"

He stopped and turned to her. "I don't know. Mal, maybe. Beth and Mary."

"The divorce papers have been served, John. It's over between us. I'm free as a bird. You do find me attractive, don't you."

He looked at her. The attraction he felt was strong. He could feel her in his arms, smell her, taste her. He continued walking.

They turned the corner onto Thurloe Street and stopped at the gate leading up the steps to his flat.

"Invite me up, John. Just this once. Please."

He shook his head. "This relationship has nowhere to go. I think that's what bothers me most." He opened the gate for her and followed her up the steps to the entry. "Neither one of us will be happy. It will just go on until one of us gets bored."

Chapter 15

Rennie stuffed rubber plugs into his ears, fired up the Garret-Hawk V-12 engine and began revving it, the noise so fierce and penetrating it vibrated the dust loose from the wooden rafters. The cylinders heated up immediately and radiated heat outward, to a network of passages carrying oil and coolant. The thick oil absorbed the heat and thinned as it flowed throughout the engine. The coolant heated even quicker, opened the thermostat and rushed through a tube up the length of the chassis, flowed through the radiator, and returned through another tube back to the engine. When the engine was sufficiently warm, he switched it off, removed the cold spark plugs, and installed a set of hot spark plugs. He fired up the engine again, revved it another 90 seconds, and switched it off again.

At this point, he usually turned to Wagner or to Young Michael and said, "She's yours, mate," and watched them speed away. But this morning, for all Rennie knew, they were still asleep at the Lion d'Or. No, this time he was taking the wheel.

He slipped on his sunglasses--the kind that wrap around the eyes and look like bug eyes--and slid his small, wiry body down into the cockpit. He didn't bother with a helmet. He fired up the engine again, revved it a few times more, and drove out of the garage. He passed the gas pumps in front and turned onto Rue Libergier, like any other car. It was a bright clear Sunday morning, still cool from the night. He checked the mirror and saw nothing behind him but the <u>Cathedrale Notre-Dame</u>, at the top of the street, its twin towers blotting out a big piece of sky. He passed restaurants and bars, shut down at this early hour, passed upstairs residences with their shutters still closed. The light was red at the next intersection. He stopped beside a blue Citroen and continued gassing the engine--to keep the plugs from fouling. The startled driver looked over to see what manner of beast was making such a horrendous racket. He looked and saw nothing of the low-slung racer. The light changed. He heard a screech of rubber and saw the darkened backside of a Formula One disappear down the street.

Rennie crossed over the Canal de l'Aisne a la Marne and turned onto the N31. He was driving through countryside now, and passed a gendarme, who didn't look twice at him. It was not that unusual for a mechanic to be seen driving a racecar to the circuit. A building with white stucco walls and red tile roof appeared off by itself on the right. Rennie recognized it immediately. It was the <u>Auberge du Circuit de Reims</u>, backdrop to racing's most infamous hairpin--Thillois. In a few hours, spectators would crowd into the Inn's portico and sip champagne anticipating that singular moment when one of the drivers missed the braking zone, skidded past the hairpin and stopped in a cloud of smoke beneath their noses. More than one French Grand Prix had been decided on this very spot.

Rennie turned left in front of the Inn and drove up what would become the Front Straight. The road was still open to traffic. A red Fiat and a white Renault zipped past going the other way. Ahead, the pits and main grandstand faced each other from opposite sides of the road. Cars were already beginning to fill the dirt parking lot behind the stands, while behind the pits the paddock was jammed with transporters and supplier trucks. Rennie drove on past the pits, rather than pull in and stop as he was supposed to do, and followed the road up a gradual rise and into a sweeping right curve. The terrain was mostly flat and waist-high in wheat. He cruised along in fourth gear at 4500 rpm--about 120 mph. It seemed slow. The road swept right again, then left. He took both turns with a slight tilting of the wheel and it seemed very slow indeed. The next turn was Muizon Hairpin. He braked and dropped down to second gear, made sure no traffic was coming from the direction of Soissons, and steered around the curve onto the back straight, to begin the two-mile run to Thillois.

"Show your stuff, old girl," Rennie cooed, leaning on the loud pedal.

The car sprung like a wild beast set free, gobbling up huge amounts of asphalt. Rennie upshifted through the gears, his head snapping back with each release of the clutch. He forced his hin down against his chest--to keep his sunglasses from being ucked off his face. Wind tore at his thick black hair, every trand feeling as if it was being ripped out by its roots. The ngine scream turned into a high, mournful howl as speed ouched 175 mph. Rennie sat pinned in the seat, frightened, nvigorated, spellbound. The engine ran flawlessly, and would un flawlessly all day long.

The previous week, he finally solved the riddle of the high-peed misfire, a problem that had plagued the engine on and off ince the team arrived in England back in April. It wasn't dirt articles getting in the system as both Hacksaw and Wagner had elieved, but a flaw in the design, as Rennie had come to uspect. As it turned out, the felt filter in the metering valve was nadequate to handle the flow of fuel as pressure mounted, and ould compress, restricting the flow of fuel to the engine. Vhenever Rennie examined the filter, it was always clean, so he idn't suspect this was the problem. When it finally dawned on im what was happening, he removed the felt, installed a large ree-flowing filter between the pump and the metering valve, and he misfire disappeared for good.

The back straight crested a low hill before dropping down to hillois. As Rennie cleared the hill, he was stunned to see the ackside of a slow-moving lorry, high as a 20-foot wall, directly n his path. With no time to brake, he whipped into the outer ane and passed the big hauler a split-second ahead of an ncoming car.

"You are one lucky son-of-a-gun," he said, and laughed all he way back to the pits.

Wagner arrived later that morning, before the preliminary vents got underway and the traffic built up. There wasn't nything for him to do but wait. He had his usual prerace jitters ut felt good. Between races, they had tested a new airfoil--a ingle wing, mounted above the engine--and picked up half-a-econd around Silverstone. But for Reims, with so few curves nd those mind-numbing straightaways, they elected not to use t. Too much drag. They reverted back to the upswept tail and or even less wind-resistance installed shorter canard wings on

the nose. The decision paid off. He was fastest qualifier. Th
big surprise was his teammate, who was starting in the third-row

French Grand Prix
Sunday, July 7

WAGNER	BOGAVANTI	PARKS
Garret-Hawk	Ferrari	BRM
2 min 3.6 sec	2 min 4.2 sec	2 min 4.9 sec

TAMBALA	EVANS
Ferrari	Lotus
2 min 5.3 sec	2 min 5.7 sec

LAFOSSE	STOCKTON	BRAVO
Matra	BRM	Garret-Hawk
2 min 6.1 sec	2 min 6.4 sec	2 min 7.2 sec

At two-fifty-nine, with the field set and the drivers inside
their cars, a short round man bearing the French Tricolor
walked with great dignity to the front of the grid. He alone wa
responsible for keeping the French Grand Prix at Reims,
somewhat dull place to watch a motor race. Champagne, fo
which Reims was known, made it tolerable. Every few years
rival organizers at Rouen or Clermont-Ferrand, offering
infinitely more picturesque venues, lured the event away. Bu
with his tenacity and connections, this single man alway
managed to bring the French Grand Prix back to its rightfu
home--to <u>Circuit de Reims</u>. After 30 years, Claude Pitou cam
to symbolize Reims. Therefore, it was only fitting that he star
the race.

With a majestic sweep of his hand, he signaled the drivers t
start their engines. The burst of 18 engines roaring to life all a
once always startled him, and he backed up a step. Then
tentatively, he leaned forward and looked over the vibrating
fuming machines.

Parks' engine wouldn't start. He raised his hand.

Pitou didn't notice, despite the Englishman's position practically under his nose, so Parks raised both hands and began waving them.

"Oh," Pitou seemed to say, seeing him at last. He turned to the pits and with a twitch of his finger beckoned the BRM crew to come forth. Obediently, two crewmen hurried out. They examined the battery and starter connections: both were tight. They shrugged and began pushing the car away.

Pitou shook his jowly face side to side. "No! No! Push-start zee car."

This was too good to be true.

"How's that again?" asked one of the crew

"Push-start zee car."

"It's okay to push-start?"

"Yes." Pitou made a pushing motion with his hands, to be certain they understood.

While everyone watched, the BRM crew pushed the green car up to a fast trot. Parks popped the clutch, the engine coughed, and didn't catch. They rolled the car back for a second try.

Lotus team manager Kevin Revette watched from the pits with arms folded. "There's always a mix up before the start at Reims," he muttered to Big Jim, "thanks to that ham-fisted Pitou."

"Looky there, Captain." Big Jim pointed to a glint of sunlight beneath Evans' Lotus. "She's over`eating."

"That's it," said Revette. "I've had it with his lunacy." He ran out to Pitou. "Are you crazy, man? These cars can't sit here with their engines running. My god, it's a hundred degrees." He pointed at the growing pool of green fluid beneath Evans' car. "That's coolant boiling out of my engine. My $18,000 dollar engine, I might add. They'll all be boiling over if you don't start this race this instant!"

"I will not start zee French Grand Prix without zee reigning world champion," sniffed Pitou. He eyed the BRM being rolled back for a third attempt.

"Push-starting is against the rules, Claude, and you know it!"

"I make zee rules here," said Pitou. He removed a white scarf and mopped his forehead.

"If you don't shove that BRM aside and start this race this instant I will issue a formal protest to the <u>FIA</u>. This will be your last French Grand Prix, Claude."

Pitou didn't respond. He knew every member of the <u>Federation Internationale de Automobile</u>. Their office was in Paris, almost next door. They were his friends, drinking pals, members of the same clubs to which he belonged. Most importantly of all, they were <u>Francais</u>. Revette was, well, an Englishman.

This time the BRM engine kicked on. Parks' crew hustled to push him back into place at the front of the grid. The English driver signaled to Pitou that all was well now.

Pitou brushed past Revette. "Out of my way. I have zee race to start." In commanding fashion, he held up the Tricolor, swung it down, and as fast as his short legs could carry him, ran for cover.

The first four rows surged away cleanly, but further back not everyone saw the flag. Some cars didn't move and were rammed from behind, others tried passing on the outside and created more chaos as everyone scrambled to get away at once. When the air cleared, four cars remained, battered and silent, the four drivers climbing out slowly. Crewmen and marshals hurried to clear the mess before the field came back around again.

Pitou didn't seem to notice. He disappeared into an upstairs room with air-conditioning and a view of the circuit. The French Grand Prix--<u>his</u> French Grand Prix--was underway. That's all that mattered.

Chapter 16

The leading four cars were running so closely together, they appeared to be coupled, as a train--an express train--circling madly beneath a fiery July sun.

From where he sat in the air-conditioned booth above track level, Edward W. Garret had a perfect view of the flat open circuit. Lap after lap, he watched the leading foursome come thundering up the front straightaway, Wagner in front, Bogavanti's Ferrari in second, Tambala's Ferrari in third, and-- god bless him--Michael Bravo in fourth.

Michael Bravo in fourth?

A month ago--even as late as two weeks ago--the very notion of Bravo running in fourth, within a wrench throw of leading a Grand Prix, was ludicrous. But Reims was Reims, a throwback to the days when European road circuits were set up for speed. It was an easy circuit to learn. It was triangular in shape and had those long, long straightaways. It was no coincidence that the leading foursome--two Garret-Hawks and two Ferraris--were off the horsepower chart as far as rival teams were concerned. Evans, for all his quickness, had not been a factor when he dropped out with overheating on lap 8. And Parks, who in practice had the speed to match the Garret-Hawk/Ferrari juggernaut, was not a factor either, having been penalized a lap for the push-start (Pitou giveth, and Pitou taketh away).

Garret watched them shoot past the pits, circle the big curve at the end of the straight, and disappear into the wheatfields. Then he raised his field glasses and peered out the backside of the booth, waiting for the cars to arrive on the back straight. In a moment they reappeared, stringing out as they sped down to Thillois at a grounding-shaking 200 mph, order unchanged. With their long, smooth fuselages and forward cockpits, they looked like low-flying fighter planes coming down to land. Braking for Thillois, their noses dropped and puffs of smoke lit from their wheels--touching down as it were. They closed rank rounding the 35-mph hairpin, and took flight once more accelerating up the front straight. Garret moved to the front of the booth to see them coming, gathering speed, four pointy noses aimed directly at him, drivers crouched low in their seats, their helmets half visible above their windscreens.

He put away his field glasses. He'd seen enough from this level. The room was refreshingly cool and comfortable, and he had all his needs met by Pitou's well-drilled staff, but it was time to get below. He loosened his tie, removed his coat, and stepped into the furnace-heat of a July afternoon in Reims, France. Trackside, keeping score on the pitboard, was his crew chief.

"Think Michael can do it?" Garret shouted.

"Finish fourth? Sure, I'd say he's got that sewn up."

"No, win the race."

Hacksaw tried to look thoughtful, but the idea of Bravo somehow taking command and winning the race was too absurd for him to consider. He shrugged. "I dunno, boss. All bunched up like that, any one of 'em can win the darn thing."

The leaders were coming. Hacksaw could hear them exit Thillois, upshifting, accelerating, growing louder. He changed the "4" to "3" on the pitboard. The message above it he left unchanged. It read:

WAG
BOG
TAM
BRA

He stepped to the edge of the track and held out the pitboard. "It's Bogo I'm worried about," he shouted. The roar of onrushing engines drowned Hacksaw's words before they reached Garret's ears. A second later, the cars blurred past at bullet-speed, followed by a tailwind that ruffled lap charts along pit row.

Garret shook his head, his ears numbed by the blast of engines. He turned to his son. "How many laps, Eddie?"

"Three."

"It's Bogavanti I'm worried about," said Hacksaw. "He's crafty, that one. Last year, he bird-dogged Lafosse the same way he's bird-dogging John now. Passed him on the last lap, too, to win the race."

* * *

Wagner knew it was a sucker's game to be leading at this stage of the game, that come the final lap, one or more of the cars behind him could slipstream past, and one of them win. Leading was a sucker's game, but he didn't know any other way. Certainly, this wasn't how he'd planned it, but he'd been trapped by circumstances, mainly of his own making. At the start, he wanted to get away quickly and break from the pack, and have the easy race Spa was supposed to have been. It almost worked. He jumped well out in front at the start, and by the time he reached the back straight he led by two seconds. Coming down to Thillois, he set up perfectly, braking firmly, but not overly hard, easing his speed down, keeping the chassis properly balanced for a smooth, swift entry into the turn. And then ... he screwed up.

If only Pitou had sent them around for a warm up lap, he would've known what to expect. The sun wreaked particular havoc on this one corner, and after two preliminary races, the surface was breaking up. Wagner laid into the curve hard and fast, tires pressed to the limit, and there was nothing to hold him. He felt the tail go, saw the world spin twice and abruptly stop. Before he could recover, Bogavanti and eight other cars filed past him. He spent the next 14 laps making up lost ground, retook the lead on lap 16, but by then he had three cars planted in his slipstream.

* * *

This time, Garret covered his ears as the leaders sped past, order unchanged--Wagner, Bogavanti, Tambala, Bravo. The tension was almost unbearable. His hands were shaking. He felt like vomiting. So much was at stake. He looked up pit lane and

135

saw Ferrari team manager Zilli, back to the wall, head tilted back, eyes closed, in seeming meditation. Garret shook his head. What does he know that I don't? Bogavanti is laying in the weeds, waiting for the right moment to spring, that's what Zilli knows. So what. Bravo has the same advantage. He could slingshot past too. Couldn't he? You bet he could.

Two laps to go.

The Public Address blared excitedly in French. Garret looked up at the speaker. The message was repeated in English. "Car number 37 has moved up to second place. Three-time world champion Giuseppe Bogavanti in car number 14 has dropped to third."

Garret spun around and looked at his son. "What'd I tell you? Give the kid some time--isn't that what I said? Give him time, and he'd come around."

"That's right, Dad, you did."

Garret rubbed his hands together. "You bet I said it, many times I said it. What do you say now, Hacksaw? Michael's in second place. I tell ya, Michael's going to win this thing before it's over."

Garret headed to the backside of the pits. Where were his field glasses when he needed them most of all? He peered across the field to the back straightaway. He squinted and saw two white-and-blue cars leading two red cars. "One-two, just like the man said," he muttered to himself. "Now, it gets interesting."

Wait. Under braking, one of the red cars passed one of the blue cars to take back second place. Was it Bravo who was passed, or Wagner? Garret rushed to the frontside of the pits to see who was leading. At such distance, the glare of afternoon sunlight made it difficult to distinguish one car from another. The scream of accelerating engines grew louder, the cars increasing in size and clarity. Garret couldn't see the number of the leading car, not yet, but he could see the color of the driver's helmet. It was black. Wagner was leading. Bravo was third. The cars ripped past. Garret felt the hot blast of their tailwind whipsaw his face.

"One lap," said Eddie.

"I know," Garret growled, "I know." He glanced at his wristwatch out of nervousness. It was almost five. He looked up to the VIP booth, where he'd left his field glasses. He'd give anything to have them now. But it was too late. The leaders were working their way around the backside of the circuit and would appear on the back straight within seconds. His euphoria had changed to dread. He looked at Hacksaw. "Can Wagner hold him?"

Hacksaw breathed deeply, thinking about it. No question. Bogavanti held the advantage. "I think so, boss."

Garret peered anxiously out the backside of the pits. Across the field, the leaders streamed down the hill, white-and-blue car, red car, white-and-blue car, red car. Braking for Thillois, they merged as one and--puff--were obscured by a cloud of dust.

"What? Oh, shit. This is crazy. I ...." Garret scrambled back to the front. "All hell's broke loose," he shouted. "Somebody's spun and caused a chain reaction."

Hacksaw squinted, looking at the hairpin. It was almost a mile away, but he saw a flicker of sunlight reflect off the movement of a car. "Somebody's coming."

Garret strained to see. "My god, what a terrible way to end a race. Can you see who it is?"

"Yeah, it's one of our cars. It's John."

"Any sign of Michael? Do you see Michael coming?"

"Two more cars are coming. One of 'em might be Michael. Wait. Dang it all. They're red. The both of 'em."

Forty feet up the track, corpulent Claude Pitou stepped out onto the tarmac. The Frenchman waved the checkered flag as Wagner flashed by. Held it up and waved it twice more, once for Bogavanti, in second, and once for Tambala, in third. Two minutes, six seconds later, he waved it again, this time for Parks, the fourth-place finisher. Where was Michael?

*　　*　　*

Wagner crossed the finish line and backed off. Bogavanti pulled up beside him and waved. The American pulled down his bandanna and smiled back at him. He thought, "yeah, you

137

almost pulled it off, Bogo. Almost. Had me under braking and then spun rounding the hairpin."

Wagner waved to the crowd, happy, tired, and relieved that it was over and that he had won. At Thillois, he saw car number 37 in the wheatfield. Michael was still seated in the cockpit, staring blankly, as if dazed. The Californian shrugged and motored on. Pulling into the pits, a human sea parted for him, and closed in around him once he stopped. He removed his goggles and helmet. His eyes searched among the faces for someone with water or champagne--anything to quench his Mojave desert-sized thirst--and stopped on a willowy red-head in a white dress.

French Grand Prix Top Six Finishers		Championship Point Leaders Race Six of Eleven	
Driver	Points	Driver	Points
Wagner	9	Wagner	33
Bagavanti	6	Parks	26
Tambala	4	Bogavanti	25
Parks	3	Evans	21
Bravo	2	Phillips	10
Giraud	1	Lafosse	10

Chapter 17

"I wish you could have seen your face," Susan laughed. "Your jaw dropped and you just sat there staring at me like I was a ghost or something. If only I'd had my camera."

Wagner smiled ruefully, glad she hadn't had her camera. "You weren't exactly the first person I expected to see in Reims, let me tell you. What brings you here, not that I'm not glad as hell to see you?"

"It was corny, John, but effective."

"What was corny?"

"The yellow roses. Don't you remember?"

Wasn't that just like him--to forget completely about it? Rather than admit it, he shrugged, acting as if, of course, he remembered. "You can't be serious, can you, expecting me to believe you came all the way to France just because I sent you a dozen flowers?"

"Why not? I figured, what the heck; if you wouldn't come to me, then I would just have to come to you."

Wagner shook his head. "You amaze me."

It had been an hour since the race, but this was the first chance they'd had to speak privately. They walked slowly along pit row, while about them tired crews were cleaning up and packing to leave. It was still broiling hot, the air filled with the dust of departing traffic. He led her back behind the pits, to a bench beneath a stand of shade trees. She sat down, and he sat beside her.

"Sometimes I think you care more about motor racing than me." She lowered her head, not believing what just had come out of her mouth. "That was awful of me to say, wasn't it?"

"After our last conversation, I kinda thought it was over between us, Susie."

"Do you want it to be over between us?"

"I sent you roses, didn't I?"

"Yes, and it was very sweet of you. Look, I know how important winning the championship is to you, and I do support you, believe me. But it's been so long since I've seen you. I've missed you, John."

Wagner nodded. "It has been a while, hasn't it? What with the way things have been going lately, with airfoils, and all the testing we're doing...."

"You don't have to explain, John."

He stretched his arms. His muscles ached from the strain and bruising of the race, and he felt very tired, and dirty. He offered her a drink from the bottle of mineral water he was nursing.

She shook her head no.

"Where are you staying, anyway?"

"Bellevue," she said.

"Bellevue? What are you doing way out there?"

"I couldn't find a room. It really is quite pretty out there. My room overlooks the vineyards."

Wagner nodded. "I want to get back to my hotel and shower and maybe lay down for a bit. There's a dinner tonight--white table cloth, candlelight, that sort of thing--in the caves. Interested?"

"Are you wearing your suit?"

"What's that got to do with it?"

"It might influence my decision," she said, teasingly.

"I am, as a matter of fact."

"This I have to see. What are the caves, anyway?"

*   *   *

A steward led them down a long flight of stairs, to a labyrinth of underground tunnels. In contrast with the heat and glare of the day, it was cool and dimly lit. Susan was glad she had brought her sweater. The caves, as the locals called them, had once been so many limestone quarry pits at the edge of town. When the champagne industry went international in the 19th century, the vintners needed vast new amounts of underground storage space and looked no further than the quarry

140

its, which they capped and connected by boring a series of tunnels.

"These particular caves contain 25 million bottles of champagne," the steward said, showing them one of the caverns. It was a large round room, hushed and solemn as the Reims' cathedral interior, with a high, dark ceiling, and rows of wooden racks that looked like church pews, pews not for seating parishioners but for stacking bottles of fermenting champagne. Susan ran her finger along the limestone wall. It was moist and chalky to the touch, and left a white film on her fingertip. The steward led them into another cavern, this one set up with a bar, and a score of tables decked in white-linen and silver candelabra. Busboys moved from table to table, lighting candles and setting up tableware. The usual crowd had gathered: drivers, team managers, officials, organizers, sponsors, journalists, and as decoration several women in long dresses. As soon as Wagner entered, a circle of people formed around him, congratulating him and shaking his hand. Susan felt herself being elbowed out of the way. Someone took her arm, as if to rescue her, a short, round man, dressed in a white dinner jacket, with a wide, ingratiating smile. "And who is this charming creature?"

"Uh, Susan Jennings. And you are?"

"Claude Pitou, your servant." He bowed stiffly, kissed her hand, and wouldn't let it go. "I see John is your escort. I am, as you say, very jealous."

Susan smiled, unsure of how to respond. "Uh, Oui."

Pitou stroked her hand. "Ah! Parlez vous Francais?"

"Oui," she said, trying gently to retrieve her hand. He wouldn't let it go. "Pauvrement."

Pitou raised an eyebrow. "Vous plaisantez. Vous avez l'accent Francais!"

Susan giggled. "Uh, C'est bien aimable a vous. S'il vous plait, nous devons parler Anglais. Je ne tiens pas a offenser John."

Pitou laughed heartily, still stroking her hand. "Vous etes bien mysterieuse, pas deplaisant. Le mystere est le secret de la romance. Acceptez ceci d'un connisseur."

Susan was beginning to feel self-conscious about this man who was holding her hand as if it were his personal property. She smiled politely. "Really, my French is awful. Please, my hand."

"Your French is charming, dear lady. As are you." He looked over at Wagner, trapped in a circle of admirers. "John does not realize how fortunate he is to have you, or he would not ignore you this way."

"You don't have to tell me," Wagner said, suddenly free of the circle. He took Susan's hand from Pitou. "I am fortunate to be with her. Very fortunate."

"I thought he would never let go of me," Susan said, after Pitou departed. Wagner found two vacant seats at the bar and they sat down. A waiter brought them two long-stemmed glasses of champagne.

"Mmm. This is good," she said.

"It's the real McCoy."

"By the way, I have a confession to make."

"A confession?"

She smiled sheepishly. "I really am here on assignment, truth be told."

"I thought so." Wagner nodded.

"I'm covering the Davis Cup match at Roland Garros between the U.S. and France."

"Whatever the reason, I'm glad you're here, Susan." He took a long, cool swallow of the golden liquid. The exhaustion, the emotional letdown he felt after every race, win or lose; it was all behind him now. He felt good. Susan was with him, and that added to his pleasure. The race had been hard fought, the outcome uncertain until the very end, but he had come out on top. That's all that mattered. Two wins in a row, three wins in five races. Yes, he felt very good. Everything was going his way now. His car was quick, and getting quicker by the week. His team was solidly behind him. He was even getting along with Old Man Garret. Another two wins would just about lock up the championship. In another month, he might be world champion. It seemed too easy.

Still, one thing bothered him. It was a nettlesome fly buzzing around in his head, that wouldn't leave him alone, that he couldn't swat. It was Irene. He couldn't believe how stupid he'd been to let her walk into his life and set up housekeeping. He didn't particularly like her, didn't really enjoy her company. But she was so damn nice to him, had done so many things for him, small things a woman does for a man. She had sewn on buttons that were missing from his shirts, bought him pairs of socks to replace all those with holes, given his flat a thorough cleaning (it needed it badly), cooked him meals. And the funny part was, he liked the attention, liked having a woman taking care of him. Strange, after all these years of confirmed bachelorhood, that as he began his forties, he should discover that he liked having someone meet him at the door when he returned home. Now, he would have to tell her to leave, to gather up her things and move out, and hope like hell that Susan didn't find out about it.

"A penny for your thoughts," Susan said.

Wagner put down his drink. "Huh?"

"You were so quiet that I was beginning to worry about you. Is something wrong?"

"Everything's fine. Couldn't be better, in fact." He looked at her, as if seeing her for the first time. Other than pale lip covering, he had never seen her in makeup before, until tonight. She was wearing red lipstick, her cheeks were lightly rouged, and she'd done something to her lashes to make them longer. Her unruly red hair was pulled back, giving prominence to her high cheekbones, and she was wearing a green gown that clung seductively to her long, thin frame. "Pitou was right," he said. "You do look lovely. Very lovely."

"Aren't you sweet." She smiled.

He kissed her, breathed in her warm scent, ran a hand over her thigh and felt the heat of skin beneath her gown. "Maybe we should leave," he said softly.

"But we just got here. And you are the winner, remember?"

"And I'm beginning to regret that ... very much."

"I think you're just horny," she said, kissing him back.

"That's it, encourage me."

143

"Look at the lovebirds. It touches my heart."

The voice had an all-too familiar Italian accent.

"Giovanni didn't tell me you were here, Susan, but he never tells me anything." Bogavanti's broad handsome face beamed. "You aren't writing another story about the luckless American, are you? Tell me it isn't so."

"It isn't so." She sipped her champagne and smiled at Wagner, amused by the Italian.

"Then why are you here? Of course. To write a story about me." He laughed. "You will find I am more charming and certainly more interesting than this bum."

Wagner cleared his throat. "Who's the girl, Bogo?"

She was blonde and full-lipped, and stood self-consciously at the Italian's side, wearing a white gown that displayed her ample bosom. Typical, thought Wagner. Bogavanti always went for the blondes, especially the young ones.

"Please, excuse my manners. This is Katherine. She is studying to become a model."

Wagner nodded. "Nice to know you, Katherine. This is Susan. She's studying to become a writer."

"Very funny," smirked Susan. "Hello, Katherine."

Katherine smiled weakly and nodded.

"Katherine does not understand the English very well yet, but she is learning."

Wagner finished his champagne. "You're the teacher, I take it."

The Italian ignored his sarcasm. "Well, my friend, we must move on. Again, congratulations. This is beginning to look like your year."

The two gripped hands, firmly. "Hell of a race, Bogo."

"Yes, but next time the outcome will be different, Giovanni."

Wagner watched Katherine and the Italian vanish in a fold of people. He looked at Susan. "I didn't know you knew Bogavanti."

"I interviewed him at Oulton Park." She giggled. "He asked me out."

"What? The bastard."

A voice boomed from across the cavern. It was Claude Pitou, the evening's host, calling the group to dinner. "Zee souffle cannot wait. Please, be seated at your table at once."

Wagner found the Garret-Hawk table, seated Susan, and was about to seat himself, when Garret pulled him aside. His breath smelled of bourbon. "Don't run off after this is over, John," he said. "I want to talk to you. It's important, so stick around."

Chapter 18

It was nearly 1 AM when Garret appeared at Wagner's table, cup of steaming coffee in each hand. He handed one cup to the Californian and sat down across from him. Except for Susan, no one else was seated at the table. Busboys worked around them, clearing away the evening's debris of soiled napkins, full ashtrays, and empty glassware.

Wagner pushed his coffee aside. "Can this wait? Susan has to get up early and drive in to Paris."

"This won't take long. You don't mind, do you Susan?"

"Not if I can find another cup of coffee around here."

Garret handed her his cup. "Here. Take mine. I've had three cups already. I hope you don't mind cream and sugar."

Susan did mind cream and sugar but took the coffee and thanked him.

Garret placed both arms on the table and leaned his massive upper body toward Wagner. "I gotta tell you, John. I'm damn pleased with my team's progress since you came aboard--three wins, and an 8-point lead in the constructors' championship." He nodded approvingly. "With five races to go, I like our chances a lot. And today, for one glorious lap, we were running one-two. Michael is starting to come on, as I always said he would. If he could have just held on and finished second it would have given his confidence the boost it sorely needs right now, the boost that can make him feel like a winner. Feel like a winner and you'll be a winner, I always say."

Wagner sipped his coffee, silent.

"I want that boy to win a Grand Prix this year."

Wagner reached for his breast pocket. Empty. It was moments like these that he missed smoking. He shook his head. "Forget it, Ed. There are lots of drivers who have been around a lot of years and never won a single Grand Prix. Good drivers too--Forgue, Gehring, Spencer."

"Don't tell me about Paul Spencer." Garret put up a meat hand. "I gave him the fastest car in Formula One last year an he didn't win a bloomin' thing. Couldn't. Didn't have the guts That's why I ended up firing him. You, you won your very firs Grand Prix in your first season of Formula One. I expect th same of Michael."

"It's not a question of guts, Mr. Garret. Look, I was 31 years-old and had plenty of experience with high-powere racecars, when I won. And it was at Sebring, a circuit I knew well. What's Bravo? Twenty-two? Until this year, he's drive nothing quicker than Formula Fords. The circuits over here ar all new to him. The kid lacks experience."

Garret leaned back in his chair, a look of satisfaction on hi face. "The facts speak for themselves, John. Young Mr. Brav was running with the leaders all afternoon, and might hav finished second if he hadn't spun."

Wagner shifted in his chair. "Right. But he did spin."

Garret frowned. "You spun today. What's the difference?"

"A lot of people spun today. It wasn't hard to do, th condition Thillois was in. But I didn't spin when it counted, an I sure as hell didn't stall my engine."

"Admit it, John, the kid drove a hell of a race today."

"He did, in a car with more horsepower than most, on circuit that favors horsepower. With experience, he might'v finished third."

Garret smiled smugly. "With experience he might hav beaten you, hotshot. Which brings me to my point. I want t speed up Bravo's progress; help him gain that experience you'r talking about. Like I said, I want him to win a Grand Prix thi year. It's going to take a team effort, and that's where you com in. Ask yourself: is there something you could have done toda to help the kid? You know, maybe let him pass you there at th end. Perhaps you could have used your experience to bloc Bogavanti and insure a one-two finish for the team. Get m drift?"

"Just give him the race, is that it?"

"I wouldn't call it that. Let me tell you, a one-two finis sure beats the hell out of the one-five we ended up with."

148

"Mr. Garret. You hired me to win races...."

"Hell, you're practically world champion and the summer isn't half over."

"I'm not world champion yet, and I'm not giving an inch to anyone until I am, not to a teammate, not to anyone."

"No man can win without a strong team behind him," said Garret calmly, still using reason. "I've given you that team, John. Hell, I've given you the quickest car in Formula One. Now, won't you give me something in return by helping Michael? This is not a lot I'm asking--one win."

Wagner felt Susan's hand slip into his.

"Michael gets my help," he said, defensiveness edging into his voice. "I help him set up his car; I show him the fastest line through the curves; I tell him where I back off, where I get back on the throttle. But there's a limit to what I can do. Six months ago, he was driving cars with a quarter of the horsepower he is now, racing guys who held down nine-to-five jobs. The kid's got talent--I'll grant you that--but he's up against the best. In a year or two, he might win a race."

Garret's patience had run out. His face flushed red. "I'm not waiting a year or two, John. I didn't want to say this, but your hardened position leaves me no choice...."

Wagner laughed nervously. "My `hardened position'?"

"Yes, your hardened position. Need I remind you that this is my team? I call the shots. Without me, you wouldn't have a snowball's chance in hell of becoming champion. I rescued your career from the scrapheap, and as long as you're a part of my team you will follow my orders. If it means helping Bravo win his first race, you will do it, or mister you can find yourself another team. Am I making myself clear?"

Wagner could put up with a lot to become champion, but Garret was pushing him. He remained calm but determined to speak his mind. "Handing Michael a win will do nothing for his confidence. He needs to earn it."

Garret rose. There would be no more discussion. "I disagree. I'm expecting great things at Silverstone. We hold the lap record there, and the kid knows the track like the back of his

149

hand. A one-two finish is not out of the question, and neither is the possibility of him winning."

Garret turned to Susan. "I apologize for the blunt language, my dear, but this is business. I'm sure you understand."

Susan nodded. She understood. Wagner's days with Garret-Hawk were numbered.

*   *   *

The lights of Reims faded in Wagner's rear-view mirror, as the road made the short climb up the Montagne de Reims. Within minutes they were above the plain, motoring through pine forest. The night air tumbling in through the Porsche's sun roof cooled quickly once they reached the higher elevation.

"Should I shut it?"

"No," Susan said softly. She tilted her head back and watched the stars dance in the night sky. Rarely had she felt this tired. She had gotten two hour's sleep on the flight over, and none since her plane set down in Paris 15 hours earlier. Her alarm was set to go off two hours from now, at 5 AM. But she had no regrets. She was glad she had driven up to Reims. Being with Wagner again had confirmed everything she'd felt about him. She just wished he wasn't a race driver.

The Porsche slowed, turned down a gravel drive and stopped in front of her hotel.

"Are you asleep?"

She smiled. "Almost."

"Shall I call room service for coffee?" she asked, once they reached her room.

Wagner shook his head. "Not for me, thanks."

She dimmed the lights and drew open the curtains, revealing Epernay's little circle of lights in the valley below. "Isn't it gorgeous," she said, feeling his strong arms encircle her.

"You're gorgeous," he breathed.

She turned to face him. "It's just as I thought."

"What?" He closed his eyes and buried his face in her hair.

"All Garret cares about is Michael. Once he starts winning, you can kiss his team goodbye."

150

"Don't talk nonsense. Garret needs me to win the championship. Michael won't be winning any time soon. Today was a fluke." He released her. "Would you rather I go?"

*   *   *

The alarm sounded at five. Susan batted it twice, found the button, and turned it off. They lay side-by side on their backs, both awake. Outside the window, the stars had vanished and the night sky had turned inky black as the first rays of dawn approached.

"Don't you have to get up?" he said, yawning.

"I do, but I don't."

"That makes sense."

"The U.S. team arrives today, and I should be there, but I don't have to be there. They don't begin play until Friday, anyway. Why don't you come with me?"

"To Paris?"

"You don't have anything better to do."

"How do you know?"

She sat up. "What do you have to do that's so important, John Wagner?"

"Well, let's see. I have to be up at Goodwood Thursday morning."

"What about the rest of the week?"

"You know, I have things to do."

"What kind of things?"

"Well, on Wednesday, I usually stop by the shop to see how the crew's doing."

"That takes all of 20 minutes, I bet. What other things do you have to do?"

"Why the third degree? I didn't say I wouldn't go."

She drew her knees up and wrapped her arms around them, enjoying having put him on the spot. "Just answer the question."

"Sometimes I make an appearance for one of our sponsors. That can kill a couple of days, what with travel and everything. And sometimes, you know, they want me to come out to their country club and play a round of golf with them."

151

"Gee, what hardship. Do you have any such appearances scheduled this week?"

"I don't think so. I'll have to check with Diane. And there's always personal business to be taken care of."

"Right. Pick up your clothes at the laundry, stop by the local pub. Admit it, John, you don't have a lot to do, other than drive racecars on the weekends."

"Think you know me pretty well, do you?"

"Like the back of my hand. Are you coming or not?"

He pulled her close to him, until her breasts were flush against his chest. "Do you really think I would miss this opportunity to be with you?"

Later that morning, having showered, Wagner went outside the room while Susan bathed. It was a bright, clear day, already hot. He walked down below the hotel to where the vineyards grew. They reached far down the hill, in neat, countless rows, to the bank of the Marne River. He walked along the edge of the vineyards, kicking up clods of dirt, Irene's face looming in his mind again, a laughing, mocking face, telling him that he was a fool, that she wasn't going to be wished away, that she would still be there when he returned, and that Susan was going to find out about their tryst.

What if she did find out? he wondered. Why should Susan care? They were adults. There was nothing binding between them, no ring, no promise, merely an agreement to see each other again. Yet it bothered him. There was something between them, something unspoken, something assumed, and in its own way binding--trust. Neither was seeing anyone, and the assumption-- the trust--was that it would continue that way, until they met again. As Wagner thought about it, he knew what really would hurt Susan was not the fact that he had been sleeping with Irene, but that what had been assumed was not true, and that she couldn't trust him.

From her room, the sound of running water stopped. He looked down at the cool flowing Marne, and imagined her stepping from the shower and toweling off. He decided he would tell her what had happened. She wouldn't like it. But it was infinitely better than risking that she find out about it from

omeone else, from, say, Irene. He walked back up the hill and
ntered the room.

Susan was in her bathrobe seated on the bed drying her hair
with a towel. She smiled. "It looks like a beautiful day outside."

"It's already hot. It's days like these I wish my Porsche had
ir conditioning."

"I'm so glad you're coming with me. Do you suppose I can
rop my rental off somewhere in Reims?"

"Sure." He looked at his watch. "We really should be
oing. I still need to check out of my hotel, remember? It could
e two before we get on the road."

Susan began brushing her hair. "What's your hurry? We
on't have to be anywhere. We have all day and nothing to do.
sn't it wonderful?"

Wagner paced. "I just want to get going."

"What about lunch?"

"I'm not hungry." He continued to pace.

"Well, I'm starving." She laughed. "Will you please sit
own. You've been going non-stop since you got up. If you're
o full of energy, why don't you find out what time the hotel
erves lunch."

He went to the door, turned around and came back. He sat
n the bed beside her. "I have something I have to tell you and
ou're not going to like it."

She stopped brushing. "What is it?"

"I've been seeing someone else."

Color drained from her face. "Someone else?"

"I don't care for her; in fact, I'm going to end it. It was just
ne of those things."

"Just ... one of those ... things?"

"I don't love her. In fact, I can't believe I let it happen."

"You've been sleeping with her?"

He sighed. "Yes."

"I see. Who is she?"

"Her name is Irene. Irene Parks. She's Mal's wife, or was.
They split up a couple months back. I dated her once, a long
ime ago, before she married Mal. I was nuts to get involved
vith her again, but it just sort of happened."

She rose and turned her face away from him.

"Until yesterday, I thought it was over between us, Susan."

"So you said."

"I didn't realize how much I cared for you. I don't want t lose you, Susan."

She faced him and began brushing her hair again. "Well, it' not as if we were married, but I would be lying if I said it didn' hurt. And if it ever happens again, it's over between us." Sh went into the bathroom and shut the door.

"I'm sorry," he said again, through the door.

She said nothing. He listened to hear if she was crying. H heard nothing. He went to the sliding glass door that faced th vineyards. It was open and he felt a hot breeze blow in throug the screen. Suddenly, he felt hungry. He went back to th bathroom door. "I'm going up to the lobby to see about lunch."

"Okay," she said in a low voice.

Chapter 19

Michael Bravo tapped the brakes and downshifted into fourth gear for Woodcote, a long, curling right-hander leading to the start-finish line at Silverstone. He turned in, clipped the marker cones on the inside and drifted out to the center of the track, smooth and steady. Then he steered back to the inside and clipped the marker cones a second time. Traveling at 130 mph, Bravo was maneuvering around bumps and ripples in the asphalt that otherwise would unsettle his machine. He was not following the obvious line through Woodcote, just the smoothest and fastest. And it had taken him three months to learn it. Nearing the end of the curve, he drifted outside and exited under full throttle, the scream of his exhaust echoing off the long line of empty grandstands facing pit straight.

Eddie peered at his stopwatch in disbelief, then whooped. "He did it. He broke the lap record. Can you believe it?"

"Hear that?" Hacksaw turned to Wagner. "Mikey's beaten your time, Big Guy. What are you going to do about it?"

Wagner was standing in the pit cubicle, amidst tool boxes and stacks of tires, changing into his street clothes. He tucked in his shirt and looked up. "Nothing."

"Nothing?" Hacksaw couldn't believe what he was hearing. "You don't mean that, do you?"

Wagner kneeled to tie his shoes. "Let the kid enjoy the moment. Tomorrow, when everybody gets here, his time won't last the morning."

Rennie was putting away his tools, within ear shot. He flashed his toothy grin. "Don't be in such an all-fire hurry to run off. Me and the boys was hoping you might tip a few with us, over at Henry V's. Like old times."

"Another time, Ren. I've got someone to pick up in Banbury, have dinner, and still make an eight-thirty curtain in London." He looked at his watch. "If I leave now, I can just make it."

"That explains it, then," said Rennie. "For a moment there, I thought you was being kindly towards our dear Michael. Is she someone we know, Johnny?"

"Yeah, it's Susan. She's here to cover the race."

*   *   *

Wagner returned to the circuit early the next morning, bought coffee for his crew, and took 1.2 seconds off Bravo's time. "Nobody's going to beat that," he said, climbing from his racecar.

Rennie nodded approvingly. "I see Susan is having a positive effect on you."

Wagner fished the cotton balls out of both ears and nodded. Yes, Susan was having a positive effect on him. She had been a little chilly leaving Reims but warmed up once they arrived in the City of Light. He spent three relaxing days with her and as he was leaving surprised her with a diamond bracelet. It set him back a grand--the most he'd ever spent on a woman--but her look of surprise and joy was worth it. Severing ties with Irene had gone as well as could be expected. She cried and felt sorry for herself, but in the end she went away quietly. Hacksaw and Ray, meanwhile, had revised the rear suspension geometry on his racecar, going to a shorter top-link to minimize camber change under heavy braking. With the very wide tires they were now running, the slightest camber change had proved critical to stopping. With the new geometry, when the tail lifted under braking, the tires stayed reasonably flat against the road. The result was a shorter stopping distance and a smoother entry into the curves. Wagner was so pleased with the change, he wondered how the Garret-Hawk would handle now at the stop-and-go circuits--Jarama and Monaco. No doubt, it would be quicker. Hacksaw and Ray planned to revise the front suspension for the next race--for the tortuous Nurburg Ring-- where Wagner was sure to be quickest now. Aerodynamically, they had done away with the upswept tail and mounted a wing above the engine--like Ferrari and Brabham--and retained the front canard wings.

156

He hadn't forgotten his conversation with Garret. The Old Man was unpredictable, certainly. But the thought that he might actually fire him seemed as remote as, well, Bravo winning the British Grand Prix. But with his teammate breaking Silverstone's lap record the day before, anything seemed possible.

"Tell me, Johnny," Rennie said, removing the engine cover, and peaking around the engine for signs of fluid leaks, "can we expect to hear wedding bells anytime soon."

Wagner rubbed the sweat from his face. "You'd better check that engine pretty good. It sounded a little rough on the cool-off lap, like the misfire's back." He winked at Hacksaw. "You don't suppose that misfire is back, do you, Ren?"

Rennie looked up, pained. "Aw, Johnny, you're no fun."

The Californian spent the afternoon session running full fuel-load tests and bedding in tires and brakes for the race. Friday, he watched his competitors attempt to beat his time. None could.

Bravo, meanwhile, knocked two-tenths-of-a-second off Wednesday's time to put himself on the outside of row two, ahead of Bogavanti and Lafosse. Wagner had never seen his teammate drive smoother and faster than he had while practicing for the British Grand Prix. He had learned the Silverstone Circuit well. Being the perimeter road of a World War Two airfield and having only eight curves--five of them right-hand, three left-hand--it was not a difficult circuit to learn, but mastering its subtleties, such as the correct line through Woodcote, took hundreds of laps. Bravo had put in those laps, and it showed, and not just in his lap times. Instead of looking down as he often did walking the paddock, as if to apologize for his presence, Bravo now walked with his head up and spoke with other drivers as an equal. Wagner was glad to see his new confidence and improved driving skills, but it also concerned him: Garret had spotted the kid's renewed confidence too.

<u>British Grand Prix</u>
Saturday, July 20

WAGNER	EVANS	PARKS
Garret-Hawk	Lotus	BRM
1 min 22.4 sec	1 min 22.8 sec	1 min 23.0 sec

PHILLIPS	BRAVO
Brabham	Garret-Hawk
1 min 23.2 sec	1 min 23.4 sec

BAGAVANTI	LAFOSSE	EDWARDS
Ferrari	Matra	Cooper
1 min 23.7 sec	1 min 23.8 sec	1 min 24.2 sec

*   *   *

A sliver of moon shone weakly in the dull night sky. On either side of the road, hedgerows streamed past, in the dark looking as high and as impenetrable as castle walls. Wagner spotted the entry into the circuit, slowed and turned in, passed behind the administration building and crossed over the bridge into the circuit infield. The long row of garages were lit up like London itself.

"I can't believe everyone is still here," Susan said, climbing from the car. "Don't they ever go home?"

Wagner nodded. "The work never stops--except for the race. Come on. Let's go in."

Minutes earlier, they had left a party hosted by one of the team's suppliers. As usual, Wagner wanted to check in with his crew before turning in for the night. Inside the garage, the two Garret-Hawks lay exposed, stripped of body panels and wheels, looking as stark as a couple of corpses cut open for examination. All the workings were visible--engine, transmission, steering, inner suspension rods, plumbing lines, cables, wires. The twang f country music blared from Hacksaw's portable tape machine. When he saw Susan was with Wagner, he switched it off.

"Hey, that's Buck Owens and the Buckaroos," rasped Walt Balchowsky. "You can't just turn that off like that."

"Shut up, you knucklehead," Hacksaw said. "Can't you see we got company? Hey, Susan, who's that bum with you there?"

"Someone I picked up at the party," she said. "He's not much on charm, but I'm kind of fond of him."

Hacksaw grinned "We knew the Big Guy would show his mug around here sooner or later, but not in such classy company. Welcome to our boudoir, Susan."

Wagner loosened his tie and looked around. When he'd left the circuit earlier, the main concern had been with the wing mounted above the engine. Fatigue cracks had been spotted where the wing joined the subframe. Balchowsky had the wing removed and was laboring over it on the workbench, amidst a jumble of files, snips, various size hammers, and a drill. Gofer Tom was feeding him rivets. Ray and Dave were huddled at the back of Bravo's car, pondering some problem. The only person missing was Rennie.

"How goes it?" Wagner asked.

Hacksaw wiped his face with a red handkerchief. "Dandy."

"Will you be here the rest of the night?" Susan looked at him sympathetically.

"Naw. What we have here tonight is pretty routine. Dave and Ray there are all done for the night. What they're lookin' at is some place to mount the oil tank, which we're planning to move from the front of the car to the rear, to put more weight on the rear tires. Racecars are never finished, you know; sort of a work in progress, you might say. And Rennie's done for the night, too. I guess he's over bugging the BRM boys. They found a problem with Mal's engine about an hour ago and will be pulling an all-nighter doing a swap job, the poor bastards. And Walt over there, God love him, should be finished up pretty soon. Just tonight he's fabricated stronger mounting brackets for the overhead wing. Otherwise, it's the usual prerace stuff. We work off a list, Susan. We check the engine over real good, and check around the engine too, looking for signs of trouble. We check all the plumbing for leaks. We take a peak inside th tranny, and check the clutch. We check the brake system, an look over the chassis pretty good for damage or cracks tha might've occurred in practice; we examine the suspension, chec the fuel system and calculate fuel mileage from fuel checks take in practice, and, of course, recharge the battery. Can't forge that. Tomorrow we'll fill up the fuel tanks, warm up the engine and have us another look around." He glanced at his watch "Right now, I'd say I'll be in bed by two, which ain't half bad i this business."

"That's certainly better than the BRM crew," Susan said.

Hacksaw chuckled. "Anything's better than that sorr bunch."

Chapter 20

Wagner sat in the reclined seat of his racecar and stared ahead vacantly, awaiting the start. It was a gray, overcast day, but rain was not forecast. Thank the good Lord for that. Rain would kill any chance of his winning. The one minute sign went up. He started his engine, began revving it, and felt heat gathering in the radiator ahead of his feet. A yard in front of him, the starter stepped onto the tarmac and looked over the field of 21 cars. Satisfied all engines were running he resumed his position at the side of the grid. Engines surged to a thundering pitch, he raised the Union Jack, counted down the final five seconds, and waved them off.

Evans' Lotus bucked and lunged forward, at the head of the herd as it stampeded around Copse Corner. Wagner followed the Scot through the left-right-left of Maggotts, Becketts and Chapel, and onto Hangar Straight. Behind him, Parks and Phillips tussled for third. Around Stowe and Club Corner, both right-handers, and through the left of Abbey, Evans stretched his lead to ten-car lengths. Approaching Woodcote to complete lap one, Wagner could see fans rise to their feet in the grandstand. He knew what they were thinking: Evans was on form today; the question now was who would finish second? Wagner smiled wryly. It wouldn't be him. Second was not in the cards. He settled in and concentrated on the little things: keeping his machine smooth and steady, holding it on a very precise line through the wide fast curves. No tail-out driving here, no slamming of throttle or jabbing of brakes, only a series of gentle, calculated actions designed to get the maximum out of his big bird without ruffling a feather.

Evans continued pulling away, and he wondered if Hacksaw had underestimated the effect of the new wing Lotus was using. True to form, Chapman had taken the concept a step further. The new wing extended five feet above the ground and was mounted at the back of the car on a pair of shafts that joined with

161

the suspension uprights, allowing downforce to be placed directly onto the rear tires. However effective it was, up high like that it looked ungainly and fragile, swaying back and forth through the curves, jiggling over bumps, as if at any second it was going to break off.

Wagner ignored the distracting wing. He braked deeper into the curves. Coming out he eased on the power sooner. His tires vibrated in protest but still gripped the road. Gradually, the gap closed. By lap seven he was glued to the Lotus-Cosworth's tail. Up close, he could smell the stink of its fumes and feel the grit of its dust, see its vibrating suspension arms, its shocks and springs oscillating like pistons, its tires lean and become distorted in the corners. Evans' blue eyes appeared in the sidemirrors. Was that surprise Wagner detected? On lap 8, exiting Chapel, he darted out from the behind the Lotus, pulled even braking for Stowe, and took the lead. The Scot came right back, trying very hard to repass him, but Wagner had hit his stride. His chassis was handling perfectly. The engine was strong, its pitch high and clean. He maintained his blistering pace until the red-and-gold car faltered slightly and fell from his slipstream. He let up very slightly after that and still the Lotus faded until it disappeared from his mirrors completely.

On lap 33, he saw the Lotus parked in the pits, driver out of car with helmet off, sweaty faced, his race over for the day. Eight pits down, Bogavanti's red machine was parked as well. Hacksaw's board showed Parks in second place, 35 seconds behind him. Wagner slowed even more and kept an eye on his pitboard for new information. Four laps later, Parks pitted, and rejoined the race, one lap down, in eight.

"An easy win," Wagner thought.

*   *   *

Garret trotted out to where Hacksaw was manning the pitboard. Everything was going perfectly. Wagner was leading, and in second was Michael Bravo.

"Signal Wagner to slow down," Garret shouted.

"He has slowed down."

162

"Then tell him to slow down more. And tell Bravo to step it up. I want him to win this race."

"What?" The crew chief felt the board drop from his hands. "Why, for heaven's sake?"

Garret frowned, mad at himself for not having discussed this with Hacksaw beforehand. "Look. I don't have time to explain. Just do as I say, okay? Don't fight me on this, Hacksaw."

Garret trotted back to the Garret-Hawk pit.

The crew chief followed and handed the pitboard to Eddie.

"What's this?" Eddie looked up. "Why are you giving this to me?"

"Are you defying my orders?" Garret barked.

"I'm taking a break," said Hacksaw. He eyed Garret. "I do that from time to time, in case you hadn't noticed. Eddie can handle the pitboard in my place."

Garret said nothing. Maybe it was better this way. Eddie would do what he was told without question. He turned to his son. "You go signal Michael to speed up, understand? I want him to win this race."

Hacksaw walked back to the paddock, found an empty packing crate amidst the transporters, and sat down. He could hear the cars roar past, smell fish being deep-fried somewhere, sense the presence of the crowd just over the wall. It seemed another world, over the wall, a world suddenly alien to him. He felt used and cheated. Over the next 15 laps, he did nothing as Wagner's 35-second lead shrunk to 10 seconds.

"I'll bet the Big Guy doesn't even have a clue," he muttered to himself. It was time to do something. But what? He returned to the pits, saw Rennie, and pulled him aside. "Listen to me, Ren, Garret's expecting me back about now. If he asks where I am, tell him I'm still in the can."

"Where are you going?"

"I'm taking a walk."

"Johnny's not going to win, is he?"

"He is if I have anything to do with it."

Hacksaw walked in the direction of Copse Corner, past the Lotus and Ferrari pits, past the Cooper and Rob Walker pits, and stopped at the end of pit row. He waited for Wagner to appear out of Woodcote, and stepped onto the tarmac. He waved his arms in great circular motions, but the Californian flew past without seeing him.

*   *   *

Gradually, lap by lap, Wagner felt his attention being drawn by something at the end of pit row. With eight laps to go, he snuck a look and was stunned to see it was his crew chief. For a brief moment, he was perplexed by what he saw. Then he looked in his sidemirror and saw Bravo following him out of Woodcote and it became painfully clear.

"I should have known. No wonder Eddie kept giving me the damn `easy' sign. Garret, you bastard, you've done it. You want me to just give the race away."

Next time past, Eddie was holding up the "yield" sign.

The frickin' yield sign.

What was he going to do? Ignore it. He couldn't disobey team orders. He had to let Bravo pass him. Garret was just short-sighted enough to fire him, if he didn't. He resisted the anger he felt igniting within and remained determinedly cold and passionless. What was important was not winning the race, but winning the championship. Finish second, take the six points, and move on.

Bravo was pinned to his tail now, but appeared to be confused. Was he supposed to pass Wagner? Take the lead? Win?

It was killing him, but Wagner raised his arm, to eliminate any doubt. Come on, Michael, pass me. Take the damn lead, for crying out loud. He saw his teammate wave back in acknowledgment. Feeling like a world-class fool, he waited for the inevitable. And waited. Bravo didn't overtake him at Stowe or Club, as Wagner expected he would, but waited until Woodcote to make his move.

Woodcote. The worst possible place.

"Not here," Wagner shouted, seeing his teammate dip inside under braking, forcing him outside, onto a washboard of bumps. Immediately, his seat and steering wheel began to shake, as if he ere strapped inside a giant vibrator. Bravo was ahead of him ow, clipping the first set of marker cones. Wagner felt his tail lide over the bumps, pulling him further outside. He steeled imself. He wasn't going to crash, by god. He was going to get ut of this mess somehow. He stayed mentally with what his car vas doing, wanting to influence its direction. He eased off the hrottle, twitched the wheel gently and nursed his tempest-tossed nachine back inside. Ahead, Bravo had drifted outside, and vas trying to steer back inside to clip the marker cones a second me, but had drifted too far out and gotten on the bumps himself. Wagner could see his tires shake, his tail slide ominously, and ne panic in Bravo's eyes as his car spun around to face him at 30 mph.

Eddie was first to see them coming. He heard the two cars ownshift once and enter the curve. To his utter dismay and orror, both cars were coming at him side-by-side, only Bravo's vas facing backwards. In another second Wagner sped past afely, but Bravo's car looped once, twice, slid along the uardrail without touching it, somehow got pointed in the right lirection, and sped on.

Wagner looked back in his mirror expecting to see a ercussion of dust and fragments from his teammate's collision vith the guardrail. Instead, he saw Michael recover and follow im out of Woodcote. It was then the terror of what almost had appened washed over him.

Eddie again held up the "yield" sign. This time, Wagner gnored it. Two laps later, Garret was trackside, shaking the itboard to emphasize the importance of his order. Wagner no onger cared. In front of 30,000 fans seated in the stands, in ront of the press box, in front of the BBC television camera, he aised his gloved hand and flipped his boss the middle finger.

British Grand Prix Top Six Finishers		Championship Point Leaders Race Seven of Eleven	
Driver	Points	Driver	Points
Wagner	9	Wagner	42
Bravo	6	Parks	30
Parks	4	Bogavanti	25
Giraud	3	Evans	21
Stockton	2	Phillips	10
Edwards	1	Lafosse	10

Chapter 21

"Dad wants to see you."

It was over. The race. The ceremony. The press interview. Now, these words greeted the race winner as he returned to the pits. It was about what he'd expected. He wetted a towel with water and wiped the dried sweat from his face. "I'm going to change first. If that's all right with your father."

Eddie nodded. "Sure. It's okay. Take your time."

Wagner unzipped his coveralls, stepped out of them, and stepped into his Levis. He slipped on his tattersall shirt and tucked it into his pants. Eddie handed him his wallet and watch and keys. "We wouldn't be winning if it wasn't for you," he said sheepishly. "I tried to tell Dad that, but he never listens to me."

"I know the feeling," said the Californian.

"I'm sorry how everything turned out, John."

Wagner stuffed his helmet and coveralls into a nylon satchel. "Yeah, so am I. Take me to your father."

He entered the transporter alone. Garret was seated at the dining table, stubby fingers clutching a glass of bourbon.

"Fix yourself something strong," the Old Man said calmly. "You're going to need it."

Wagner sat down and faced him. "I was disappointed not to see you at the ceremony."

"I'll bet you were." Garret threw down a swallow.

Wagner peered directly into Garret's eyes. "What's the problem, Ed? Today makes three-straight, and you got your one-two, like you wanted. You should be happy."

Garret's face reddened. "You disobeyed my orders. I also think you caused the kid to spin, but I can't prove it."

"You do, huh? Have you even spoken with Michael since the race? He practically broke down on the podium apologizing to me. I followed your orders, but Michael chose the worst possible place to pass me. Why? I don't know, but I'm sure his

167

lack of experience had something to do with it. We both could have been killed. Do you know that? Do you care? Jesus, Ed, I think the thing that frustrates me most about you is that you have no idea what it's like out there. It's not easy. And sometimes it's damn scary. Bravo spun right in front of me. I still don't know how I missed him."

"You ignored my orders and flipped me off in front of the whole damn world. You should be begging me to keep your ride, which I hoped you'd have sense enough to do. But no." His voice grew louder. "Instead you're insolent, thinking you're somehow above it all, that you can disobey my expressed orders and just waltz in here as if nothing has happened. Well, I have news for you, Mr. Wagner: you're finished. I'm firing you--effective immediately."

It was what Wagner expected, but the words still surprised him. He stood up suddenly and banged his head on the low ceiling. "You can't fire me," he said, rubbing his scalp. "We have a contract, remember?"

Garret laughed. "I'll pay you for the rest of the year; that fulfills my obligation. I just won't have a car for you to drive. It's over, hotshot. Your services are no longer needed."

"What about the press?"

"I don't give a tinker's damn about the press. When my car wins the constructor's championship, those same journalists will be singing my praise. I can imagine what they'll write about you." Garret chuckled. "Three-time loser."

Wagner glanced at the dark bottles on the bar behind Garret.

"Want that drink now, hot shot?" Garret asked, bemused.

Wagner sighed. "Look, Ed. You want the championship as bad as I do. This is crazy, what you're doing. What are you going to tell your sponsors? What are you going to tell Herb Cook?"

Garret smiled, the man with all the answers. "Why should I concern myself with him? Garret-Hawk will win the constructor's championship. As far as Mr. Cook is concerned, he was paying me to field a second car anyway. Until he stepped in, I planned to run just one car, for Michael. I hired you only after Cook agreed to finance a second car. Now, without you, I go back to running one car. We still win the championship, so Cook has nothing to bitch about. Everybody gets what he wants--except you. Good luck finding a decent ride at mid season."

"Your car hasn't won the constructors' championship yet, Ed. If you think Michael can deliver those kinds of points, you're sadly mistaken."

Garret rose. "He finished second today, didn't he? He's confident now, a winner."

"Right. On a circuit he's practiced on all season, after all the top drivers dropped out. Wait till the Nurburg Ring. He'll be fortunate if he can finish sixth. Then there's Monza and Mosport, two more circuits he's never seen. That leaves Watkins Glen. Good luck, Ed."

"No," said Garret, opening the door for him. "It's you who needs luck."

*　　*　　*

It was late, and in Silverstone village a pub called Henry V's was emptying fast. Wagner was seated in a booth with Susan at his side. She still had a story to write but she wasn't deserting her man at maybe his worst hour. Nearly everyone connected with the race had stopped by to express regrets. Hacksaw, Rennie, and the crew said Garret would come to his senses and take him back, knowing in their hearts it would never happen. Dan Phillips offered him his car for the duration of the season, forgetting both were under contract to different oil companies, while BBC television commentator Peter Cunningham offered to help him get a job in broadcasting, should he decide to retire. But most, like Giuseppe Bogavanti, merely shook their heads and encouraged him to hang in there, that something would work out.

Susan sat quietly beside him and listened to them all. With the race long since over, and traffic having cleared from the roads back to London, everyone was departing. Susan had waited them out. Now it was her turn. She slipped a hand around his. "How are you feeling? Do you want to leave?"

"Why don't you go," he said wearily. "I'll call you in the morning. Right now, I feel like just sitting here awhile longer."

"I'm not leaving until you leave." She moved closer and kissed him. "I love you, John Wagner, in case you didn't know."

Wagner sipped his beer. "I know."

She stroked his leg. "I have a suggestion. Please think about it before answering, okay?"

He turned to her, curious. "Okay. What is it?"

She smiled, gathering her courage. "I've been thinking. I don't know how to say this exactly, except to let it just come out, so here goes. Maybe, maybe this just might be a good time for you to retire."

"Retire?" He spit out the word contemptuously. "I'm not going to retire."

"I said to think about it first, remember? It's clear you're the best driver. What more do you have to prove? You're without a team. You'll only embarrass yourself driving for some lesser team, which is your only option. Why not get out now while you're on top? Besides, it would give us a chance to be together. I miss you so much, John. And I worry about you constantly, ever since your accident in Spain."

"Listen, if I walk away now, it will be one more opportunity down the drain. Please, try to understand. I want this championship very badly. It's all I've ever wanted, going back to the Speedster days. I've come too far, made too many sacrifices, to quit now."

"You would have me," she said.

"I've thought about quitting, sure," he continued, not hearing her. "But it's got to be at the right time. Right now, I'm at the top of my game, and the championship is within my reach. I've got to finish the season, see this thing through. Besides, I love racing. It's my life. I don't know what I'd do, if I quit."

Susan was not surprised by his response, but she was hurt by it nonetheless. Somewhere within her she harbored the idea that he would retire to be with her. That thought seemed very foolish to her now. He had no intention of retiring, even if he did win the championship. He would go on racing as long as his skills were sharp, as long as he still got a kick out of it. The only

170

question now was whether she wanted to make it her life, and be forever waiting for him, forever worrying about him, living not for herself but for him.

"You're right, John," she sighed. "I really should go."

*   *   *

As long as Wagner had known Peter Cunningham, the bearded ex-GP race driver turned BBC race commentator, Cunningham bragged he could make the drive from Silverstone to London in one hour flat. No one else could do it. Wagner's best time was 67 minutes. He didn't know the roads as well as Cunningham, and he was always a bit cautious, thinking too much, backing off the gas when he should have been stomping on it. But tonight would be different. Standing in the pub parking lot, the time had come to beat Cunningham's record. His nerves tingled with electricity, despite a dousing of alcohol, and he had the proper I-don't-give-a-damn attitude. His pent-up anger needed release. What better way to siphon it off than by doing the one thing he truly understood--going like hell.

He opened the door of his Porsche and was greeted by the familiar smell of leather. He sat down into the cold seat, inserted the key, turned it, and felt the six-cylinder engine fire up behind him. With night rides down Diablo Pass playing in his head, he revved the engine repeatedly, bringing it up to temperature. After a few minutes, he engaged first gear and smiled. Just like old times. Swinging out of the parking lot, he noted the time: 1:50 PM.

He stayed off the M1, which was well patrolled, and followed a maze of backroads into the city. It was moonless and very dark. With headlights penetrating the darkness, he burst through patches of fog, leap-frogged humped-back bridges, and slid around narrow curves. Going twice the posted speed limit, the slightest bumps and dips made a springboard of the 911S's suspension, at times launching him a foot off the road. The tires hissed angrily over the damp pavement--four treadprints, each no larger than the size of his hand. Those four small treadprints were all that was keeping him from sliding off the road, and his

171

senses were so keen he could feel them clawing the curves, as if indeed, they were his very outstretched hands. There were no other cars to distract him, no lights but that of an occasional house, no traffic signals, nothing to brake for but curves and roundabouts. Every so often he came upon the dim street light of a village, which he slowed for. On the other side, under the cover of darkness again, he jammed back on the gas and watched the road unravel before him.

As much as he buried himself in his driving, he couldn't escape his thoughts. His anger at Garret--and at himself for not controlling his emotions and following team orders--had subsided. Like a once raging fire, these thoughts now burned as embers. In its place were thoughts that cut deeper and created questions. What was he doing with his life? Did he really have to be world champion? His single-minded determination had brought him to the brink once more, only to have the prize snatched away again. True, four races remained, but without top team behind him, what chance did he really have? Maybe Susan was right. Maybe it was time to get out. He had the respect of his peers, that's all that ever really mattered to him. Men like Bogavanti and Parks; they knew how quick he was. Hell, he was the only driver Evans respected--or feared. Except for racing, his life was empty, a hollow shell. Except for a bookcase full of trophies, he really had nothing to show for 40 years of living. He had no house, no investments, just two Porsches and a beater Mustang. He had never had a lasting relationship with a woman. Susan was going to leave him, he could see that in her eyes tonight. Yes, he had a son, but not by choice; a son who called someone else "Dad." Since seeing Ron's photograph, he had begun thinking about him, and wondered if maybe he had run away from something good. As he reflected on it, that seemed to be his life's story: always running away from something, avoiding attachments, not facing problems; or running after something and never quite catching it. Always running--going like hell--that's what he did best. He was doing it now. For some reason, he found fulfillment in the running, and maybe not in the having or the getting. He wondered what it would be like to just stand still, and have time

172

for a lasting relationship--with Susan perhaps--and to have a child, one that he would be there for and guide growing up. One thing seemed obvious: the running had gotten him nowhere.

It seemed only a few minutes and he crested a low hill and saw the lights of London shimmering in the darkness. Other cars began to appear on the road now, which he weaved around with alacrity. Entering the city limits, he checked his watch: 12:44 AM. Fifty-four minutes.

"Beat that, Cunningham."

When he reached his flat all of his thoughts had played out and his mind was ready to shut down. He crawled into bed and fell asleep instantly.

Chapter 22

The underground train glided to a stop at South Kensington station. Susan stepped off and walked briskly up two flights of stairs to the street level arcade. Beneath its glass roof were several shops, deserted after the morning rush. Out of habit, she looked in the window of a pastry shop. The pastries with chocolate glaze looked all too inviting. She was debating whether or not to buy some when she realized someone was staring at her. It was another woman, a very pretty woman with short dark hair and red-red lipstick. To Susan's surprise, she walked up to her and spoke.

"You're Susan Jennings, aren't you?"

"Have we met?"

"No. But I recognize who you are. You write for SportsWeek, don't you? I've enjoyed your work very much."

"Thank you."

"Well, I must be running. It's nice to meet you. Bye."

Susan watched her hurry down the stairs to the underground trains. Then it hit her: how did this woman know who she was? One of the nice things about being a magazine writer was visual anonymity: no one knew what she looked like. How did this woman recognize her?

She ordered a half-dozen pastries and forgot about the incident. She pushed through the glass doors facing Thurloe Street. Across the way were white row houses. She located number 29C and pressed the buzzer.

A familiar voice came on the scratchy intercom: "Yes."

"It's me, Susan."

"Be right down."

It had been 10 days since the British Grand Prix, and much had happened. The British press had expressed outrage over Wagner's firing, saying Garret's action represented all that was wrong with America, while newspapers in the States relegated the story to the back pages of the sports section. Herb Cook of Unirich Tire ranted and raved and threatened to withdraw sponsorship if Garret didn't reinstate Wagner immediately. With the constructor's championship nearly in his pocket, Garret had the upper hand, and Cook's threats amounted to nothing. The day after the race, calls started coming in, from team owners, sponsors, suppliers, promoters, offering advise, wanting to know what he planned to do, would he retire or continue pursuing the world championship? Some had a stake in his decision, so he had to give a definite answer. When asked if he would be competing in the German Grand Prix, he said yes. Later, at a quieter time, when he had time to reflect, he cursed himself. When it came right down to it, he didn't have the guts to quit.

For a few days, he appeared headed back to Brabham, his old team. Both were contracted to Unirich Tire, but not, unfortunately, to the same oil company. That left the independents. Rob Walker would have taken him in a heartbeat if Walker hadn't been under contract to Dunlop. Wagner decided to go with Scuderia Jano, which was conveniently without a tire contract. The owner, Alberto Jano, had been Ferrari's chief engineer when Wagner raced for the Maranello firm, and was a friend. Jano had his own company now. Wagner drove to Jano's headquarters in Milan and signed a contract for the duration of the season, making Unirich part of the deal as sponsor and tire supplier. Wagner rented an apartment in Milan and drove back to England to move his things.

At SportsWeek, meanwhile, Jeremy Sterns was heartsick over the firing. His dream of seeing his old pal finally win a championship was thwarted once more. "John's snakebit," he told Susan when she filed her story on Wagner's firing. On the other hand, as editor, he saw a great story about to unfold as Wagner scrambled to pick up the pieces. Sterns even managed to talk his boss into covering it. Susan was given the assignment to report on the remaining four races. She took a few days off, then flew back to England and set up office in SportsWeek's

London bureau. She called Wagner once he returned from Milan and was surprised to learn he was moving the next day.

"I can't believe you're doing this," she said, climbing the stairs to his third-floor flat. "It's so ... sudden."

Wagner opened the door for her. "There's nothing keeping me here. Milan's my home now. That's where my new team is, that's where I'll be testing. What's in the bag?"

"Pastries. I saw them in the window across the street and couldn't resist. I bought enough for both of us. Help yourself."

He reached in and took one. "Chocolate, huh? What is it with women and chocolate?"

"Shut up. Do you have coffee to go with these?"

"Not made."

"I'll brew some." She looked around the living room. It was littered with boxes, half of them packed. The bookshelves were empty and the walls were bare. "You've been busy."

"I don't have much time. The movers will be here in the morning, and the day after I've got to be at the Ring."

"You're always on the go, John Wagner. I hope you have time for lunch--Jeremy's treat."

"How is Jeremy these days?"

"Fine. What about lunch?"

"It'll have to be someplace close."

"Any suggestions?"

"The Brig & Age is over on the next block--pub food."

"Do they have salads?"

"Salads. Sandwiches. Pickled pigsfeet."

"Yuck. Where's your coffee maker?"

Susan brewed a pot and poured them both a cup. They finished the pastries and Wagner went back to packing. Susan peeked into his bedroom. The unmade bed was strewn with the contents of the closet. She walked to the window and looked out. Below, nestled between buildings, was a small garden of red geranium and blue lobelia that someone was lovingly maintaining. She turned back to the room and her eyes were

drawn to the clothes piled high on the bed. "Would you like m
to pack these?"

* * *

"What I want to know is, can you still win the championshi
driving for an independent like Jano?"

Wagner shoveled a portion of steak-and-kidney pie into hi
mouth and nodded. It was lunch hour, and the Brig & Age wa
crowded and smoky, but Wagner knew the owner and he'd pu
them in a private room that was quieter and free of tobacc
smoke.

"Jano's car is a Brabham BT19 with some hard miles on it,"
he said, "but it's a car I know. It's lightweight and handles wel
I tested it last weekend at Monza. It won't win any races, but
don't need to win races. What I need is to finish consistently i
the points--finish third or fourth a couple of times, that should d
it--and hope like hell Evans or Bogavanti or Parks doesn't ge
hot and put together a string of wins. It'll be tight, but I can wi
this thing."

"You mean the decision will come down to Watkins Glen?"

"Yeah, probably."

"You haven't had much luck there."

Wagner said nothing. He took another bite of pie and chase
it with beer.

Susan brushed back a lock of red curls. "This is all s
needless. If that darned Garret hadn't fired you, none of thi
would have to happen. You wouldn't have to move to Milan an
drive some second-rate racecar, and there wouldn't be thi
prolonged drama of whether or not you become champion."

Wagner raised an eyebrow. "You sound surprised, Susie
Aren't you the one who said Garret would dump me?"

She looked at her half-eaten salad. "I guess I still can'
believe he would do something that stupid. It's so childish.
swear, boys and their toys."

Wagner wiped his mouth and pushed his plate aside. "I'l
bet you've seen lots of coaches get the ax, and not all of then
with losing records. Don't tell me petty grudges and personalit
178

conflicts didn't enter into it. Enzo Ferrari would not re-sign the greatest driver I ever saw--Juan Fangio--after Fangio won a world championship for him."

"Why?"

"Because Fangio was getting all the credit. So what does Enzo do? He fires the guy. Fangio goes across town to Maserati, who are delighted to have him, and wins another championship. Ferrari? He doesn't win another Grand Prix for two years, and another championship for five. Garret reminds me a lot of Ferrari. He thinks I'm getting too much credit for his team's turnaround. Anyway, there's no sense dwelling on me being fired. Right now, my biggest concern is picking up points in Germany. Which reminds me: how are you getting there?"

"To Germany? I'm flying."

"Why don't you come with me? I'm driving the Porsche. The weather should be nice and I would enjoy your company."

*   *   *

The movers arrived, and Wagner watched them carry his belongings down to the street and load them into a white van. Then he shut the door forever on his home of five years and walked six blocks to the Ennismore Gardens Mews, where he kept his Porsche. He had a local garage wash it and change the oil, then he picked up Susan at her hotel in Mayfair. They departed London and drove down through the wooded Kent countryside to the Dover coast. They caught the one o'clock ferry to Calais and made the crossing in fog.

Away from Calais, on the Flemish plain, the fog vanished and the sun shone hot and bright, as in a van Gogh painting. Endless miles of green farmland greeted them reminding Susan of the American midwest, where she was raised. Except for an occasional farmhouse and barn, which were all roofed with orange tiles, the terrain could have passed for much of Illinois, Indiana, and Ohio. Shortly after 5 PM, the smokey Liege skyline loomed on the horizon. The plain ended here and the Ardennes began. They crossed the gray Meuse River and turned down one of Liege's tree-lined streets, hunting for a place to dine.

Susan had done a lot of soul-searching since that night at Henry V's. She had just about decided to end their relationship when Jeremy assigned her coverage of the last four races. "I'll make a decision later," she thought, hurriedly packing her bags. Being with Wagner again made her forget about leaving him.

"I have a five-week break after the race," Wagner said, as they sat down to dinner. "How about asking Jeremy for some time off? We could go somewhere. To the Bahamas, maybe."

Susan thought a moment, chin cupped in her hands, a slight smile on her face. She needed a vacation, and this sounded like just the ticket, but in her heart of hearts she knew she had to leave him, sooner or later, and that such a holiday would make their parting so much harder. Better sooner than later.

"I would love to," she heard herself say.

Chapter 23

It was a cool morning in the Eifel Mountains of West Germany, and a breeze stirred the pines on the surrounding hills. Wagner drummed his fingers on the padded steering wheel, waiting for the first practice session to begin. It seemed that's all he ever did was wait. Wait for practice. Wait while the crew worked on his car. Wait for the race to begin. After the race, wait for traffic to clear so he could drive back to the hotel and start waiting for the next race. Waiting. Always waiting. He hated it.

"Go easy, Johnny. If the car doesn't feel right, bring it back in. No heroics. Understand?"

Wagner cupped his eyes from the sun's brightness and looked up at the man speaking to him. "Still the mother hen, eh, Berto?"

Alberto Jano smiled ruefully. Yes, he was still the mother hen. He couldn't help it when race drivers placed so much faith in him. As an engineer, he knew all too well of the many dark deep secrets of his racecars--of the thousands of critical bolts and welds and rivets that held them together; of the incredible stresses placed on the chassis, and of how much it could withstand. Yes, there were so many parts to worry about, that could break or come loose.

"Remember, we are not here to win the race," Jano said, "but to finish in the points."

Wagner nodded perfunctorily. "Third place, Berto?"

"That is our plan, remember? Your plan."

The course clerk signaled the track was open. The wait was over. Time to go like hell. Wagner ran his finger down a row of switches, flipping them on. The fuel pump began ticking. He pressed the starter button. The magnesium V-8 engine coughed, let out a high piercing cry, and came to life.

Jano said something, his words drowned out by the engine's shrieks, but Wagner could read his lips: "Go easy, Johnny."

He accelerated away, made the loop at the South Curve, sped back behind the pits, and rounded the North Curve. The heart of the 14.2-mile <u>Nurburg Ring</u> opened with a succession of sweeping downhill curves. He was in no hurry, feeling his way along while bedding in new brakes and tires. Tall pines flashed overhead, shutting out much of the sunlight. Pine needles swirled beneath his wheels and scattered behind him. It would be several laps before all the dust and debris were blown away and a solid film of rubber was laid down. Until then, the circuit would feel slippery and lap times would be high.

At Hocheichen, he burst back into sunlight, upshifted to fifth gear and accelerated up the fast rise to Flugplatz (literally, Fly Place). He wasn't ready to fly just yet, and rolled over the crest with tires firmly grounded. Two right-handers followed in quick succession, followed by a left, putting him on a long, gently curving, uphill section, bordered by rolling meadows. He scanned the gauges--everything checked. The speck of another racecar winked in his mirror. He didn't know who it was, nor did he care.

The old Brabham felt not half-bad, he decided. It was a spaceframe chassis, an old-fashioned chassis; not as rock-solid as a monocoque, but solid enough, with front coil spring-shocks mounted outside in the windstream, where God intended them to be. He upped his speed past 100 mph, became airborne over a rise, and landed without bottoming out. He upped his speed even more and felt the wings kick in, making the chassis feel heavier and the tires stickier. It seemed to him that the only serious drawback to Jano's Brabham was its engine, a three-liter V-8 Jano produced in his factory. It had good low-end torque, but lacked the exhilarating rush of horsepower of the higher-revving V-12s and Cosworth V-8. If only he could talk Jano into switching to the BRM V-12 or Cosworth V-8....

The road dipped down to the Aremburg bridge, where a tricky right-hander awaited him. With perfectly timed, precise motions, he braked, downshifted twice, turned in, and--nuts, wrong gear--felt the Brabham whip sideways. He downshifted another gear and angled out of the curve under increasing power,

aw something gray, solid, and much too close to his outside
wheels flash past, and realized it was a cement bridge girder.

"Go easy, Johnny," he could hear Jano telling him.

The road leveled off briefly, then plunged downhill again,
through a tunnel of pines. The Foxhole. The car in his mirror
grew larger. Lunging up the next hill, he could make out its
colors--gold nose, red fuselage.

No. It wasn't.

Driver in yellow helmet. It was. Evans.

Wagner's jaw hardened. "If he thinks he's passing me...."

The Lotus drew closer through the tight, slippery Adenauer-
forst esse curve, as Wagner's hands whipped the steering wheel
back and forth. At the top of the next hill, setting up for the fast
Metzgesfeld left-hander, he felt a jolt from behind. He glanced
in the mirror and detected a grin on Evans' face. The bastard.
Feeling sweat bead on his face, he dropped a gear and steered
into the curve, sliding, sliding, trying to hold the line.
Something inside caught his eye, something red and gold. What
the hell? He turned to see Evans' Lotus buck crazily going by
him, its inside tires riding the grass verge. As it went ahead, one
of its tires kicked up a large stone. Wagner could see it clearly--
rising, spinning, coming directly at his face. There was no
avoiding it. He closed his eyes and felt it strike his goggles with
the force of a hard-thrown fist; opening them he saw his right
lens spider-webbed with cracks, but intact.

Ahead, Evans set up for the sharp Kallenhard right-hander,
turned in, and disappeared around the hedges. Following his
line, Wagner braked, downshifted, turned in, and--nuts, wrong
gear again--felt his car whip sideways. Would he never get used
to the Brabham's gear ratio? He dropped another gear but this
time there was no saving himself. A high earthen bank rushed at
him. With a thunk, his outside tires struck curbstones, bounced
and climbed the bank. Brush slapped against the fiberglass body
and disappeared beneath him. The trunk of a tree seemed to
drop out of the sky and land in his path. Instinctively, he flung
the wheel to avoid it. To his surprise, the car responded, and the
tree flashed off to his left. The curve opened. He straightened

the wheel and rolled off the bank as if he had taken Kallenhar
this way a thousand times.

"This is madness," he thought. "I can't keep up with Evan
in this junkheap."

Evans cut the next corner so tightly his inside wheels slice
into the hedges. Leaves swirled flying past Wagner's head as h
too buried his inside tires into the hedges. The road plunge
downhill again. This was the Adenau Descent, the mos
dangerous section of the circuit. Diablo Pass with hedgerow
Back and forth across the road, he followed Evans from hedge t
hedge, both cars burrowing grooves into the shrubbery. Ever
few seconds he could see daylight flash beneath the red-and-gol
machine as it lifted and took flight over high spots in the road
see flames shoot from its tailpipes between gear changes. /
grass valley, far to their left, appeared through a gap in th
hedges. Every few seconds it reappeared, closer than before
until finally they were in it. Nose-to-tail, the two cars blew ove
the Adenau Bridge--the half-way point--and bounded up the nex
hill, beginning the long climb to the Hohe-Acht summit.

Evans was drawing away. Around the Bergwerk hairpin
densely wooded valley lurked, where the road rose and dippe
repeatedly--like the back of a serpent--creating a series o
humps, or--more precisely--jumps, where racecars soared a
much as five feet above the ground, in distances of up to 20 feet
Wagner clung to the steering wheel, resigned to watching Evan
draw away. But over the first jump, the Lotus landed heavily i
a shower of sparks. Wagner recognized the problem instantly-
the ride-height was too low. Evans took the next jump slowe
and Wagner repassed him. At the top of the valley, braking for a
hairpin right, he looked back in his mirror and saw nothing bu
empty road.

"It isn't over yet," he muttered.

He accelerated uphill to the next hairpin, a looping, bowl
shaped left-hander called the Karussell, where he saw
photographers on the rim above the curve, aiming their camera
at him. He braked, inched over to the left, and felt his car drop
down into the banked curve. A ribbon of jointed cement began
thumping rhythmically beneath his wheels. Holding the engine

184

at mid-throttle, he downshifted directly to second gear and stayed well down in the groove. As the suspension compressed under mounting g-loads, every joint and crack in the cement jolted his spine and lower back. Coming off the curve, he opened the throttle fully and felt a moment's weightlessness as the springs rebounded and the chassis lifted. He smiled thinking of Evans' belly pan scraping cement as the Scot rounded the Karussell behind him.

The road continued to climb, reached the summit, and plunged down a new set of roller-coaster curves. The hump at Brunnchen Bridge sent him soaring once more, followed by more tight curves, another tight, steeply banked turn, called Swallows Tail, and then the long Tiergarten Straight began.

Evans reappeared in his mirror and closed at the rate of a brisk walk. Off to the right, the high dark walls of the Nurburg Castle jutted from the skyline of pines. Evans was nearly wheel-to-wheel with him now. The Tiergarten Bridge winked into view, disappeared as the road dipped, and reappeared at the top of the next rise, larger and closer. Almost at lap's end. He could still win this private little race. With some guile. Past the bridge, he let his Brabham drift over towards the Lotus, forcing Evans to back off and take a slower line into the next curve. Coming out, the control tower and empty grandstands rose into view. He leaned on the steering wheel. "Come on, baby. Faster."

Evans drew up beside him again. It was going to be close. The start-finish line skipped beneath their tires with Wagner still in front, by inches.

*   *   *

The Californian climbed from the car, removed his helmet and goggles, and looked down to the Lotus pit, where Evans was climbing from his car.

"Nailed your ass, didn't I?" he called down to the Scot. In a quieter voice, one that Evans couldn't hear, he added, "And it doesn't mean a stinkin' thing, does it? You bastard, Sunday you're going to win the race without me."

185

Evans smiled and nodded back. He saw the Scot turn to Revette and with animated hands begin to vent his feelings about some problem he was having with his car, no doubt telling him that it was bottoming out badly, and how dare they send him out at the Nurburg Ring without first raising the ride height. Wagner sighed. "To have such problems."

"How is the car, Johnny?" Alberto Jano's round, balding head peered up at Wagner with questioning eyes. "Not so bad for such an old woman, yes, my friend?"

"The water temperature was rising toward the end of the lap, and I can feel something clunking in front, like the frame has a broken weld in it somewhere, and it pushes when I get on the throttle early, but that could be the result of the broken weld." He winked at Jano. "Other than that, yes, it's not so bad for such an old woman."

Jano scribbled down what was said. "Anything else?"

"That's enough, isn't it. How soon before I go back out?"

"One hour. Maximum. I promise."

"Make that thirty minutes," Wagner said.

Jano nodded. "Yes. Thirty minutes. Maximum. I promise."

Wagner watched Jano's crew push the Brabham away, took one look at his broken goggles, and threw them in the trash. Then he headed in the direction of the Garret-Hawk pit.

"Well, look who's here." Hacksaw grinned and pumped his hand. "Nice to see you, Big Guy. How's it going with Jano's outfit?"

"The car could use some poke, but it handles all right. How's things with you?"

Hacksaw furrowed his brow and sighed. "Oh, you know, it's Mikey's first time on the Ring, and you know how that goes."

"How's he handling the pressure?"

"Not real good, sorry to say. I've talked to him some, but I can't say it's done a lot of good. I guess the Old Man's filled his head with a lot of rah-rah crap about being number-one, and stepping up; nonsense like that, you know, that will get Mikey killed. It's a real shame, all that's happened, and may still happen. I'm leaving this outfit once the season ends and I get my bonus."

"You mean, <u>if</u> you get your bonus. Garret hasn't won the constructor's title yet."

"I know, but I've got my fingers crossed."

Number 36--Wagner's ex-racer--was parked on pit lane, silent and cold. The white-and-blue paint glistened in the morning sunlight.

"I see you're taking good car of my car," Wagner said, touching its chrome roll bar.

Hacksaw shook his head sadly. "I wish it was still your car. We revised the front geometry like we planned, taking out that dreaded anti-dive. It ended up being more work than we thought. Me and Walt about came to blows a couple of times. But the job's done, for all the good it will do us now. I can only guess what that car would do in your hands here at the Ring. But we'll never know now, will we?"

"No, we won't." Wagner looked at his watch. "I better head back. It was good seeing you, Hacksaw."

"What's your hurry?" Rennie stuck his head out of the pit box and grinned toothily. Ray appeared too. They stepped over the counter and shook Wagner's hand.

"Strange seeing you in a red car again," said Rennie. "There's no mistaking it for a Ferrari, is there? How much does Jano's little putt-putt motor put out--Three-thirty, or three-thirty-five horses?"

"Enough to whip your butts."

"Aye, agreed," said Rennie, "under the circumstances. Which reminds me: we got this little bet going? Interested?"

"What kind of bet?"

"Whether or not Michael will break nine minutes," said Ray. "I got five dollars that says he won't."

"You guys, I don't believe it." Wagner turned to Hacksaw. "Are you aware of this?"

The crew chief shrugged. "I got five bucks on Mikey breaking nine minutes by this afternoon."

* * *

Rain was forecast for all of Saturday, the second and final day of practice. If drivers expected to improve their times, it was now or never. In the first hour, Evans became the first driver to break eight minutes, with 7 min 53.1 sec. Parks was next quickest, with 8 min 4.5 sec, followed by Bogavanti, with 8 min 7.9 sec. Wagner was sixth fastest, with 8 min 14.4 sec. In the second hour, word came that someone had crashed heavily at Flugplatz. Wagner drove past the spot and saw where a car had punched through the hedgerows, saw a wrecker and an ambulance, but saw no evidence of whom the unlucky driver was.

Later, he learned the unlucky driver was Michael Bravo.

* * *

Wagner showered and began dressing for his dinner-date with Susan. He had just stepped into his slacks when someone knocked on the door. He put on a shirt and opened it.

It was Eddie. "Can we talk. Off the record, I mean?"

Wagner motioned him in. "You've got five minutes, then I've got to go."

"I thought it was nice of you to go see Michael in the hospital this afternoon."

"The kid's damn lucky to be alive, that's all I have to say. But that isn't why you came here. What is it that you want?"

"First, my father didn't send me here. In fact, he wouldn't like it that I was here."

Wagner buttoned his shirt. "Go on."

"Second, I opposed my father's decision to fire you; I thought it was a big mistake. I also didn't agree with him ordering you to slow down so Bravo could win. But it's his team, and he's entitled to run it the way he sees fit."

188

Wagner tucked in his shirt. "Okay, you didn't agree with our father. What's the point?"

"The point is this: Michael's through for the season, so we've hired Guy Forgue to replace him in tomorrow's race. If Forgue doesn't finish in the top six Dad won't sign him for Monza. That means we will need a driver. I'm going to recommend you."

"Your father fired me, remember? What makes you think he's going to take me back?"

"Bravo's accident was a big shock to him."

"Two broken legs and a concussion, I hope to shout it was," Wagner said.

"If I approach him in the right way," Eddie continued, "I think he might reconsider. He wants that constructor's championship pretty bad."

Wagner knotted his tie in the mirror. "It's out of the question, Eddie. I've signed a contract with Jano for the rest of the season."

"So, that doesn't mean anything."

Wagner whirled around. There was anger in his eyes. "A contract means nothing to you Garrets. What do you propose to do with Jano? Pay him off, too?"

"Rumor has it Jano's bankrupt. His team doesn't have the money to finish the season."

Wagner slipped on his blue blazer. "Sorry, but I don't believe it. If Jano had money problems, he would have told me. Time's up, Eddie."

*　*　*

It rained all day Saturday. Friday's times determined the starting grid for Sunday's race.

German Grand Prix
Sunday, August 4

EVANS	**PARKS**	**BOGAVANTI**
Lotus	BRM	Ferrari
7 min 53.1 sec	8 min 4.5 sec	8 min 7.9 sec

PHILLIPS	**EDWARDS**
Brabham	Cooper
8 min 9.3 sec	8 min 13.1 sec

WAGNER	**LAFOSSE**	**TAMBALA**
Brabham	Matra	Ferrari
8 min 14.4 sec	8 min 18.7 sec	8 min 20.1 sec

Chapter 24

Alberto Jano stood in the shelter of a vendor's umbrella, rain splashing at his feet. The rain showed no sign of letting up. All around the garage quadrangle doors were pulled down to keep the rain out.

"Coffee, Johnny?" he said, stirring his cup. "You look like you need a cup."

Wagner adjusted the baseball cap on his head, the one bearing the Unirich logo. "It's raining, Berto, and it's gonna rain all during the race."

"I can see that it's raining, Johnny."

"Rain can work to our advantage, <u>if</u> we have the right tires. Know what I mean? There'll be confusion in the pits. No one's going to stand out in the rain checking the brand of our tires. I say we make the switch."

"To Dunlop wets? That is what you are suggesting?"

Wagner nodded.

Little gears turned in Jano's engineer mind, and stopped once an answer was formulated. "We have a contract with Unirich. We have no choice but to run their tires."

"Look, on Unirich wets, I don't have a prayer of finishing in the points. On Dunlops, I might win this frickin' race."

Jano smirked. "I doubt that."

"Why not? I've won here twice. I know this place better than anyone else. Second place, for sure. Can you imagine us finishing in second place? Six points? It'll practically guarantee me the championship."

"Yes, Johnny, I know, I know, but Cook's technical people are everywhere. I was talking to one not one minute ago, before you arrived. Please, forget this foolish idea."

"I can't. Listen, a set got swapped onto my car by mistake a couple months back, right here, at the Ring. No one noticed. But I noticed. I've gotta have those tires."

191

"And what if Cook finds out? Humph. Tell me, where are you going get these tires? From the Dunlop distributor? Within five minutes it will be the talk of the paddock."

Wagner grinned crookedly. "I can get the tires, and no one will ever find out where. Look, if Cook's people find out, let me handle it. Me and Herb go way back. You tell them it was my decision and that you knew absolutely nothing about it."

"Tell them that I was on a coffee break, perhaps?"

"Why not?"

"The simple-minded owner who knows nothing of what his team is doing was on a coffee break. Is that what I tell them?"

"You won't have to tell them because they won't find out. Trust me."

* * *

Giuseppe Bogavanti was dressed in a red silk robe, dining on a breakfast of fried eggs mixed with red peppers, spicy sausage, bread dipped in olive oil, and thick, unsweetened coffee. A dark cloud seemed to be hanging over his head.

"Why should I get you these tires?" he said, between bites of egg.

Wagner smiled crookedly. "You owe me one."

"I owe you one." He nodded thoughtfully, then smiled. "One what?"

"Friends, Bogo, remember?"

The Italian wiped his mouth. "Friends? You would cut my throat without hesitation, if you had to, as I would yours." He looked out the window at the falling rain and sighed. "It's days like these, I think of so many other things I would rather be doing with my life."

"Don't give me that. I remember when you used to look up at the sky and rub your hands gleefully at the slightest raindrop."

"An act, Giovanni, that's all it ever was. I've always hated the rain. Only that crazy man Evans likes the rain."

"Can you get me the tires or do I look elsewhere?"

"If I should get you these tires, it would be a violation of your contract, would it not? Where would you and Jano be without a tire contract?"

"Let me and Jano worry about that."

"This race is not so important as to risk losing a sponsor as big as Unirich. Perhaps you want to think about this, eh?"

"I have thought about it. Can you get me a set or not?"

The Italian picked up the telephone receiver. "Ah, Giovanni, you and I, we see the world so much more differently." He dialed, waited for someone to answer, then spoke quickly in Italian. He placed a hand over the mouthpiece. "The tires will be outside your garage in 10 minutes. If you say where you got them, I <u>will</u> cut your throat."

Wagner rose. "You're a sweetheart, Bogo." At the door, he nearly collided with Carlo Tambala, who was entering. There was panic in Tambala's dark eyes, and a screaming baby in his arms.

"Carmelita will not stop crying," he said excitedly. "She no take the bottle and her mother went out. I do not know what to do. Please, Giuseppe, do something."

Bogavanti looked up at the heavens. "Why is it they always come to me with their problems?" He held out his arms. "Bring her to me." The baby stopped crying once in his arms, and began to coo. "Yes, yes, my dear little one. Giuseppe understands."

*   *   *

Rain. It seemed to curve as it fell, and flew at him horizontally. It sprayed with jet-like force off the spinning wheels of the cars in front of him. It blew in through every hole and seam inside the cockpit. It dripped from his chin, beaded on his instrument panel, sidemirrors, and goggles. The race wasn't 90 seconds old, and he was drenched to the skin, and might've begun to shiver if it weren't for the furnace-like heat of the radiator just ahead of his feet. He followed what little he could see of Lafosse's Matra. Past the Hocheichen esse curves he eased open the throttle for the uphill run to Flugplatz. Midway

193

up the hill, the road crossed a narrow bridge, which wasn't normally a concern, except at this very moment Tambala's Ferrari was at his side, trying to pass him here. The bridge appeared to be wide enough for two cars, but in the blinding spray it looked chancy. It was too soon to be taking a risk such as this. Knowing races are never won on the first lap, and often lost, he let the Ferrari forge ahead.

He stayed with the Italian that first lap, as he passed Lafosse's Matra and Edwards' Cooper. "I've got to repass this guy and somehow make it stick," he thought.

On lap 2, entering the fast Pflanzgarten left-hander, Tambala spun around backwards, slid for a hundred feet pointed that way, and stopped short of ramming a stone wall.

"That ought to scare some sense into him," Wagner thought, looking at the shrinking Ferrari in his mirror. "The crazy bastard."

With clear road ahead, he got down to business. He calculated his position. He'd passed Lafosse and Edwards, and now Tambala. That put him in fourth place. Rolling onto the Tiergarten Straight, he spotted a car far ahead, shedding great clouds of spray that hung in the air like sheets of linen, sheets he tattered going through. He guessed the gap was six seconds. That's got to be Parks up ahead, he thought. Or Phillips. Or Bogavanti. Maybe all three.

Approaching the Tiergarten Bridge, like some bad dream back to haunt him, Tambala's screaming, rain-streaked Ferrari reappeared at his side again, tires flinging spray like pinwheels. He glanced over at the red car, startled to be meeting the Italian's eyes. They were dark, crazy eyes, like those of a cornered animal.

He let the red car speed ahead, watched it round the next curve, and wondered how many more times he could do this and still expect to finish second or third. It wasn't long, and Tambala spun again.

"That's it," thought Wagner. "That's got to be the last I see of him. I hope." He pushed on, every few seconds peering at one of his sidemirrors, to be sure. A lap later, about to begin the Adenau Descent, the red car reappeared in the mists behind him.

"No. Not again. That crazy bastard wants to kill himself--
nd take me with him."

The ball of spray that was Parks' BRM was directly in front
f him now. He passed the green car and worked very hard
istancing himself from Tambala. The backside of Phillips'
netallic green Brabham appeared at the center of another ball of
pray. He passed it too. Approaching the Adenau Descent
gain, a marshal in yellow raincoat stepped from the rain
rantically waving a yellow flag. Wagner reduced speed.
'urther ahead, parked at the edge of the road with red lights
lashing, were a tow truck and an ambulance. Several men with
opes and a stretcher were starting down the hillside. Wagner
ringed when he saw where some poor devil had left the road,
nd the eery feeling came over him that he would not be seeing
'ambala's Ferrari in his mirror again.

The sky grew darker. Rain fell harder. Puddles began to
ppear, and rivers began to wash over some sections of road.
Vagner kept pushing, hoping to catch Bogavanti, in second. A
ap later, approaching the Pflanzgarten left-hander, he saw yet
nother car that had left the road, a dark green car, with two
vheels torn off, and the driver, now out of the car, standing
eside it. Wagner recognized the car and the driver immediately.

"Parks. He's all right, thank god."

He remembered Parks' girlfriend, sitting back in the cold
lamp pits. Poor Claudia. Mal hadn't come around on the last
ap. She had to be worried sick about him. He also thought of
,aura Tambala. If it was Carlo who had gone off at the Adenau
)escent, he hadn't passed the pits in some time either. Both
vomen would be getting conflicting reports about what had
happened. Everyone would smile and assure them that all was
vell, that a driver had been seen walking from the crash, but
nside they would know this was fiction and fear the worst. It
vould be several hours before they would know the exact fate of
heir man.

At Adenau Descent, Wagner was shown the yellow flag
gain. The ambulance had departed and now pieces of the
hassis were being hauled up and stacked onto the wrecker. The
mashed body panels were red, indicating the car was either

195

Tambala's Ferrari or one of two red BRMs entered by Italian industrialist Dominic Martini.

Then he saw the number 12 on one of the panels. Tambala's number.

It was after this that Wagner began to feel it, a clunking sensation every time the Brabham lifted over a crest and landed back on its wheels. After a particularly fierce landing something broke loose and fell between his knees.

"What the hell?"

A frame tube? With his left hand, he tried to grab it but it was too far forward. It began rolling back and forth between his knees every time he rounded a corner.

Along pit row the flood lights had come on. Jano was standing in the rain holding up the pitboard. The message:

3
-118 Bog
6

Third. He knew that, but Bogavanti was two-minutes ahead of him? For a guy who hated the rain, he certainly wasn't driving like it. More likely, another of the Italian's psyche jobs. There was no way Wagner was going to catch him now, even with six laps remaining. Visibility was down to 100 feet or less, he was tiring, and road conditions were getting worse by the lap.

Third place. It wasn't what he wanted, but it would do.

With three laps remaining, even that began to slip away. A wheel vibration set in. Whenever his speed reached 100 mph his right front wheel shook so badly he had no choice but to slow down. He thought about pitting, but knew Jano didn't have another Dunlop tire to replace it with. It wasn't long, and Phillips' Brabham appeared out of the mists behind him. Instinctively, he speeded up but the vibration was so intense now it felt as if the tire would rip the suspension apart. He backed off and Phillips passed him.

Fourth place.

The race was nearing three hours when he received the white flag. One lap to go. Near the Karussell, he came upon a car

196

going very slowly. High wing at the back. Red and gold paint. Driver in yellow helmet.

Evans.

The Scot was limping along on a flat tire. He'd led every lap but the one that counted.

Wagner passed him and calculated the new order: Bogavanti in front, Phillips in second, and he in third.

Third place. He'd take it. Gladly.

Coming up the hill, he leaned the old Brabham into the Karussell and felt the rhythmic thumping of cement joints beneath his wheels. He geared down to second and felt G-forces pull at him. The end of the curve rolled into view. He pressed the throttle fully and ... what the hell?

The engine faltered, sputtered like it was running out of fuel, and cleared itself. Sputtered again and cleared itself. Sputtered and cleared itself again, back and forth like that, jerking him up the hill.

Was he running out of fuel? Or had water gotten into the electrics. That had to be it. Water had shorted the automatic switch-over to the last fuel cell, that's why the engine was sputtering. No problem. There was a manual override. Flip the handle and he was home free.

He reached under the dashboard, fumbled for the handle, found it, and gave it a tug. Nuts. It wouldn't budge. He tried again--still stuck. The engine was stumbling badly now, running on fumes. He pulled harder, putting muscle into it. This time the handle turned ... and twisted off in his hand. He looked at it, not believing this could happen, and flung it into the hedges.

Third place, hell. In about a minute he would be walking.

The sputtering Brabham crested Hohe-Acht and died completely coming down the backside, freewheeling through a long section of downhill curves. He could hear his tires hissing on the wet pavement, hear raindrops drumming on the fiberglass body. A few hardy fans above the road called to him in German. He could only guess what they were saying, but he waved back. Down through Wippermann, over Brunnchen Bridge. The road flattened. The free ride was over. He coasted to a stop under a stand of dripping firs.

197

He felt exhaustion coming on. With great effort, he wrenched himself out of the cramped cockpit, his limbs stiff with fatigue. He sat up on the roll bar, hoisted one leg over the side and then the other, stepping into the mud, and took a few stiff, painful steps. Rain beat on him mercilessly, running in tiny torrents down the creases of his soaked uniform. Lafosse raced by, now in third, and Lehmann, the West German, now in fourth. They took no notice of him. Stragglers sped past, some one- and two-laps down. Wagner waved, hoping one of them would stop and give him a lift back to the pits, but they sped by, caught up in their own private dramas. He started walking and heard another car approach, clippity-cloppeting along on a flat tire, the tire so frazzled it was now all but gone.

Evans stopped. Was that a smile Wagner detected on his face? "Would you like a ride?" the Scot asked.

Evans crossed the finish line in fifth place and earned two points. His passenger was credited with seventh place and earned nothing.

German Grand Prix Top Six Finishers		Championship Point Leaders Race Eight of Eleven	
Driver	Points	Driver	Points
Bogavanti	9	Wagner	42
Phillips	6	Bogavanti	34
Lafosse	4	Parks	30
Lehmann	3	Evans	23
Evans	2	Phillips	16
Giraud	1	Lafosse	14

*   *   *

Hundreds of people stood in the rain to greet Bogavanti as he pulled into the pits. Zilli was a sad ship in a sea of happy faces. He watched his driver remove his helmet, laugh and open his arms as if to embrace the entire crowd. Zilli and three officials moved in and pulled him away. Phillips and Lafosse--the second- and third-place finishers--were waiting for him to join them on the podium. Bogavanti stopped at the steps and turned to Zilli, his old friend. "Ludovico, something is wrong. You must tell me what it is."

Zilli looked down, unable to face him. "It is Carlo."

Bogavanti's smile vanished. He looked imploringly at Zilli. "Carlo?"

"I am sorry, Giuseppe."

"Carlo?" he said faintly. "No."

Zilli's great stony face softened. "They are waiting for you, Giuseppe. You must go. You are the winner."

Bogavanti fell into Zilli's arms and sobbed tearfully: "Sometimes, there are no winners."

*   *   *

Laura Tambala was the last to know. When her man had failed to come around again, she, like Claudia, waited anxiously for some word, some scrap of information. She was seated with several other drivers' wives and girlfriends. The other women tried to cheer her with encouraging words. Carlo had merely broken down on the circuit, they said. Or spun off harmlessly somewhere. But when an ambulance and a wrecker were dispatched, and over an hour passed, and still no word came, she became deeply concerned. Finally, the race ended, and the other women dispersed, leaving Claudia and Laura alone. They looked at each other, one Italian, the other English, unable to communicate. But their eyes spoke plenty.

When news came, it was the wives of two former world champions who delivered it. Patty Phillips and Mireille Lafosse had been down this road many times, both as bearer and recipient. Patty had the easy job. She smiled reassuringly at Claudia, led her away and told her Mal had been released from the hospital and was unhurt. Because Mireille spoke excellent Italian, she had the thankless task of telling Laura the fate of her husband. She could have made it easy on herself and told Laura that Carlo had been taken to a hospital, which was true, and that his condition was unknown, which wasn't true. Mireille saw no sense in being dishonest and, worse, leaving the task to some poor German doctor who didn't speak Italian. Her heart went out to the young mother, who looked no older than 19, and she gave it to her straight.

Susan Jennings saw Laura Tambala crying inconsolably in Mireille Lafosse's arms, Patty Phillips having taken the baby. She felt sick and angry all at once. She knew death could happen any time yet it had caught her off guard. These past few weeks, in Wagner's steady company, she'd been lulled to sleep, intoxicated by the atmosphere, the tension, the human drama that played out on race weekend. She couldn't imagine anything bad happening to any of the drivers, most of whom she had come to know and like. If any of the drivers talked about the dangers at all, it was in a joking manner. Even Bravo's accident on Friday, as terrible as it was, hadn't awakened her. Now, seeing Laura crying and unable to attend to her own baby, and knowing Carlo's body was lying on a cold slab somewhere, made her angry with herself for having been fooled. It wasn't right, a young life being snuffed out so needlessly. She made no attempt to hide her feelings from Wagner.

"What's going to happen to Laura Tambala?" she demanded, teary-eyed and shaking. "And that poor little baby girl. She will grow up without her daddy, thanks to this cruel sport of yours."

"Carlo made a mistake," he said, measuring his words. "He was over his head and he made a mistake."

"Well, he didn't deserve to die for it, did he?"

"No, he didn't. But it's the risk we all take. He knew the risk. He accepted it."

"What other sport asks its participants to take such risks?"

Wagner's legs felt like jelly. He sat down and looked up at her. "Susan, we've been down this road before...."

"Other than war, what other occupation has such risks? Can you tell me, please?"

Wagner sighed. "I know you're upset, Susan...."

She sat beside him and put her hand on his knee. "Don't you see, John? This is what I fear will happen to you? That you will die one of these Sunday afternoons. How can I love you when you put yourself at risk all the time?"

*   *   *

Jeremy Sterns sat glumly on the sofa, resting his chin in his hand. Every Sunday afternoon, all summer long, he'd watched all the Chicago television sportscasts, and not once had even one of the sportscasters given the results of that day's Grand Prix. Sure, they gave all the baseball scores, results of golf and tennis tournaments, horse races, even bowling scores, for crying out loud, but motor racing? Forget it. Like newspapers, the stations got race results off the wires--plus footage from the network feeds--and ignored it. But not this Sunday afternoon. The German Grand Prix headlined the sports report because someone had been killed. It didn't matter that none of the sportscasters had ever heard of Carlo Tambala before, but with sad eyes they looked into the camera and spoke as if they had known the Italian since he first started racing go-karts in Genoa, Italy. Two sportscasters failed to mention who had won the race. And the one who did, pronounced Bogavanti's name with a hard g and got the o-sound wrong.

"You're disgusting," Sterns cried at his television set. "Every one of you. You're all a bunch of blow-dried jock sniffers."

Chapter 25

In sharp contrast with the rain and dreariness of Sunday, Monday was bright and sunny. Wagner was down in the Sport-Hotel dining room sipping coffee and reading the <u>Times of London</u>. Occasionally he looked out the window at the Nurburg Castle. Except for Susan, who had slept in after working late on her story, everyone connected with the race had checked out of the hotel. He flipped to news of the race. At the top of the page the headline read: "Bogavanti Wins Rain-Soaked German Grand Prix." Below it was a photo of Bogavanti, wreath around his neck, sobbing at the news of Tambala's death.

Further down a second photo showed Evans crossing the finish line with Wagner straddling the engine. The caption heading: "Wagner Luck Strikes Again."

"Have you read the story about Jano yet?" Susan said, looking over his shoulder. Next to the race report was a second story, headed: "Ex-Ferrari Engineer to Declare Bankruptcy."

She sat down beside him. "According to the story, Jano is broke. Maybe Eddie was right."

Wagner didn't look up. "Until Jano tells me, it's only a rumor as far as I'm concerned."

"But what if it's true, John? What will you do?"

He said nothing.

She placed her hand on his arm. "I'm sorry about what I said yesterday." She smiled. "I'm sure the last thing you needed was for me to unload on you. I truly am sorry."

He looked at her for the first time. "Everyone's emotions were a little raw." He stopped a waiter. "Get the lady some coffee, will you, please."

"No, thank you," Susan said. "I had coffee with breakfast, in my room."

The waiter nodded and moved on.

"I can't believe some of the things I said," she continued. "I'm so embarrassed. You must think I'm terrible."

He took a swallow of coffee, said nothing, and went back to reading the paper.

At noon, he drove her to the Cologne airport, kissed her goodby and promised to call her in two days to set up their Bahamas vacation. Then he drove on to Milan and to an uncertain future.

*   *   *

Jano Automobili occupied a two-story brick building in an industrial section of Milan. The small company produced 400 luxury sports coupes and roadsters annually, plus 40 race cars, mostly Formula Threes. When Jano left Ferrari to found his own company, he did so with the twofold ambition of beating his former boss on the race track and of outselling him in the lucrative luxury sports car market. His philosophy was simple: win on Sunday, sell on Monday. Jano started quickly, having a team of Formula Ones and sports prototypes ready for competition within 12 months. But it was too much, too soon, and the cars were embarrassingly slow and unreliable. When his biggest backer died suddenly, Jano was forced to cut back. He gave up building his own Formula One chassis, and competed with year-old Brabhams, powered by a V-8 engine produced by his factory, but even this combination failed to win races. Meanwhile, his luxury sports coupes and roadsters cost more to build than anticipated and could not be priced competitively with Ferrari. Coupled with Jano's failure to win on Sunday, his cars were not selling on Monday, or any other day of the week. Jano made more cutbacks, but his tiny company couldn't withstand the mounting debt. His final bid to save the enterprise was to sign Wagner and resurrect his Formula One team, hoping Wagner's name and success on the track would boost sales and maybe attract another backer. When Jano returned from Germany with a disappointing seventh-place finish, his remaining backers said it was time to fold.

As soon as Wagner arrived in Milan, Jano called him to his office. Suspecting the worst, the American drove to the plant and parked inside the chain-link fence that surrounded the building. He walked through an arch and into the central courtyard and discovered the usual hum of activity was absent. He entered a side door and walked upstairs to Jano's second floor office. It was furnished simply with an oak desk, coffee table, and brown leather chairs. A large window overlooked the courtyard. On the wall behind Jano's desk hung an oil painting of a shark-nosed Ferrari 156 on the banking at Monza. It was the only memento of Jano's 16 years working for the patriarch of Italian motor racing, Enzo Ferrari.

Jano did not rise when the American entered, but merely motioned him to a seat facing his desk. Jano had just returned from Tambala's funeral and Wagner hoped that was the reason for the somber mood that seemed to permeate the place.

"You like being direct," Jano said, "so I will not mince words. I must turn over my company to my creditors. Effective immediately, Jano Automobili no longer exists." He wiped his eyes with a handkerchief. "I owe you a tremendous apology, John. You came to Milan thinking you had a car for the rest of the season. I did not intentionally mislead you. At the time I thought everything would work out. Perhaps if we had finished third in Germany, I would have been given more time. But that wasn't to be."

"What about the money from Unirich?" Wagner asked. "Didn't that help?"

Jano smiled through his tears. "That was only a drop in the bucket. My company has very big debts, John. If it had been enough, I never would have let you switch tires." He wiped his eyes again. "I did enjoy your little game. Under the circumstances, it was a necessary gamble. You know, we came within five miles of finishing third. Five miles more and I might still have the company."

"What will you do now, Alberto?"

"I can always go back to Ferrari, as much as I despise the man, or to several other companies that would gladly take me." He looked at Wagner with concern. "You need to think about yourself, Johnny. You still have a championship to win."

"Believe me, I know. The first thing I'm going to do is call Eddie Garret and see if his father will take me back."

"Is that possible?"

"Eddie thinks so. He approached me in Germany and said his father may have had a change of heart since Bravo's accident. I told him I had a contract with you and that it was out of the question."

"That is fantastic, John. Call him at once. Here, use my telephone."

Wagner still remembered the number of Garret-Hawk's London headquarters, and dialed long distance. He waited while operators connected him.

Eddie picked up the telephone on the other end. "I wish I had some good news for you," he said, after hearing Jano was folding. "My father still thinks he doesn't need you. I even asked him if an apology from you would make him reconsider. He said no. Right now he's in the States trying to sign someone else. It's a real shame. With you driving, we were just about unbeatable. Now, I doubt if we'll win another race this year. Of course, Dad doesn't want to hear that."

Wagner looked at Jano and shook his head.

The Italian sighed heavily.

"Thanks for trying, Eddie. I'm curious. Any idea who the driver is?"

"None. Dad's keeping it a secret. Good luck, John. I hope you still win the championship. No one deserves it more than you."

Wagner thanked him and hung up.

"Let me call Andre Sendak in Brussels," Jano said, picking up the phone. "Andre is an old friend and Equipe Nationale Belge is under contract to Unirich. Since Forgue left, Andre has only one driver."

Wagner waved his hand with contempt. "Forget it. Equipe Belge is the bottom of the barrel. Andre runs a couple of old Cooper-Maseratis--pure junk. Forgue couldn't leave fast enough."

Jano put down the receiver, a puzzled look on his face. "Who does that leave? Dominic Martini is under contract to Dunlop, so is Rob Walker. Wait. Brian McLaughlin."

"Where have you been, Berto? McLaughlin folded last year. He's back peddling stock again."

"Then who does that leave?"

Wagner rose. "I don't know. No one, I guess."

"It leaves Equipe Nationale Belge, that's who. Maybe if Andre had you as his driver, he might be encouraged to spend the extra money to hire a top engineer and more mechanics."

"And spend money on new racecars too? He would need to do that too. Forget it. Sendak is just trying to survive. Besides, I could do all those things myself, and do a better job of it too, if that's what it's going to take." He looked through the window down at the courtyard below. Two men were pushing Jano's red Brabham into a van. "Maybe that's what I should do. It's about the only choice I have, at this point."

"You mean start your own team?" Jano's eyebrows raised a notch.

Wagner turned to face him. "Why not? I could buy a couple of engines from Cosworth, dig up a chassis somewhere, a year-old Lotus or Brabham, something with good bones...."

"Johnny, you don't know what you are saying. The costs will eat you up. You have no crew, no tools or equipment, no transporter, no shop to work on the cars. There is so much you would need. I could go on and on. But money, Johnny, that is what makes it all possible. Where will you get that kind of money?"

"Unirich will help with some of the expenses," he said, looking down on the courtyard below. The two men were now loading spare parts into the van. "I'll hire a crew and find a place for them to work, but first I'll need a chassis. What's happening to that one?"

Jano looked down into the courtyard. "All my cars were appraised yesterday. The Brabham was assigned no value so I'm shipping it to a broker in Modena. You don't want it."

"Maybe I do--if the price is right. Hell, I almost finished third in the sucker. Wings have been fabricated. Put a Cosworth in back and who knows?"

"No, no, no. Please, listen to me. You do not want that car. The frame has been broken and welded so many times it looks

207

arthritic. Do you know what one appraiser told me? He said it would make a nice planter."

Wagner wasn't amused. He would hire a proven miracle worker--Hacksaw Gilbert. Hacksaw would make a new frame and have the car ready for the next race. He would have to talk him into quitting Garret, but that wouldn't be hard. He could visualize Jano's Brabham on the grid at Monza already, painted America's colors. The idea made sense. It excited him. "Give me a price."

Jano shook his head. "I should never have let you race that car, Johnny. The frame is so very bad."

"A price, Berto."

Jano walked back behind his desk and sat down. He folded his hands on the desk. "Nothing."

"Be serious."

"I am quite serious. Let's say it's my way of repaying you for all that has gone wrong." He nodded slightly. "Of course, once you have a look inside the car, you will see I have done you no favor."

Wagner returned to his apartment in Milan and spent the afternoon on the telephone. He called Hacksaw first. The crew chief was in transit so Wagner left a message. Next, he called Herb Cook at Unirich's headquarters in Akron, Ohio. Cook was between meetings and seemed irritated by his call. The Unirich boss said he would call back when he had time to talk. After that, Wagner contacted North Coast Oil and two other suppliers with whom he had contracts. Combined, they agreed to fork over $5000 per race for the privilege of seeing their decals on his car. It wasn't much, considering the costs of running a team, but it was a start. The big money--the money he was counting on-- would come from Unirich. Next, he arranged shipment of the ex-Jano Brabham to Los Angeles. He ordered three engines from Cosworth, one for each race, plus a pair of Hewland transaxles, setting him back $70,000. Both companies wanted cash on delivery. He had $68,000 in the bank. He called Katie, his mother, who agreed to lend him the difference. He also informed her the barn behind her house was about to become the headquarters of Team Wagner. He called the movers who had

208

shipped his belongings from South Kensington to Milan and asked them to return and ship them to California. Thank goodness he hadn't had time to unpack. He remembered his Porsche. What would he do with it now? Sell it? Or ship it to American too? Right now, he needed the cash more than the car, so selling it made sense. He called a Porsche dealership in Milan who, learning Wagner was the owner, offered to pay good money for it, sight unseen. The next call he dreaded; it was to Susan Jennings, to cancel their holiday. He certainly didn't have time for her now. She wasn't in her office, so he left a message.

*　　*　　*

The return calls started coming at 8 PM. The first was from Hacksaw.

"I got your message, Big Guy. What's up?"

"Jano's bankrupt, that's what's up. I've decided to carry on with his car and form my own team."

"You're kidding?"

"I'm going to need a crew chief. As far as I'm concerned, the job's yours."

After a long pause, Hacksaw responded: "I'd love to be a part of it, I really would, but, you know, I'm sorta locked in with Garret."

"You're going to quit at the end of the season. You told me that. What's the difference, then or now?"

"A bonus check. Look, I've got two daughters in college, my wife's just bought us a new house, and I got my mother's medical bills. I need that bonus money. I get it only if I stay."

"You mean you get it only if Garret-Hawk wins the constructor's championship. Face it, Hacksaw, it's not going to happen. Garret's lost Bravo and fired Forgue; now he's trying to hire lord-knows-who for a driver, and whoever it is, I guarantee you he won't have Formula One experience, so you can just kiss that bonus check goodbye."

"What you're saying is probably true. But right now Garret's chances look better than yours. Sorry to have to put it that way."

"Hacksaw, I need you. I can't win the championship without you. Okay, you lose a bonus check maybe, but if you join me I'll give you half of the team. You've always wanted your own team; here's your chance. It's not much right now, but if we win the championship it could snowball into something, especially the way tire companies are throwing money around these days."

"Your team could fold tomorrow, John. With Garret, at least, I can count on a paycheck twice a month."

Wagner said nothing. If Hacksaw wouldn't join him, he would have to find someone else. There was always someone else, maybe not as talented, but there would be someone else. With or without Hacksaw, he was determined to do this, to put together a team and find a way to win. But it would have been so much easier with Hacksaw at his side.

"My heart is with you, Big Guy," said the crew chief. "But I gotta stay put."

Twenty minutes later, Herb Cook called. He didn't sound happy. "I've been meaning to speak with you," he growled.

"Thanks for calling me back, Herb. Before you say anything, I have some bad news; you probably already know by now--Jano's folded. As crazy as it sounds, I'm without a team again."

"You're also without a tire contract."

"What?"

"I found out about the Dunlops, John-boy. Oh, yes. One of my technical guys saw them on your car when it was towed back to the pits. What the hell kind of stunt was that? After all I've done for you? Damn it, John. I've been more than your sponsor. I've been your friend. And this is how you thank me. What the hell am I supposed to tell my board of directors? They'll think I'm one Class-A fool, that's what they'll think. Thank God you didn't finish, that's all I have to say. Thank God you didn't finish, because I'd sure as hell would have sued your ass for breach of contract."

Wagner sat down on one of the packing crates, trying to think of some reply. The best he could manage was, "I can explain, Herb."

"You can explain? You think an explanation will fix everything? Explanations are excuses. I don't accept them from my sales directors and I sure as hell won't accept one from you. I'm tearing up your contract. You'll never get another red cent out of Unirich. Not another red cent." Click. The line went dead.

It wasn't five seconds and the telephone rang again.

It was Susan.

What would he say? That without Hacksaw Gilbert or backing from Unirich he was starting his own team? That he was pinning his hopes on a three-year old Brabham and, win or lose, after it was all over he would be out $100,000 at the very least? That he had no crew, no equipment, no transporter, and, in all probability, no chance? And because of this, he was cancelling their vacation?

Or, having thought about it, he had decided she was right: it was time to retire. Yes, and he was calling his travel agent to arrange their vacation. Oh, and would she marry him? He had $68,000 in the bank, enough to buy a very nice home in the suburbs, plus furniture, and her very own Porsche--and not a damned 912, but a 911--and whatever else she wanted, if she would say yes.

In the second or two before speaking, every possible response that came into his head sounded ridiculous. He didn't know what to say. So he started slowly, from the beginning.

"I have some bad news, Susan."

"Let me guess--Jano's folded."

"There's more, lots more...."

Chapter 26

A bronze haze hung over the Los Angeles basin that was usual for this time of year in the City of Angels. The commercial jetliner Wagner was riding skimmed over the haze for a moment, as if debating whether or not it wanted to make the plunge. Finally, the nose dipped and the plane was in it. On the ground, it was the kind of air that made the lungs ache walking up a single flight of stairs. This was not a day for heavy exertion, but Wagner had no choice. The Jano Brabham and three large wooden crates awaited him in an airport warehouse.

He rented a van and backed it around to the warehouse loading dock. A beefy worker in a sleeveless shirt greeted him. He had the shaggy blond-brown hair and deep tan of a surfer, and obviously lifted weights. Ex-football player, Wagner guessed, junior college level, no higher. In his early 20s, wondering what to do with the rest of his life now that his playing days were over.

"You look familiar," said beef-boy.

Wagner handed him a receipt. "I'm here for the racecar and three crates."

"Hey, I know who you are now. You're John Wagner. You race over in Europe. So that's your car, huh? Where's your crew? Shouldn't they be picking up this stuff?"

"I don't have a crew. I would appreciate it if you could help me load."

"Sure." He stuck out a big hand. "Name's Ted."

"Hello, Ted."

Using a dolly, one by one they wheeled the heavy crates into the van, grunting and sweating with each trip. Lastly, they pushed the Brabham into the van.

"This thing looks rough," said Ted, looking the car over. "I thought racecars looked sharper than this."

Wagner didn't answer. At the moment, he was more concerned with tying the car down than with how it looked.

"Here, let me help you," said Ted, grabbing a piece of rope "Got someone on the other end to help you unload?"

"Can't say that I do."

"I'm off in 30 minutes. How about if I come with you an help you unload? I could return the van back here and save yo a trip."

Wagner eyed Ted closely, unsure of how to respond.

"I got nothin' better to do," said Ted.

The High Desert baked and shimmered in 110 degree hea The big van rattled and absorbed heat like a sponge. Anythin, inside the cab made of metal was too hot to touch. They reache Lancaster and turned east on Avenue J. Within a few miles the reached the alfalfa fields. The cool, moist air wafting in off th irrigated fields felt like air conditioning. A few miles and th van slowed and turned up the gravel drive to Edington Farm Katie was waiting with tall glasses of lemonade. Ted downe his in a single gulp, stifled a burp, and asked the driver what h planned to do for a crew.

Wagner knew of people to call, mechanics who'd kicke around Southern California for years, preparing sports cars fo races at Pomona, Riverside, Willow Springs and the like mechanics who had never advanced to the next level. They wer good mechanics who loved their work but hadn't gotten th breaks, or had settled down with families and didn't want to liv on the road. They weren't in Hacksaw's league, but who was?

"I'm not a mechanic or nothin'," said Ted, "but I could do . lot of odd jobs for you. You know, sweep up, clean parts, d heavy lifting, run errands, whatever you asked. I can quit my jo and start tomorrow. I'm not married or nothin', and I worl cheap."

Wagner looked at the Brabham and the three large woode crates. There was unpacking, organizing, cleaning, sweeping and a thousand other little jobs that needed doing. Sooner o later, he would need a gofer.

"Go apply for a passport, then come see me."

"Huh? A what?"

"A passport. We fly to Italy in four weeks. If you want t go, you'll need a passport."

After everything was unloaded and Ted had departed with the van, Wagner made an inventory inspection, starting with the Brabham. He removed all the body panels. Inside the cockpit, near the pedals, still lay the tube that had broken off during the race. It was a section of frame, as he'd suspected. He looked around the frame to see where it had been attached and discovered evidence of a prior crash. The broken frame tube was one of several that had been used to rebuild the damaged area. It was a patch job, done in a rush, probably the night before some race, to make the car "a starting-money special", no more, no less. The team returned to Milan no doubt intending to effect a permanent repair but probably were put on another job and never got back to it. Jano's people were spread pretty thin, as he was short of cash. That explained it, but it sure as hell didn't excuse it. The frame was on the verge of collapse. Wagner shook his head angrily. "My god, Berto, the least you could have done was to have told me."

Next, he pried open the three wooden crates. They contained spare parts: two sets of dinged magnesium wheels, narrow and out of date; a transaxle; several greasy boxes of gears; three clutch discs, two of them worn; various suspension arms, some bent, probably from the same crash that damaged the frame; a spare set of half shafts; a set of front uprights; four sets of brake discs, all worn below spec; a set of coil springs; several sets of shocks; a smashed water radiator; extra fiberglass body panels; plus a multitude of lesser parts: a steering wheel, a seat, side mirrors, gauges, boxes of brake pads, spark plugs, universal joints; and cans of various size nuts, bolts, and washers, all mixed together. He removed the parts and had them spread out over the floor when Katie appeared at the door.

"Dinner's ready, John."

Wagner stood back and surveyed the scene. Jano's red Brabham was nicked and patched and sagged in front, a tired old race horse ready for the glue factory. Half of the spare parts were worn or damaged.

"It's all just so much junk," he said, in a depressed, tired voice. "Yep. This is it. Team Wagner. And who do I have for a crew? Ted."

The following morning, as the first rays of sunlight shown on the High Desert, Katie knocked lightly on his bedroom door. "John? Are you awake? Someone's come up the drive."

Wagner looked at the clock on the nightstand. It was 6:06 AM. He threw off the covers disgustedly. "It's Ted, the big jerk. Why on earth he's here at this hour is beyond me." He slipped into his trousers, grabbed a shirt and headed downstairs. He yanked back the dead bolt and pulled open the big front door.

"For crying out loud, Ted...."

Hacksaw's blue eyes appraised him coolly through horn-rimmed glasses. "Excuse me? Is this the Wagner residence?"

"Hacksaw?"

"At your service."

Wagner shut the door behind him. "I'm glad as hell to see you, pal, but what the devil are you doing here?"

"It's a long story, Big Guy, but I can sum it up in two words: 'Tony Dayton.'"

"You're kidding? The Indy driver? Garret's hired an Indy driver?"

"Don't that beat all?"

"You were his crew chief, weren't you, when he won Indy?"

"Two times. In six years, we had one losing season, and what does the guy do? Fire me."

Wagner nodded. "I heard he's an ornery bastard."

"Garret firing you was bad enough, but signing that jackass was just too much. Bonus or no bonus, I couldn't leave fast enough. I got into Denver yesterday, threw some tools into my truck--plus a little surprise I have for you--kissed my wife goodbye, and drove all night to get here. Is that coffee I smell brewing? And sausage?"

"What kind of surprise?"

Katie appeared from the kitchen, wiping her hands on her apron. "Shall I set another place?"

*   *   *

"My lord, will you look at all the room in here." Hacksaw heard his voice echo. Except for Katie's green Jaguar sedan, the

216

Brabham and its spare parts, the barn was completely empty. The floor was paved. Small windows along the south wall let in shafts of light. Along the west wall was a paint booth, metal work benches, shelves and cabinets. In the corner was a small, walled-in office.

"There's about 5000 square feet in here," Wagner said. "My dad collected cars and had about 20 of 'em in here at one time. There's a kitchen, bedrooms, and a bath upstairs. You can stay there. I'll have meals catered--not that I can afford it--and a maid come in daily to make the bed and clean up."

Hacksaw walked to the center of the barn and turned completely around, wonder in his eyes. "I feel like I died and gone to heaven. I might not ever want to leave."

Wagner nodded. "You might change your mind once you have a better look at the Brabham."

Hacksaw looked the car over, shaking his head constantly. "I can't believe you drove this thing and lived to tell about it. There's almost nothin' here that's salvageable."

"Can you do something with it in time for Monza?"

"Yeah, it'd take some doing, but you'd still have yourself a racecar with a spaceframe. Which brings me to the surprise I have waiting outside in my truck. Come on."

Hacksaw's truck was a long stepvan that doubled as a machine shop and tool repository. Strewn in the walkway were crates of parts and what looked like a monocoque chassis. It was just the bare hull and it showed signs of having been crashed.

"Let me guess," said Wagner. "This is your surprise."

"Yep."

"What is it? Or should I say, what was it?"

"A Lotus 38."

"An Indy car?"

"Yep. Finished second in sixty-six. Dayton bought it off Chapman and crashed it a week later at Milwaukee. Burned his hands pretty good trying to get out. I built a duplicate which won Indy the following year. This here sat around Dayton's shop for awhile. I ended up buying it off him thinking sooner or later I would rebuild it and start my own team. Well, that time has come."

"You're kidding? This?"

"It may not look like much, but I can have you a racecar in four weeks. Most of the suspension is in those boxes there, and what we don't have we can make. We'll have to lighten her up a little and shorten the wheelbase, but that should be no problem. Walt Balchowsky will be here in a couple days to hammer us out a magnesium skin."

Wagner chuckled. "Fat Walt?"

"Yep. He's the only one I could talk into coming with me, but he's the one we need most. And I think I got us a suspension man, too, one who can weld and fabricate titanium. What concerns me is finding us an engine. I hope you got something lined up in that department or we're up a creek."

"I ordered three Cosworth DFVs and a pair of Hewland gearboxes. The engines will be tuned and ready to go. All we got to do is bolt them in."

"Sounds good."

"Maybe it's not so good."

Hacksaw's eyes narrowed. "What do you mean?"

"The engines and trans cleaned out all of my cash. That's not all."

"You mean there's more?"

"Unirich dropped me."

Hacksaw raised an eyebrow. "Oh? Any more bad news?"

"That's about it. For now."

Hacksaw hitched up his pants. "Well, I can go without a paycheck for a while, seeing as the team is half-mine. But we'll need to pay Walt and the boys. They won't hang around here without a paycheck."

"We'll get starting money at each race, and money from my other sponsors, but all it amounts to is petty cash. The rest I can borrow from my mother. In the end, I'll be in hock up to my ears."

"You mean, we'll be in hock. Are you sure you want to go through with this, Big Guy?"

"Why? You want to change your mind?"

"No. I just want to be sure you're prepared to do this thing right. I didn't come here to lose."

"Good, because I don't intend to lose. Not this time."

* * *

It was hot, dirty work, cleaning the barn and getting it organized to begin rebuilding a racecar. Ted did the heavy lifting and much of the grunt work, but it was sweaty work for all of them. Around three, Wagner went to the house for ice water, heard the phone ring, and picked it up.

"John, is that you?"

There was no mistaking the voice, even after 14 years. "How are you, Tina."

"Omigod. It is you, John. I don't believe it. Did you get the photo I sent? The one of Ron?"

"Yeah. He looks like a nice kid."

Tina's voice hardened. "I sent that photo four months ago, John. At least you could have had the courtesy to write back and thank me."

Wagner sensed any response he might give would lead to heated words. She hadn't changed. What was the point of them talking, if it meant quarreling again? "I'll tell Katie you called. Take care, Tina."

"No, wait. Don't hang up. I'm sorry, John. I shouldn't have said that." She paused, thankful he was still on the line. "Can you see him? He's almost grown, and it's incredible how much he looks like you--tall and thin."

"You mean skinny, don't you?"

Tina laughed. It was a musical laugh, the way he remembered it.

"Okay. He is skinny, and such a nice boy. Please, come see him. It would mean so much to him, meeting his real father."

"I would like to see him, Tina, but I can't imagine why he would be interested in me. I've been out of the picture an awful long time."

"He's at that age where he's curious about you, John. And he knows you're back in the Valley. In a couple weeks he starts

219

his senior year of high school. Please come. It would mean so much to him."

"A lot of water has gone under the bridge, Tina. I really don't see the point."

"He's your son, John. Isn't that the point? Time goes by so quickly. Before you know it, he'll be married and have children of his own, and then it won't matter anymore."

Wagner looked out the window. The door to the barn was open. He could see Hacksaw and Ted inside working. "How do you want to arrange it? Should I come to you, or maybe your husband would prefer a neutral site?"

"Come here, why don't you? It's only Ronnie and me now. Steve and I divorced years ago."

Chapter 27

Tina lived in the shadow of the San Gabriel Mountains--in Palmdale--a medium-sized town 20 minutes south of Lancaster. For Wagner, it was a trip back in time. He remembered their first date, cruising the drive-ins with her in his Deuce coupe, and, of course, parked at the top of Diablo Pass. Hell, that's how he found the mountain road, looking for a secluded place to park. Inevitably, he remembered the bad times too, the rushed marriage, the army years, the baby, and divorce. It happened so long ago. He was different then, a kid--not much older than Ron was now--with different dreams, different goals, a different outlook on life. He loved fast cars--that much hadn't changed-- but he hadn't yet dreamed of racing Formula Ones, or of winning the world championship. His goal was to run the service department of his father's dealership. Then came the Porsche Speedster, and everything changed. The Speedster was his ticket out of the marriage, out of the dealership, and out of Lancaster-- and into the life he now lived.

He was nearing the house and beginning to feel nervous about seeing Tina again. He couldn't imagine what she looked like now. In his mind, she was still a girl of 21, still had the dew of youth on her face, still had the long black hair. And Ron? The last time he saw him he was in diapers. Now he was 17. He could be any teenager he saw on the street. Meeting him would be like meeting a complete stranger.

Tina's house was in a tract development that butted up against the desert. The streets were anything but desert-like, with well-watered lawns, and trees and shrubbery brought in from somewhere else. Her house was at the end of a cul-de-sac. It was tan with brown trim, had manicured shrubs, perfectly aligned rows of flowers, and the greenest lawn on the block. He parked his Mustang at the curb and walked up the driveway. Near the house, he could smell the freshly cut grass and the rich brown earth of the flower beds. It was a very still afternoon, without a hint of wind, pleasantly warm. He knocked.

Tina opened the door, the same lovely girl he remembered, only now her hair was short and backcombed, and she wore, perhaps, too much mascara. She smiled warmly and crows-feet appeared at the corners of her eyes. She hadn't gained an ounce of fat and still had the same firm well-rounded figure of a girl of perhaps 18.

"You haven't changed a bit," she said. "Same crooked smile, same lanky arms and legs. You look even more like Gary Cooper." She pecked him on the cheek. "Thanks for coming."

"My pleasure," he said, wrapping his arms around her. "You look wonderful, Tina." He breathed in her warm, perfumed scent. "Has it really been 15 years?"

She pushed him away. "Don't get carried away. Yes, it's been all of that. Come in."

The house was as neat as the front yard. Too neat. But that was Tina. The living room looked out onto a patio dominated by a red-brick barbecue.

"Ronnie is out with his friends right now," she said. "I think he's a little nervous about meeting you. He should be back anytime. Will you stay for dinner? I was thinking we could grill some steaks, like old times."

Wagner smiled. Steaks--that was the other thing he and Tina had in common--a love of red meat. Living on army wages, steaks had been the one luxury of their married years. Tina even bought a small charcoal grill on which to broil them. Sunday afternoons, she fired up the grill, put potatoes in the oven to bake, and tossed a big green salad coated thickly in thousand island dressing. They lived like strangers during the week, but on those Sunday afternoons, with steaks sizzling on the grill and beer on ice, they drew close again. Sometimes, the renewed good feelings even carried over to Monday.

"I would like that," he said.

She went to the kitchen and returned with two bottles of beer. She handed him one and pointed to a big upholstered recliner.

"Have a seat."

222

She sat on the sofa facing him, back straight, shoulders squared. Her white sleeveless blouse accentuated her smooth bronze skin. Wagner took a gulp of beer and imagined touching that skin again; running his hands over her smooth firm arms, lightly touching her small neck, feeling her cheeks, kissing her small mouth.

"You never married again, did you?" she said.

He leaned back in the recliner. "No, I never did."

"Not the marrying kind, huh?"

"I guess not, although it wasn't a conscious thing. I just never found anybody that really interested me."

"Ronnie has been following your career for a couple years now and is talking about becoming a race driver himself. What do you think about that? Should I encourage him?"

"If he wants to race, he won't need encouragement. Do you want him to race?"

"Do you?"

Wagner leveled his eyes at her. "Tina, I haven't seen the kid in 15 years, remember? I'm not his parent, or even his father; not really."

"No, you're not. You abdicated that responsibility long ago. Steve is his father. They're still very close, you know. But lately he's been asking about you, wanting to know what you were like and why we split up. Every month, he goes out and buys <u>Road & Track</u> and reads the race reports over and over again. All he talks about is you and Evans and Parks and Boga-what's-his-name."

"Bogavanti."

"Right. I mean, they're--you and the others--are like gods to him. The fact that you're his father, I think, he finds just so incredible. And now he wants to be a race driver like you." She frowned at the irony. "I guess I should have seen it coming."

"What would you like me to tell him?"

She clutched her hands together until her knuckles turned white. "I don't know. But I don't want him to be a race driver, or a cop, which is the other thing he's been talking about. I've tried so hard to bring him up right, keep him out of trouble. He's such a sweet boy. He's even talking about enlisting in the

Marines--after graduation--and going to Vietnam. He's a lot like Steve--very gung-ho. I don't want him to go to Vietnam but I can't talk him out of it. I.." She paused, and looked at him with worried eyes. "How do you feel about the war?"

"Vietnam? I know it's gone on for an awful long time, and kid's are protesting, but to be honest, I don't know much more about it than that."

"Well, you had better learn more about it, because your son may be fighting over there one of these days. Frankly, I don't want him to go."

Wagner swallowed the last of his beer. "He's going to have to go in the service some time."

She took his empty bottle and went into the kitchen. "I know, but I would rather have him go to college first."

"That makes sense. By the time he graduates, this thing in Vietnam will be over."

"I doubt that. I read somewhere that they've been fighting over there for a thousand years. What makes our government think they can stop it?"

"What do you do, Tina, if you don't mind my asking?"

She returned and handed him another beer. "I raise Ronnie," she said, an edge in her voice. "That's enough." Her voice softened. "Actually, I'm a secretary for a building contractor. It's a good job, and I have a lot of responsibility. He even involves me on business deals."

"Does he pay you well?"

"Well enough."

"What's his name?"

"Bill. Bill Schroeder. I've been seeing him socially for some time now."

"Marriage?"

"Maybe. When he leaves his wife."

"He's married?"

"It's not what you think. He takes very good care of me; gives me things, takes me places. We spent a week in Hawaii recently. He'll leave her, when the time is right. What about you? Are you seeing someone? I bet you could get any girl you want, and probably do."

224

Wagner jolted forward in the recliner. "What do you think I do--sleep with a different girl every night?"

Tina smiled, triumphant in his reaction. "I've followed your career over the years. You really have gone far, John Wagner, farther than I ever thought you would."

"Is that a compliment? Or a crack?"

"Take it any way you like."

He looked at his watch. "When is Ron coming back? You did tell him I was coming?"

Tina's smile disappeared. She rose, her face tight as a fist. "Of course, I told him. Why do you think I invited you here, anyway? I don't like your question."

A car rumbled into the driveway. A car door shut and footsteps approached the house.

"That must be Ronnie," she whispered.

Wagner put down his bottle. He rose and tucked in the back of his shirt, which had pulled out slightly.

The door opened and a tall youth entered. He looked just like his picture, only his hair crept over his ears now.

"This is your father, Ronnie."

It was not the awkward moment it might have been, or an emotional reunion of father and son. Steve Reynolds was the boy's father now, and Wagner was not foolish enough to think he could change that, nor did he want to. He greeted the teenager casually, like a friend, not his son. Ron, who at first seemed shy, was relieved with this approach, and warmed up immediately, responding not to John Wagner, long lost father, but to John Wagner, famous race driver. Ron turned fan as conversation inevitably shifted to Wagner's career. It wasn't but a few minutes and the boy had him outside to show off his Camaro. It was metallic blue, had black interior and a four-speed Muncie floor shift.

"I want you to drive it," Ron said, handing him the keys.

Wagner looked at Tina with questioning eyes, and she nodded approval.

"We won't be gone long, Mom," Ron said, as they backed out of the driveway.

Wagner liked the car immediately. It was equipped with 327 cubic-inch engine that delivered more horsepower than the average Joe would ever need. He drove it up into the foothills above Palmdale, where traffic was scarce, and turned onto Angeles Forest Highway, a snaking mountain road that took them high above the desert.

"What do you think of my car?" shouted Ron. He looked at the speedometer as it inched past 90 mph.

Wagner glanced over with a devilish grin. "The horsepower is positively lethal."

For all its brute horsepower, the suspension was mushy and the tires moaned like a wounded animal when pressed in the curves. After repeated braking, the drum brakes began to overheat and fade. Wagner was disappointed but not surprised. The Camaro was typical of Detroit muscle cars: all engine and no brakes or suspension. He reduced speed and cruised through the few curves leading to the mountain top. At the top, he pulled over.

"Enough about me," he said, switching off the ignition. "Tell me about yourself, Ron."

"What's there to tell?" he said in a breaking high-low voice that most teenage boys suffer through at some point. "I'm starting my senior year in a couple weeks."

"How are your grades?"

"I'm no Einstein, but I do okay. I like math."

"What about college?"

"Maybe. But I might skip it and become a cop, like my dad."

"College helps."

"I know."

"And it will keep you out of the army--for four years anyway. And when you do go in, you go in as an officer."

"Mom told you, didn't she? She's worried about me going to Vietnam. When I told her I was thinking of enlisting in the Marines, she flipped out. Did she tell you I wanted to be a race driver too."

Wagner nodded. "Yeah. She did."

"You're not against it, are you?"

226

"I am, as a matter of fact."

"That's so hypocritical. You're a race driver. And don't tell me it's too dangerous. I know it's dangerous. But what isn't? Heck, my dad--I mean, Steve--he's a cop. He's seen guys killed. Kids my own age are getting killed in Vietnam every day. The way you handled my Camaro just now, I want to be able to do that. I want you to teach me how."

"I didn't do anything," snapped Wagner, annoyed. He started the engine, turned the car around and started back down the hill. Why am I so stupid, he thought. I should never have set foot in this blasted car. Tina's going to be mad as hell when she finds out I hot-footed it up here. "Where did you get the money to buy this car, anyway, if you don't mind me asking?"

"Mom bought it for me. She said every boy should have a car for his senior year of high school. Don't you like it?"

"I like it fine, but do me a favor, will you? When we get back, don't tell her I raced this thing. Let that be our little secret, okay?"

Ron smiled knowingly. "Okay. You know what, John? You're all right. I bet you'll even change your mind and help me when I start racing--on the sly, of course, so mom doesn't find out."

Wagner shook his head. Ron was a sharp kid. He had him figured out already.

The steaks were New York strip, nicely marbled, and grilled medium rare, the way they loved them. They dined on the patio and watched the desert sky turn lavender as the sun dropped behind the San Gabriel Mountains. Being with Tina again, and getting to know his son, Wagner had a taste of the life he might have had, had he stayed. Tina certainly was very well preserved. He felt a twinge of regret.

"He's a fine young man," he said, after Ron went in to shower.

Tina had just returned from washing the dishes. She sat down beside him and squeezed his hand. "I'm glad you think so. But I won't kid you--it hasn't been easy."

"I just have one question," he said.

She looked at him with questioning eyes. "What is it?"

"Why on earth did you buy him that Camaro?"

* * *

Team Wagner had grown to a crew of four. There was Ted, gofer and clean up guy; Hacksaw Gilbert, designer, fabricator, machinist, mechanic, and benign dictator; Walt Balchowsky, sheet metal fabricator and organizer of the weekly poker games; and Nigel Long, an Englishman with 12-years Formula One experience, brake and suspension expert, machinist, fabricator, and titanium specialist. That was it. That was Team Wagner, about to take on the might of BRM, Ferrari, and Lotus.

Chapter 28

Susan was unsmiling. "I can't stay. I was in L.A. to interview the Rams' new head coach and Jeremy suggested I come up and see how your team is doing. That's the only reason I came."

Wagner had just arrived at Edington Farm himself, having returned that afternoon from a sales convention in Pittsburgh where he'd made an appearance for one of his sponsors. He was drained from the flight, but perked up seeing her. He grinned crookedly. "It's great to see you, Susie. How about dinner?"

The Italian Grand Prix was a week away. Susan was determined to see the car, get a few quotes, and leave.

"Thank you, no."

"We could drive out to Michel's and enjoy the lake while we eat. Let me shower first; it won't take but a sec."

"John, please. I said no."

Wagner looked at his watch. It was almost five. "What are you going to do? Drive back to L.A. tonight? Then what? Order something up to your room? Come on. It'll give us a chance to talk."

Susan watched him walk quickly to the house. She shook her head. "He didn't hear a word I said."

Hacksaw walked up behind her. "John's been a real bear to be around lately, snapping at everyone all the time, wanting everything done yesterday. Me and the boys was kinda glad to see him leave for a couple of days, if you know what I mean. It's good to see him acting more like his old self again. Let me show you what we've been doing here the last couple of weeks."

He started with the monocoque tub. It had been rebuilt and given a magnesium outer skin, for lightness. "We used magnesium and aluminum wherever we could, given the time we had, to lighten everything up."

"It's painted blue," Susan said, surprised. "I thought the U.S. colors were white with blue trim."

"They are. Ted screwed up. I taught him how to use the spray gun and gave him the paint and said `go to it', but he got the colors ass backwards. No time to repaint it now, I guess."

"Actually, I like the new color."

Hacksaw grinned. "Yeah, so does John. One thing's for sure, with this new color scheme, no one's gonna be mistaking us for that other American outfit."

He showed her Nigel Long's handiwork. The Englishman had fabricated new suspension arms out of thin-wall tubing and the front upper rocker-type a-arms out of titanium, for lightness.

"This used to be an Indy car," Hacksaw said, "built to carry more fuel and a heavier engine and to meet a higher minimum weight requirement, so we been lobbing off pounds here and there and everywhere, and shifting some things around to improve weight distribution, like moving the oil tank from the front to the back, to get more weight over the rear tires. But the main thing we've done is make the car lighter, which is like adding horsepower. When we're done, we should be just under 1200 pounds dry, which is about what the Lotus 49B weighs, so weight-wise we'll be right there."

Susan looked at the workmanship as he talked. The new suspension components glistened from hand-finishing and reminded her of jewelry. And the monocoque tub looked as smooth and unified as a single formed piece, as from a mold.

Off by itself, under a gray tarp, was the Speedster. As Hacksaw talked, Susan's eyes became drawn to it. She could see its partially exposed aluminum wheels and fat black tires. As she stared at it, Hacksaw's words became distant and unintelligible.

"Will we make Monza?" Wagner asked, returning. His hair was combed and still wet from the shower and he was dressed in a fresh blue shirt, tan slacks, and brown loafers. "That's all I want to know."

The crew chief removed his glasses and examined the lenses. "I've got to clean these suckers one of these days. They're gettin' disgusting."

Wagner turned to Susan. "What did he tell you? Will we make Monza or not?"

"He gave me a definite 'Maybe.'"

"That's good enough for me." He took her arm. "Come on. Let's not keep Michel waiting."

It was a clear, bright summer afternoon, hot, but not roasting hot, the desert air dry and soft and scented with sage. After the uncertainty and doubt of a month ago, Wagner felt in control of his destiny again. He had a dedicated team behind him, he was calling the shots, and the rebuild of the Lotus 38 was on target. In the Cosworth V-8, he had a strong and reliable engine. Instead of dreading the final three races, he was looking forward to them. True, he didn't have a major sponsor behind him, and in the end he still would be in debt. So what. Staying in the game was what mattered.

Susan hadn't uttered a word of complaint when he cancelled their vacation, but he knew she was deeply upset with him. He'd meant to call her and make things right once he got to California, but the weeks flew by and the next thing he knew she was back again, having come to him once more. Ostensibly it was to check on the team, but he held out hope she had really come to see him. He couldn't be sure. She was cool, distant, and the gleam in her eye she always had for him was gone. Tonight, somehow, he would have to win her back.

It wasn't long and they were back within the confines of Elizabeth Lake Canyon, turning down the narrow drive to the weathered old A-frame house that was Michel's. Michel greeted them with the same sad eyes and slight smile, seated them at the same table as before, beneath the high wood rafters. Sunlight glittered on the water exactly as before. Wagner placed their orders. Michel returned moments later with an iced tea for her and beer for him.

"Thanks for insisting I come," she said.

"Did I insist?" He sipped his beer.

"You insisted."

"Well, I knew you were pretty upset with me, and I guess I figured we should talk about it."

She turned to look at the lake. She sighed. "I don't know about us, John."

Wagner cradled her hands in his. He looked into her hazel eyes and saw the tinge of green they possessed. "Susie, I'm sorry about cancelling out. Believe me, I didn't want to. It's just that everything sort of fell apart after I got to Milan. I had to do something. I couldn't stand by and watch another championship slip away."

"I know," she said. "and I understand completely. You're not going to let anything interfere with winning the title; me, or anything else."

He let go of her hands. "It isn't that way, Susan."

"It isn't?"

"No. I want the championship, sure, but not at the expense of losing you."

"You sure don't act like it. You know, you could have at least called me once in awhile. You promised to come and see me and never did." Her jaw hardened. "You never did, John. The only time we ever did get together was when I came to you."

Wagner looked at his beer. "I wanted to, but, you know something always happened. The development of wings changed everything. I had to test, or risk falling behind. Not a day went by that I didn't think about you."

"Why didn't you call more?"

He shook his head. "I don't know."

"I understand, John, I truly do, it just took me awhile to realize how you really are. You don't need me. You may think you need me, but all your actions say you don't. I would be lying if I said I wasn't hurt by it--I was, very much. But I'm over it now."

"You mean you're over me, don't you?"

"You aren't really surprised, are you?"

Wagner said nothing.

"I also know about Irene."

"Irene? I told you about Irene."

"The second time, I mean."

"The second time? What are you talking about?"

"After you told me about her, you slept with her again. That second time."

"Where did you get that idea?"

232

"I ran into her, across the street from your flat. I didn't know who she was at the time, but later I put it together. It was Irene Parks, and she was coming from your flat."

"Susie. You're drawing the wrong conclusion."

"Don't lie to me, John. One of the things I admire about you is your honesty. Please don't destroy that too."

Michel arrived with their dinners. "Trout Almondine for mademoiselle and New York strip steak for monsieur." He smiled his cool sad smile. "Will there be anything else?"

"The lady will have another iced tea, and I'll have another one of these." He held up his empty beer glass.

Susan watched Michel depart, then turned back to him. "I know Irene means nothing to you. You love motor racing, first and foremost, which is wonderful. Very few people are lucky enough to love what they do. I just don't want to play second fiddle to your one great love."

Wagner shook his head slowly. "I don't know what to say. You've got me covered at every front. No matter what I say, you've got a response. I love racing more than you, I've been sleeping with Irene again, I don't call, I don't come, but, by god, I am honest. But to hear you tell it, I'm about to destroy that too. What can I say, without sounding like a bum?"

Susan looked at him without emotion. She didn't say anything, but Wagner saw something flicker in her eyes, some stray emotion she couldn't control.

"I can only say one thing," he said, "and that is this--I love you. I didn't realize it until today. I do love you, Susan, more than anything in the world. As for Irene, you're right, I did sleep with her again. That woman is like the devil sometimes, always coming around. It was right after Garret fired me. We kind of picked up again for awhile."

Susan stood up and covered her mouth. "You mean it's true?"

"Susan."

She ran to the ladies room.

Michel rushed over. "Is everything all right?"

233

Wagner's eyes narrowed, looking inward. He shook his head. "I don't know--yes, everything is all right. I'm sorry, Michel. We'll leave."

"No. Is okay."

Susan emerged, composed again.

"Come on, I'll take you back, if that's what you want."

She sat down. There were no tears in her eyes, but there was a tear in her voice. "No, I'm fine."

"I am going to retire ... one of these days."

"I know you are, but I'm not going to wait around for you, John. I was crazy about you, and maybe I loved you. You seemed decent and I thought there was something special between us. We did a few things together, which I will always cherish, but...."

Michel returned. He looked at their meals. They were untouched. "Let me take les diners away. They are cold."

"No, they're fine," Wagner said, distractedly. He looked up. "Everything's fine, Michel, just fine. Okay?"

Michel smiled politely, sensed he wasn't wanted and departed.

"Look, I've got an idea," he said. "How about if I come see you in Chicago after the season's over? We can start over again. I understand Fall is a good time to see the Windy City."

"It's not a windy city. It sounds nice but it will end up being another of your empty promises. Something unforeseen will come up at the last minute and stop you; a sponsor needing to see you, a race somewhere, some business deal. You'll apologize and feel badly about it, but still you will go. And, besides, too much has happened. Pardon my frankness, but I never wanted to become involved with a race driver." Tears reappeared in her eyes. "Oh, John, we never had a future. We're too different, too independent."

Wagner looked at his steak. The juices around the edge were beginning to congeal and turn white. He saw Michel and flagged him over.

"These could use a little reheating."

"Yes, thank you," said Michel, relieved. He removed their dinners.

Wagner looked at Susan, expecting her to say something. She said nothing. He took a swallow of beer and glanced out at the lake. "Actually, one of the things I liked about you was your independence. I liked the fact you weren't calling me all the time. I guess, in the end, you made it too easy for me not to do anything, so I ended up doing nothing. It was never intentional; it just sort of happened. I got caught up trying to win the championship, and, you know, I've been living alone for so long I guess I'm comfortable being this way. But I can change. I will change, for you."

"It's more than that," she said. "I knew when this thing started that we would be apart most of the time. I knew how much you wanted to be champion--that winning is a full-time commitment--and I accepted it. But that was then. Now, now, I realize, I can't live that way. I can't be the housewife who stays home with the children and lives her days like she was a widow. I realize now that I need my man to be around all the time, and not off somewhere. I want a marriage. A true marriage, with a husband who is home every night."

"That sounds fine, Susan, but I don't get it. You're not exactly home every night yourself. What are you saying? That you're going to quit being a sports writer? I thought you loved what you did. I thought that's why we were such a good fit. You had your career, and I had mine."

"I thought so too, but I've changed my mind. I guess one of the things I've learned from this is that when I do find the man I love I will quit my job. I have you to thank for that."

Wagner finished his beer. He was growing tired of the discussion, growing tired of her. Where was the tough/soft girl he had begun to love, the practical forthright girl, the one without illusions. She was starting to sound like every girl he had ever known. If she couldn't change him, she would find someone else to fit her ideal of what she thought love and marriage should be.

"You know what I think," he said. "I think you still love me, or you wouldn't feel this way. I think you've been hurt and you're reacting, instead of thinking clearly."

"You couldn't be more wrong, John."

Michel returned with their dinners. "Trout Almondine for Mademoiselle and New York strip steak for Monsieur."

"These aren't the dishes I sent back," Wagner said.

Michel smiled patiently. "Of course, they are not. I do not reheat le poisson, and the steak was not satisfactory, oui?"

"The steak was fine."

"No more discussion. Eat, please. Bon appetit."

Wagner looked at Susan. "Bon appetit."

The summer sun was still above the rim of the San Gabriel Mountains. They ate without speaking. Michel returned to recite a list of deserts, but neither had an appetite for sugary things.

"You've seen some of the most difficult circuits in the world," Wagner said, laying aside his napkin. He felt edgy. He had the need to drive fast. "How about seeing Diablo Pass, and making a comparison?"

Susan felt something deep inside her stir. Wagner wasn't going to drive slowly this time. The idea was frightening--and exciting. She looked him squarely in the eyes. "You're on."

*   *   *

Back and forth the road went. Trees and mountain cuts whipped past. Susan sat snugly in the bucket seat and took it all in. It seemed only a few minutes and the Speedster crested the mountain pass. The dark hills she remembered were now bathed in the last rays of sunlight, rugged and steep and covered with silver-green sagebrush. In the gloaming below, the waters backed up behind Bouquet Canyon Reservoir were black. Like a hawk closing in on a kill, the Porsche swooped down to the first curve. Susan didn't see any possible way they could slow in time for the curve. When she was certain all was lost and they would die horribly, a calm came over the car as Wagner braked and downshifted. The Speedster leaned slightly and glided through the curve gracefully; no squealing tires, no jerky motions, no panic. Curves began coming in rapid succession: combination left-right, taken very fast, then a hard left, tail drifting out, followed by a hard right, tail drifting the opposite

236

ray, then a series of steep downhill esse curves. It was like schussing down a ski slope, breathless, fast, quick cuts back and forth, ever downward. Wagner's hands and feet were busy, his movements fluid and unhurried. The engine screamed behind them. The chassis leaned this way and that, vibrating, bouncing, but with purpose and precision. Near the bottom, they burst through a mountain cut and the vast black reservoir filled their eyes. As quickly as it appeared, it disappeared as the road circled back around the hill and dropped down to a final hairpin curve. The Porsche rolled through it as effortlessly as the others. It was over. Susan looked back up the mountain they had just come down, stunned they had reached the bottom so quickly, relieved it was over. Now she knew what it was all about. Wagner pulled off the road and stopped.

"That wasn't at all what I expected," she said, feeling out of breath. "It was so smooth. You must have been taking it easy for me."

He smiled crookedly. "Lady, that's as fast as I can drive." He took a deep breath. His face became serious. "Look, I don't want us to end this way. I meant what I said--I love you. Maybe I didn't realize it before, but I do now. Maybe I did some things wrong, but I won't do them again."

She looked down at her hands, folded them, and said nothing.

"I'm going to pursue you, Susie. I'm going to run and not stop until you're mine."

"That's the problem, John, you're always running. If you had me again, you would go off running after something else. Nothing would change."

* * *

Ron Wagner dropped by Edington Farm after school most days, and on weekends. He brought his friends, too, which turned the gravel parking area in front of Katie's house into a kind of showplace for high performance cars. On any given afternoon, there would be a bevy of Chevelles and Mustangs, jacked up to accommodate oversize tires; '56 and '57 Chevies, a

237

mint '31 Ford roadster that caught Wagner's eye, a few Pontiac GTOs, even a lowered yellow Buick Riviera with windows tinted black. But having curious teenagers stepping over parts and asking non-stop questions got to be too much for the work weary crew. Wagner took his son aside and told him he could stay, but his friends had to go.

Hacksaw and the crew were not too surprised to learn Wagner had a son. They hadn't known him that long. But Hacksaw, who had raised two daughters was very disappointed that Wagner hadn't stuck around and been a father to the boy.

"How could you up and walk out on your own son like that, Big John? It's inhuman."

Wagner shrugged. "Never thought about it, I guess."

"Never thought about? He's your own flesh and blood, for crying out loud. Weren't you ever the least bit curious about him?"

Wagner sighed. "Listen, Hacksaw, no one knows better than me that it was a mistake, okay? I keep thinking I have to make it up to him in some way, but there's no way that I can. What's done is done. He calls me 'John' and there is someone else he calls 'Dad'. You think I like that? You think I feel good about that? I keep thinking I'm just a curiosity to him, that once the novelty wears off, he'll forget about me, and that he probably should."

"I don't think so," Hacksaw said.

"Why not?"

"He wants to be like you."

With the monocoque tub finished and painted, final assembly went quickly. The Cosworth engine was installed and new plumbing, cables and wires were routed. The suspension and brakes were installed. Once the tires were installed, Wagner and Nigel Long set the ride height, adjusted the camber and toe in, and selected the anti roll-bar stiffness. The settings were mostly an educated guess. Fine tuning would be done at the circuit. Unfortunately, it would have to be done at Monza, on race weekend, because there wasn't time for testing at Willow Springs. The crew worked 48-hours straight to have the car finished by Wednesday, travel day. The final task was

238

fabricating the exhaust headers; funneling 12 tubes of equal length into four megaphones. Balchowsky didn't complete this job until seven o'clock Wednesday morning, five hours before their departure from LAX. The crew was exhausted and dirty and scratching several days' growth of whiskers, but exhilarated they'd made the deadline.

"It was tight," said Hacksaw, "but we made it. Barely. Right now, I could use a shower and about 24 hours of sleep."

Wagner looked into his bleary eyes. "Sleep on the plane. I want to fire this baby up."

"Forget it," Hacksaw protested. "The brakes need bleeding and there's no gas in the tanks. Hell, we barely got enough time to load up and make the flight as it is. And I want everyone to shower. I don't relish sitting on the plane with this smelly bunch for 12 hours, you included, John."

"There's time, don't worry. I'll siphon off some gasoline from the Speedster. Add coolant and for god's sake make sure there's enough oil in the engine. I don't want to blow our first engine before we even get on the damn race track."

With eight gallons of gasoline in the tank, and coolant and oil added, Wagner flipped on the fuel pump: nothing happened. Hacksaw checked electrical connections and discovered that the battery was missing. There was a mounting place for it on the side of the transaxle, with special brackets that Hacksaw had fabricated himself. The brackets hung loosely, holding nothing.

"Where the hell's the battery, for pete's sake? Ted, I asked you to install the battery this morning. I guess I should have done it myself."

"Oh, shit," said Ted, turning red. "I knew there was something I forgot to do."

With the battery installed, the fuel pumps ticked for what seemed like a minute, until fuel reached the injector pumps. Wagner pressed the starter button. The compact V-8 revolved, sucking in air and fuel and expelling it. Wagner cursed, still pressing the starter button, worried the battery would run down. Finally, the engine kicked, backfired once, shooting a flame out one of the velocity stacks, and came to life. Hacksaw and Fat Walt went around checking water and oil connections. Nigel

Long monitored the gauges. Wagner kicked off his work boots grabbed his helmet and slipped into the cockpit. He worked the steering wheel back and forth, tried the brakes, depressed the clutch and tried each of the five forward gears, revving the engine constantly.

"The brakes need bleeding," Hacksaw yelled, reminding him.

"Screw 'em." Wagner drove out of the barn, past the house, and down the gravel drive to the highway.

"Where's he going?" Ted asked, wide-eyed.

"Test drive," grunted Fat Walt.

"But that's illegal, isn't it?" Ted looked at the crew with questioning eyes. "I mean, the car doesn't have plates or nothin', and no muffler, and ... what if the cops get him?"

The crew's laughter was drowned by the scream of high-pitched exhaust as Wagner accelerated east on Avenue J, away from Lancaster. Gradually, the scream faded, as he put miles of distance behind him.

The flat two-lane road was clear as far as he could see. He upshifted to fifth gear and watched the tach climb to 9000 RPM--150 mph. Wind whipped his face, the chassis bucked over every crack and lump in the road, and alfalfa fields streaked past in two green blurs on either side of him. He was so into it--rocketing down a public road in a Formula One--that he felt like following the road clear to the very end of the paving, a distance of another 14 miles. But he doubted there was fuel enough in the tanks to get him back. Hacksaw was right; the brakes did need bleeding. The pedal was soft as mush. He pumped it several times, slowed and stopped near a small irrigation reservoir. He looked for cars, saw none, and turned around. He nailed the gas, let the tires spin, and laid down a pair of 200-foot-long strips of rubber. In seconds he was back up to 150 mph, blinded by wind and feeling giddy as a kid with a new toy.

Chapter 29

"Hello. Is anybody home?" Giuseppe Bogavanti's dark eyes peered inside the Team Wagner garage. It was Friday morning, an hour before the first practice session was to begin for the Italian Grand Prix. It was bright outside, and it took a moment for the Italian's eyes to adjust to the dim light inside the garage. The air inside was cool and pungent with smells of gasoline, rubber, and new paint.

"So, this is the new American racecar, eh?" he said, running his hand over the bright finish. The dark blue paint was accented with a white center stripe. Painted on the nose and sides were white balls, where Ted was painting in the number 48 in big black letters. The canard wings in front and the wing over the engine were also painted white. On either side of the car were three decals, one for each of the team's sponsors. "It looks very nice, but is it quick?"

"Quick enough to give that Ferrari of yours some heat." Wagner put out his hand. "Nice to see you, pal."

The Italian shook his hand, nodding. "Some heat, yes. I will try to remember that."

"Listen, Bogo, I'm glad you stopped by. I need your help."

"My help? Not again."

"I just came from the Dunlop distributer and they say I owe them $800. You didn't tell me I actually had to pay for those tires I got in Germany."

"Tell them to bill Jano."

"That's just it. Jano's folded, so they're after me. Look, I need tires, at least three sets this weekend, possibly four. I can't afford $800 a pop, plus another $800 on top of that. That's four grand."

"Racing is expensive, Giovanni."

"Look at my car. There's room on the front and rear wings for their decal. Talk to them, will you?"

"You should have listened to me. Honor your contract, isn't that what I said?"

"Don't give me that crap, Bogo. Can you help me or not?"

"I thought I did help you."

"You can do something, with all your connections. Friends, remember?"

The Italian rolled his eyes "Ah, to have such friends. Yes, I will talk to them. But that is it. No more favors."

"Thanks, pal. I knew I could count on you."

"Now, may I ask you something?"

"Shoot."

"Maria is planning a very special dinner for Saturday evening, and she would like you to come."

"Be delighted. Who else is coming?"

"Susan."

"That's it? No one else?"

The Italian nodded.

"You're kidding?

"Why would I kid about something like that?"

"It's over between us."

"Impossible. Maria has made arrangements to send the girls away for the evening. Today she is at the market buying the meat. She is looking forward to meeting this girl of yours, Giovanni. I can't tell her you are not coming. You must come, the two of you. I insist."

"It wouldn't be right. Besides, she wouldn't come, anyway. She's hard-headed. Like me."

"She loves you, John. I saw it in her eyes that night in the caves. Love like hers doesn't go away. Let me to talk to her."

"No. Let me talk to her. I'll get her to come. Somehow."

The Italian's broad face broke into a smile. "Good. Now, let me see about getting you some free tires."

*   *   *

Claudia Liebermann hadn't missed a race since meeting Mal Parks in Belgium, and had joined the ranks of pit women. A perky pixie of a girl, she sat up on the pit counter displaying her

242

retty legs and keeping lap charts for her boyfriend. Mal, who
ad always been oblivious to women on race weekend, was with
er every minute he was not in the cockpit. They spoke in
hispers, as if keeping secrets from the world, and were forever
neaking kisses. BRM Team Manager Vic Watson, and the
3RM mechanics, were finding it difficult to adjust to the new
rrangement. This wasn't like Mal. He even looked different.
lis blond hair was no longer short and greased down. He was
etting it grow, and it partially covered his ears and collar. Every
norning, before coming out to the circuit, he used a blow dryer
) make his hair fluffy. When he put on his helmet, a little flip
f blond hair stuck out at the back.

Friday morning, during the first practice session, the new-
ook Mal took his BRM out onto the circuit and within eight laps
owered the lap record by a full second. Vic Watson scratched
is head. The new Mal maybe was quicker than the old Mal.

*　　*　　*

Dunlop agreed to waive the $800, if Wagner agreed to
urchase their tires for the remainder of the year at a reduced
rice of $400 per set--and, of course, display their decals. Word
ot around to the other tire suppliers--Wagner needed rubber--
nd a Goodyear rep arrived at the Team Wagner garage offering
he very deal the Californian was seeking: free tires in exchange
or decal placement on the wings. Keith O'Leary, Director of
Racing for Unirich, and a long-time friend of Wagner's, came
round, too. He had a determined look on his florid Irish face.

"Look, John, all could be forgiven if you run our tires this
veekend."

"On whose authority?"

"My own and no one else's. If you do run our tires, I'll talk
o Akron and see what more can be done."

Wagner was impatient. "Look, Goodyear's talking contract
or next season, putting serious money in my pocket to run their
rand. Can you match that?"

"Talking? Or have they made you a definite offer?"

"Talk, so far."

"Talk is cheap, John. They're waiting to see how you do Stick with me, friend. If I can't do anything for you, Goodyear will still be around, believe me. Give us this one race, at least You owe us that much."

"You can't do anything, Keith. I spoke with Herb directly He said--and I quote--'not another red cent.' What makes you think you can change his mind?"

"I'm well aware of what he told you. If I approach him right, he might have a lapse of memory. It wouldn't be the first time."

Wagner knew O'Leary was right. Cook was mercurial and talked tough, but he was smart too, smart enough to know when a position was no longer tenable. Like any smart general, he knew when to retreat. "Okay, Keith. You've got yourself a deal I'll run your tires. For this one race. After that, we'll see. But want you to know it's costing me $800."

"What are you talking about--$800?"

"It's what I owe Dunlop. Can you do anything?"

O'Leary frowned as only an Irishman can frown. "You are joking, aren't you? You violated our contract, and now you're asking Unirich to pay for it? You're pushing the limit of my patience, John; quite severely, I might add."

Wagner grinned crookedly. "It never hurts to asks."

*　　*　　*

For a good old boy like Tony Dayton, bred on the unforgiving, rutted dirt tracks of small-town America, Formula One was child's play, or so he was fond of saying. But behind the swagger and bravado lurked a shrewd and calculating man who knew Grand Prix racing was no place for him. Dayton was a winner in whatever he drove--midgets, sprints, champ cars stockers, even sports cars--and that was why Garret hired him But until now, he had avoided Formula One, knowing he couldn't slip behind the wheel and expect to win races as he had done in so many other types of racecars. He knew Formula One took time to master. And that was the problem. The Texan had neither the humility nor the patience to devote two years to

244

earning a whole new game. He accepted Garret's offer because Garret's car was a winner and he was familiar with two of the circuits--Mosport and Watkins Glen. And that the third circuit--Monza--wouldn't be difficult to learn. But most importantly--and the decider for Dayton--Garret was paying him $25,000 per race. Old Tony knew he was putting his reputation on the line, but he didn't have the heart to walk away from $75,000. Wearing a cowboy hat and snakeskin boots, he drew stares at Monza. He tried driving the Garret-Hawk the same way he drove champ cars--tail out, hell-bent-for-leather--and the car simply wouldn't perform. He spun and flat-spotted a set of tires, spun again and flat-spotted a second set of tires, then blew his first engine. That was the morning session. He settled down in the afternoon session, tried a more gentle style, and managed a respectable 1 min 28.5 sec--and blew his second engine. He might have been three for three in blown engines had he not had a three o'clock flight to catch at Malpensa Airport. He had another race the following afternoon in Indianapolis, Indiana--the Hoosier Hundred--on a one-mile dirt oval. He would be back in time for Sunday's Grand Prix, but unbeknownst to him or Garret his plan had a flaw.

*　*　*

Somewhere amidst the concentrated activity of Friday's practice sessions, amidst the harried mechanics and over-officious race officials, amidst the boorish Italian police who seemed to be everywhere, and the excitable <u>Tifosi</u> who were everywhere, Susan went about gathering information for her story. In the morning, she roamed the pits, gathering quotes from Evans and Parks and Bogavanti. In the afternoon, she joined her photographer at the sweeping Curva Grande and the tricky Parabolica, marveling at the drivers' coolness and skill as they set-up and rounded these curves on the barest limit of adhesion. Wagner caught occasional glimpses of her walking the paddock and interviewing people. He kept expecting her to stop in, but she never did. He stayed late at the circuit, shared a spaghetti dinner in the garage with his crew, and returned to his hotel around 11 PM. He was dirty and tired, when he picked up his key from the front desk. The clerk gave him Susan's room number. He was going to ring her, until he discovered her room was on the same floor as his. He knocked instead.

He heard papers rustle, then footsteps. The door opened. The woman looking out at him was wearing glasses. Her red tangled hair was piled high on her head. "Oh, it's you," she said, absent-mindedly.

"Expecting someone else?"

She folded her arms and leaned against the door jam. "I wasn't expecting anyone, not that it's any of your business. Why are you here?"

"To say hello. I didn't know you wore glasses."

Susan took them off. "Oh, these. They're reading glasses." She looked down both ends of the hall. "Why don't you come in a minute."

Wagner stepped in. He saw the piles of paper. "Working on your story?"

"No, something else." She stretched tiredly. "I'm writing a novel. Please, sit down."

He sat on the edge of the bed and cupped his hands. "Bogo has invited us to dinner tomorrow night."

"Us? As in you and me? I hope you said no."

"I want you to come, Susie--for Maria's sake."

She sat in her chair. Her robe flapped opened at the top. Instinctively, she pulled it closed, although there was nothing underneath to see but flannel pajamas. "Who is Maria?"

"His wife."

"His wife? You mean he's married? Who was that hot little number we met in Reims?"

"Who knows. One of the many."

"That guy, I swear."

"Look, Susie. Don't fight it. The guy has a few mistresses. Maria knows it. Everybody knows it. It's just the way it is."

She rose. "Forget it. I'm not going."

"Maria's going to a lot of trouble. They're friends of mine, old friends of mine, since my days with Ferrari. She wants to meet you."

246

"Why doesn't she leave him, for heaven's sakes?"

"That's their business, Susan. Maria's a terrific cook. It should be an enjoyable evening. What do you say?"

She crossed her arms. "I'll think about it."

"Fine. You think about it." He rose. "I'll pick you up at eight. I might even wear my suit."

"John?" she said, as he opened the door.

He faced her. "What?"

"I'll be ready."

Chapter 30

The road to Bogavanti's villa wound through orange and lemon groves, and vineyards where laborers picked grapes in the lingering sunlight. Below the road, Lake Como shimmered in silver coolness. Riding in Wagner's borrowed Ferrari roadster, Susan closed her eyes and breathed it all in. She would miss his life of fast cars and fast driving as surely as she would miss him. Maybe she would buy a Porsche, she thought. A bright red one, like the Ferrari she was riding in.

Bogavanti saw them coming up the long drive to his house. He stepped down from the porch and opened Susan's door. "You look beautiful," he said, admiring her strapless white gown, especially her cleavage, slight as it was. He kissed her cheek and turned to his old friend. "Nice car, Giovanni. Enzo would be proud."

Wagner removed his sunglasses to have a better look at the house. It was an imposing two-story structure, with cream-colored stone facade and doric columns on either side of the large entry.

"Nice place, Bogo. Wish I could afford it."

"You should endorse more products, Giovanni; that's where the real money is. I could never afford this on what Ferrari pays me, although this is quite modest compared to some of the villas in the area. A British king built this for his mistress in the 18th century."

"Why am I not surprised?" Susan said softly, following Bogavanti into his home.

Maria was petite, darkly beautiful, and hard working. With the aid of a single maid, she kept the large house and raised five daughters. The dinner she served--veal cooked in white wine with ham, bacon, sage, and rosemary; steamed summer vegetables; and polenta--she prepared herself. Dinner was served on the patio, overlooking the lake, where the scent of jasmine was strong.

"It was wonderful of you to invite us," Susan said, taking up a fork.

"It was nothing," said Bogavanti.

"That is not true," interrupted Maria. "It was a lot of work but I enjoyed doing it. Since John left Ferrari, I rarely see him anymore. And it is a pleasure to have you here, Susan. John is fortunate to have you. Aren't you, John."

"I am." He looked at Susan. "Very lucky."

"How long have you been seeing each other?" Maria took a bite of veal and chewed it thoughtfully.

"Well," said her husband, looking at her. "Does the veal meet your standard?"

"It is satisfactory," Maria said without emotion.

Bogavanti lifted a glass of wine. "Maria says the veal is satisfactory. Let us drink a toast." He raised his glass. "To the veal."

"To answer your question," Wagner said, after the toast, "we've been seeing each other since April--on and off."

"More `on' than `off,' I hope," Maria added, tartly.

"Actually," said Susan, playing along with the charade, "almost all of my assignments are in the States, and with John in Europe all summer, it's been difficult to see one another."

"Have you thought of quitting?" Maria smiled at Susan. "So you and John could be together."

"Not really. You see, writing about sports is not merely a job, it's what I love doing. Sometimes, I can't believe they actually pay me to do it."

"But what about children? You do want to have children?"

"Maybe."

"Maybe?" Maria's face frowned with disdain. "What kind of marriage will you have without children? Children are the cement of marriage. It's what binds a man and woman together."

Wagner put down his fork. "Who said anything about marriage?"

Bogavanti smiled at his wife patiently. "Ah, Maria, my dear one, not everyone wants to have children, as you and I did. I

John wanted a family, he would have married--years ago. And Susan is a career woman. Career women rarely have children."

Maria looked at Wagner. "You want to have children, don't you John?"

Wagner smiled, imagining the surprised looks on their faces should he tell them he had a son. He would, at the right time. This wasn't the right time. He straightened his tie. "Children? I don't know."

"I do." Susan looked at him with steady eyes. "I want kids. But not by an absent husband."

"Yes, I know what you mean." Maria patted her husband on the hand. "But my Giuseppe will be retiring soon, and be always at my side. Won't you, darling?"

Bogavanti smiled. "Of course, my love."

"Tell this man of yours," Maria said with a nod towards Wagner, "that if he's serious about you he will retire and be always at your side."

"She already has," Wagner said, and dropped his fork. It clanked loudly on the glass table.

*   *   *

It began at dawn.

The Tifosi crowded through the gates of the <u>Autodromo Nazionale di Monza</u> and like streams of ants flowed to all points of the 3.6-mile circuit. They filled grandstands, lined up four- and five-deep behind chain-link fences, climbed trees, found lodgement atop billboards and poles, ventured anywhere and everywhere to get a better view of the action. If they trespassed into a restricted area, a few thousand lira were pressed into a policeman's palm and the transgression was ignored. At eleven o'clock, the first of several preliminary events got underway, and the smoke of speeding cars mixed with the sultry air and hung like a pall over the wooded dells of the one-time royal park.

To Wagner, it seemed the three o'clock start would never come. He needed solitude before the race and there was none. He had no transporter to hide in and his hotel was across town. Ninety minutes before the race, one of his friends with North

Coast Oil offered him sanctuary in their transporter. He gratefully accepted, and entered the big rig about the time Tony Dayton and Edward W. Garret were sitting down to a hastily-called meeting with the course clerk.

*　*　*

"I must inform you," said the clerk, his hands clasped before him on his desk, "that Mr. Dayton cannot drive in today's race. The rule is quite clear. A driver cannot compete in a Grand Prix within 24 hours of competing in another race."

Dayton jumped to his feet, as if to grab the $25,000 he saw flying out the window. "That's got to be the most dumb-ass thing I ever heard. And why not?"

"Because you are not properly rested."

Dayton turned to Garret. "Do I look rested to you?"

"Absolutely." Garret did not take his eyes off the official. "Mister, my driver just spent 10 hours sleeping on an airplane. I'm also aware of the rule and happen to know it's seldom, if ever, enforced. Why are you singling me out?"

"I cannot speak for other circuits, only Monza. I am certain Mr. Dayton is sufficiently rested. However, should he have an accident today--through no fault of his own, of course--the blame would rest on this office for having relaxed the rules. So, you see...."

"That's baloney," Dayton said.

"Excuse me?" said the course clerk, not comprehending the metaphor.

"I know what this is really about. You're afraid a real racecar driver is gonna whip these Formula One sissies."

*　*　*

Wagner stepped outside and pushed his way through the crowd, ignoring calls for his autograph. The pits were rife with the usual pre-race tension. Hacksaw and the others nodded to him and said nothing. He put on his helmet and gloves, grabbed a spare set of goggles, and followed his crew as they pushed his blue Lotus to the front of the starting grid.

Italian Grand Prix
Sunday, September 8

PARKS	EVANS	WAGNER
BRM	Lotus	Lotus
1 min 26.1 sec	1 min 26.2 sec	1 min 26.3 sec

PHILLIPS	LAFOSSE
Brabham	Matra
1 min 26.4 sec	1 min 26.6 sec

BOGAVANTI	STOCKTON	EDWARDS
Ferrari	BRM	Cooper
1 min 26.7 sec	1 min 26.9 sec	1 min 27.0 sec

He settled into the cockpit and waited. Hacksaw held a sun umbrella over him. His only real concern was the water temperature--the engine had been running on the hot side.

Engines started. The field stormed away for a warmup lap, returned to the grid, and engines switched off. Some drivers climbed out. Wagner stayed seated. Gofer Ted rubbed down the finish for what seemed the fiftieth time while Nigel and Fat Walt made sure everything was tight and fastened down, retorqued the wheels and checked air pressure. Hacksaw leaned in close to the driver. Wagner expected him to say something, but the crew chief merely observed the water temperature. It was normal, but it didn't change the crew chief's worried look.

Two minutes. Drivers returned to their cars. One minute. Engines restarted. Crewmen retreated to the sideline. Seconds ticked down. The starter waved the flag. Wagner jumped away in a smooth burst of power, leading the pack into Curva Grande. Coming out, he glanced in his mirror. Evans and Parks were hard on his tail, followed by Phillips, Lafosse, Bogavanti, and Stockton. He checked the water temperature. Okay so far.

253

Ahead, the twin Lesmo curves appeared first as a clearing in the trees, then as a tongue of asphalt bearing hard to the right. He eased on the brakes, bringing his speed down gently, downshifted to third gear and turned in. Coming out, he accelerated, upshifted to fourth, and rounded the second Lesmo with foot hard to the floor. Exiting, his tires shook and shafts of light burst through the treetops and danced on the finish of his car. Evans and Parks sparred with one another in his mirror, while the others fell back in a long broken line. At 170 mph, the dip under the old circuit banking passed with a queasy toss of his stomach. He tapped the brakes to settle the chassis and leaned into the fast Ascari left-hander. He felt the tail twitch, wanting to slide, the tires right there, on the edge. Off to his right, the woods fell away revealing the paddock garages and backside of the pits. Accelerating back up to 170 mph, he drifted over to the left for the Parabolica, a looping right-hander that would take him back to the front straight. Holding his machine smooth and steady, he braked, downshifted directly to second gear and pitched the Lotus into the curve. The chassis leaned hard. He squeezed the throttle, gaining speed rapidly as the curve opened onto the front straight. The pits and main grandstand rolled back into view, grew to towering proportions, and flashed behind him.

For several laps, he played cat-and-mouse with Evans and Parks while his water temperature gradually crept up. By lap eight, it was dangerously high. He reduced RPM, and immediately Evans and Parks whooshed past without so much as a glance. Nuts. There was no staying with them, not if he expected to finish. By limiting the engine to 9800 RPM on the straights, the water temperature gradually dropped to normal.

In his mirror, like a pack of hungry wolves, Phillips, Lafosse, Bogavanti and Stockton, closed in for the kill. When they caught him on lap 16, the four cars swept past so fast he had to scramble to catch their slipstream. In traffic again, his water temperature climbed again. He felt sick and disgusted. Should he drop out of the slipstream and fall further behind, or hang on and hope for the best? He was debating this when the tail of Bogavanti's Ferrari began to smoke. The red car pitted. That ut him sixth. He looked past Stockton and Lafosse and saw hillips' metallic-green Brabham leading the pack.

"The hell with it," he thought. "I'm going to pass this bunch nd run in clean air." He upped his RPM, swung out to pass tockton's BRM, only to have the Welsh driver block him.

"Here we go again," he muttered. "I should have punched ut Pete's lights at Spa, and I wouldn't be having this trouble ow."

He tried again and was blocked again. He glanced at his vater temperature. The needle was so high it was running out of umbers. He slipstreamed the Welsh driver out of the Parabolica nd feinted a pass to the right, then to the left, then back to the ight. A hole opened and he passed him, shaking his fist as he vent by. The bastard. Taking Lafosse was a snap. That left hillips. He was setting him up when his eyes were drawn to his nirror. A white substance billowed from his tail.

Steam.

He pitted clinging to the remote chance Hacksaw would find loose hose connection or something as simple, repair it quickly nd send him on his way again. He stayed seated while the crew hief removed the engine cover and looked around. Meanwhile, 'at Walt kneeled at the back of the car and peered inside one of he exhaust pipes. Speckled on the patina of carbon were tiny eads of water.

"Headgasket," snorted Fat Walk.

Hacksaw replaced the engine cover. "Hear that, John?"

All of the worry and sweat and anguish of the past five veeks, all of the aggravating problems overcome at Monza, all f the tension and build-up before the race, had all come to othing. Wagner climbed from the cockpit slowly, feeling as if e would explode from sheer frustration. A green car slowed nd dipped into the BRM pits, misfiring badly. Wagner removed is helmet and handed it to Hacksaw.

"Take this," he said, walking in the direction of the BRM pit.

"Hey, where are you going?"

"I have a score to settle."

Stockton climbed from his car startled to see Wagner's lushed face leering at him.

"Take off your helmet, Pete."

Vic Watson stepped between them. "John, what are you doing here? What is the meaning of this?"

"Stay out of this, Vic. Pete, take off your helmet."

"You don't belong here, John," yelled Watson. "Leave."

Stockton removed his helmet coolly and grinned. "You wouldn't."

"Yeah? Watch this." Wagner swung.

Stockton ducked and the Californian missed and reeled over from the force of his swing. He turned around and swung again only to be stunned by two quick blows to his face, neither one of which did he see. His knees buckled and he found himself seated on the pit apron quite involuntarily.

Still grinning, the welshman put out his hand. "Better get up before someone runs over you, mate. Here, let me help you."

Wagner pushed his hand away. "Get away from me."

"Have it your way."

Wagner stood up, weaving like a drunkard. Funny. He didn't feel hurt. In fact, he didn't feel anything. Why couldn't he stand up straight? He leaned toward Stockton. "I ought to pound you in the ground."

"You better get something for that left eye," he said. "It looks rather nasty."

"Come on, Big Guy," said Hacksaw, appearing out of nowhere. He wrapped an arm around Wagner's shoulder. "This just ain't your day."

Italian Grand Prix Top Six Finishers		Championship Point Leaders Race Nine of Eleven	
Driver	Points	Driver	Points
Evans	9	Wagner	42
Parks	6	Parks	36
Phillips	4	Bagavanti	34
Lafosse	3	Evans	32
Edwards	2	Phillips	20
Giraud	1	Lafosse	17

Chapter 31

It was the end of summer, but the countryside surrounding Akron, Ohio was its usual spring green. Most U.S. tire makers were headquartered here, under a skyline of smokestacks at the city's edge. The commercial jetliner Wagner was aboard flew directly over Akron, made a half-circle above the cornfields west of town, and touched down at Akron-Canton airport. A limousine waited there to take him to the Unirich World Headquarters on East Market Street. When he arrived, he was escorted to the president's suite on the fourth floor, where Herb Cook stood motionless over his putter. Cook looked as lean and hungry as ever, his salt-and-pepper hair perhaps having a little more salt and a little less pepper than the last time Wagner saw him.

"How was your flight?"

"For once the sky wasn't overcast coming in."

Cook tapped the ball wide of the cup and scowled. "Damn." He laid his putter aside and motioned the driver to a sitting area. Outside his big window smokestacks churned out black smoke.

"We call that the `lake effect.' Depressing as hell, let me tell you. Coffee?"

Wagner seated himself. "Nothing, thanks."

Cook pulled up a chair and faced him. "What happened to your eye?"

Wagner touched his left eye. The skin around it was black, but the swelling was down. He'd been keeping it hidden behind sunglasses, but it didn't seem appropriate to wear them meeting with the president of a four-billion dollar company. "I bumped into someone's fist."

Cook chuckled. "I should say you did. Never take on anyone bigger than yourself, John-boy."

"He was about a foot shorter than me, to tell you the truth."

"I hope he got the worst of it."

"Never touched him--too quick. Fighting was never my game, anyway."

Cook removed a pack of cigarettes from his breast pocket and offered him one. "Still quit?"

"Yeah."

"Good for you." Cook lit up and inhaled. "Let me tell you something. I was damned pleased to see you run our tires at Monza." He exhaled and watched the smoke rise. "Damned pleased. That's the kind of loyalty that could almost make me forget about Germany." He paused and looked Wagner hard in the eyes. "Almost. I'm still mad as hell at you, but as a businessman I can't ignore the fact that you still might become champion. You've put together a team, and stolen Hacksaw out from under Garret's nose. You know, on top of being a damn good race driver, you might have a head for business."

Wagner shifted uneasily on the sofa. "I was lucky."

"Lucky, hell." Cook blew a smoke ring. "I don't believe in luck. The luckiest people in this world are the ones who are the hardest working. Always have been. Always will be. You sure you don't want a cup of coffee?"

"I'm sure."

Cook snuffed out his cigarette. "Well, I want some. Janet."

A well preserved woman of about 40 appeared in the doorway. Her blond hair was combed back and tied in a bun, giving prominence to her pinched nose and pointed chin.

"Janet, get me some coffee, will you? A pot and a couple cups." He looked at Wagner. "You take cream and sugar, don't you?"

"No."

"No cream or sugar, Janet."

Cook leaned back. "Now, about why you're here. Have you ever thought about Indy? Racing there, I mean?"

"No. Can't say that I have."

"You should, because Unirich is testing tires right now for next year's `500.' And we're signing up top drivers, like Tony Dayton. He's been tough to corner, but I think we've hooked him with the Formula One deal. He likes our tires, but I'd hate to tell you what it's costing us."

"Driving for Garret, you mean?"

Cook nodded.

"I can't believe you would be part of that, Herb, after what Garret did to me."

"It's business, John, pure and simple. Like I said, I wanted Dayton running our tires at Indy next year and saw this as a way to bring him over to our side. I had to sweeten the deal with some cash, but it worked out."

"How much cash?"

"That is none of your business."

Wagner folded his arms. "Why am I here?"

Cook reached into his coat pocket and removed an envelope. "Here."

Wagner took the envelope and stared at it a moment.

"Go ahead, open it."

It was a check for $20,000. Wagner nodded.

"Try to look happy, John. I went to a lot of trouble to get that for you. I may be president of this company, but it doesn't mean I can do whatever I want. A lot of people around here didn't want you back, and one of them was the CEO. I did what I could, which is pretty damn good, considering. And thank Mr. O'Leary next time you see him."

Wagner fingered the check and considered giving it back. Goodyear was up the street. He could go there and maybe cut a better deal.

"You mentioned Indy," he said. "Is Unirich bailing out of Formula One?"

"No, but Indy's where we'll be allocating much of our racing budget over the next few years. Since Goodyear's come into the game, the battle's heating up. We've jumped in and already we've got the best guy--Tony Dayton. And we're talking to Ed Garret about building six or seven Indy cars for next year, so our drivers will have top equipment. One of those cars will go to Tony, and one could go to you, if you decide to run Indy. Think about it. A brand new racecar and a couple of turbo Fords, all at no cost. Plus a healthy retainer. Imagine following up your world championship with a win at Indy? It's enough to make your mouth water."

259

Janet returned with the coffee. She set the pot and cups on the coffee table between them and departed.

Cook sipped his coffee and looked at the driver. "Well, what do say?"

"I say she's very attractive."

"I think so."

"Sleeping with her?"

"That is none of your damn business." He looked at his watch. "I have a meeting in exactly 12 minutes. Do we have a deal or don't we?"

Wagner folded the check. "Let me have one of your cigarettes and I'll think about it."

Chapter 32

As the first rays of sunlight crept over the California High Desert, three trucks departed Edington Farm and drove east; Hacksaw's stepvan, with enough tools and equipment to outfit a respectably-sized auto repair shop; a second van loaded with spare parts including a pair of Cosworth V-8s; and a pickup pulling a trailer carrying an open-wheeled racecar. Nightfall, three days later, they arrived in Bowmanville, a sleepy town on the north shore of Lake Ontario, and checked into the Bowmanville Lodge. The following morning, they reached their destination: Motorsport Park, Willowdale, Ontario, or, as it is better known, Mosport. It was deserted.

Where was everyone? Wagner climbed from the truck and looked around. Was the Canadian Grand Prix being held elsewhere this year? At St. Jovite, another day's journey further east? Had he somehow gotten it wrong? "We might as well turn around and go home," he said. "We won't make St. Jovite until nightfall, which means we lose the first day of practice. We can't lose a day of practice and expect to compete. I swear. Can't one thing go right, one stinking little thing?"

The dull roar of a diesel engine sounded in the distance. Wagner looked back down the road, hoping it was what he thought it was. Whatever it was, it was coming their way.

"Well, I'll be darned," said Hacksaw.

"I'll be darned too." Wagner shook his head. "For a second there, I thought I was going nuts."

"I think we're all going a little nuts," said the crew chief. "It goes with the job."

Two big tractor trailers roared up the hill, passed through the paddock gate, parked side-by-side, and disgorged their cargo; three cars each for the factory teams--British Racing Motors, Scuderia Ferrari, Matra Sport, Repco Brabham, Team Lotus, and Cooper Cars; and two each for the independents--R.R.C. Walker Racing Team, Scuderia Dominic Martini, Equipe Nationale

Belge, and one car each for Rolf Gehring and Mark Ryan. Garret-Hawk's white and blue transporter was next to arrive, followed by supplier trucks and big fuel rigs, unloading truckloads of tires, drums of fuel and lubricants, and a warehouse of equipment. Tents went up, booths opened, and banners were raised, much as a circus-come-to-town. An engine started, and another, and another. The crisp morning air filled with the acrid smells of hot exhaust and burning oil. One-by-one, drivers slipped into their machines and darted away.

Wagner bedded in new brakes and tires, increased speed, and spun in Turn One, a harmless, embarrassing spin. He turned his machine around and drove slowly back to the pits.

"The damn track's bumpier than hell," he said, "especially One and Three. I'm getting beat around so much I can hardly keep the sucker on the road. It's pushing bad, it keeps popping out of second, and there's a vibration in the rear at anything over 7000 RPM in fifth gear."

Hacksaw hitched up his pants and gave him his best irritated look. "You got any good news, fella?"

"Yeah," the driver smirked. "The overheating's gone. You fixed it."

In the afternoon session, the car was better, but under hard braking the nose was diving. Rather than pit and waste more time changing the setup, Wagner tried finessing the brakes, easing them on early and not as hard, which cost him a couple tenths, but kept chassis attitude flatter going into the curves. The suspension didn't shake as much over the bumps, thanks to softer springs, so he was getting better grip and cornering faster. As he went round and round, adjusting to the new setup, he found his rhythm. He pitted again, lowered tire pressure slightly and adjusted the tail wing to give the rear tires a tad more bite. With this setup, he felt comfortable, and pushed the car to the edge, where his heartbeat quickened. Walking a tightrope, he managed two quick laps without a bobble, and pitted again. A Unirich tire technician took a reading of his tires and handed him the numbers. The driver nodded. He turned to Ted.

"Well? What's my quick time?"

Ted was the chosen one--timekeeper. He looked up, slightly befuddled. "Huh?"

"My quick time, please?"

"Uh, lessee, a minute twenty-six-point-eight."

"That isn't right."

Ted ran his finger down the numbers. "Wait a sec. A minute nineteen-nine. That's your quickest time. One minute, nineteen point nine seconds."

Wagner grabbed a towel and rubbed the sweat out of his hair. "The car still pushes in One and Three, and we haven't played with the wings much. I can knock another half-second off that time easy, maybe a full second, if we get everything right."

More changes were made and Wagner went back out again. He was warming up the tires and brakes when a familiar car appeared in his mirror.

Number 36.

He could see Tony Dayton's white helmet and trademark red bandanna pulled tightly across his mouth, and a determined look in his eyes. The Texan stayed glued to his tail, following him from curve to curve. Wagner speeded up, and Dayton speeded up. He slowed again, and Dayton slowed. Coming into Turn Two, Dayton pulled even with him, stayed there a moment, and fell back again. He did the same thing at Turn Five. Coming up the hill, the Texan blew past, his V-12 sounding shrill and clear. Wagner watched the white-and-blue car veer through Turn Six and disappear over a crest in the road. On the backside of the crest, braking for Turn Eight, Wagner's eyes were drawn to an explosion of dust and debris, outside the curve.

"Dayton. Shit."

He stopped quickly and jumped from his car, running to the crash. Amidst the dust and steam and smoke he could see the Texan trying to free himself from the cockpit.

"My legs are pinned," he yelled, more angry than hurt. A section of twisted guardrail lay across the chassis midsection, inches from Dayton's face. The engine was silent, but leaking fuel was spreading on the ground, towards the still-glowing exhaust headers.

263

"Hang on, Tony. I'll get you outta there."

"I am hanging on. I ain't got no choice. Just make it quick, hear?"

Wagner leaped over the guardrail, ripped off what was left of the cowl and peered inside the chassis. A bulkhead was folded over the Texan's legs. Hacksaw had fabricated it from aluminum to save weight. Wagner gave the member a pull and felt the soft metal bend back. Dayton's knees were bloody but he pulled them free. Wagner stepped back over the rail and helped him stand up. "Can you walk, cowboy?"

"Hell yes." Dayton stepped from the cockpit and fell face-first in the dirt.

Wagner dragged him up. "You sure?"

"I said I can walk, didn't I?" he hissed through clenched teeth. He took another step and bent over in agony, but stayed on his feet. He rose slightly, took another step, and another, limping slowly away from the wreckage that had been his racecar.

A fire truck arrived and doused the car with white foam until it looked like so much vanilla ice cream.

"Listen, partner, thanks for getting me the hell out of there," Dayton rasped between breaths. "For a second there, I thought I was a goner."

"What happened?"

"Aw, the dang nose keeps lifting on me ever' time I come over that dang hill there. This time the car kinda took off on me." He chuckled, then grimaced from pain. "For a second there, I thought I was gonna fly all the way back home to Fort Worth. I do swear, these are the damnedest little cars. Sorry I got in your face on the track a moment ago. You don't rattle easy, do you?"

"Want some advice?"

"Not really, but go ahead."

"You're hitting the hill too fast. Back off early--before you crest it--and don't get on the brakes until you're on the backside. Let the car sort of flow over the top, know what I mean? Then brake. It'll seem slow at first, but you'll hit Eight smoother and pick up a couple of tenths."

An ambulance veered off the track and bounded toward them in a cloud of dust, red lights flashing.

"Here comes my ride. You put yourself at risk a moment ago. Old Tony don't forget about things like that."

Chapter 33

Susan looked at her watch. It was twelve-sixteen. Wagner was late.

It was Saturday, the second day of practice, and it was warm and pleasant where she was sitting. Wagner had agreed to meet her for an interview at noon, at the outdoor cafe behind the pits. She had her portable tape recorder set up and her notes out. Where was he?

She ordered a second coke and wished she were somewhere else, somewhere far from this place, on another assignment, covering baseball, or football, anything but motor racing and John Wagner.

"Sorry I'm late," he said, appearing at last. He sat in the chair beside her. "I just came from the administration office. My life's been a lot more hectic these days, now that I'm running things. How are you, Susie? You look terrific."

She didn't smile. "I'm fine. What happened to your eye?"

He touched it. "This? You should have seen it two weeks ago."

"Don't tell me you got into a fight?"

"One swing and it was over--for me. Pete Stockton. How was I to know the guy boxed in the Olympics?"

"Who started it? Not you, I hope."

"Me?" He chuckled. "I'm a little old for that, don't you think?"

"You did start it, didn't you?"

"Let's just say he finished it, and let it go at that."

Susan smiled faintly. "What am I going to do with you?"

"Something wonderful, I hope."

She looked at her notepad. "While I was sitting here waiting, I did some calculating. Did you know that if you win tomorrow, and Parks finishes no higher than third, you'll be champion? The only way Evans or Bogavanti can stay in contention is if you finish second or worse."

He nodded, looked at his hands, and looked at her. "Mind I change subjects? What are you doing tonight?"

"John, please."

"I was thinking maybe we could drive in to Toronto and have dinner somewhere. There's a jazz club I know about where we might have coffee afterwards."

"I don't see any point to it."

"It might be fun. What's wrong with that?"

"Well, for one thing, you have a race tomorrow."

"Yeah, and tonight I don't want to think about it."

"... And for another I have a story to write. If I don't do some writing tonight I'll only have more work tomorrow when I'm under the gun of a deadline. And ..." her voice trailed off, "I want to move on emotionally."

"I miss you, Susie."

"Get over it."

"I miss hearing your voice, I miss touching your hair, I miss all those unpredictable things you do."

Were those tears he saw forming in her eyes? He clutched her hands. "Listen to me, Susie...."

She pulled away. "No, you listen to me. I'm not going to be like Maria Bogavanti, sitting at home worrying about you while you're out running around, or like Laura Tambala attending your funeral."

He sat back. "I bet you'd look lovely in black."

"I won't attend your funeral, John Wagner."

A hardness came over his face. "Not all race drivers die, Susie. You want to know why Carlo died? He made a mistake. He was driving over his head and it caught up with him. Hell, the guy spun right in front of me, a couple of times. You'd think it would have scared the hell out of him, and maybe put some sense in his head, but he kept right on driving like a madman. was scared out there, and not just of him, but of the conditions. I've always been a little scared, because I know how easy it is to get killed. I know just how fine the line is between winning and crashing, and I respect the hell out of it. Carlo? He respected nothing that day, and it reached out and bit him." He looked around. "Where's the waiter? I'm ready to order."

268

The mood had changed. Wagner made no more mention of dinner. They ordered lunch and Susan interviewed him while they ate. Afterwards, he excused himself and left her with her tape recorder and her notes and the wrappers and paper cups of what had been their lunch.

Practice resumed in the afternoon. As he had been both days, Wagner was quickest.

Canadian Grand Prix
Sunday, September 22

WAGNER	EVANS	BOGAVANTI
Lotus	Lotus	Ferrari
1 min 18.8 sec	1 min 19.1 sec	1 min 19.6 sec

PARKS	PHILLIPS
BRM	Brabham
1 min 19.8 sec	1 min 20.0 sec

EDWARDS	LAFOSSE	STOCKTON
Cooper	Matra	BRM
1 min 20.4 sec	1 min 20.5 sec	1 min 20.8 sec

The race was underway. Wagner glanced in his mirror at the cars fighting for position behind him: Evans, Bogavanti and Parks, then Phillips, Edwards, Lafosse, Stockton and Greenman, a gap, then Phil Hill subbing in the second Ferrari, Giraud, and Tony Dayton in the lone Garret-Hawk, then Pisecky, Gehring, van Zwet and Lehmann, Fillol, Chasseuil and Valenti. Bringing up the rear was the South African, Mark Ryan, in a very tired and very old Cooper-Climax.

Coming up the hill, Wagner backed off for Turn Eight and felt his body become light cresting the low hill where Dayton had gone off. As the chassis sat back down, he eased on the brakes and leaned his machine into the fast right-hander. Exiting, he set up quickly for Turns Nine and Ten that formed an esse curve that put him back on Pit Straight. Evans' red-and-gold machine clung to his tail, but the others were falling back, knotting up in groups of three-and-four.

It wasn't long and backmarkers began arriving in his path. First was Ryan, whom he passed quickly, then Valenti, Chasseui, and Fillol, in a tight group. Passing them took care. He looked back, and Evans was still with him. The next group was spread out and arrived like dodgem cars--dart left to pass Lehmann's white Brabham, cut right to get around van Zwet's Walker Lotus, right again, to pass Gehring's lumbering Cooper-Maserati. Wagner looked back again. A gap had opened between him and Evans.

Good. He was losing him.

On lap nine, more cars arrived: Jan Pisecky in one of the red BRMs, Jacques Giraud in the second Matra, and Hill's Ferrari. Pisecky was an easy pick-off, but Giraud and Hill were driving factory cars and tougher to get around. Evans closed the gap again. Was there no shaking this guy?

The next car was Dayton's Garret-Hawk. Wagner caught him coming back up the hill, followed him over the crest into Eight--Dayton took it smooth and fast--and around Nine and Ten and onto Pit Straight. Was the Texan going to let him pass, or make him fight for it?

Pay back time, Tony, remember?

Rolling off One, the Texan raised a hand and pointed to his left. Dayton was letting him by. Attaboy, Tony. After I'm past, if it's not too much trouble, would you hold up Evans for awhile? For, say, the remainder of the race?

Cresting the hill, he pulled even with the Garret-Hawk. As the road fell away into the fast left-hander, he felt his machine lean to one side, felt his tires strain to hug the curve. Something caught his eye, something shiny and spinning, inside the curve. Was that the wheel of another car trying to pass him here? There wasn't room. Evans was forcing his way into a lane that didn't exist. In that brief instant, with both cars suspended in the curve--suspended in time--if he could have, he would have reached out and pulled Evans from his machine and crushed out his life and felt good about it. In the next instant, their wheels touched and the delicate balance of grip was broken.

270

The world upshifted into hyper-speed, blurring past Wagner's eyes in a kaleidoscope of colors, while time itself continued to tick excruciatingly slowly. He was all too aware of what was happening, aware that he might hit something, might flip over, be thrown from the car, hurt or killed. He saw Dayton speed on, unscathed, while Evans was spinning somewhere off to his right. He hung on to the steering wheel, felt his tires scrub into the gravel verge, heard the buckshot sound of gravel beating against the magnesium exterior. Having spent its energy, his car slid to a stop. The engine stumbled, about to die. He gassed it, but nothing happened. The pedal was stuck. Nuts. Stones must have lodged in the throttle slides and jammed it, he thought. He pressed harder and felt the throttle cable snap and the pedal collapse to the floor. The engine went silent.

Across the road, Evans righted his machine and sped away.

Wagner climbed from his car, stunned not so much by what had happened but by the outcome. No one had been killed or even injured. He hadn't caused the accident, and yet he was the one out of the race.

Canadian Grand Prix Top Six Finishers		Championship Point Leaders Race Ten of Eleven	
Driver	Points	Driver	Points
Evans	9	Wagner	42
Bogavanti	6	Evans	41
Parks	4	Bogavanti	40
Edwards	3	Parks	40
Phillips	2	Phillips	22
Pisecky	1	Lafosse	17

Chapter 34

The big trucks that had picked up the racecars from Kennedy Airport and brought them to Mosport, turned around Monday morning and brought them down to Watkins Glen. That same day, the Garret-Hawk transporter and Team Wagner caravan made the same journey. The following morning, the teams gathered under the big steel roof of the Glen Technical Center where, for the last time, preparation began again.

Team Wagner had the routine down to a science by now. They stripped the car, had parts magnafluxed or zygloed, others inspected visually for wear and damage. Fat Walt had the thankless task of removing the inspection plates and fuel bladders from the monocoque tub, stuffing one of his large arms inside the tub, and, wielding a small metal mallet, tapping out all the dings and dents inflicted at Mosport. Around the front bulkhead, he discovered a series of rivets that had popped loose from the soft outer skin. Repairing this required new fabrication that added several days to his work. When the job was done, the tub was repainted and the painstaking process began of piecing the car back together. Sunday afternoon, with the race still one week away, the car was finished and the crew found themselves with something they hadn't enjoyed in eight weeks--free time. It was a strange and empty feeling, and a wonderful feeling.

Free time was the last thing Wagner wanted, because it meant time to think and to worry, and he did not want to think and to worry. Monday morning, after a mere half-day of rest, he dragged his crew back to the circuit and began testing. Testing meant wear and tear on the light, fragile machine, which meant more repairs and modifications that extended into each night. Wagner was concerned not at all when he spun off the track and a suspension arm ripped loose from the tub. It meant another long night of work, which meant instant blissful sleep the moment his head hit the pillow.

On Friday, marshals took their posts around the circuit, timers gathered in the booth above Pit Straight, and practice began officially for the United States Grand Prix. By then, Wagner's machine felt as comfortable as an old boot, a well-stitched, highly-polished old boot. He went out and lowered the lap record by two seconds. No one else was close. At the end of the session, he walked up the hill to the Press Office to see if Susan had arrived.

*　*　*

"What do you think of it?"

Wagner walked around the car slowly, admiring its flawless finish, the flawless fit of its doors, the clean simplicity of the design. It was not the 911S, but the less expensive and less powerful 912, painted fire-engine red. He opened a door, looked inside, and got a heady whiff of new-car smell.

"I don't believe it, Susie. You did it. You actually went out and bought yourself a Porsche."

"I picked it up last week. I just love it, don't you? Here." She tossed him the keys. "Take it for a spin."

Wagner inched the 912 past incoming traffic, and turned west on Bronson Hill Road, away from Watkins Glen. The trees were at their autumn peak--bright reds and shining golds.

"How's the team doing?" she asked. "I see you were fastest this morning."

"Yeah, the car's quick, but I'm disappointed with my time. Yesterday, I was a second quicker."

"Your black eye is gone, too."

He touched the skin below his left eye. "Yeah, I kinda miss seeing it in the morning when I shave."

She smirked. "I'll bet you do."

They were passing through farmland now, low, rolling hills flush with corn stalks as tall as a man, corn soon to be harvested for feed.

"You know," she said, "I can't believe the season is almost over. This Sunday is it."

Wagner's jaw tightened. "I just hope we get it right this time."

Susan touched his hand. "You will, John. After all you've been through, I can't imagine you losing the championship now."

"What about <u>after</u> Sunday? Will I see you again?"

She looked away. "Let's not talk about that now."

"Why not talk about it now? I don't want you to just walk out of my life, Susie."

She looked out the window and said nothing.

"After the race we could drive your Porsche back to Chicago. Whatever happens, my team won't need me. I'll ask Sterns to give you the week off. We could go anywhere you like, up to Mackinac Island, maybe, or stay in the city. I'm all yours."

Susan brushed a wrinkle out of her dress distractedly. "Nothing will have changed, John."

He turned to her and winked. "I might be world champion."

"You know what I mean."

He pulled over and stopped. "Listen, I am serious about retiring--even if I don't win the championship on Sunday."

"It won't change anything."

"I don't understand, Susan. I thought you wanted me to retire?"

"It doesn't matter anymore."

"It doesn't matter anymore? What's that supposed to mean?"

"I wish you would retire, John. Not for my sake, but for yours. But whether you do or not, it won't change how I feel."

"And how do you feel?"

She crossed her arms. "Do I have to spell it out for you?"

"I wish you would."

"I don't love you."

He turned the Porsche around and started back to the circuit. "I don't believe you."

She said nothing. She sat with her arms crossed, looking out the window.

"There's a restaurant down by the marina," he said. "I was there the other night and had the trout." He looked at her for reaction. She continued looking out the window.

"Believe it or not, I kind of liked it," he said, "probably because I was thinking about you. It came with broccoli and rice, which I ate, every bite."

"You mean you didn't have a baked potato loaded with lots of butter and sour cream?"

"A guy can change, can't he? Tell you what. I'll have the trout again, if you'll have dinner with me tonight."

"With broccoli and rice?"

"With broccoli and rice."

"Eat every bite?"

He frowned. "Yes, mother."

"And have wine instead of beer?"

"You're asking a lot, lady."

*　　*　　*

It didn't make sense. The chassis was handling perfectly. The engine was strong. He was driving as smooth and precise as ever. And yet his laps times were progressively slower.

"Something's wrong with the car," he said, after practice was over. "I can't put my finger on it but I know this much: I'm losing 100 RPM up the Front Straight."

Hacksaw hitched up his pants. "I don't know if we need to get in a big sweat over this, Big Guy. What are we talking about? A couple tenths? Heck, a gust of wind could do that to you, or putting a wheel wrong in a corner somewhere."

"I wish it were just a couple of tenths," Wagner sighed. "What was my quick time this morning, Ted?"

"A minute-four-point-five-seven."

"Yeah, and that was the quickest time of the morning," added Hacksaw. "Like I said...."

"That was this morning," snapped Wagner. "What about this afternoon, Ted?"

276

"Let's see, you did a minute five-six-two, a minute five-one-nine, a minute seven-seven-one, and ... looking further down, well, your best time was ... well, it was a minute-five-one-nine."

Wagner rubbed his face. "And my quick time yesterday? A minute three-seven something, wasn't it?"

"Uh, let's see. A minute three-seven-two."

"I'm not within two seconds of that now. Hell, I was gassin' it out there this afternoon, and I can't get close to that time. Explain that? I should be in the minute-threes, or at the very least, the minute-fours."

"It's hotter this afternoon than it was yesterday," Hacksaw, said, trying to be rational about it. "The air's not as dense, so the engine can't put out as much. The track's hotter and maybe gotten some oil on it."

"Tell Evans that," said Wagner. "Have you seen his time this afternoon? A minute-four-point-two-oh. That number just sticks in my head like a bad dream. Evans. If there's one guy I got to worry about on Sunday, it's him. Nuts." He paced the length of the car. "Listen, I want you guys to go over this car with a fine-tooth comb. Check the chassis. It's been banged up and rebuilt so many times I don't want to think about it. Make sure it's not off somewhere. It wouldn't take much. Check the suspension. Measure everything."

"We have measured everything," Balchowsky grumbled.

"Measure it again. It's probably some chicken-shit thing that's slowing us down. Find it. Fix it." He grabbed his windbreaker off the tool box. "One more thing. This is Watkins Glen. It hasn't exactly been kind to me over the years. Twice, I came here leading in points, and both times someone else ended up with all the marbles." He started to leave. "I don't know what it is about this place."

"Hey, where do you think you're going?" Hacksaw called to him.

277

Wagner smiled. "Cook's in town and wants to buy me a drink. After that, I'm having dinner with a lady. Don't sweat it. I'll be back."

*   *   *

Herb Cook had more than a drink in mind; he wanted to discuss plans for next season, over dinner. Plans for Garret-Hawk to build Indy cars had never gotten past negotiations. Edward W. Garret kept pushing up the price and Cook lost patience. Hacksaw Gilbert was the real talent behind Garret anyway, and since he'd moved to Team Wagner, Cook found it easy to cut off talks. Wagner tried, but there was no getting out of dinner. Cook was talking big money, which he couldn't ignore. He didn't mention his dinner-date with Susan. Around seven, he excused himself, found a pay phone, and dialed the Glen Motor Inn.

Chapter 35

"I'm going to nail it this time." Wagner braked midway into the Turn One right-hander, grabbed third gear and felt the chassis shake accelerating up the hill. From his low seating position, he couldn't see the entry into The Esses, but he could sense it. Cresting the hill, the car lifted and he felt his body tighten. He eased back on the power and steered into the left-hander. Inside the curve, the yellow-and-red stripped curb slithered into view. He nudged it with his inside front tire. As the chassis settled back on its springs, he upshifted to fourth and set up for the second half of The Esses, a climbing right-hander. Pressing the gas fully now, the engine screaming at his back, he turned in, clipped the apex, and drifted outside.

"I can't do it any smoother than that," he thought. Under the pull of fierce acceleration, he relaxed his neck, allowing his head to rest back against the roll bar. It was a cool and overcast morning. On either side, trees whipped past in smears of red and gold. The race was a day away, but already cars and campers filled the clearings. Smoke from campfires wafted among the trees. He felt the straightaway level off, about to dip into the Loop. A millisecond before he braked, he checked the tach.

Ninety-four-hundred RPM.

Not even close.

He returned to the pits and stayed seated as a tire engineer went around taking temperature readings off each of his tires. The engineer scrawled the readings on a sheet of paper and handed it to him. He looked at them out of courtesy, then folded the paper and put them in his pocket. Tires weren't the problem.

"Well, let's have it," he said, climbing from the car slowly. "Give me the bad news."

"A minute-six point-one-one." Ted sighed wearily.

Wagner rubbed his neck. "Sounds about right."

His crew moved around the car, slowly and without enthusiasm, removing the engine cover and nose cone. They'd been up most the night and were cold and tired. And out c answers.

"Somebody say something." Wagner took a swig of water "The silence is killing me."

Hacksaw exhaled. "Hell, I don't know, Big Guy. We'v checked everything there is to check, replaced everything there i to replace. All we can do is push her back up to the Tech Cente and try something else."

A car rounded the Ninety and screamed past. A white-and blue car. Wagner listened as the Public Address announced th time: "One-minute-four-point-eight-three, for three-time Ind winner Tony Dayton."

"Hear that? Tony's two-tenths off my quick time. Hell, th guy couldn't even keep his car on the road up at Mosport ... an a damned Indy driver, too. Nuts."

"No one said the man didn't have talent," Hacksaw said.

Balchowsky cleared his throat, spit on the ground, an rasped: "Know what I think?"

"No, and I don't care," Wagner said, annoyed.

Balchowsky picked at his teeth. "I think you're a little tight that's what I think. Why don't you go somewhere and you res your head awhile. It might do you some good. And I know i will do us some good not having you around here questionin every damn thing we do. Frankly, I'm pretty tired of it."

"He's right," Hacksaw said. "Get out of here. Go thin about something else for a while. We'll find whatever' wrong."

"I wish I could believe that." Wagner grabbed hi windbreaker. "This is Watkins Glen, remember?" He looked a the racecar one last time then headed out through the back of th pits. Midway across the paddock, he heard someone call hi name.

"John. Hey, John. Wait up."

Wagner turned to look. Could it be? Michael Bravo? H still had casts on both legs and was walking with the support o crutches. And there was a girl at his side.

Bravo smiled warmly. "It's good to see you, man. Geez how you been?"

"Hello, Michael. How are the legs mending?"

Bravo tapped one of the casts with his finger. "These come off next week."

"That's great news."

"You bet it is. And guess what else? Ferrari has invited me to Italy for a tryout. What do you think of that? Me, driving for Ferrari next year? Pretty incredible, huh?"

Wagner nodded. "I hope it works out." He looked at the girl. "Are you going to introduce us?"

"Oh, hey, yeah, this is Lisa," Bravo said. "She's sorta been taking care of me these past two months, and, uh, well, we're planning on getting married."

Lisa extended her hand. She was not pretty, with a long nose, crooked teeth and faded-blue eyes, but she had a warm, giving smile that said `I like you.'"

"Congratulations, to the both of you. When's the big day?"

"We're thinking some time in the Spring," Lisa said.

"How about you?" Bravo asked. "Still seeing Susan?"

"Kind of, yeah. It's hard to say what's going on between us, actually."

"That bad, huh?"

Wagner scratched his neck. "Yeah, I don't know."

"Look, I just wanted to wish you the best for tomorrow, and tell you how much it meant to me to be your teammate," said Bravo. "I didn't tell you this before, but growing up I was your biggest fan, and couldn't believe that I ended up being on the same team with you, and...." Bravo paused, choking on his words.

Wagner nodded. "Thanks, Michael."

"And ... who knows, maybe we'll be teammates again some day, you know? Under better circumstances."

"Maybe we will, Michael. Maybe we will."

A helicopter was shuttling guests back and forth between the circuit and the Glen Motor Inn. Wagner boarded the chopper, felt it lift off, soar high over the circuit, and glide northward. Seneca Lake's dark waters appeared, stretching far off to the north. The helicopter drifted over the lake's western shoreline and descended. Wagner looked down at the Glen Motor Inn parking lot. It gleamed with cars, but one car in particular drew his eyes, one with a bright metallic blue finish and a long hood. "Can't be," he thought. "There must be a thousand like it on the road. It better not be."

As soon as the copter sat down, he jumped out, located the Camaro, and examined its plates. California plates.

He walked swiftly to the hotel entrance. In the lobby, looking more like some lost 14-year-old than the 17-year-old that he was, was Ron Wagner.

"Dad--John, man, am I glad to see you."

Wagner didn't smile. "Where's your mother? She had better be around here somewhere, that's all I got to say."

"It's okay. She knows I'm here."

"She knows you drove all the way here by yourself? Do you expect me to believe that?"

"I left her a note."

"You left her a note? Damn it, Ron, she's gotta be worried sick. How could you do this to her? Well, you can't stay here, if that's what you think. You're going to have to turn around and drive right back to California. No, you're going to fly back. Jesus, Ron. I don't have time for this."

He grabbed his son's arm and started walking. "Come on. We're calling your mother right now." He led Ron to his room. There was no answer at Tina's house. He tried Ron's stepfather. There was no answer there, either. He hung up the phone. "I'll try again later." He sighed. "Get your bags. You can stay here until I figure out something. This is absolutely the worst thing you could have done to your mother. I hope you know that."

"I don't blame you for being mad, John, but I couldn't stay home. If you and Mom had stayed together, I would be here now."

"No, you would be in school now, where you belong."

"It's not fair that I should be cheated out of this ... because of something that happened between you and Mom 15 years ago."

Wagner didn't answer. He thought better of telling his son that if he hadn't left his mother 15 years ago he would be running a car dealership in downtown Lancaster, California, and wouldn't be here himself.

282

Chapter 36

Susan didn't have much to ask him, and Wagner wasn't talkative. It was gray and cold, and the last time they would be meeting for an interview. It seemed depressing to be ending this way.

"I do have one last question," she said, after they had eaten lunch. "What will happen to your team after the race is over?"

He smiled slightly. "Funny you should ask. Last night, Herb Cook unveiled Unirich's plans for next season. He wants my team to build racecars for next year's Indy 500. Some of the cars will go to drivers like Tony Dayton, while at least two will be entered by my team. We'll also send a pair of cars to Europe to compete. There are a lot of details to work out, but I kind of like the idea. Of course, it could all go down the toilet tomorrow if I don't win."

"Why should it matter if you win or lose?"

"Winning is the calling card in this business. It's what pays the bills. Cook's talking a multi-million dollar deal. He's not going to be able to sell it in-house if I don't win the championship. The deal will go to someone else. Mind if I change subjects?"

She didn't answer. She knew what was coming.

"Look," he said. "I'm sorry about last night. I was meeting with Cook. I couldn't just walk away."

"It's not just last night. Racing is your life, John. It's what you love. Even if you do retire, you'll always be involved with it in some way. Half the time, you'll be in Europe or Indianapolis or somewhere. I bet your time for next week is already blocked out. Even if I accepted your invitation, you couldn't go with me back to Chicago. Could you?"

Wagner said nothing.

"Could you?"

He sighed. "I got a meeting in Akron first thing Tuesday morning."

*   *   *

This time up the Front Straight he couldn't crack 9300 RPM. Not too surprised, he returned to the pits, switched off the engine, and climbed out as his crew moved around the car lifeless as zombies.

"Don't all speak up at once," he said, removing his helmet. He grabbed a towel to dry his hair. Only his hair wasn't wet. He hadn't even worked up a sweat.

"I don't know what to say," sighed Hacksaw. "We changed the suspension some. We took out just about all the wing. I swear, I been in this business a long time and I never seen anything quite like this."

"Maybe it ain't the car, George." Balchowsky looked at the crew chief for reaction. There was none.

"What the hell is that supposed to mean, Walt?" Wagner glared at him.

"You've been a little tight lately, like I said."

"Not that shit again, Walt."

"Face it, John. You've been feeling the pressure, these past few weeks, and you said yourself this place ain't exactly been kind to you. You're uptight, and it's costing you a fraction here and there. Hell, a tenth here, a tenth there, it adds up to whole second in a big hurry."

"Uptight my ass. I'm losing RPM. Explain that."

"Everybody knows The Esses are the key to this circuit. Screw up on 'em and there ain't no way to make it up. You'll drop Rs like there's no tomorrow and you're lap times will go all to hell."

"You think I'd don't know what the hell I'm doing out there, is that what you're saying?"

"I didn't say that, John. I said you were maybe a little tight...."

"Shut up, Walt. You've had your say. I want to hear from the others. Hacksaw. Nigel. You, too, Ted. You think it's me?"

Nigel Long stared at the ground. "I don't know," he said, not looking up. "I'm no race driver. The chassis's straight. The suspension's on. The wings, maybe, but we turned them and made them practically flat. I don't know."

"Ted?"

Gofer Ted smiled vacuously, and shrugged. "I, uh, geez, John. I don't know nothin'."

"Hacksaw?"

Hacksaw's blue eyes narrowed. "Aw, hell," he said, after running it through his mind. "You're not some rookie who can't hold his pee."

"I take that as a vote of confidence." Wagner looked up and down pit row. "Where are we on the starting grid? Ted?"

"Huh?"

"The starting grid, Ted. Look at the lap charts. Where are we?"

He flipped through them. "Fifth."

"We've fallen that far, have we?" Wagner shook his head. "I guess I'm not too surprised. We have a spare engine, don't we?"

"Used 'em all up," said Hacksaw. "Hell, if we'd had another, I'da changed that too."

Wagner rubbed his jaw. "Nuts. That leaves us with no choice but to install one of the old engines."

"No, we can't do that." Hacksaw raised his eyebrows. "Besides, you said yourself the engine felt strong."

"Maybe there's something wrong with it, something I'm not detecting. How about the engine we ran up at Mosport? What's it got--100 miles on it, 150 max?"

The crew chief nodded. "Something like that, but it sucked up some stones in Canada, remember? Hell, the valves and piston tops..."

"Pull the heads and check for damage. I doubt if you'll find any. If everything looks good, put the sucker in. If there is damage, we'll go with what we got."

*   *   *

It was a quarter-past midnight. The circuit infield was dotted with the light of trailers and motorhomes and campfires. Rock music and laughter sounded faintly from a party somewhere back in the woods. Down at the circuit gate, cars trickled in and would continue to do so throughout the night. Wagner departed the Tech Center, climbed aboard Hacksaw's stepvan, fired up the motor, and headed back to the Glen Motor Inn--alone. The engine swap was complete. The crew was staying behind, putting in one last all-nighter to make absolutely certain the racecar was bullet-proof.

He felt tired, but was keyed up from the work, and the restlessness he felt before every race was already at work. Walking through the lobby, he heard country and western music blare from the bar downstairs, and decided a beer or two would help precipitate a mood for sleep.

Then he remembered.

Ron.

He'd forgotten completely about him. What had the kid done about dinner? Was he still in the room? Was he all right? He passed the bar and walked to his room, inserted his key in the lock, but before he could turn the knob the door opened and there facing him was ... Tina.

*   *   *

There wasn't a chair or stool that wasn't taken inside the bar, so Wagner ordered two bottles of beer and motioned Tina outside into the hall.

"It's quieter out here anyway," he said, handing her a bottle. "So, tell me, what happened? How'd you find us? I tried calling you earlier. Now I know why you weren't home."

"I tore out of Palmdale as soon as I found his note," she said. 'I could have wrung his little neck. You know, I've never been further east than Phoenix, but I was determined to drive the face of the earth if I had to, to find him. Once I got here, I checked every motel and hotel around here figuring wherever you were staying, that's where I would find Ron." She clinked her bottle against his. "Thanks for taking him in. By the way, who's sleeping on the floor tonight?"

"Not me." Wagner smiled.

"There isn't a vacant room within 50 miles of here," she said. "So I guess I'll just have to sleep on the floor."

"No, you won't," he said. "I know the owner. He usually keeps one or two rooms open for just such emergencies."

A couple exited the bar. They stepped aside to let them pass.

"Isn't there someplace else we can go?" she said. "I feel silly standing out here blocking traffic."

He pointed to the back door. "There are some tables and chairs outside--if you don't mind the cold."

They had been seated but a minute when Tina pulled her jacket up around her neck. "Look, why don't you see the manager about getting me that room, okay? I'm freezing my butt off out here."

Wagner looked at his half-empty bottle. "Shall I get us a couple more of these?"

"You'd better."

The room was small, taken up mostly by a queen bed and a bureau. Near the door was a small table and two chairs. Wagner placed two unopened beers on the table and sat down. Tina removed her coat and sat opposite him. She looked at his grease-stained coveralls. "You're a mess."

"I'm also tired," he said. "It's finally hit me. I'll finish my beer and let you get some sleep."

Tina left her chair and came to him. Slowly, carefully, she began undoing his coveralls.

"What are you doing?"

"Getting you out of these."

He watched her. "Are you sure you want to do this?"

"As sure as anything I've ever done."

Once she had the top open, she reached her arms inside and circled them around his bare chest. "Mm. You feel good." Softly, tenderly, she kissed his shoulders, neck, face and, at last, his mouth.

Wagner pulled her closer, suddenly needing her very badly. She was so beautiful, her skin so warm and inviting. Clothes began peeling off. All the years that had passed were as nothing, as they fell back into their old pattern of love-making. They both squirmed and gasped between kisses, until Wagner pulled away.

He couldn't go through with it. The attraction was purely physical and that's all it had ever been. Their lovemaking wouldn't stop here. It would continue tomorrow night and begin again in California and lead to nothing because there was no love in it. He had been down this road one too many times before.

"What is it?" said Tina. "What's wrong?"

He shook his head. "You are still the sexiest woman I have ever known, but we can't do this."

"What do you mean? You're feeling what I'm feeling. It isn't wrong. Let it happen."

"I want to, believe me, I want to."

"Is it someone else?"

"Yes ... and no."

"Yes and no? What the hell kind of answer is that?"

"It means I love someone else ... and that I don't want to get started with you again."

Tina buttoned up her blouse and rose to her feet. Tears rolled down her cheeks. "Listen, buddy, just because we make love doesn't mean anything is starting. I'm not about to get started with you again. You hurt me, really and truly hurt me, and I won't let anyone do that to me again."

Wagner fastened up his coveralls. "I wish it weren't this way, Tina."

"So do I. Now get out of my room."

Chapter 37

Wagner had one final piece of business prior to the race--making an appearance before a group of Unirich executives. He left the Tech Center and headed towards a large orange-and-blue striped tent behind the main grandstand. As he entered a stocky man in a three-piece suit who was leaving bumped into him accidently.

"Watch where you're going, bub," grumbled the stocky man. He looked up, stunned to see it was the Californian. "Oh, it's you."

"Hello, Ed. How the hell are you, pal?"

Garret brushed past. "Always the smart ass."

Inside, casually-dressed sales directors and vice presidents mingled, swapping stories and drinking beer. Holding court in the center, was Herb Cook, his hollow cheeks quivering as he talked.

"John, it's about time you got here," Cook shouted. "Come on over here." He grabbed Wagner by the shoulder and pulled him close. "Listen up, men. This guy standing here next to me is the next world champion. Let's hear it for John Wagner."

The executives clapped approval.

"Me and him go way back, to my days as sales director out in L.A.. It's been what--12 or 13 years, John?"

"Something like that."

"Yeah, it's been all of that. Of course, way back then, he was racing Porsches and nobody knew who he was, but I knew who he was, because he used to clean my clock regularly. Who would have guessed that we'd be standing here today, me as company president, and him as maybe the best damn race driver on the planet?"

The executives clapped approval again. Cook turned to the driver and spoke in a hushed voice. "How's it going? I hear you guys are having trouble."

"Everything's fine. We're ready to go."

Cook turned back to his executives. "As all of you know, Unirich is building tires for next year's Indy 500. Right now, John and I are working on a deal that will have his new company building state-of-the-art Indy cars for the Big Race, for people like three-time Indy winner Tony Dayton and, if I can talk him into it, John, here, will drive one of them. Wouldn't that be something? America's two best race drivers in next year's 500, on our brand, and one of them winning?"

The executives clapped louder this time, some whistling their approval.

"Don't con me, John-boy," Cook whispered. "Will you win or not? Everything is hinging on it."

* * *

Wagner pulled on his helmet, fastened the strap, and was about to step into his machine when he felt a hand grab him by the shoulder.

It was Tony Dayton. The Texan had on his white helmet, and his trademark red bandanna drawn up around his mouth making him look like the Lone Ranger. "I still owe you one, partner," he said.

"You paid me back, remember?"

"That little old pass you made? That don't count. You spun."

"We're even, Tony, as far as I'm concerned."

The Texan winked. "Whatever you say, partner. Best of luck today, hear?"

"You too."

Wagner slid down behind the wheel and checked everything in the cockpit to be certain all was as it should be. He closed his eyes. The seconds seemed to drag, feeling more like minutes than seconds. He was in no hurry.

The first three rows shaped up this way:

<u>United States Grand Prix</u>
Sunday, October 6

EVANS
Lotus
1 min 4.20 sec

BOGAVANTI
Ferrari
1 min 4.27 sec

PARKS
BRM
1 min 4.28 sec

PHILLIPS
Brabham
1 min 4.37 sec

WAGNER
Lotus
1 min 4.57 sec

DAYTON
Garret-Hawk
1 min 4.81 sec

The signal to start engines was given. He pulled his white bandanna up around his mouth and tugged at each glove to be certain they were taut as a second layer of skin. This was it. Time to go like hell. He flipped on a row of switches. The little kitchen that was his cockpit came alive. He pressed the starter button. Behind him, the Cosworth V-8 spun to life, emitting a high, sweet growl. Hacksaw leaned in and shouted "Good luck." The crew vanished. He grasped the steering wheel and jabbed the throttle repeatedly, feeling the engine's raw power, at his command. This was what he lived for. Everything else was just waiting. Championship or not, he wasn't going to retire after today. He knew that now.

The starter took his position at the front of the grid. He looked over the field of 20 cars, the green flag clutched in his right hand, a cigar clutched in his teeth. Tex Hopkins, in white suit and white cowboy boots, was the most flamboyant race starter in motor racing. He threw his cigar aside and counted down the final seconds. Engines rose to a deafening pitch. Crewmen held their breath. Fans rose in unison. Hopkins leaped high into the air with both arms extended and seemed to

hang there a moment. Before his feet touched ground, h
whipped down the green flag.

The United States Grand Prix was on.

Wagner surged forward amidst the thunder of cars. He trie
following Evans into Turn One and maybe grabbing secon
place but Parks slid over to fill his lane. To his right, Dayto
found an opening and squeezed past Parks and Phillips to tak
third as the field rounded the first turn. Pounding up the hill, th
order was Evans, Bogavanti, Dayton, Parks, Phillips, an
Wagner. Up through the Esses, the field ran tightly together bu
accelerating up the Front Straightaway began to string out.

Wagner upshifted to fifth, slipped into the vacuum of a
behind Phillips' Brabham, and felt an instant boost of power. H
checked his mirror. Greenman's Lotus was riding his vacuum
All the cars were running in single-file order now, drafting on
another up the straight. Bearing down on the Loop, Wagne
passed Phillips under braking.

Fifth.

Drafting Phillips and now Parks up the Front Straight, h
wasn't able to get an accurate tachometer reading so didn't kno
if the engine swap had made the slightest difference. But
didn't concern him. At the moment, his concern was gettin
around Parks. He looked past the Englishman, to get a read o
the others. Already, Evans' Lotus held a substantial lead ove
Bogavanti's second-place car. Dayton, in third after a brillian
start, had lost steam and fallen back into Parks' clutches
Wagner had to admit he was doing a masterful job of holding u
the Englishman, and might have been amused if the Texa
wasn't holding up him as well.

Laps began clicking by with startling regularity. It wasn'
until lap 12 that Parks finally passed Dayton.

"Nuts. Now it's my turn to deal with the cowboy," Wagne
thought. But at the very next corner, Dayton let him pass.

"Now we're even," muttered Wagner, giving him a wave o
thanks.

Fourth.

A gap opened between his car and Parks' BRM. Speedin
up the Front Straightaway, he was picking up enough of th

Englishman's draft to still not get a clear reading on his engine's performance. He kept his right foot planted and gradually closed the gap. On lap 22 he passed Parks.

Third.

Bogavanti's blood-red Ferrari was next. Giuseppe Bogavanti. His oldest friend on the circuit. As teammates in the early sixties, the Californian was always quicker, but it was the Italian who won most of the races. It seemed little had changed since then. Bogavanti had all those trophies, but Wagner was still quicker. On lap 31, winging down into the Loop, he passed the three-time world champion.

Second.

He was running alone, without the aid of a slipstream. Next time up the Front Straight, he watched his tach closely to see if it would reach 9600 RPM. The needle swept past 9300 RPM, past 9400 RPM, past 9500 RPM, and nudged 9600 RPM a split second before he bore down on the brakes. Dead on perfect. It had been the engine.

Next time past the pits, Hacksaw showed him this:

Evans
-14

Fourteen seconds. It might as well have been fourteen minutes. Evans had the bit between his teeth and surely sensed victory. How could he catch him now?

* * *

Susan was stationed on the knoll above Turn One where she could see the drivers brake, turn in, and accelerate uphill into the Esses. It was as good a spot as any for what was to be her final race. No way was she going to let Jeremy talk her into another motor racing assignment. Her vantage point gave her a bird's-eye view of how the drivers negotiated this critical corner. At first, their techniques all looked the same, but closer observation revealed vast differences. Lining the inside of the curve, a row of hay bales told the story. Some drivers cut to within inches of

293

the bales, others allowed themselves a foot or more of room, while still others varied their line from lap to lap; cutting within inches one time, by as much as a foot the next time. The difference between Wagner and Evans was so minute at first she didn't see it. Only after careful observation did the difference become clear, and it amazed her. Both drivers cornered on the identical line, entering the curve with power on, each time cutting within a whisker of the bales. Only Wagner's inside tires always brushed past the bales without actually touching them. Evans, on the other hand, clipped the bales ever-so-slightly and each time corrected the wheel a fraction to compensate. That was the extent of difference. Wagner was that tiny bit better.

For more than an hour she watched Wagner whittle away at Evans' lead, certain the Californian would catch him. But with five laps to go, and Evans still leading by four seconds, it was clear to her the better driver would not be crowned world champion today.

*　*　*

Backmarkers. That was all Evans had had to deal with all afternoon. Another loomed in his path, one more to be picked off. Seeing the white-and-blue paint scheme and number 36 emblazoned on its flanks, for a split second he thought it was Wagner. Then he saw the driver's white helmet and realized it wasn't Wagner but that swaggering loudmouth, Tony Dayton. Blasting up the Front Straight, he reeled the Texan in like a fish on a hook. Bearing down on the Loop, he darted inside for the pass only to see the Garret-Hawk cut in front of him. Evans stood on the brakes to keep from hitting him.

"Look in the mirror, you stupid clot. Somebody's trying to pass you."

Evans tried again at Big Bend and again at the Ninety, and both times Dayton cut in front of him.

"I don't believe it. The bloody idiot. He's blocking me. He's actually blocking me."

294

Accelerating up Pit Straight, Evans shook his fist so the officials could see what was happening. Somebody blue-flag this idiot.

Dayton didn't care if they blue-flagged him or not. His engine had lost its edge from over-revving an hour ago, so they could black-flag him for all he cared. It was payback time. Whipping through the Esses, he looked back in his mirror, past Evans' Lotus, and saw Wagner's big blue machine closing in fast. Yessir. Old Tony's tactics were about to pay off big time. Accelerating up the Front Straight, his sick engine was at a disadvantage and Evans flashed past in an angry blur of red and gold, but Wagner was right behind him. He watched the two cars hunker down braking for the Loop and swoop nose-to-tail into the circular right-hander.

"Now, we're even," the Texan muttered with a grin.

*   *   *

Wagner laid on the throttle too eagerly coming off the Loop and slid wide. Powering onto the back straightaway, he watched the backside of Evans' Lotus shrink. Using all the road, he whipped through the fast left-hander behind the pits and into Big Bend, the sweeping downhill right-hander. The last corner was the Ninety. Coming in, he braked hard, geared down, and stormed around it. Exiting onto Pit Straight, he saw Evans' Lotus at the opposite end, setting up for Turn One.

Hacksaw stepped out on the tarmac and pointed emphatically at the pitboard.

Two laps.

"I know, Hacksaw. I'm peddling as fast as I can," Wagner muttered.

Next time, Tex Hopkins was there to greet him, with the white flag.

One lap.

Evans was closer now, but was there enough race track to catch him? And if he did catch him, could he pass him?

He leaned into Turn One and accelerated up the hill into The Esses, at the turn-in feathering the throttle as the chassis lifted.

Then full power through the next turn and up the long Front Straight. On either side, fans waved to him, rooting him on. They were his fans, Americans, like himself, and the United States Grand Prix was his race. He wasn't going to lose the championship here. Not on home soil. Not again.

He ran the tach past 9600 RPM, to 9700 RPM, going deep into the braking zone, deeper than ever before. Everything was coming at him so fast, but at the center of the blur the world was focused and still, at his control. He braked midway into the Loop, sliding, but on line. The back straight loomed and disappeared quickly beneath his wheels. The backside of the pits appeared, far off below the road. In another 20 seconds, one of them would be taking the checker first.

He could see Evans' worried glances in the sidemirrors. One chance. That's all he wanted. One chance at Evans. He rounded Big Bend on the Scot's tail.

Under hard braking for The Ninety, the Lotus moved over to the right to seal off the inside passing lane. Slick move, thought Wagner, but not slick enough. He moved further right. Braking, his inside wheels could not find traction on the bits of rubber and small stones strewn there. In an instant, he was sideways, his nose veering toward the midsection of Evans' Lotus. He saw the Scot's hands spinning the steering wheel frantically, then a blur of color, dust and bits as the Lotus spun too and slid backwards off the track.

Wagner's head jerked forward violently as his car screeched suddenly to a halt. Stunned, he looked up and saw Tex Hopkins gaping at him, 100 yards away. He pumped the accelerator to keep his stumbling engine running, engaged first, and sprung for the checker. A flash of motion caught his eye. Evans' Lotus, bouncing, picking up speed, working his way back onto the road. The next moment his tires encountered asphalt and smoothed out, at Wagner's side.

Tex Hopkins leaped high in the air and waved the flag as they sped past, with no idea of who had won.

Chapter 38

Opinion was divided over who crossed the finish line first. It looked like a dead heat to Tex Hopkins and to three other officials standing at the finish line. Wagner and Evans were no help. They each thought the other had won.

The officials had made the egregious oversight of not having photographer at the finish line, so they scratched their heads for solution. Several options were put forth, including a coin toss. Then someone named Elsie Brandon stepped forward claiming she had photographed the finish. She wasn't confident of the photo quality, or even certain if she had captured the exact moment both cars crossed the finish line, but to the desperate officials Elsie Brandon was a godsend.

While Wagner and Evans and everyone else waited, the precious film was taken to the press darkroom and developed. While the negatives were still wet with solution, each frame was held up to the light and examined. There were snapshots of Miss Brandon's aunt and uncle who lived in Ithaca, photos of Seneca Lake and, finally, five snapshots of the race. The final frame captured the finish. Because they were looking at a small negative, it was difficult to tell who led crossing the line. So, while everyone waited a little longer, a print was made. Eyes peered closely into the solution as an image gradually appeared. Darker images appeared first, such as the nose of Wagner's car, which was dark blue. Still no clue. Then the lighter images slowly filled in, such as the gold nose of Evans' car, and the white finish line. The finish line was about a foot ahead of the noses of both cars, with one nose--the dark nose--leading by mere inches.

United States Grand Prix Top Six Finishers		Championship Point Leaders Race Eleven of Eleven	
Driver	Points	Driver	Points
Wagner	9	Wagner	51
Evans	6	Evans	47
Parks	4	Parks	44
Phillips	3	Bogavanti	40
Lafosse	2	Phillips	25
Edwards	1	Lafosse	19

* * *

Wagner was given a lap of honor in the big gold Lincoln convertible he'd been awarded for winning the race. He sat up where everyone could see him, but told the driver to wait while he looked in the crowd for his son. He spotted Ron with his mother and invited them both to join him. They sat on either side of him and waved back to the crowd, looking every bit a family.

Later, amongst much joking and laughter, he met with the press.

"I guess from now on `Wagner Luck' is going to mean good luck, wouldn't you say, John?" said one of the journalists.

Wagner smiled. "Whoever said otherwise?"

He noticed Susan in the back of the room scribbling notes. He caught her eye and winked. She smiled back and said something which he took to mean "congratulations." It was the last time he saw her.

After that, Cook escorted him to a private celebration in the Unirich corporate motorhome. Only Hacksaw, Keith O'Leary and three Unirich senior executives were invited. Before the first round of drinks was consumed, someone pounded on the door. Edward W. Garret entered with Al Fornier, a member of Formula One's governing body. Smiles and laughter ceased as the two men stepped up into the cabin.

"Relax," Garret said. "We're not here to spoil your little party." His hard face crinkled into a smile as he put a meaty arm around Wagner. "John, here, has earned the right to be called champion. Congratulations, boy. You've done America proud. Now, I want Al Fornier to complete the honors by awarding me the constructors' championship."

Cook was annoyed with Garret's intrusion--and bewildered. By his calculations, Garret-Hawk won the constructors' championship, making it a landmark day and advertising bonanza for Unirich Tire.

"What's the problem?" asked Cook, puffing on a cigarette. "Garret-Hawk has 51 points and Lotus has 50."

Garret smiled, trying to be patient with the uninformed, even if the uniformed was his biggest sponsor. "You're right, Herb. I do have 51 points. The question is, how many points has Lotus? By Al's calculation, Lotus has 59 points."

"Fifty-nine?" barked Cook. "How the hell did he come up with 59?"

Garret smiled, still patient and not wanting to offend anyone while seeking a favorable decision. "Al says John's car is a Lotus. If true, Chapman would pick up an additional nine points and win the championship. The car started life as a Lotus, an Indy Lotus. Am I correct, Hacksaw?"

"The chassis is a Lotus 38."

"You mean `was,'" said Garret. "It's my understanding this car was extensively modified." He turned to Wagner. "It's your team, John. What you tell Mr. Fornier here will determine who is constructors' champion." Garret's face had a thin smile, but his eyes were cold and imploring, almost demanding in their gaze.

For a moment Wagner relished the thought of denying Garret the constructors' championship, as a payback for all the grief he had caused him. Being put in such a position--and by Garret---was too good to be true. But the idea of being vindictive, of getting even during this magical moment, was at odds with everything he was feeling. He was buoyant with goodwill, walking on clouds, and Garret wanted to ground him with decisions and break the mood. No way. Besides, he couldn't say for sure what the chassis was. Only Hacksaw could do that. He shrugged and deferred to his crew chief.

"It's a Lotus," Hacksaw answered. "Plain and simple."

"Now wait just a minute," Garret said, trying hard to keep his smile. "That car was stripped and rebuilt from the ground up. Hell, most of the sheet metal was produced right here in the good old U.S. of A."

"Let me tell you what we did to it," said Hacksaw, gesturing with his hands. "We gutted it all right and rebuilt much of it with new metal, true."

"Right," said Garret. "Refabrication. New metal. Hell, old Colin wouldn't recognize half the parts on your car."

"May I say something?" interrupted Fornier. "The final decision rests with me, after all."

"Please do." Garret was beginning to show his anger.

"Tell me, did you alter the suspension pickup points, or any of the basic design?"

"Not in the slightest."

"So, in other words, while much of the chassis has indeed been refabricated, it still matches Lotus 38 blueprints?"

"To a tee."

"I see. All of the basic components--steering rack, suspension arms, uprights, body panels, are interchangeable with Lotus 38 factory components?"

"Yessir."

"Well, there you have it, gentlemen. The chassis is a Lotus. I'm sorry, Ed, but Lotus Cars is constructors' champion. I'll give Colin the news."

"You do that," Garret said angrily. Without another word, he exited the motorhome.

*   *   *

The celebration moved to the Glen Motor Inn and continued through the awards banquet and into the wee hours of Monday morning. Everyone found something to celebrate. Bogavanti was happy to see his ex-teammate finally win a championship. Colin Chapman was delighted to win another constructors' title,

300

while Evans suggested kiddingly that he and Wagner were "co-champions." Parks, Lafosse, and Phillips, all one-time champions, welcomed the American to their exclusive club. And Tony Dayton, who had never met a party he didn't like, disobeyed Garret's expressed order and joined in the celebrating. He kidded Wagner about coming to Indy and driving "a real racecar." To his surprise, Wagner said he might do just that, as early as next May. Congratulatory telegrams arrived from all over the world, from people as diverse as Alberto Jano and Jeremy Sterns.

The killjoy was Susan's absence. Wagner called her hotel room before the banquet but she had already checked out. She had seen him win the championship, but she didn't stay for the celebrating. She didn't even say goodbye.

Tuesday morning in Akron, Ohio, Wagner met with Herb Cook's people to work out the details of his new team. Cook chose the name: American Racing Specialists, or ARS, for short. Wagner caught up with his team back at Edington Farm. There was unpacking to do, squaring of accounts with suppliers, and paying each team member a hefty bonus, thanks to Watkins Glen's $50,000 winner's purse. Meanwhile, Hacksaw opened up the Cosworth they had replaced and discovered two broken valve springs. Had they not changed it, Wagner wouldn't have finished.

The new team shaped up as Cook envisioned it, with nine cars to be built the first year: three for Grand Prix, and six for Indy. While Unirich Tire was supplying the start-up capital, the enterprise would be the sole property of John Wagner and Hacksaw Gilbert. Almost as good, the team would be headquartered in Denver, Colorado, Hacksaw's hometown. The barn at Edington Farm, although spacious, was too small for the new operation; furthermore, Katie had decided to sell the farm and move to Carmel-by-the-Sea. Her famous son would have to find someplace else to store his Speedster. Meanwhile, Wagner and Hacksaw flew to Denver, bought a suitable lot, and hired an architect to design a facility.

October ended with news from Europe--happy and sad. The happy news was Bogavanti's retirement. The Italian had finally decided to hang up his helmet--after Maria threatened to leave him and move the children to Switzerland. The sad news brought Wagner and Bogavanti to England for the funeral of their friend and competitor, Malcolm Parks. Coming home late one evening, poor Mal and Claudia were struck head on by a lorry. Wagner could not remember a sadder funeral. Irene cried inconsolably while Joseph Parks, devastated by the loss of his only son, fought back tears and thanked everyone for coming. It had been decided the two girls, Beth and Mary, would move to Paris and live with Mal's parents.

In early November, Garret surprised the racing world by announcing the disbandment of the Garret-Hawk racing team. Citing recent profit losses, he said he needed to devote full time to his business, and promised that his racing team would be back and stronger than ever--in a year or two.

It was at Tina's house Thanksgiving Day that it hit Wagner how very much he had missed. All those years he was away could never be brought back, never be relived. Ron was nearly a man. That's how he would know him. He would never know him as a 5-year-old, an eight-year-old, a twelve-year-old, never share those things a father shares with his young son, never share those memories that bind. Not with Ron, but he still could have them, with a second child. There was still time. If he stopped the running. If he retired from motor racing.

With a sense of urgency, he called Susan several times but she was never in, nor did she return his calls. Since she wouldn't take or return his calls, there was only one thing to do--see her personally. A week before Christmas, Jeremy assured him she would be in the office all that week. Wagner boarded a Douglas DC-9 out of Los Angeles. He smiled as the plane lifted and swooped out over the blue-green Pacific. Susan would certainly be surprised to see him, as surprised as he was when she dropped in on him at Reims. He tried to imagine the startled look on her face when he walked into her office unannounced. He didn't know if news of his retirement would win her back, or a proposal of marriage, but it was worth a try.

North of Santa Catalina, the jetliner made a u-turn and headed inland. Passing over Los Angeles, the pilot backed off

302

he throttle to reduce noise. The big plane slowed and seemed to ang in the sky, making Wagner nervous. Some things never hange. Sure, he'd retired, but he would always hate standing till. A few minutes later the DC-9 crossed the San Gabriel Mountains and the jets went to full thrust and he felt himself eing pulled gently back into his seat. That was more like it. He losed his eyes, pressed the recline button and said, "Go like ell, plane."

END

About the Author

Richard Nisley is a native Californian who makes his home in a suburb of Chicago. He's married and has two sons, ages 4 and 9. Mr. Nisley has written about topics as diverse as classical music and the history of the Illinois and Michigan Canal, and has contributed to such magazines as Car and Driver, Record Review, and Porsche Panorama. <u>The Ragged Edge</u> is his first book.

CPSIA information can be obtained at www.ICGtesting.com
Printed in the USA
BVOW010436130312

285025BV00001B/2/A